W9-AMA-871

KIM CHANCE

Mendota Heights, Minnesota

Keeper © 2018 by Kim Chance. All rights reserved. No part of this book may be used or reproduced in any manner whatsoever, including Internet usage, without written permission from Flux, except in the case of brief quotations embodied in critical articles and reviews.

First Edition
First Printing, 2018

Book design by Jake Slavik
Cover design by Jake Slavik
Cover images by Oleg Breslavtsev/iStockphoto; lfistand/iStockphoto; Dudarev Mikhail/Shutterstock Images; Zajcsik/Pixabay

Flux, an imprint of North Star Editions, Inc.

This is a work of fiction. Names, characters, places, and incidents are either the product of the author's imagination or are used fictitiously, and any resemblance to actual persons living or dead, business establishments, events, or locales is entirely coincidental. Cover models used for illustrative purposes only and may not endorse or represent the book's subject.

Library of Congress Cataloging-in-Publication Data
Names: Chance, Kim, author.
Title: Keeper / Kim Chance.
Description: First edition. | Mendota Heights, MN : Jolly Fish Press, [2018]
Summary: Sixteen-year-old bookworm Lainey Styles discovers she is a Keeper--a witch with the exclusive ability to unlock and wield a powerful spell book that has since been stolen by a malevolent wizard--but with the help of some friends Lainey attempts to steal it back.
Identifiers: LCCN 2017041834 (print) | LCCN 2017054364 (ebook) | ISBN 9781635830132 (hosted ebook) | ISBN 9781635830125 (pbk. : alk. paper)
Subjects: | CYAC: Witches--Fiction. | Wizards--Fiction. | Magic--Fiction.
Classification: LCC PZ7.1.C478 (ebook) | LCC PZ7.1.C478 Ke 2018 (print) | DDC [Fic]--dc23
LC record available at https://lccn.loc.gov/2017041834

Flux
North Star Editions, Inc.
2297 Waters Drive
Mendota Heights, MN 55120
www.fluxnow.com

Printed in the United States of America

For Jim, of course.

CHAPTER ONE

The Dragon's Horde was as crowded as a Walmart on Black Friday.

By a sheer stroke of luck, I'd managed to claim the last square inch of standing room left in the place. Wedged between a metal rack of colorful anime novels and a life-size cardboard cutout of Captain America, I used my SAT prep book as a barrier between me and the throng of cosplayers and super-nerds swarming the comic book store.

It was Superhero Saturday, and the tiny shop was packed with every die-hard fan within a fifty-mile radius. A hazard of living in a small town, I guess. With so little to do in Lothbrook, Georgia, the Horde's monthly meet-up event was as big a deal as the San Diego Comic Con.

"Pandemonium," I muttered as two brightly-colored, spandex-wearing individuals began a heated debate over which was better—Marvel or DC. "Noun. Wild and noisy disorder; uproar."

I rolled my eyes and tried to tune out the noise. I needed

to have fifty new vocabulary words memorized by the end of the night, and the chaos around me was making it difficult to concentrate.

I cannot believe I let Maggie talk me into this. I groaned, burying my face deeper into the prep book. *That girl owes me so big—like "name her firstborn after me" kind of big.*

I eyed my best friend standing a few feet away, talking animatedly to a boy with sandy brown hair and glasses. He was wearing a black Star Wars t-shirt and a newsy hat and looked exactly like the Pokémon-loving type of guy she usually gravitated toward.

Maggie was grinning and twisting a loose thread from her worn Batman t-shirt around her finger. Her thick black curls bounced around her shoulders—almost in response to her enthusiasm—and her light brown cheeks were tinged with pink. She practically glowed.

"Aww," I said, turning to the cutout of Captain America. "Look! Nerd flirting at its best!" I chuckled at my own joke before turning my attention back to the list of words.

"Superfluous. Adjective. Means additional or unnecess—Argh!" I squealed as a large, burly-looking dude dressed like the Hulk bumped into me, sending my SAT book flying and knocking me right into Captain America.

The guy gave me a rather authentic grunt as I struggled to keep myself and the Captain in the upright position.

"Sorry," he gruffed, handing me back my prep book.

"No worries," I said, with a wave of my hand.

He grunted again and then ambled toward his friends, a

group of guys all wearing various forms of tights and Avengers gear. I took it as my cue to get a little fresh air.

Weaving in and out of the crowd, I paid little attention to the people around me. My goal, the wide double doors, was only a few steps away.

"Now where are ye going, yon pretty lady?" A guy dressed as Thor—complete with thunder hammer and winged helmet—blocked my path. His phony accent was as ridiculous as the rest of his costume. "Ye should stay a while. I can show thou how I work my hammer." He gave me a wide, toothy grin and jerked his head so that the rounded arc of his hair flipped back into place.

I rolled my eyes. "Save it, Thunder God. I don't date guys who are more hair obsessed than I am. Maybe next time."

I moved to sidestep him.

"Don't be like that." Thor stepped in front of me again, dropping the accent this time. "I'm just looking for my own Jane Foster, darlin', and I think she might be you." He winked at me.

If that's supposed to be a panty-dropper, then this guy is more clueless than I thought. I rolled my eyes and tried again to step around him, but he was quick, holding out his hammer to block my path. This time he waggled his eyebrows at me.

I sighed. Clearly, Thor wasn't taking the hint. I looked past him, hoping to see Maggie or some other form of escape.

I spotted it standing a few feet away.

A tall guy in a dark gray t-shirt leaned against the wall with his arms crossed. He wasn't talking to anyone, and he looked about as thrilled as I was to be stuck in this circus of spandex. It was worth a shot.

"Babe!" I called over Thor's shoulder. "There you are!" I pushed past Thor and walked over to the guy. His eyes narrowed in confusion, and I gave him what I hoped was a pleading look. "I've been looking for you!" I pulled him off the wall and linked my arm through his. Then I turned back to Thor and smiled widely.

Thor narrowed his eyes in suspicion, and my heart flickered with panic as the boy pulled his arm from mine. But then he snaked it around my shoulders and pulled me close.

"Sorry, babe," he said, his voice deeper than I expected. "I got a little distracted by all the hair tossing." He looked pointedly at Thor, and then stared down at me, a crooked smile on his lips. This time my heart flip-flopped for a different reason.

I turned back to Thor, a triumphant smirk on my face.

He swung his hammer from one hand to the other, glared at me, and then stalked off.

I quickly stepped out of the stranger's arms. "Sorry about all that." I shrugged. "Who knew Thor was such an arrogant asshole in real life?"

The boy in gray stared at me, his blue eyes bright with amusement. There was a faint streak of purple on his pale cheek, a bruise I hadn't noticed initially. I wanted to ask about it, and there was a strange urge flowing through my fingers to reach out and brush his cheek, but I stopped myself on both counts. *What the hell, Styles! Get a grip!*

"It must be all the hair spray affecting his brain," he said, his smile widening.

My cheeks grew warm. "So . . . you a big comic book fan?"

"I appreciate them, but big crowds like this? Not really my scene. A friend of mine paid me twenty bucks to drive him here tonight."

"Yeah, not really my scene either. I'm more of a small group kind of gal."

He chuckled and pointed to my prep book. "Doing a little light reading?"

"You can never be too prepared," I said, my cheeks blazing hotter. "The test is in two days. I'm graduating early, and I have to get at least a 2200 to get into my top schools. The science programs are pretty competitive." *Oh my God. Could you sound like a bigger nerd?*

He nodded politely. "That's pretty impressive."

"I've moved around a lot," I said with a shrug. "Tons of sleepy little towns where nothing ever happens. I want to get out and see the world, ya know? So many things to see and discover. I figured why wait?" *Stop. Just stop.* I wanted to smack myself. Of all my quirks, nervous word-vomiting was definitely my least favorite.

"I think that's really cool," he said, and then we stood there staring awkwardly at each other for a moment as if neither of us knew what to say next.

"So . . . thank you," I finally blurted out, much louder than I meant to.

"Happy to help." He smiled, and that strange sensation

washed over me again. It was like the cool underside of the pillow after a long day or the way hot cocoa warms you from the inside out after you've been out in the cold for too long.

There was something oddly familiar about him, but I couldn't quite pinpoint what it was. "I'm sorry, but have we met before?" I asked.

His smile faltered and his eyes seemed to cloud over. "No, I don't think so." He looked down at his feet, scuffing the tile with his shoe. When he looked back up again, however, his smile had returned.

"Right," I said. "Well, I really appreciate your help. My name's Lainey, by the way." I held out my hand.

"Nice to meet you, Lainey." He took my hand in his. "I'm Ty."

"Lainey!"

I jumped as Maggie ran over and grabbed me by the arm, spinning me around in a circle. "Guess what?" she squealed. "That guy I was talking to just asked me to go grab a coffee with him!"

"That's great, Mags," I said, pulling myself from her grip with a laugh. I turned back to where Ty had been standing, but the patch of wall he'd occupied was empty. I scanned the crowd, but there wasn't a single stitch of gray in the sea of color. He was gone.

I sighed and turned back to Maggie, who proceeded to tell me every single detail of her conversation with Heath, the boy in the newsy hat.

"I told him I'd have to take a rain check, of course, but it was so nice to be asked!"

I frowned. "Wait, why didn't you say yes?"

"I promised I'd quiz you on your words if you came with me," Maggie said with a shrug. "What kind of best friend would I be if I bailed on you like that?"

"And what kind of friend would *I* be if I didn't let you off the hook." I smiled at her. "You should go."

Maggie narrowed her eyes at me. "Are you sure? Because *you*, Lainey Styles, are the true love of my life, and you come first."

I grinned. "I'm totally sure. I need to be home early tonight anyway. Go have fun."

"It's just so rare to find someone who actually understands that Gwen Stacy was Peter Parker's one true love. Everyone is always Team Mary Jane."

"See? You *have* to go."

Maggie squealed again and threw her arms around me, hugging me tightly. "You're the best!"

"Have fun—and text me when you get home."

"Will do, Styles. Love you!" Maggie yelled over her shoulder as she scampered off.

"Well," I said, hugging my SAT prep book to my chest, "guess it's just you and me, then." I sighed again and made my way toward the door.

Outside, the night air was crisp with a slight chill. Coats were usually unnecessary until the dead of winter—a "perk" of living in the Deep South—but October had brought with it some unseasonably cool temperatures. I wasn't complaining; it was nice to be able to walk outside for ten minutes and not need a shower afterward.

The parking lot was less chaotic than inside the shop, but there were still dozens of people milling about. I dodged around a lightsaber fight and a very serious-looking game of Magic: The Gathering and made my way toward the sidewalk. My beat-up red Ford Escort was parked around the corner a few blocks down the street.

Lainey.

I jumped at the sound of my name and turned around. There was a family with two small children standing a few paces away and a group of middle-school-aged boys, but no one I recognized.

I looked around, shrugged, and kept walking.

Lainey.

This time the melodic, yet pleading voice was so close, it was as if someone were whispering in my ear. I shrieked a little and whirled around. "Maggie?"

There was no sign of her. A massive case of the heebie-jeebies pricked at my spine, but I shook it off, squeezing my SAT prep book a little tighter to my chest. There was a round of loud shouting as the lightsaber duel intensified, and more people were pouring out into the parking lot.

I shook my head. Maybe all the studying was starting to have an adverse effect on my brain. "Adverse," I muttered, turning back toward the street. "Preventing success or development; harmful; unfavorable."

A tall figure emerged from the shadows of the building. She stood apart from the crowd, her long skirt rustling around her legs like a bell in the breeze.

I stared at her. Her costume wasn't one I'd seen before. She looked like she stepped off the page of a history book instead of a comic. There was something about her that held my attention; it was as if an invisible tether was linking us together. I couldn't look away.

As she stepped forward into a pool of light from one of the parking lot streetlights, all the blood drained from my face.

She looked older than me, but only by a few years, with long dark hair and hollow, sunken eyes, but it wasn't her face that sent my heart into my feet. Her dress and long green overcoat were stained crimson with blood.

She stood there staring at me with sad eyes, blood pouring through her fingers from a wound in her stomach.

I gasped and stumbled backward, dropping my SAT book on my foot in the process.

"Are you okay?" The mother of the small children was staring at me, her eyebrows knitted together.

"That woman over there," I said, nearly choking on the words. "She's hurt!" I turned and pointed toward the shadows. "I saw—" I broke off.

There was no one there.

"Sweetheart, are you sure you're okay?" The mother's

wide eyes searched my face. "You look like you've seen a ghost."

My eyes darted around the parking lot. But there was no blood, no body, no indication I had seen anything at all.

"Sorry," I managed to squeak. "I thought I saw something."

I didn't bother with further explanation. I ducked my head and made a beeline for the sidewalk. My knees wobbled as I half ran to my car. Blood pounded in my ears, and a thick layer of goose bumps covered my skin.

Just think of something else. Anything else.

My brain was muddled but immediately began supplying me with the words I had been cramming into my head for weeks.

"Consternation. Noun. A feeling of anxiety or disbelief over something unexpected. Trepidation. Noun. A feeling of—"

LAINEY!

The scream roared to life in my ears, and I took off running. I jammed my hand into my pocket for my keys and collided with the driver's side door. I fumbled for the right key, my hands shaking so badly I could barely hold on to them.

I forced the key into the lock. My hand wrapped around the door handle, pulling it open, but then I stopped. The dim light from the streetlamp was casting just enough glow to see hazy reflections in the window. The outline of my head and shoulders was familiar enough, but something was moving behind me.

I squeezed my eyes shut. *It's not real. Just a really good costume. An early Halloween prank, even. You're exhausted and your brain is playing tricks on you. It's not real.*

I turned around and opened my eyes. The bloody woman was standing right in front of me. Her deep green eyes, the same color as the ornate, pulsating stone that hung from her neck, burned into mine. Something inside me crumpled, like a wall that I'd never known was standing. Every cell in my body pulled me toward the woman. The magnetism between us crackled through my veins.

I opened my mouth, but before I had the chance to scream, her icy hand shot out and gripped my arm above the elbow.

The moment our skin touched, a wave of electric energy shot up my arm and surged through my body. I cried out as a blistering light exploded before my eyes. My limbs quaked and the heat intensified, engulfing me in a fire that threatened to incinerate me from the inside out. I fell to the asphalt, collapsing against the inferno raging beneath my skin. The wave of electricity intensified with each beat of my heart. I cried out again.

Then, as quickly as it had begun, the pain disappeared. The world faded away, and everything went black.

CHAPTER TWO

When the darkness finally lifted, my cheek was pressed against something rough and gritty. The air around me was thick with the tang of newly poured asphalt.

I was lying on the ground beside my parked car. The driver's side door was slightly ajar, and the repetitive beeping of the door alert blended with the sound of the cicadas buzzing in my ears. My vision was blurry, and I blinked several times until the swirl of color in front of my face morphed into something more recognizable.

Tiny bits of gravel were digging into my skin, so I shifted slightly and a low, involuntary groan rumbled in my throat. It was like I had been hit by a truck—or better yet, as Maggie would say, it was as if I'd found myself on the receiving end of a Hulk Smash. Everything hurt.

I sat up slowly, trying not to exacerbate the pounding in my temple. I glanced around to make sure I was alone and then managed to pick myself up off the ground, crawl inside my car, and push the door lock down before completely losing it. The bloody woman's face was seared into my eyeballs; she was everywhere I looked.

Tears poured down my cheeks, and my chest ached as I gasped for breath. I gripped the steering wheel, if only to still my shaking hands. I panted for air but couldn't get enough. Black splotches dotted my vision.

You're having a panic attack. The voice inside my head was calm and matter-of-fact. The rest of me, however, was in complete freak-out mode.

Breathe! my brain urged, but my body was less than co-operative. My arms and legs were so heavy I could barely lift them.

It wasn't real, the voice whispered to me. *Calm down. It was just a figment of your imagination. It wasn't real.*

"It—wasn't—real," I wheezed. *Breathe. Just breathe.*

In my mind, that soothing voice of reason repeated those words over and over again. *In through the nose and out through the mouth. Just breathe.*

After several agonizing minutes, the tightness in my chest lessened. Relief flooded through me, though my entire body was still trembling.

"It wasn't real," I whispered. "It wasn't real." But the words sounded strange. My lie was hardly convincing.

When I finally got my breathing down to a normal pace, I wiped my cheeks with the back of my hand and blinked away the remaining tears.

"Okay, Lainey, calm down and figure this out." I gulped

down a breath of air and began methodically going over the details in my head, trying to objectively look for something that might explain what had happened. *There has to be a logical explanation for this.*

"Step one, look at the evidence." I shivered as I pictured the woman, the feel of her icy skin against mine. "Step two, form a hypothesis."

The scientific method had never failed me before, and already my nerves seemed a bit calmer. "Probably just a bad combination of stress and exhaustion," I continued. "People see weird stuff like this all the time, right?"

My hands still gripped the steering wheel, but at least they weren't shaking anymore. My breathing had evened out. The more I talked myself through it, the more I could— almost—start to believe it was all just some joke, just a dream or a hallucination my overworked brain had conjured up in the heat of the moment.

Most of the remaining pain in my body had started fading away, dulling into a more manageable ache. My left arm, though, was throbbing.

I glanced down—and yelped. Right above my elbow, in the very spot the woman's fingers had wrapped around my skin, was an angry, red handprint. The mark, raised and puffy, was the exact silhouette of five slender fingers, not much bigger than my own. I prodded the skin gently with one fingertip and hissed through my teeth; the spot was tender to the touch. It looked and felt like a bad burn, but the pain radiated much deeper.

A fresh layer of goose bumps covered my skin. All former thoughts of reason and logic evaporated. The voice inside my head began its calming mantra once more—*It's not real. It's not real. It's not real*—but this time it lacked the confidence and conviction it had before.

There was only one thing I knew to do.

Tearing my eyes away from the handprint, I pulled out my cell phone and tapped the first picture on my list of favorites.

"Hey Styles! What's up? Did you make it home okay?" Maggie's cheerful voice on the other end of the line was so comforting, I nearly burst into tears again.

"Maggie," I breathed into the phone. "I'm so sorry, but I really need you. I'm freaking out. Can you come meet me?"

"What happened? Are you okay?"

I bit my lip, unable to hold back the tears any longer. "No," I whispered into the phone. "I'm not."

❧ • ☙

The playground was deserted. Even with silver patches of moonlight filtering through the trees, the place was dark and a little eerie without a bunch of noisy kids running around.

I hadn't wanted to stay at the comic book shop, and I couldn't go home, considering the state I was in, so Maggie had suggested the old playground near my house. It was familiar and soothing in a way. Yet every time a squirrel moved in the trees overhead or the swings squeaked in the wind, I nearly jumped out of my skin.

I sat shivering on the edge of the sandbox and gripped the worn plywood edges.

"God, Maggie. Where are you?" I grumbled, checking the time on my phone. The playground was only a few miles from the coffeehouse Maggie had gone to with Heath.

"Lainey!"

Maggie's curls swayed side to side as she hurried toward me, her brow furrowed. A lump formed in my throat. I swallowed hard, but it barely budged.

"What happened?" She plopped down beside me and reached for my hand.

It took everything I had not to start crying. "Just promise me you won't say anything, okay? Not to anyone."

Maggie nodded and drew an X across her heart with her finger. "It's rule number one in the best friend handbook."

I took a deep breath and scoured my vocabulary for the perfect words. Ironically, despite the hundreds of flashcards I had made, I was drawing a blank. "It doesn't make any sense, not even to me."

"Just tell me, Lainey. We'll figure it out together." She squeezed my hand.

"I think I might have witnessed some kind of crime."

Maggie's shoulders stiffened. "What?"

"I was walking to my car." My voice cracked. "It was really dark and there was this woman. . ." My hands started to shake. "She was covered in blood. So much blood!"

Maggie was frozen beside me, her eyes wide.

"But when I tried to get help," I continued, the words rushing from my lips, "There . . ." The words stuck in my throat. "There was no one there." My voice came out as a whisper, but the words seemed to hang thick in the air as if I had shouted them.

Maggie was still unmoving, her face a mixture of confusion and awe. I could almost see the wheels turning in her brain as she tried to process the information. I sat still and tried to let her make sense of what I told her, but seeing her speechless was really freaking me out. *What if she doesn't believe me? What if she thinks I am completely crazy? What if I am crazy?*

Finally, she took a steadying breath and asked, "No one else saw her?"

"No," I squeaked.

Maggie nodded slowly. "I think you better go back and tell me the whole story."

I went back to the beginning, right after I walked out of the comic book shop. I rehashed every single detail—the woman's appearance, the strange connection I'd felt, her sudden disappearance, and how I had run for my car and seen her behind me.

"Oh my God," Maggie said when I stopped speaking. "That's—"

"Crazy?" I finished for her, letting out a huff. "There's more." I pushed up the sleeve of the hoodie I'd thrown on in the car.

"Holy crapkittens, Styles!" She yanked my arm forward to get a closer look. "Does it hurt?"

"It feels better now than it did half an hour ago, but it still stings."

Maggie's already wide eyes practically bugged out of her head. "I can't believe this."

"Well, that makes two of us."

"So she just grabbed you, gave you the Dr. Doom treatment, and then you passed out?"

"Well, yes. But . . ."

"But what?"

I hesitated, but finally spit it out. "I heard her voice in my head. . . . She knew my name. It was like she was trying to tell me something." I looked down at the ground. "But I couldn't understand."

"You've been working really hard lately, staying up late, studying a lot." Maggie was chewing on her bottom lip. "Is it possible that . . ."

"That I made it up? That it was just some weird mind trick?" I gripped the wood beneath my fingers even tighter. "I don't know, Mags. I don't know what to think." Heat rippled through me. "I keep looking for a logical explanation. Maybe it was an early Halloween prank or some figment of my imagination. But the voice in my head and *this.*" I thrust my arm out. "There's nothing logical about it."

Maggie paused, thinking. Then she took a deep breath. "Well, we have to start thinking a little less logically, then." She pulled out the comic book she had shoved in her back pocket and tapped the cover. "I'm sure Peter Parker was as confused as you were when he suddenly woke up with superpowers."

"You can't compare what happened to me to a comic book," I scoffed. "It's not like I got bitten by a magical spider."

"First of all, that spider was radioactive, not magical, but you're missing the point." She pointed to the cover again and rolled her eyes. "Maybe there are things in the world that you can't explain and you just have to believe they're possible."

"You sound like a fortune cookie."

"Try to stop being . . . *you* for a second," Maggie said, ignoring me. "Throw logic and reason out the window."

I scoffed. That was like asking me to stop breathing. Yet, she had a point. If logic couldn't explain it, then there was nothing left to turn to—except, of course, the impossible. I sighed.

"Do you think . . . maybe it was a ghost?"

"That makes more sense than anything else." Maggie's face lit up at the suggestion. "And you know, small towns are known for paranormal activity. Wasn't Mr. Reinhard saying just the other day that Sherman burned down most of Lothbrook during his march through Georgia? I bet—"

"It was just a thought," I broke in, fighting the urge to laugh. "A stupid idea, really. Forget I mentioned it."

"Don't do that," Maggie said. "Don't play it off like it's nothing. It can't hurt to explore all the possibilities, right? Now, think. Is there anything else you can remember about her that might help us figure out who she is and why she attacked you?"

"No," I said. "I told you everything."

"Hmmm, okay. Well, I'm sure we can figure it all out."

"Oh yeah? How?"

"What about the census records at the library? You said it looked like she was from the olden days. Maybe there's some kind of record of her or her family."

"It's possible, I guess, but I don't even know her name. And it's not like we can look up 'the dead girl who attacked me' in the index," I countered.

Maggie pushed the hair from her eyes and leaned forward. "Well, you know, if we could somehow figure out where this gal is buried, we can salt her bones, burn them, and—"

My mouth dropped open. "Are you serious right now?"

"What? I've been marathoning *Supernatural*. There was this one episode where Sam and Dean—"

"Wait. *Supernatural?* Seriously, Mags?"

She pursed her lips. "Don't start with me, Styles. That show is legit."

I groaned and dropped my head in my hands.

"Okay, fine. No bones, no fires," Maggie said, yanking on my arm. "That means the first step should probably be to try and contact her. This woman obviously reached out to you for a reason. Don't you want to find out what that reason is?"

"Of course I do. But I seriously doubt a TV show is gonna help us."

"You underestimate the sheer awesomeness of the Winchester brothers," Maggie said with a dreamy smile. "But look, we could try a more classic approach."

"Such as?"

"What about a spirit board?"

"A Ouija board? We used to play with those at all our old middle school sleepovers. They never worked."

"That's because we were too chicken to ask it anything important. Come on, Styles. I know we're totally outside your comfort zone, but you have to try. Why are you fighting this so much?"

I chewed on my bottom lip for a few seconds before answering. "I guess I'm just a little . . ."

"Scared?"

"Yeah. I mean, I'm used to relying on books for everything. Concrete facts, hard evidence—things that can't be disputed. None of this makes any sense, and I don't do well with . . . with stuff like this."

"What? *You?*" Maggie interjected, feigning shock. "I never would've guessed that."

"You know what I mean. I just have a feeling that this, whatever this is, is big. And it makes me really nervous."

"I know it's kinda freaky, but that doesn't mean it's bad. Maybe something incredible is about to happen. Hell, for all we know, you could be turning into some kind of ghost-seeing mutant with special powers." Her eyes sparkled with excitement.

I cracked a small smile. "Well, when you put it that way . . ."

"I have one more idea," Maggie said. "And this one doesn't involve a television show or a board game."

"I'm all ears."

"What if you talked to Serena?"

I thought of my uncle's girlfriend, with her long skirts and tarot cards. "Absolutely not."

"What? Why?"

"Because she's completely nuts, that's why." I'd known Serena my whole life. Hell, she was practically family, but I'd never been able to buy into all her talk about the worlds outside our own. She marched to her own beat, and I was cool with that, but asking me to learn the rhythm? *That's* where I drew the line.

"All I'm saying is it couldn't hurt to talk to her. Weird is kind of her area of expertise."

"No." I shook my head. "I don't think so. Maybe we should just try the library after all."

Maggie sighed. "Fine. We can go and look in the archives for old newspaper photographs or something that might help us figure out who this woman is and what she wants."

The whole thing still sounded crazy, but what other choice did I have? I glanced uneasily at the handprint on my arm. My fingers were itching to tug my sleeve over it and pretend it didn't exist, but a wave of determination washed over me. I ground my teeth and glared at it instead. There had to be an explanation for what had happened to me, and I was going to find it.

"Sounds like a plan."

CHAPTER THREE

It didn't take long for the calm I'd felt while talking to Maggie to evaporate. As soon as I left the playground, my mind began to hurl questions at me—questions with no answers. By the time I arrived home, my nerves felt like I had been running over them with a cheese grater.

I pulled myself from the car and turned to see my uncle Gareth sitting on the front porch. He was holding a book in one hand and a mug of coffee in the other. Considering the late hour, it could mean only one thing.

"Oh, come on," I groaned as I stomped up the steps and plopped down in the chair beside him. "Again? She just did one last week."

Gareth smiled sheepishly but didn't look up from his book. "She had a feeling. You know the drill."

I rolled my eyes. "Why can't you date someone normal?"

He ignored me, but he did reach over to give me a sympathetic pat on the shoulder. "She brought cookies, if that helps."

"Snickerdoodles?"

"They are your favorite, aren't they?"

I nodded and let out a sigh. Serena might be bat-shit crazy, but she was a hell of a baker. "Fine."

"That's my girl." Gareth grinned at me, the glint in his eyes making him look much younger than his forty-two years.

We don't look much alike. Gareth is tall and brawny with honey-colored hair, tan skin, and dark chocolate-colored eyes. I'm on the short side with long, wavy brown hair, hazel eyes, and a fair complexion. I look mostly like my mom, but I have my dad's smile.

Gareth's and my mannerisms are the same, though, and we have the exact same sense of humor. We can even finish each other's sentences. Serena jokes that we share a brain. I guess that's what happens when your whole family consists of a single person. Gareth took me in after my parents died, and it had been just the two of us—and his kooky girlfriend, Serena—ever since. Our relationship had always been more like friends or roommates than uncle and niece, but I liked it that way. Life with Gareth was easy.

I leaned my head against the back of the wicker chair and sighed. Sitting beside Gareth on the porch, listening to the soft slithering sound of his pages turning was peaceful, but my mind still flashed with images of the woman, or ghost, or whatever it was. The handprint on my arm stung under the fabric of my hoodie.

"You okay, kid?" Gareth was looking at me over the top of his book.

"I think I'm just a little stressed about the SATs," It wasn't exactly a lie.

"You're going to do great," he said, giving my shoulder a squeeze. "You've been studying for months."

"I know. I guess I'm just. . ." I bit down on my bottom lip. "I'm just worried." *About more things than one.*

"Everything will work out exactly as it's supposed to. You can't control what happens to you, only how you react to it." He smiled at me. "Besides, you have nothing to worry about. You asked for a dictionary and a set of encyclopedias for your eighth birthday. I'm pretty sure you're gonna kill it."

The memory made me laugh. Though the encyclopedias had passed on, I still had that same worn-out Webster's sitting on my desk in my room. "Thanks. You're right. I just need to relax a little."

"Exactly." Gareth turned back to his book. "Now, why don't you head in for some of those cookies? Serena should be finished up by now."

"Aren't you coming?"

"I'm right behind you."

I stood up and walked toward the door. Part of me was dying to turn around, jump into his lap like I used to do as a kid, and tell him how scared and confused I was. But the other half screamed at me to walk inside and not say anything that might land me in a padded room.

With a huff, I walked inside. The house smelled strongly of burnt sage. Serena, or Madam Serena Morales as her customers call her, was in the living room. A dozen or more candles lined the room, casting shadows against the walls. The light wrapped around her, giving her russet brown skin a soft glow. Her large brown eyes were wide and focused, and she was swaying back and forth, her shiny dark hair swishing around her shoulders in a perfect line. She was clutching a bundle of burning sage and mumbling some kind of incantation under her breath.

If I hadn't seen it a thousand times before, I would've laughed, but Serena and Gareth had been together for as long as I could remember, and these cleansing rituals had become commonplace in our house.

"Hi, Serena," I called out as I passed through to the kitchen.

She blinked and turned to smile at me. "Lainey! Just in time! I've just finished the cleansing ritual. Your house is officially spirit free!" She swept across the floor with that ridiculous flamboyant walk she somehow made look natural and began to blow out the candles. "Don't you just love the energy of a clean house? It's absolutely exhilarating. Can you feel it?"

"Yeah, definitely." I snorted down a laugh. Not that Serena noticed. She continued flouncing around the room, sweeping her long skirt around her legs like a matador does his muleta.

"You know what I think we should do?" Serena skipped back over to me. "I think we should form a serenity circle. We haven't done one in months!"

"Um . . . that sounds really great, but I've got a lot of

studying to do. I think I'm gonna grab a few cookies and then head up to bed."

Serena put a palm against my cheek, her forehead creased as she peered into my face. "You know your aura *is* looking a little cloudy. Perhaps a good night's rest is what you need."

"Or maybe she just needs to stop stressing and stuff her face full of cookies instead," Gareth's voice rang out from the entryway. He walked into the living room with his book in his hand and a grin on his face.

Serena scoffed at Gareth and smiled, but it didn't quite reach her eyes. "Yes, cookies and rest. Just what the doctor ordered." She turned away from me then and shot Gareth a look I didn't understand before turning her attention back to the candles.

Gareth looked back at her, his own face unreadable. I wondered if this was one of those weird couple moments when they were having a conversation without saying actual words. I watched them for a few seconds before deciding to retreat to the kitchen. A plate of snickerdoodle cookies sat on the counter. I grabbed a handful and headed upstairs for my room.

As soon as I shut the door and sat on the edge of my bed, all the fear and confusion I'd felt outside the comic book shop returned, coiling low in my gut. My heart was thumping, so I shoved a warm cookie into my mouth as a distraction. My eyes roamed around the room as I chewed.

My bedroom wasn't large, but I loved the sense of home it gave me—something I'd rarely felt at all the other houses we'd lived in. Maybe it was because I knew I'd get to stay in this one longer than a few months. Gareth had always claimed the job market was unstable, but after fourteen moves in the last five years alone, I'd made him swear to stay put long enough for me to finish high school in one place. He'd agreed and had kept his promise for more than two years now, but I wasn't taking any chances—thus the goal of early graduation.

The bulletin board above my desk was covered in brochures from colleges around the country. The thought of being alone and on my own both terrified and thrilled me, but I was eager to leave Lothbrook behind. There was so much of the world I hadn't seen yet, and the scientist in me was eager to explore and experiment—and maybe make an important discovery or two! I'd been nothing more than a bookworm and a nomad my entire life; I was ready for a big change.

There has to be something else out there for me, I thought, staring at the brochures. *It's time I found out what.*

Swallowing the last of my cookie, I grabbed my dictionary off the desk, the blue one Gareth had given me, and thumbed through it. *Just get back to studying, Styles. Everything else will keep for a bit.*

"Ambiguous. Adjective," I said out loud, letting the familiar words soothe me. "Meaning unclear or vague." I flipped to a new page. "Irrevocable. Adjective. Meaning permanent or unchanging."

When I turned the next page, a worn photograph fell

into my lap. I knew what it was without even looking at it, but my heart still wrenched as I turned it over. It was the last picture ever taken of my parents and me. Gareth had given it to me several years back. My mother and father were standing underneath a tall tree with red and orange leaves. My father was grinning at the camera, holding me, only a bundled infant at the time. My mother wasn't looking at the camera. She was looking lovingly at my father, her eyes wide and bright.

It was comforting to see their faces, despite the familiar pang in my chest every time I thought about them not being here.

I was just about to shove the photograph back into the dictionary when a tiny detail caught my eye. I moved the photograph closer to my face, blinking to clear away any tears that might affect my vision.

I gasped, dropping the photo as if it were on fire.

"No," I whispered. "There's no way." I stared at the photo lying facedown on the carpet.

I reached down and gingerly picked up the photograph. The faces were the same, radiant and smiling, but that wasn't what had my heart threatening to beat out of my chest.

Around my mother's neck was a silver necklace, and hanging from the necklace was an oval-shaped emerald pendant.

I recognized the necklace. I'd seen it only hours before.

It was the very same emerald amulet that had hung from the bloody woman's throat.

CHAPTER FOUR

The electric guitar riffs coming from my alarm clock were loud enough to wake the dead. I fumbled for the snooze button, muttering curses under my breath.

When the room was silent, I collapsed back against my pillow, pulling the blanket over my head. I groaned, my stomach rolling with the nausea that comes from lack of sleep.

In the last forty-eight hours, I had spent every spare minute searching the Internet for anything that might explain my encounter with the blood-covered woman. I'd also been canvasing my house for clues as to why the necklace in the picture of my mom and the one the woman wore were the same. Yet, the only thing I'd found in my searches was way too many disturbing websites and a hella ton of dust mites.

I'd almost asked Gareth about the photograph, but every time I mentioned my parents, especially my mom, he always looked so sad. I hated seeing the grief—still fresh after all these years—in his eyes, so I usually didn't bring them up.

Besides, I was still convinced there was some kind of logical explanation for it all. I just had to find it.

But what about the handprint on your arm? What does it mean? How is it possible that the woman you saw was wearing the same necklace as your mother?

The voice in my head repeated the same three questions that'd kept me tossing and turning all night long. "I just want to sleep," I grumbled. "I just want it all to go away."

Thankfully, the alarm wailed again, pushing away everything except my annoyance. The opening strains of an AC/DC song blasted through the speakers, and I slapped at the clock like I'd been doing for the past half hour. *Why the hell is my alarm on anyway? It's Saturday.* I closed my eyes and snuggled deeper under the covers—and immediately jolted upright.

"Shit!" I shouted when the realization dawned on me. There was a reason I had set my alarm for bright and early on a Saturday, why I had set it to the local classic rock station—something I couldn't possibly sleep through. Today was the day of the SAT.

The clock beside me read 7:45. The test was scheduled to begin in fifteen minutes! Throwing the covers back, I leapt out of bed, shucked off my pajamas, and grabbed the first pieces of clothing my fingers touched. After throwing my hair into a messy bun, I grabbed my backpack and flew out the front door, slamming it behind me.

I drove as fast as I dared, trying to ignore the roar of

anxiety screaming inside my head. The clock on my dashboard read 7:51.

The high school was only few miles away, but there was no way I was going to make it in time. The red light in front of me seemed to be taking its sweet time, and I slammed my fist against the steering wheel. "Turn green already!" The light changed colors, almost as if in response to my demand, and I let out a tiny smile of satisfaction before stomping on the gas pedal.

I managed to make it a few hundred yards before being stopped by another light. I groaned and gripped the steering wheel to keep from beating the crap out of it.

The clock now read 7:55.

"Green!" I yelled through the windshield. The light obligingly changed. I sped down the street, praying I wouldn't catch any more lights or run into a cop.

I was less than two minutes away from the school when flashing red lights and lowering metal arms indicated an oncoming train. I came to a complete stop, exactly one intersection away from my turn, and burst into tears. The morning freighters were famous for being incredibly slow and miles long.

The clock read 7:58.

I dropped my head to the steering wheel and tried not to choke on my tears. All that studying, all the stress and worry, the months of preparation—all for nothing.

I pounded my fist against the dash. This was entirely my

fault. If I hadn't been so distracted, I wouldn't be missing the most important test of my life.

The ever-reliable voice of reason inside my head began whispering condolences, but I shook my head to silence the sound. It didn't matter that the test would be offered again next month. Early acceptance depended on this round of scores. I wanted to punch myself in the face.

Just ten minutes, I agonized. *If I had just gotten up ten minutes sooner.*

Warmth flooded through my body—probably some rush of endorphins in response to my panic. I sucked in a few ragged breaths. There wasn't anything else I could do. It might be possible to sweet-talk the officials into letting me enter the testing room late, but I doubted it.

The train was still moving in front of me, but I could see the final car getting closer. This train was much shorter than the ones that usually backed up traffic for miles. Some kind of small miracle. Not that it mattered. Especially since—

I froze, staring at the clock on my dash. The bright green numbers now read 7:48.

What the hell?

I pulled my cell phone from where I had tossed it into the cup holder and tapped the screen. 7:48.

My stomach flip-flopped. *Maybe I just read the clock wrong?* I thought of that sign hanging in the counselor's office about stress and its effect on the teenage mind. I imagined my poor little overworked brain collapsing on the sofa with a cold compress pressed against it. "Even brains make mistakes, okay!" it yelled before bursting into tears.

I let out a small chuckle, ignoring the chill inching its way down my spine.

The train was past me now, and the metal arm barricades were beginning to lift. I pressed down on my gas pedal, driving on autopilot as my thoughts whirled around like a tornado. I parked in the student parking lot and sat musing as people walked toward the door. *My mind was definitely just playing tricks on me. Yes, that's it. Just some weird twist of brain matter.*

I shook my head and straightened my shoulders. "Focus, Styles," I said, double-checking my backpack for my calculator and No. 2 pencils.

I began to recite vocabulary in my head like a mantra. *Implausible. Adjective. Meaning not realistic or believable. Indiscernible. Adjective. Defined as impossible to see, hear, or know clearly. Consequential. Adjective. Important or significant.*

I just needed to focus on one thing at a time. Something inside me wailed in protest, but I ignored it. I had to get through the test. Everything else had to wait.

I crossed the parking lot still murmuring vocabulary words under my breath and walked purposefully through the doors.

❧ • ☙

When they released us from the testing room, I was relieved. I felt good about the test, but the constant battle between the ability to think critically and the distractions floating around my brain had given me a wicked headache.

I wanted nothing more than to go home, curl up in my bed, and stay there until further notice. The handprint on my arm had been stinging all morning, and if I didn't already have plans to meet Maggie at the library, I would've done just that.

I parked my car at the end of already busy Main Street and headed down the crowded sidewalk toward the town library. Lothbrook wasn't a big town, but it was well known for its antiques and local cuisine. The quaint row of buildings was colorful and bright, each one with its own unique character and charm. The large window displays were all decorated in the cheerful oranges and yellows of fall, and pockets of tourists meandered down the walkway, window shopping and enjoying the smell of cinnamon and banana that wafted through the open door of Gertrude's Bakery— one of Lothbrook's most iconic locations. Main Street hadn't changed much in the last few decades, and the classic "Leave it to Beaver" feel of the place drew folks from all over Georgia. Weekends on Main Street were always busy affairs.

I dodged around an older couple feeding a parking meter and pulled my phone out of my backpack so I could text Maggie and let her know I was almost there. As the screen lit up, a weird sensation floated over me. All of the hair on the back of my neck stood up. I swallowed and looked up from the screen.

The blood-covered woman from the comic book shop was standing on the opposite sidewalk, her long, dark hair blowing in the breeze. Her sad face locked on mine, and the amulet around her neck pulsed like a heartbeat.

Lainey.

The whispered echo of my name boomed in my ears as black splotches appeared in front of my eyes. I blinked, trying to clear them away, but it didn't help. In seconds, my entire field of vision was nothing but darkness. Before I could so much as whimper, the darkness shifted, giving way to a cyclone of colors that swirled in front of my eyes and spun into life. The swirl took shape, and small bursts of recognizable matter exploded into the darkness.

A cluster of tall trees. A red-tinted moon. A strange symbol. The acrid tang of smoke stung my nose.

I gasped, but as soon as they had come, the flashes were gone, replaced again by the familiar sights of Main Street. The woman was closer now, standing in the middle of the street with her dark green eyes trained on my face. The look in her eyes made my stomach twist, and I staggered backward, accidentally plowing into the couple at the meter.

"Oh my gosh, I am so sorry," I said, trying to find my balance. "*So* sorry." The man and his wife were both giving me disapproving looks, but they seemed pacified enough with my apology not to scold me. As they pushed past me, I heard the woman mutter something about teenage drug use. Under different circumstances, I would've laughed, but my tongue was sticking to the roof of my mouth. I glanced back to the street, expecting to see those intense green eyes staring back at me, but it was empty.

I let out the breath I was holding. *You're just stressed. An aftereffect from the test this morning. A figment of your imagination.*

The voice of reason was back, soothing me with exactly what I wanted to hear, but the feeling coiling in my gut was hard to ignore. *Just seeing things,* the voice whispered.

"Am I?" I grumbled, shaking my head.

Trying to ignore the uneasiness that wrapped around me, I turned my attention back to my phone. I had barely swiped my finger across the screen when loud shouting and the clanging of trash bins startled me so much I dropped my phone with a smack on the concrete sidewalk.

Hissing under my breath, I scooped the phone off the pavement, praying to the Goddess of Expensive Cellular Products that the screen wasn't busted. Thankfully, it wasn't. The noise was coming from the tiny alleyway in between one of the antique shops and Auntie Marmalade's House of Fritters.

I turned to see what all the commotion was about and caught a flash of white as a body went flying up against one of the brick walls. I gasped and rushed over for a closer look. I glanced around, but no one else seemed to notice what was happening.

At the end of the alley, there was a group of guys shuffling around, throwing punches and cursing loudly. I watched the majority form a lose circle around a single fighter wearing a leather jacket and dark gray t-shirt. *Three against one.* They were circling around the boy in gray, taunting and jeering. It reminded me of how a house cat toys with its prey before consuming it.

The boy in gray took off his jacket and tossed it behind him. He stood with his back to me, his body rigid and tense. *What's he doing? Why doesn't he run?*

Before I had time to question it further, the boy launched himself into the fray with a battle-like cry that reverberated off the brick walls. In less than a second, he punched his nearest opponent in the chin, sending him flying backward into the chain-link fence that blocked off the back entrance of the alley. Then he turned and jabbed a second boy in the stomach before delivering a quick blow to the boy's face. The boy shrieked as blood poured from his nose.

I couldn't move from my spot on the sidewalk. I was glued to the fight, watching as the boy in gray whirled around, his movements lithe and graceful. He was outnumbered, but far from outmatched. In fact, he seemed to be *enjoying* the fight. His laughter contrasted jarringly with the shouts of the other boys.

The fight continued, the other boys refusing to back down, though it seemed they were no match for the boy in gray—despite their advantage in number. Suddenly, two of the larger boys grabbed the boy in gray from behind and pinned his arms behind his back. He struggled but was unable to pull free. The last boy, tall with stringy blond hair, the apparent leader of the group, grabbed something off the ground: a piece of silver that glinted slightly in the dim light. It looked like a sharp piece of metal, a fragment from a broken pipe.

My stomach did a somersault, and my feet were already moving by the time my brain decided to catch up. "Hey!" I shouted. "Hey!"

The boys at the end of the alley all turned to look at me, their faces a mixture of shock and confusion. "Shit," I said. *Now what, Styles?*

It was just enough of a diversion, though, and the boy in gray took advantage of it, throwing his body weight backward and slamming his captors into the brick wall behind them. The blond boy lunged forward, swiping the piece of metal through the air, but his arm was easily deflected by the boy in gray. The two began to grapple, the silver of the pipe slicing through the air.

"Shit!" I said again. I took a step forward, though I had no idea what I planned to do.

Half my mind was already supplying me with visions of the murder I was surely about to witness, and the other half was screaming at me to stop staring like an idiot and call the cops.

I had one foot poised to take another step when the back door to Auntie Marmalade's opened and Auntie Marmalade herself came pouring out yelling like a banshee and swinging her rolling pin as if it were a baseball bat.

The three boys, the leader with the pipe and his two

minions, scattered like ants, running in all directions. Two of the male servers who worked for Auntie Marmalade—they looked more like bouncers, really—took off after them.

The boy in gray, however, was standing still amid the chaos staring right at me. He took a step forward and when his face hit a patch of sunlight, I let out small gasp. I recognized him.

The boy in gray was Ty, the guy I had met two nights ago at the comic book shop.

I stood there staring at him, not knowing whether I should wave like we were old pals or pretend I didn't have a clue who he was. He was taller than I remembered, and I couldn't help but admire his broad shoulders and the way his tangled, almost too-long black hair was sticking to his forehead and curling around his ears and the nape of his neck.

He didn't break my gaze, but one corner of his mouth quirked up into a grin. The smile lasted only a second and was replaced with a furrowed brow, but it still made my heart do a little jig.

With a small inclination of his head, the boy walked right past Auntie Marmalade, still brandishing her rolling pin, and stalked over to the fence at the end of the alley. Without a single look back, he hopped over the chain link and headed toward the opposite road.

I blinked

What just happened? Why did Auntie Marmalade let him pass? Did she know him?

"Are you all right, ma'am?" One of the servers was standing at my elbow looking concerned.

"I'm fine, thanks."

He nodded at me and walked over to Auntie Marmalade. "They were too fast; we couldn't catch them. One ran down Main, the other two hopped in a car a few blocks away."

Auntie Marmalade grunted and murmured something along the lines of "stupid punks" under her breath.

"What about the other guy?" I piped up.

The server looked confused. "The other one?"

"Yeah, the one in the gray shirt." The server gave me a long, blank stare. "You know," I continued. "Gray t-shirt? Black hair? Tall with broad shoulders, a crooked yet mildly seductive smile that kinda makes you feel like a popsicle on the fourth of July?" I stopped myself. *Geez, Styles. Word vomit, much?* "Ignore that last part." I indicated the server. "He walked right past you."

The server was staring at me like I had sprouted a second head. Auntie Marmalade, who was cradling her rolling pin to her chest like a baby, offered me a sympathetic smile. "You poor dear. You must be in shock. Come inside and I'll make you up a plate of nice, hot fritters."

"Oh, no, thank you, ma'am. I'm fine, really." I thought about how Ty had walked so casually past Auntie Marmalade, as if she couldn't even see him at all, and hopped the fence.

"As if she couldn't even see him," I muttered, under my breath.

"What was that, dear?"

"Nothing." I shook my head.

The servers followed Auntie Marmalade back into the restaurant, and I was left alone in the alley feeling very much like I had entered the Twilight Zone.

On the ground by the wall, a lump of material was lying in the dirt. It was Ty's leather jacket. "Okay," I said, picking it up. "So I'm not completely crazy. He *was* here." I wiped the dirt off the jacket and, feeling slightly ridiculous, folded it over my arm and continued toward the library.

The sidewalk was more tightly packed with people now. I weaved in and out of the foot traffic, trying to make sense of all the mayhem that whirled around inside my head. I was so preoccupied with my thoughts, I didn't notice when the man in front of me came to a complete stop.

Like an idiot, I slammed into his back and fell backward onto the pavement. The man whirled around and gave me a dirty look.

"Sorry!" I squeaked, trying to appear demure.

He harrumphed at me and kept walking. The palms of my hands were slightly skinned from where I had landed on them, and my elbow was throbbing. "Ow," I groaned, rubbing the spot gently. I stood up, assessing myself for more damage, and wiped the dirt off my jeans.

When I straightened, Ty was standing in front of me, an amused expression in his eyes. The bruise on his cheek, the one I had noticed at the comic book shop, had faded to a greenish-yellow color, but a new one was forming around his left eye.

I started a little. "How long have you been standing there?"

"Long enough to see you wipe out on your ass."

"I didn't wipe out," I said, matter-of-factly. "I was testing the sidewalk for durability. You'll be happy to know that this particular patch of concrete is in fact safe for pedestrians." I cocked an eyebrow at him. "You're welcome."

He let out a deep chuckle, and my cheeks warmed at the sound of it. I wasn't sure if he recognized me from the comic book store or not, and despite my initial emboldened response I had absolutely no idea what to say next. *Should I ask him about the fight?*

"Well, now that I know the sidewalks are passable, I better get going. See you around."

He waved, then turned and starting walking toward the street.

I stared at his retreating back.

"Wait!" I called out. "Wait! So that's it?"

He turned around to face me, walking backward. His face was lit with a grin. "Were you expecting something else?"

"Well, you could at least give me a high five or something. I saved your life, after all." *And I wouldn't mind knowing how you managed to go all Harry Potter with an invisibility cloak back there.*

Ty stopped, his features suddenly highlighted by a patch of fading sunlight. "You saved *my* life?"

"That guy had a weapon," I replied matter-of-factly,

pushing back my shoulders. "He could've killed you." At this point, I wasn't sure the other boys actually had a real chance of *killing* this mysterious boy in front of me, but the fact remained that without my brilliant—okay, slightly stupid—interference, the fight could've ended differently.

Ty walked toward me, each step slow and methodical, his face bright with amusement. "Trust me, he couldn't have killed me."

I rolled my eyes, though I had to admit I was the tiniest bit impressed by how certain he seemed of his abilities in the fight. "You're kinda cocky, aren't you?"

"Not at all," he said, without a single ounce of arrogance in his voice, as if he were stating a fact. "And why don't we just call it even. Had any more troubles with Thor lately?"

"So you *do* recognize me!"

"Of course . . . *babe.*"

I had no control over the stupid smile that crossed my face. "We're even."

"All the same, thank you, Lainey. It's not every day such a pretty girl saves my life." He winked at me.

He remembers my name! My stupid smile got even bigger.

"Oh!" I turned around and walked back the few paces to where I'd fallen and scooped up his leather jacket from where I had dropped it. When I turned back to face Ty, though, he was already rounding the next corner out of sight.

"Wait!" I called after him. "I have your jacket!" But he was already gone.

❧ ⋅ ❧

"Geez, Styles! Where have you been? I've been blowing up your phone for the last fifteen minutes. I was getting ready to send a search party."

I held my hand up and tried to catch my breath. After Ty had disappeared, I ran the rest of the way to the library.

"I'm so sorry, Mags. I got . . . distracted."

Maggie raised an eyebrow. "Distracted?"

"Yeah, on the way over here there was this fight and that guy from—"

"A guy, huh?"

I rolled my eyes. How very like Maggie to completely skip over all the other details and go straight to the "guy."

"It wasn't like that, okay. It was . . . interesting."

"Oh-kay." Maggie stared at me, but decided to move on. "Any news on the ghost front?"

My face fell. The fight had been a welcome distraction.

"Actually, yeah." I reached into my bag and pulled out the photograph of my mom. "See the necklace in the picture?"

Maggie nodded.

"The woman I've been seeing is wearing the exact same one. I saw it when she appeared the first time and then again today."

"You saw her again?"

I hesitated. The voice in my head urged me to deny it, but instead I nodded my head. "On the sidewalk. I was heading here. And I saw . . . something else too. Flashes. Tidbits of . . . memory or something. I could smell smoke."

"Weird," Maggie said, staring at me with wide eyes. She took the picture from my hand and stared at it. "Any idea what this means?"

I bit down hard on my lower lip. I had an idea, but I didn't want to say it out loud, and the words were like peanut butter sitting on my tongue. "I think she and my mom are connected somehow."

"Holy crapkittens, Styles. That's . . . that's just crazy."

"Tell me about it."

I must have look panicked or wounded in some way because Maggie leaned over and gave me a quick hug. "Look, no matter what, I've got your back. We'll figure all this out together, okay? I promise."

"No offense, Mags, but I don't think that's a promise you can keep."

"Well, I'm gonna try."

I'd always admired Maggie's determination—even if it was fueled by mule-headed stubbornness. In this case, I was grateful for it. I took a deep breath. "So what now?"

Maggie looped her arm through mine and steered me toward the double doors of the library. "We'll just have to April O'Neal this thing until we find the answers."

"Just like that, huh?"

She grinned. "Yup. Just like that."

"You're something else, Mags."

"Is that a nice way of saying I'm totally crazy?"

"Well . . ." I smiled.

Maggie shook her head at me. "Oh, Styles. If I ask you to hop on a Nozgul and fly into the fiery depths of Mordor with me, *then* you can call me crazy. But for now, let's just go with cheerfully optimistic."

I let out a loud laugh. "Fair enough."

CHAPTER FIVE

I slammed the door shut behind me. The door frame rattled, and the picture of me holding a hot pink fishing pole and small catfish from the line fell off the wall. The glass shattered into pieces against the hardwood floor. "Perfect," I muttered, massaging my temples. "That's just freaking perfect."

As I bent and began picking the shards of glass off the floor, I couldn't help but notice the irony of the situation. The library had been a complete bust. Maggie and I hadn't found anything remotely helpful, and I had driven home with a knot in my stomach that grew bigger with each passing mile. Just like the glass, the shred of hope I had been clinging to—the one that told me we would find some kind of logical answer—was broken. I was out of ideas, out of clues, and very likely out of my own damn mind.

A small sliver of glass sliced through the pad of my fingertip, and I hissed as a thick droplet of blood rolled down my finger. I was still holding a small pile of glass pieces in my other hand, so I glanced around for something to stanch the blood.

"Here." Gareth walked over and knelt beside me, a box of tissues in his hand.

"Thanks," I said, wrapping the tissue around my finger. "Sorry about the picture."

Gareth shrugged. "Frames can be replaced." He narrowed his eyes, looking closely at my face. "You okay?"

I nodded. "Gareth, can I ask you something?"

"Of course."

Should I tell him? What if he thinks I'm completely nuts? I took a deep breath. "Do you believe in fate? I mean . . . do things happen for a reason, or is everything just some cosmic hodgepodge of random, unrelated events?" The words came pouring out. I studied Gareth's face for a reaction, but he didn't seem surprised or confused by the question.

"I think we all have a path we're destined to follow. The people we meet, the places we go, the things we experience . . . Nothing is by chance." He paused. "However, whether or not we choose to follow that path is another matter entirely."

"What do you mean?"

"A person's destiny isn't a concrete certainty. There are people who live their entire lives and never fulfill their true purpose. Free will and choice, you see, are powerful tools of alteration. A simple choice can change everything."

"So, when crazy things happen," I questioned, "it's up to the person to choose how they want to react . . . and that choice ultimately determines their future, right?"

"Exactly." Gareth smiled at me. "If a man were told he might die on an airplane, then he could choose not to travel by air or take his chances. Either choice would drastically alter his future. Thus, the powerful nature of free will."

I nodded, relief welling up inside of me. It was a comforting thought, though I still had a nagging feeling. "But what if free will isn't part of the equation?"

Gareth raised his eyebrows.

"I mean," I continued, "what if something happened that you had no control over—something that made no sense. Something even free will couldn't stop?"

A strange look passed over Gareth's face. Confusion, maybe? "Well, there are, of course, some very powerful forces at work in the universe . . ." He trailed off. "Are you sure everything's okay? Did something happen with the test? When you called, I thought you said you did well."

"No, the test was fine. Just have a lot on my mind, I guess." I swallowed. "The future and all that." The lie came naturally. *Real brave, Lainey. Real brave.*

Gareth's face relaxed, and understanding washed over his features. "I keep telling you, kid, you have nothing to worry about. And you've got time, you know. You don't have to have all the answers right now."

I snorted. "Don't you know me? I've had my life mapped out since I was old enough to make my first to-do list."

"That may be so," Gareth said with a chuckle, squeezing my shoulder. "But your future is far from decided."

"That's what terrifies me."

"Just remember: you can't control what happens to you, but you can control how you react to it. *Those* choices are what will determine your destiny."

"Gee, thanks, Yoda," I joked, trying to ignore the knot in my stomach. "You make it sound so simple."

"Simple it is," Gareth said, imitating Yoda's gravelly voice. "Trust me, you should."

I laughed and let him pull me in for a hug.

"Now, what do you say we get this glass cleaned up and order a pizza? Serena is on her way over and we can watch terrible movies and eat greasy carbs together."

"I like the way you think." I grinned. The knot in my stomach was still there, but the weight of it didn't seem quite as heavy.

I stood up, unzipping the jacket I hadn't yet removed. "I'll go get the broom. Is the dustpan still in the pantry?"

I looked at Gareth. His shoulders were tense, and I couldn't read the expression in his eyes. He was staring at the handprint—now faded, but still visible—on my arm.

"Lainey—" he began.

"It's nothing," I squeaked. "Maggie and I were messing around. You know how she gets." I forced out a dry laugh. *More lies.* "Serves me right for having an easily excited best friend."

"Maggie did that?"

"Oh, yeah. Something about a new Avengers movie. She saw the trailer and freaked out." I sounded so sure I almost convinced myself. "So, the dustpan?"

Gareth stared for a moment before finally swallowing. "On the bottom shelf in the pantry."

"Right." I shuffled toward the kitchen. I pulled the broom and dustpan from their respective places and also grabbed a clean sweatshirt from the basket on the laundry machine. I threw it over my head, making sure the handprint was no longer visible.

I'll tell him the truth when I know what's going on, I promised, hoping to placate the guilt stirred up by all the lies. *I will tell him.*

I let out a long breath and walked back into the hallway, a forced smile plastered on my face. "So the real question is," I said, "cheese or pepperoni?"

❧ • ❦

"Mom! Mom!"

I ran through the darkness, my arms reaching and clawing through the blackness in front of me, but touching nothing. "Mom, where you?"

Her face appeared, the one that looked so much like my own, but the lovely smile I'd seen in pictures was gone. Her lips were curled back in a scream, her eyes seeing beyond me.

"Lainey!" she cried. "Run!"

I didn't wait to see what the danger was. I ran as fast as I could in the darkness, my mother's frantic voice in my ear. "Run, Lainey!"

I saw a sphere of light ahead, and I dashed toward it. It bobbed against the darkness, and I threw myself forward, desperate to catch the light.

I landed on a patch of grass.

Trees surrounded me on three sides. In front of me was a large white plantation house.

And standing in front of the house was my mother. Fear still danced in her eyes, but there was a calmness about her.

"Mom?" I didn't understand what was happening.

She stepped toward me, holding out her hand. I reached for her, but someone stepped out from behind me, getting to my mother before I had the chance to grasp her outstretched fingers.

The bloody woman from the road turned to face me, her bright green eyes trained on my face. She held out a hand to me, the emerald amulet around her neck glowing brightly. "Lainey."

"Leave me alone!" I screeched, shoving past her. "Mom!"

But my mother was already gone.

Sweat poured down my face and neck as I sat straight up in bed. Gasping for a breath of air, I gripped the wad of crumpled bedsheets and waited for it to fill my lungs. A few seconds passed and I could breathe, but I couldn't shake the images of my mother and the bloody woman from my nightmare.

The photograph of my mother and father sat on my bed-side table. A silver stream of moonlight fell perfectly against the picture, illuminating my mother's face. My eyes focused on the emerald amulet around her neck.

"What does it mean, Mom?" I whispered, hot tears filling my eyes. "What's happening to me?"

I sucked in another breath and fell back against my pillow, tearing my eyes away from the picture.

I wish you were here, Mom.

॰ • ॰

Come on," I murmured. "Brew faster."

The next morning, I stood bleary-eyed next to the ancient lime-green coffeepot on the counter, gripping my empty mug like the Jaws of Life. I wasn't much of a coffee drinker, but on mornings like this, when exhaustion clung to me like a second skin, I made an exception.

I hadn't slept well. No, that was an understatement. I hadn't slept *at all.* Right after I'd crawled into bed, the familiar black spots had appeared and my mind started alternating between flashes of things I couldn't explain and nightmares of my mother and the bloody woman.

By the time the images had finally faded away, I couldn't get my mind to shut off. Exhausted, I was depending on a cup—or two—of coffee to make me feel more human and less like a zombie.

Refusing to wait any longer, I yanked the coffeepot out midstream. I ignored the hissing sound the coffee made when it hit the burner and filled my mug. The hot liquid nearly scalded my throat when I took a few desperate swigs, but knowing the caffeine was working its way through my system gave me the jump start I needed.

Back upstairs, I dressed without really thinking about what I was putting on. I was aiming for comfort: a soft t-shirt, faded blue jeans, and red Chucks. My favorite black cardigan, however, was MIA. Swearing under my breath, I searched for an alternative. My eyes fell on the leather jacket lying on the corner of the bed. Ty's jacket.

It was absolutely ridiculous, but I had slept with the damn thing. The scent of spearmint and leather had been oddly comforting when I finally woke from the nightmares, and it occurred to me that it might have the same calming effect during daylight hours. So, given that I was feeling as cheerful as a cactus, I threw on the jacket and decided to hell with my sanity.

A car horn sounded outside. I stomped down the stairs and grabbed my backpack from the landing. Outside, Maggie's yellow '74 VW beetle was idling by the curb, the engine sputtering and coughing.

I yanked the rusted passenger door open and plopped down inside, throwing my bag onto the backseat.

"Hey now, easy on ole Delilah! She's fragile!" Maggie complained.

"Excuse me, I forgot your car is practically a senior citizen."

"Well, good morning to you too, grumpy pants." Maggie

pursed her lips, trying not to laugh, and shifted into drive, the whole car vibrating and shaking. "Sorry I'm late, but you know Delilah's not a morning person. It took a while to get her going."

I rolled my eyes. Delilah was about as reliable as a tin can. "Battery again?"

"Yeah, needs a new connector. I'll swing by Joe's house later and see how far a few bats of my eyelashes will get me. I bet he has some spare parts from his dad's shop." She grinned wickedly, and I snorted.

"You don't play fair. Joe's been in love with you since elementary school."

Maggie shrugged. "All's fair in love and car repair."

I rolled my eyes again but did manage to crack a tiny smile.

"So," Maggie began after turning on the main road, "I see we're going for the hot biker chick look today." The smirk on her face was one of pure amusement.

"Oh, don't even start with me. I know it's stupid, but—"

"Hey now," Maggie interrupted. "You don't have to explain anything to me. If I managed to meet some gorgeous mystery guy in this town, I'd probably steal more than his jacket." She waggled her eyebrows. She'd finally managed to coax out the details about my encounter with Ty and had done little else but tease me about it.

"Oh, good gravy!" I said, the tips of my ears growing hot. "I didn't steal it. He left it. I'm just . . . keeping it for him till he wants it back."

"Keeping it warm, you mean?"

I groaned. "I know it makes no sense," I said, pulling the jacket a little tighter around my shoulders, "but in a strange way, it kinda makes me feel better. After the library and everything . . . knowing that we're no closer to figuring out what's going on . . . I don't know. I guess I just felt like wearing it. That sounds really stupid, doesn't it?"

"Like I said, you don't have to explain anything to me, Styles." Maggie smiled as she pulled the car into the student parking lot. "Our friendship is a no-judgment zone. Besides, if the hot boy takes your mind off all the other crap, then I'm all for it." She drove down the aisles of the parking lot, looking for a space. "Hell, he could've been a figment of your imagination for all I know, but at least the thought of him is keeping you from freaking out."

I coughed, nearly choking on spittle. "Uh . . . well, I can definitely vouch for the fact that he was real enough."

Maggie looked over at me quizzically.

In the penultimate spot in the long row of parked cars, clashing violently with the familiar hand-me-down cars and a bunch of rusty trucks, was a shiny black car. It wasn't a fancy model or anything, but it was easily the newest and nicest vehicle in the lot, and more than one person stopped to check it out on the way into the building. But it wasn't the car that made my mouth drop open in shock. It was the guy leaning up against it.

"Because he's standing right over there." I cocked my head in his direction.

He was standing there in a pair of loose blue jeans and a long-sleeved black Henley. He was facing the building and wearing a pair of sunglasses, but it was undoubtedly him.

Maggie began to slow the car down, seeing an empty parking spot adjacent to the black car.

"Maggie! What are you doing?" I shrieked, ducking down in my seat.

"I'm parking! Don't you want to talk to him?"

"NO! Keep going!"

"Are you serious, right now? I never get a space this close to the building!"

"YES!"

Maggie stifled a giggle, but gave the Beetle a little bit of gas and headed toward the opposite side of the lot. "Of course, you realize you owe me huge best friend points for letting go of such a primo space so you can duck and cover from the guy you won't admit you're swooning over."

I ignored her, covering my face with my hands. "What is he doing here?"

"Well," Maggie said, still trying not to laugh, "you *could* ask him. But that would require actual face-to-face communication, and clearly you're not up for that."

I turned and glared at her. "Just tell me if you can still see him."

Maggie craned her neck toward the window looking back in the direction of the black car. "No, I don't see him anymore. The bell's about to ring though. Maybe he's already inside."

Thank God for small miracles. "Good."

"So, are you gonna explain what this sudden shyness is about? I mean, I thought you'd be kinda excited to see him again."

"I am. I mean, I think I am. I just . . . I don't know. I just don't have time to deal with this right now.

Maggie chuckled. "Don't you at least want to talk to him?"

I thought of our previous encounters, and the heat from my ears spread to my neck and cheeks. I shook my head. "No," I said, pulling my backpack from the backseat. "Come on, we're gonna be late."

We headed inside, making our way through the packed hallways. I was fully prepared to dive into the nearest doorway if I had to, but thankfully there was no sign of Ty.

At my locker, I crammed my books inside at warp speed. All I could think about was hightailing it to English class without being seen. I slammed the locker door shut, the metal clanging loudly, and hurried down the hall toward my classroom.

I ran around the corner and sighed with relief when the class door came into view. Just a few more steps and I would be home free.

But my feeling of relief popped like a bubble when the familiar tenor of two little words broke through my thoughts.

"Nice jacket."

I let out a squeal and spun around like a ninja, my arms up and ready for attack.

"Easy there, Karate Kid." Ty was leaning against a row

of lockers, his arms folded across his chest, the corner of his mouth slanted up in amusement.

"What are you doing here?" I asked, my heart racing.

"Heading to English. Same as you."

I rolled my eyes. "You know what I mean. What are you doing *here?* At my school."

"Well, according to this," Ty said, pulling a crumpled schedule from his back pocket, "it's *our* school."

"You go here?"

"Well," Ty said, pushing off from the wall, "my parole officer thought it would be a good idea for me to get a little education. Makes me look better to the judge."

I sucked in a breath of air—a little too quickly, in fact, which resulted in a small fit of coughing and sputtering. *Parole officer?*

"You all right?"

I waved my hand in dismissal as one last cough shook my shoulders. "Yeah," I managed, my voice strained. "Allergies." I stood up a little straighter and tried to play it cool, though I was secretly hoping a freak sinkhole would suddenly open up and swallow me whole.

"Right." Ty watched me for a moment, a full grin of amusement on his face, before finally leaning forward. "You know I was kidding, right?" He smirked. "I haven't talked to my parole officer in months."

"Oh," I shrugged. "Of course. Right."

Ty chuckled again. "Look, it's pretty basic. I'm eighteen

years old. If I want to graduate, I kinda have to attend this little establishment."

"Right. So you obviously just moved here. I mean, Lothbrook's a pretty small town. Everyone knows everyone—that kind of thing. I haven't really seen you around much."

Ty shrugged. "I guess I make it a habit of staying out of the spotlight."

"Yeah, except for those random fights in the alleyways," I pointed out. "Right? I'm assuming from the color wheel that is your face that it's a pastime of yours."

Ty laughed and a slight flush colored his cheeks—which in fact was covered in various degrees of fading bruises. "Sometimes I make an exception."

I resisted the urge to stick out my tongue. *Geez, when did I turn into a five-year-old?* Ty's knack of answering questions with complete non-answers was getting on my nerves, though. "Has anyone ever told you that you're kind of frustrating?"

Ty smirked again and moved a little closer. He smelled like laundry detergent. He leaned toward me. "Not today. But it's still early."

Narrowing my eyes, I put my hands on my hips, meeting his challenge. The tips of my ears blazed hot—though I wasn't sure if it was my annoyance or his proximity.

Behind me, someone cleared her throat.

Mrs. Runyan, my English teacher, was staring at me from the door of the classroom. "Ms. Styles, are you planning on joining us for class today?"

"Yes, I am. Sorry, Mrs. Runyan." I dashed into the

classroom and plopped down in my seat without waiting to see if Ty would follow. My seat in the back of the room was directly underneath the air conditioning vent, and despite the heat still burning my face, the cool air made me shiver. Mrs. Runyan led Ty into the room and pointed him in the direction of an empty seat. Ty caught my eye as he made his way down the aisle and grinned before settling in at his desk.

I pretended not to notice.

At the front of the room, Mrs. Runyan began giving directions for an upcoming persuasive essay. Her even monotone droned on and on about the role of persuasive writing and how to make and argue a claim.

While she lectured, I made a valiant effort to pay attention and stay focused, but my eyelids were drooping. The caffeine rush from the coffee was fading fast, and the insomnia-induced drowsiness was getting harder to fight.

Using the beefy boy in front of me for cover, I put my head on my desk and closed my eyes. *Just a few minutes . . . Just a few minutes to rest my eyes.*

Mrs. Runyan's voice was already fading into the background.

Just a few minutes.

And with that, everything around me faded away.

CHAPTER SIX

JOSEPHINE

A thick plume of smoke blackened the sky.
Josephine's heart pounded against her ribcage, and every visceral cell in her body screamed for her to run.

The warning of the blood moon—the very thing that had driven her from her bed in the first place—was lost behind the pillar of charcoal haze. An eerie orange glow broke through the trees as a symphony of discordant sounds sliced through the air, shattering the usual quiet of the night.

Josephine broke into a run, ignoring the pain of the branches that clawed her bare skin. She had forgotten her slippers when she left the house, and now the soft soles of her feet were paying the price. Blood squished between her toes, but she didn't stop running. Cold fear crawled up and down her spine, a strange juxtaposition against the heat that coursed through her body as she ran.

Her neat braid was coming undone, and long tendrils of dark hair whipped around her face. The emerald amulet hanging around her neck thumped painfully against her chest as she ran.

She was getting closer now. The sounds were becoming more defined: the horses whining in the stables, their frantic squeals sharp and panicked, the loud pop and crack of wood burning, glass breaking.

She burst through the tree line, her eyes wide and searching.

Bright orange flames danced, almost mesmerizingly, along the woodwork, igniting everything they touched. There was no saving it. The house that had taken two years to build, the place that had become her home, was lost. In minutes it would be nothing but a pile of ash and blackened rock. Josephine bit back a scream as the inferno burned.

Several feet away, two men dressed in black surveyed the work of the flames. She had never seen them before.

Where are father and mother? What about Mercy? The servants? Her mind was racing. *Henry! Oh God, where's Henry?* An image of their earlier rendezvous flashed before her eyes. The picnic by the river. His sweet smile. The caress of his warm lips against hers. A sharp pang pierced her chest at the thought of her beloved. She couldn't stand still any longer.

Without even thinking about her actions, she sprinted toward the house, her long nightgown billowing around her like a sail.

One of the men cried out as she raced past, but they wouldn't be able to stop her—she was too fast.

Inside the house, the scorching air was thick with smoke, and her lungs screamed for oxygen. Her eyes watered from the thick smoke, making the limited visibility even worse. She tried to find her bearings, but she could hardly see two feet in front of her.

"Mother!" she cried out, choking and gasping. "Father! Are you here?"

She kept moving forward.

With every rapid heartbeat, a spasm of pain ricocheted through her skull. The loud sounds that had been deafening only moments before were now distorted and muted, as though she were swimming and her head had slipped beneath the surface of the water.

She stumbled forward, losing her footing.

"Josephine!" a familiar voice called to her as she fell. "Josephine, you have to get out of here! Hurry!"

A hand grabbed her wrist, yanking her through the burning wreckage and out through the service door. Once outside, clean air filled her lungs, and she choked and gagged until her throat was raw.

"What were you doing, girl? Trying to get yourself killed?"

Josephine looked up and almost burst into tears. The man standing before her with his full beard and thick wavy hair was as familiar to her as her own reflection.

"Father!" She threw herself into his arms. His dark green

overcoat was singed and covered in soot, but he quickly removed it and covered Josephine's bare arms with it.

"Jo, you must listen to me. You are in grave danger."

"Father, I don't understand. What's happening? Where's Mama? What about—"

"He found us."

He found us. The sobering words crashed upon her like a bucket of ice-cold water. Her heart, already pounding with adrenaline, slammed against her rib cage, making her gasp. *"No* . . . please, Father, tell me it isn't true."

"I wish I could." His face held such sadness, such utter defeat, Josephine had to squeeze her eyes shut to keep from weeping. "I'm so sorry, Josephine. I tried to protect you, to protect my family. . . but I've failed."

His words were like iron pokers to her heart. "Father? Oh God, what of the others? Of Mother? Of Mercy? Of . . . of . . ." She trailed off as her father slowly shook his head, his eyes swimming in pools of tears.

"No . . . No!" A wail of pain tore from her lips. Had it not been for his strong arms around her, she would have collapsed.

"Josephine, listen to me. You have to go! You must run! More of his men are coming. You don't have much time." His face, streaked with ash and tears, was as grim and serious as she had ever seen it.

"No, Father, I can't leave you."

"You must." He gingerly fingered the amulet at her throat. "You have to protect it, keep it safe. No matter what, it must be protected at all costs."

"But I'm so afraid." The whispered words reverberated throughout her body as the truth of them resonated deep within her bones. She shivered.

Her father kissed her quickly on the forehead. "I know, my darling girl, but you must be brave. You know what to do. Now, go. Quickly!"

Josephine threw her arms around her father again, not minding that his arms nearly crushed her. "This is not good-bye, Father. I will see you again soon."

"Go, Jo! Run!"

With his urgent cry echoing in her ear, Josephine picked up what was left of her tattered nightgown and fled.

She hadn't gone very far when a shadow stepped out from behind a tall tree. A sharp yank of her arm brought her to an abrupt stop, and she screamed. One of the men in black had her arm in a vice, a cruel sneer across his face.

"And just where you do think you're going, girl?" he drawled, pulling her closer in his iron grip. His hot breath sent a wave of panic down her spine. Josephine tried to pull free, but the man was twice her size. He laughed, his eyes shining. He pulled her even closer. She could see the stubble on his chin and a symbol of interlocking triangles in the soft skin of his neck. *His* mark.

"Let me go!" she cried, trying with all of her might to force herself free.

He laughed again, his fingers gripping her arm so tightly she was sure her bones would break. "Oh, the Master will like you, he will." He sniffed her hair, and Josephine shrieked.

Then the man coughed and bright red blood exploded from his lips. Tiny crimson beads splattered against Josephine's face and body, staining her nightgown red. The man sputtered and grew limp. When he slumped forward, Josephine's knees buckled under the weight. She screamed and struggled to free herself from underneath the man's body.

Someone yanked the man off her. There was a knife plunged deep into his back.

Another hand reached for her. She batted it away, fighting to be free.

"Jo!" her father yelled in her ear, the grip on her tightening. "You must run! Go now! Hurry!"

Then a loud *crack* shot through the darkness and ricocheted back off the tree line.

The sound of a gunshot.

The sound of *death*.

The hand that held her arm jerked once, then relaxed.

The cacophony of angry sounds died away . . . except for one. Cruel, delighted laughter echoed across the trees, ringing in Josephine's ears.

She opened her eyes. The smoke made it difficult to see, but when her eyes adjusted, another man was lying on the ground next to the man in black.

A man with curly dark hair and a face that was the perfect mirror of her own.

A man with wide emerald-colored eyes now opened forever to the sky, as a pool of crimson blood stained the grass beneath him.

CHAPTER SEVEN

An earsplitting scream shattered the quiet of the room. It echoed across the walls and filled the small space.

I jolted upright in my desk.

Every single pair of eyes in the room was staring in my direction, and it took me way longer than it should have to realize that the screaming was coming from *me*.

I clamped my jaw shut, effectively cutting off the sound from my throat. But the damage was already done. Even Mrs. Runyan, who was known for her imperturbable temperament, was staring at me with wide, concerned eyes, her mouth open midsentence.

Beads of sweat rolled down my back, and my heart raced, the sound thudding like a drum in my ears. Time itself seemed to slow down as I scanned the faces of those around me. Hot tears welled up in my eyes; my cheeks and neck were blazing.

In the corner of the room, Ty leaned forward in his seat. When our eyes met, I lost it.

It was all too much.

I shoved back my chair, sending it toppling over, and ran from the room. Mrs. Runyan was calling my name down the hall, but I didn't care. I had to get out of there.

I kept running, giving no thought to the puzzled expressions of the people I passed in the hall.

Up ahead were the double doors that led outside to the student parking lot. Flinging them open, I ran into the blinding sun. There was no one to be seen in the parking lot, and I jogged through the cars until I collapsed, gasping for air, in between two cars. My whole body shook, and hot tears burned my eyes. I blinked them away, refusing to let them fall. I *hated* crying—especially in front of people—but all things considered, I couldn't not cry. A single tear slipped past my defenses and down my cheek. My mind was racing, and even after I managed to gulp down a few mouthfuls of air, I couldn't stop the onslaught of emotions crashing down upon me.

I was absolutely *mortified*.

Thinking about how everyone in the room had looked at me like I was crazy made my face and neck burn. I rubbed at my temples and forced myself to take a few deep breaths.

Ty's face floated into my thoughts. I groaned, recalling his bewildered expression. Of all the people in the world to have witnessed what was undoubtedly the most embarrassing thing that had ever happened to me, why did it have to be him? My heart raced even faster.

I rocked back on my heels and tried to calm down.

Everyone had embarrassing moments. I couldn't be the only person in history to have a nightmare in the middle of English class, right?

Overhead, the sun was high in the sky, and even though it was early, it was already shaping up to be a fairly warm day. I peeled Ty's leather jacket from my shoulders and held it in my hands, running my fingers over the worn leather.

Nice jacket.

The words came back to me, and before I even realized what was happening, my shoulders were shaking with laughter.

He must think I am a complete and utter freak. First, I get busted wearing his jacket, which I didn't even bother offering to return, and then he sees me screaming like a maniac in the middle of first period. I laughed even harder, wiping my eyes again with my fingers. "Guess I don't have to worry about him asking for my number," I mumbled under my breath.

It felt good to laugh, but the small reprieve was already fading away.

What had just happened? It was obviously a nightmare, but it wasn't my nightmare. It was *her* nightmare—*Josephine's* nightmare, her name now so clear in my mind, much like her face.

I shivered as the horrific images flashed through my brain. The image of Josephine's father, prostrate in death, caused my eyes to well up with tears again. I was only a baby when my parents died, but I knew well the hole left by that kind of loss, and the feeling made my chest ache.

I stared at the pavement, willing my supposedly intelligent brain to find the missing piece of logic or reason that would make this whole screwed-up situation make sense. But there was nothing.

Well, it's official. The only logical explanation to be had is that I am completely losing my mind.

I sighed and contemplated my next move. There was no way I was going back to English class, and since I hadn't bothered to grab my backpack—where I kept my cell phone during school hours—I didn't have any way to get in touch with Maggie.

I stood up and dusted myself off. The only option was to head to the nurse's station. If I claimed "female issues," she'd probably let me hide out in her office for a few periods. I might even be able to get a good nap in.

I was congratulating myself on the excellent idea—particularly the nap part—when the car next to me beeped. I turned around and realized I was standing next to the black car I had noticed earlier that morning.

Ty's car.

"Sorry, I couldn't resist."

He was standing on the other side of the car with both arms raised in mock surrender, the keys dangling from one hand. He had a concerned look in his eyes, but that crooked smile of his made it less obvious.

"Very funny," I deadpanned. *Seriously? Of all the people to find me . . .*

Ty chuckled quietly before glancing down at his shoes. When he looked back up at me, his smile was gone. My cheeks burned again as he stared at me. I was pretty sure my complexion was beginning to resemble a plum.

"You okay?" he asked.

I shifted from one foot to the other. I had hoped maybe he would do me a solid and pretend the whole debacle in class had never happened, but since that was no longer an option, I thought for a minute about how to answer him.

"Yes," I finally replied, "I'm fine." The truth wasn't worth telling.

He studied me for a moment. "You're lying."

"What?" I snapped.

"You're lying," he repeated, his voice low and even.

"You don't know that."

"Actually, I do."

"Oh yeah?" I challenged. "And how exactly would you know that?"

Ty shrugged. "Because people only say they're fine when they're really not."

"You're assuming things."

"Am I wrong?" Ty looked pointedly at me.

Dammit. Anger surged through me. "You know what? You don't know me. You don't know one single thing about me. I know you think you're witty and clever and all, but that doesn't make you an authority on all things *Lainey*."

"I don't claim to be an authority on anything, actually," Ty replied, his face serious. "I'm just good at seeing what's right in front of me."

"Oh, really? And what exactly do you see?"

Ty tilted his head to the side and then back again. "Well, for starters, I see a girl who is having a pretty shitty morning."

In spite of myself, I let out a small laugh—though it sounded more like a snort. "Yeah? Was screaming in the middle of class your first clue?"

"That *was* a pretty good indicator."

"Fair enough." I looked down at my shoes. "What else do you see?"

Ty toyed with the keys in his hand. "Well, you know," he said, with a smirk, "I'd tell you, but I'd have to kill you."

"Why can't you tell me?"

"Because where would the fun be in that?" he teased.

I wasn't sure whether to laugh or be seriously annoyed, so I sighed instead. How was it possible that one person could be both infuriating and almost charming at the same time? I suddenly had the strongest urge to fling myself across the small expanse of pavement between us. Part of me wanted to hug him or something, while the other half of me wanted very much to slap that smug look off his face. It was both amusing and confusing. *More proof that I am certifiably insane.*

"You're right," I blurted out, desperate to keep myself from doing something I would later regret. "I'm not fine."

Ty nodded. "I know."

Back up at the main building, the bell rang shrilly, and

people began pouring out of the double doors, heading toward the gym and athletic buildings. Panic washed over me as more and more people spilled out into the sunlight. I wasn't ready to face the gossip storm that was surely in full swing by now. I looked at Ty, trying not to choke on my anxiety.

"You know," he said, unlocking his car and tossing his books inside, "I think I've had enough school for today." He locked the car again and started walking toward the road.

"You've only been to one period!"

Ty turned around, grinning wildly. "Like I said, that's enough for one day."

"Well, where are you going?"

Ty gestured to the road. "Think I'll head into town."

"What about your car?"

"Eh, I'll get it later. It's a nice day for a stroll, don't you think?"

I stood watching, slightly stunned, as Ty turned back around and started walking toward the parking lot exit.

"You could come with me, you know," he called over his shoulder.

I bit my lip. Skipping school was a stupid idea. I couldn't afford to get behind in my classes. Skipping school with a guy I barely knew? An even worse idea. I should probably just go back inside and face the music. That was the logical thing to do, after all.

"Hey!" I called out to Ty's retreating back. "Wait for me. I'm coming."

CHAPTER EIGHT

"Are you sure about this?" I watched uncertainly as Ty wrapped my right hand with a thin cotton band.

"Trust me," he replied, not bothering to look up. "You'll thank me for this later."

I sighed and continued to watch as he meticulously worked the band. The stretchy fabric, wrapped around my wrist and then woven between my fingers, was taut and supportive, but not to the point where it constricted my circulation.

When he was finished, Ty secured the band and reached for my other hand. He gave it the same treatment, and then stepped back to admire his handiwork. He nodded once, satisfied.

"Follow me," he called over his shoulder as he walked toward the back corner of the room.

When I decided to follow Ty into town, the old gym on Elm Avenue was the last place I expected to end up, but stranger things had happened, and it seemed a moot point to question his confident smile. So, despite how awkward I felt with my hands wrapped up like burritos, I dutifully followed behind him.

Half a dozen cylindrical black bags were suspended from the ceiling by thick metal chains. Ty walked among them, running his hand along the synthetic fabric, until finally selecting a bag toward the end of the row. "Here," he said, handing me a pair of thick padded gloves. "Put these on."

"More?"

Ty chuckled. "The goal is to blow off some steam, not break your hands." He helped me pull the gloves tight and then wrapped the Velcro safety bands securely around my wrists. "All right, you're good to go." He stepped away from the bag. "Go ahead. Hit it."

I eyed the heavy bag. "How's this supposed to help again?"

"Just try it."

I huffed but rolled up on the balls of my feet, the way I'd seen boxers do on television, and took a tentative swing at the bag. It was surprisingly satisfying. I took another swing.

"Keep your wrists tight," Ty instructed over my shoulder. "It'll give you more control."

I adjusted. "Like this?"

"Exactly. Now, don't be afraid of the bag. Really hit it."

I nodded and took another swing, this one with more force. The resulting smack echoed in my ears. I hit the bag again. And then again.

"Maintain control of the bag. Don't let it swing back and forth so much."

I adjusted my stance again, following Ty's directions, and threw another punch. And another.

Every time my fist made contact with the bag, it was gratifying, like taking a deep breath after being underwater. The tension drained from my body with every swing. Beads of sweat rolled down my spine, and the muscles in my arms were starting to ache, but I didn't stop. Over and over, I hit the bag. The adrenaline coursed through my veins, forcing every ounce of frustration out of my body with each resounding smack.

I took another swing. Faster this time.

Another swing. Harder than the last.

Everything else faded away. It was just me and the bag.

It wasn't until I was completely spent that I sank to the floor, my chest heaving, my arms throbbing and achy.

"Lainey?"

I swallowed hard, an ache settling in my throat.

"Are you okay?" Ty knelt next to me, a warm hand on my shoulder, his eyes full of concern.

"I'm fine." He didn't look convinced. "Really, I'm okay. It's just . . . that was amazing." I rocked back on my heels and looked up at him with a wide smile. "To be able to let go like that, to just take it all out on the bag . . ."

Ty nodded. "It sure beats yelling at guys you barely know in the parking lot, huh?" He winked at me, smiling.

I winced. "I'm really sorry. I don't usually blow up like that, but things have been crazy lately and . . ."

"You don't have to explain. I get it."

"You do?"

"Yeah," he replied, plainly. "I do."

He didn't bother offering anything else in the way of explanation, and I blinked, feeling slightly frustrated as I watched him walk back toward the bags.

For the last hour or so, I'd been trying to figure Ty out, trying to determine what was behind those piercing eyes and crooked smile. But every time I was close to forming some sort of conclusion about him, he would say something that would completely change my mind. I wanted to write him off as just some typical teenage guy with a cocky sense of humor and an affinity for dark-colored t-shirts, but it was becoming very obvious that this guy wasn't as typical as I thought.

"So," I asked, eager to keep the conversation going, "do you come here a lot?"

"A couple times a week." He smiled again. "I help train some of the new guys, and Mike, the owner, lets me work out for free."

"Oh, so are you like some professional fighter or something?"

"No, nothing like that." Ty laughed. He got up and walked over to a red Igloo cooler and poured each of us a small paper cup full of water. "It's just in my blood." He handed me one of the cups. "My father taught me."

I took a sip of my water. "And now you can kick butt and take names?"

He laughed. "Yeah, I guess. Something like that."

"Want to show me some of your moves?" I nodded toward the bag.

Ty raised an eyebrow. "What for? You've seen me fight."

"True, but come on," I prodded, handing him the padded gloves. "Don't all badasses jump at the opportunity to show off for a girl?"

Ty thought for a minute and then laughed. "Only for the pretty ones," he said with a wink as he took the gloves from my outstretched hand.

The tips of my ears began to burn, and I gulped down another sip of water to hide the goofy grin on my face.

Jumping to his feet, Ty walked to the corner of the room and grabbed two cotton bands. He wrapped his own hands in record time and strapped the gloves securely to his wrists.

He stepped up to the bag and took a deep breath. He walked slowly around it, almost like an animal stalking its prey, his shoulders tensed in preparation. Then with another deep breath, he struck the bag.

I watched, awestruck, as he moved around it, his arms darting and swinging in perfect precision. His face was a mask of pure concentration, his eyes blazing with intensity. The muscles in his chest and back strained against the thin fabric of his t-shirt. His movements, though clearly practiced and purposeful, were full of power and intensity and looked almost graceful. The intricate patterns of his footwork and the staccato rhythm of his fists making contact with the bag were mesmerizing.

I knew nothing about fighting, what made someone good or bad, but from where I stood, Ty wasn't just an amazing fighter—he was a force of nature.

I didn't realize my mouth was hanging open until Ty delivered a final punch to the bag and whirled around to face me, sweat pouring down his face, his eyes shining and bright.

"Wow," I managed to force out, snapping my lips back together.

Ty waved his hand in dismissal and walked over to the Igloo again and downed several cups of water.

"No, seriously." I stood up. "That was amazing."

He shrugged. "My dad was a good teacher."

"I can tell. Does he still train with you?"

Ty's face fell. "No, he, uh . . . he passed away."

My stomach lurched, like someone had knocked the wind out of me. "Oh God, I'm so sorry. I didn't mean to . . ."

"It's okay," Ty interrupted. "Really."

I nodded, though I still felt like a jerk for bringing it up. "I am sorry though."

Ty sighed and walked back toward the bag, placing his hands tentatively on the fabric, his face pained and thoughtful. I watched him, chewing my bottom lip and silently berating myself for bringing it up. His expression was one I knew well.

I wasn't sure whether I should say something or just keep

my big fat mouth shut. "It's just my uncle and me," I finally blurted out.

Ty turned his head, his eyes asking the obvious question.

"Car accident," I confirmed. "When I was little."

This time it was Ty who looked sympathetic.

"I don't remember them much," I continued softly. "But my uncle says that my laugh is exactly like my dad's. And that I'm stubborn like my mom."

A few long seconds passed by.

"He loved corny jokes," I continued, not really knowing why. "And my mom was a really terrible baker."

Holy shit, Styles. Could you have made things any more awkward? I looked down at my hands, heat rising in my cheeks. I stood up, trying not to meet Ty's eyes. "I'm sorry. I don't know why I told you that."

"I'm glad you did." There was something in Ty's voice that made me look up again. He was still staring, but there was the hint of a smile across his lips. "My dad had a thing for 90s sitcoms."

The look on his face resonated deep within my core, and I realized that what I heard in his voice, what I was seeing in his eyes, was something I'd never experienced with anyone before: *understanding.* I smiled back.

My heart was beating ninety to nothing, and I fanned my face with my hand.

"So the street fighting," I said, wincing at the shrill squeak of my voice. "Why do you do it?"

Ty cocked his head.

"I mean," I continued, seeing his confusion, "from what I just saw, you could kick someone's ass in like five seconds. But back in the alley, you let them think they could win."

"You think I was holding back?"

I rolled my eyes. "I heard you laughing."

This time it was Ty's cheeks that turned pink. "You heard that, huh?" He reached up and rubbed the back of his neck. "Uh . . . would you believe me if I said it was fun?"

I pointed at the punching bag. "That thing made me feel like a million bucks, and while I've never done it myself, I can see how smashing someone in the face might be equally if not more satisfying." I giggled at the sheepish expression on his face.

Ty cocked his head and moved to stand in front of me. "You know something, Lainey? You surprise me." He quickly held up a hand. "In a good way, I mean."

My smile grew bigger. I wasn't offended at all. "I could easily say the same for you." Flirting was not my forte, but somehow I was managing to hold my own. It made my stomach jump around like a game of double Dutch.

"Here," Ty said, pulling my bundled hands toward him. "Let me."

With nimble fingers, he expertly unwrapped the bands from my hands. My heart was already beating fast, but as his fingers skimmed my skin, it began to race.

"Thanks," I said, when he was finished. "For bringing me here today."

"Of course." Ty's voice was low, and it sent a shiver

dancing across my skin. As I drew in a shaky breath, he reached out and carefully tucked a loose strand of hair from my ponytail behind my ear. His fingertips grazed my earlobe, and a sharp jolt of electricity shocked us both.

Ty jerked his hand away, and I reached up to smooth my hair. "Sorry about that," I said. "Damn static cling." I laughed, but the sound was all wrong.

Ty looked at me for a moment with wide, almost surprised eyes. Then a shadow crossed his face, and he stalked to the corner of the room where we had stashed our belongings. "I should probably be getting you back to school," he called over his shoulder, not bothering to look at me again.

What just happened? I looked down at my empty hands—the hands that seconds before I had imagined entangled in the dark locks that now swept over his eyes. I was hardly an expert on guys, but I'd felt a connection with Ty, and from the look in his eyes, he felt it too. So what had gone wrong? The emptiness pounding in my fingertips was hard to ignore. Frowning, I shoved my hands in the front pockets of my jeans.

"Yeah," I replied, trying to sound as nonchalant as possible. "Yeah, that's probably a good idea. I've got some studying to do, and Maggie is probably freaking out right now."

I wanted to say something, apologize for making things weird if that's what happened, but I had no idea what to say.

Ty turned to me, what looked like a strained smile on his face. "You ready?"

I nodded and followed him toward the door, my usual stress mechanism kicking in.

Awkward. Adjective. Meaning to feel displeasure or embarrassment; uncomfortable.

Ty didn't say anything else, so when he held the door open for me, I let out a sigh and stepped into the bright sunlight.

CHAPTER NINE

"Well," I said, plopping down next to Maggie in our usual cafeteria booth, "I think it's safe to say this day wins the award for 'Worst. Day. Ever.'" I groaned and covered my face with my hands.

Maggie gave me a sympathetic pat on the back. "Come on, Styles. It's not so bad."

"Not so bad? Mags, I fell asleep and screamed bloody murder in the middle of my English class."

"No one can blame you for that. Mrs. Runyan gives everyone nightmares."

I snorted. "Well, what about the part where I managed to make myself look like a gigantic idiot in front of the really hot guy I don't want to admit I'm crushing on?"

"I knew it," Maggie said with a grin. "Honestly, I really wouldn't worry about it. Clark Kent embarrassed himself all the time in front of Lois Lane and they still managed to make it work." She waved her hand. "I hardly think anything you've done today qualifies as catastrophic."

I sighed. "Look, I know you're trying to make me feel better, but I seriously doubt there's anything you could say that would make me even halfway reconsider my plan to go home and stay there until I'm thirty."

"Well . . ." Maggie leaned forward, her eyes dancing. "What if I told you I had some information about your mystery man?"

My head perked up. "What kind of information?"

"Personal information. Like the kind you would find in—let's say, someone's *personal* file."

"Personal file? But how would you . . ." My mouth dropped open. "You didn't!"

Her sheepish grin was the only response.

"Maggie!"

"What? All the office aides do it!" she said with a shrug, not the least bit bothered by the fact that she had broken a rule, much less that there were laws about that sort of thing.

"You could get suspended!"

"I'd have to get caught first. Look, you're my best friend, and I wasn't about to let some random—albeit seriously hot— guy come swinging into the picture without digging up some information on him."

I shook my head. "Maggie, I—"

"I know, I know. You're welcome. Now do you want to hear this or not?"

I cracked a smile. There really was no stopping her once she got going. "Proceed."

"Thank you. So his name is Tyler Marek, and he

apparently just moved here a few weeks ago. He's living with a friend of the family—some guy who owns a gym in town."

"The one he took me to today?"

"I would assume so. And apparently, he hasn't been enrolled in school for a while."

"That's weird," I said. "Did the file say why?"

"No, but I bet it has something to do with his father's death." Maggie leaned forward, her voice no louder than a whisper. "According to the file, his dad was murdered a while back."

"Murdered?"

"Yep. There was some kind of evaluation report from the counselor."

Holy shit. It all made sense now. The look in his eyes, the tightened expression. No wonder he looked as if someone had punched him in the stomach when I asked about his dad.

"That's awful. Was there anything else?"

Maggie shook her head. "Unfortunately, no. His file was pretty sparse. But hey, at least now we know he's not a serial killer or some kind of psychopath, right?"

"Um, I guess." I put my head back down on the table. "Although now I feel like an even bigger idiot."

Maggie gave me another pat on the shoulder. "Like I said, all things considered, it's not so bad."

"And what exactly would you classify as *bad?*"

She thought for a minute. "Well, when Jason Aaron tricked Wolverine into killing his own offspring, *that* was pretty bad. And when Spiderman gave up his marriage to Mary Jane to the demon Mephisto in order to save Aunt May's life, I cried for days. Oh! And Tony Stark's battle with alcoholism—that was awful! And then there was—"

"Okay, okay! Point made!" I said, laughing. "Forget I asked!"

Maggie gave a satisfied smile and took a big bite out of her ham and cheese sandwich. "I also think I might have a lead on your whole ghost thing. What did you say her name was again?"

"Josephine."

"Well, I think I found a way to get in contact with her."

I stared at Maggie. "Contact *Josephine?* Seriously?"

She smiled sheepishly and pulled a rumpled piece of paper out of her messenger bag. She took a breath and slid it across the table.

I scanned the paper. It was an article about the moon's orbit and its close proximity to the earth. I looked up. "Oh! There's going to be a Supermoon on Friday."

"Right! And according to my research, most paranormal activity coincides with some sort of celestial phenomena. Solstice, equinox." Maggie began to tick items off on her fingers. "Eclipse. I think that's when the veil between us and the spirit world gets . . . lifted. Or something like that." She shrugged. "So, it should be easier for us to contact her. I think we should go to the cemetery and give it a shot."

I blinked. "The veil between us and the spirit world?"

"Yes, the veil. Try to keep up, Styles. We've already missed the Autumnal equinox, and Halloween is still two weeks away. I think this is the closest thing we're gonna get." Maggie looked at me expectantly. "So what do you say? Are you in?"

I thought about it for a moment. "A good scientist examines the evidence, right? Well, a dead girl attacked me on the road, I'm having visions or dreams about said dead girl, and so far, despite everything I've tried, all I've figured out is that there's some connection between her and my mom." I let out a breath and shrugged. "I need answers. I need to find out why all of this has happened and what is has to do with my mom. This goes beyond logic and reason, so I need to look at the other variables."

I tapped the paper. "If we're gonna do this, we better start researching supermoons."

Maggie squealed and clapped me on the back. "That's the spirit, Styles!" She laughed. "See what I did there?

Maggie was too busy cracking up at her own joke to notice that I wasn't laughing.

Someone moved beside me. I had looked up, making eye contact.

Standing a few feet away, and staring directly at me, was Josephine.

∾•∾

The paper fluttered slightly, before landing on my desk. The flash of white startled me enough to erase the image of *her* face. Even though three days had passed since that day in the cafeteria, Josephine was still everywhere I looked. I would turn the corner, and there she'd be, staring at me with those sad, knowing eyes of hers. It was seriously creeping the hell out of me.

"Just think of it like this, Styles. You're like that kid from the *Sixth Sense!* How freaking cool is that?" Maggie had said. She, of course, grew more ecstatic after every new Josephine sighting. I, however, did not.

I glanced at the paper, my eyes slow to focus. It was my latest history essay about the Great Depression and FDR's New Deal. But the grade circled in red ink at the top right corner was foreign to me. C+. I double-checked the name to make sure I had the correct paper. My stomach flip-flopped at the sight of my name written in my own, curling script. I'd never gotten a C before. Not even close.

I eyed the book sitting on the corner of my desk. *Supermoons: Warnings from Beyond the Grave?* Several pages of notes stuck out from the corners.

It had been an easy transition for me—throwing myself into the research—and I didn't realize how much my focus had shifted until now. My Ivy League dreams sputtered to life in my mind, but that red "C" glared at me from the corner of the page.

"Damn you, Josephine," I muttered under my breath, fighting the urge the crumple the paper. A lump was forming in my throat, but I swallowed a few times to dislodge it.

It's one paper. Don't panic, the voice inside my head

reasoned as I shoved the paper into my binder, the lump growing bigger. *Just one paper.*

"Yeah, but scientists don't get Cs," I muttered, silencing the voice.

When the shrill bell rang signaling the end of class, I stood quickly, eager to escape.

"Lainey?" Mr. Reinhard, my history teacher, called out. He was staring at me over the rim of his reading glasses. "Can you stay for a few moments, please? I'd like to speak with you."

"Yes, sir?"

Mr. Reinhard trained his eyes on me, his forehead furrowed. "Lainey, about your latest essay. I—"

"I know what you're going to say," I interrupted, "but please. I know it wasn't my best. It's been a weird few days. I haven't been sleeping well, and I—" I broke off, not sure how to explain it further. "I'm just off my game right now, Mr. R."

Mr. Reinhard nodded. "We all have off days, Lainey, but I'm concerned. This week, you've seemed really distracted. I've never known you to get anything less than an A."

His voice was kind, but that only made the lump in my throat triple in size. "I know. I'll try harder."

Mr. Reinhard raised an eyebrow. "Is everything okay at home, Lainey? I heard about what happened in your English class when you—well, have you considered speaking with someone? Our counselor, Mrs. Fox—"

I shook my head. "It was just a nightmare. Stupid, really. I'm fine. I'll do much better on the next essay, I promise."

The lines around Mr. Reinhard's eyes softened and he sighed. "Just go home tonight and get some rest. Okay? I think you need it."

When he dismissed me, I practically ran toward the exit. I needed some fresh air.

Hissing through gritted teeth, I waited until I was safely out of the building before I let out a frustrated yell. A few people walking by stared at me, but I didn't care.

There was a small grove of trees up ahead and a courtyard with benches and tables designated for students. It was mostly empty; a couple was making out on one of the benches, and one of the art kids was stretched out on the grass, sketching in a notebook. There was also someone else, a guy, propped up against one of the trees, his face hidden behind a book.

Plopping down on a patch of shaded grass, I closed my eyes and let out a long huff.

"Bad day?" a voice called out.

You have got to be kidding me. I opened my eyes and sure enough, a familiar pair of blue eyes were looking straight at me. Ty was leaning around his open book, the usual smirk on his lips.

"How do you keep doing that?" I demanded.

He raised an eyebrow at me.

"Popping up out of nowhere." I waved my hand as if it were the most obvious thing in the world. "And always when I'm at my worst." Ty chuckled and moved to sit across from me, ignoring my question. He pulled a brown paper sack from his backpack and handed me something wrapped in plastic wrap.

"A sandwich?"

"It might not be the answer to your problems," Ty said, unwrapping his own sandwich. "But I personally believe that life is a whole lot more manageable on a full stomach." He took a bite of his sandwich and nodded at me as if he were the authority on such matters.

I looked down at the sandwich in my hand. It was peanut butter and grape jelly—my favorite. My stomach rumbled at the sight of it.

I rolled my eyes, feeling ridiculous, and took a bite. It was actually quite satisfying, and I took another bite without any hesitation.

"You wanna talk about it?"

I swallowed. "Not really."

Ty nodded and took another bite, chewing slowly.

We sat there without speaking, both of us focusing on our food.

Maybe it was because he didn't push me, didn't ask me questions I couldn't answer, but as I sat there, the tension in my shoulders eased, and with each bite of the sandwich, the lump in my throat slowly dissolved. There were no expectations to meet, no obstacles to overcome. It was just easy. Sitting next to Ty, eating PB&J was the most normal thing I'd done in a while.

The calm was unfortunately short-lived, however. Something tugged at me; the last remnants of the handprint on my arm—now almost completely faded—tingled. I looked up, nearly choking on my next bite of sandwich. Josephine stood a few feet away. She stared at me as usual, but it wasn't the normal look of intensity I'd become accustomed to. It was something much deeper. It took me a minute to place it, but when I did, it nearly took my breath away. The look on her face was sadness—the kind you feel deep within your soul. It made my chest ache.

Lainey. Josephine reached out a hand to me. Her eyes pleaded with mine. *Lainey.*

"Hey." Ty nudged his shoulder against mine.

I tore my eyes away from Josephine's face.

"You okay?"

I nodded. "Fine. Just a lot on my mind." When I looked back, Josephine was gone. I sighed and turned my attention back to my sandwich. *I have to figure all this out. I just have to.*

As I swallowed my last bite, my eyes fell upon the book in Ty's lap, the one he'd been reading before I showed up. It was a worn paperback, several of the pages loose and sticking out of the top. The cover was half missing, but I knew it well.

"The Great Gatsby?" I asked, pointing at the book.

Ty smiled, somewhat sheepishly, and picked up the book in his hands. "Fitzgerald is a favorite of mine."

I smiled back. "Mine too."

Ty had also finished his sandwich and was busy placing our empty plastic wrap back in the brown bag. When he had shoved the trash back into his backpack, he picked up the book and looked at me. He smiled at me, opening to the page he had dog-eared, and then began reading aloud.

I couldn't help but stare. How was it possible that this mysterious boy who picked fights for fun understood the simple satisfaction of a peanut butter and jelly sandwich and the peaceful calm that came from reading beautiful prose?

Who are you? I mused, watching as he read.

He was a natural reader, his voice automatically rising and falling with the cadences of Fitzgerald's style. His face was bright, and I could tell he was enjoying the story as much as I was. *What a mystery you are, Tyler Marek.* I smiled and lay back on the grass to listen, enjoying the stillness of the moment.

When the bell rang, Ty finished the page he was on and closed the book with a gentle snap. "Feel any better?"

"Yeah, I do." I sat up, fighting a yawn. I peeked over my shoulder, but Josephine was still nowhere to be seen. I let out the breath I was holding. "Thank you for the sandwich . . . and for reading. It was really nice."

Ty nodded his head. "You're welcome."

I stood up and dusted the grass from my clothes. "Chem for me next. You?"

Ty followed suit. "History." He looped the straps of his backpack over his shoulders. "Can I walk you to class?"

My heart gave a tiny flutter. "Sure."

We didn't say anything as we headed toward the building, but there wasn't any need to. I think we both felt the ease of just walking beside one another.

When we walked through the double doors, I saw Maggie pacing back and forth in front of her locker.

"Styles?" she yelled, waving at me. "Where the hell have you been?"

She stomped over, almost skidding to a stop when she saw who I was standing next to.

Ty chuckled under his breath beside me.

"Ty, this is Maggie," I said, stifling my own laugh at the wide expression in her eyes. "Maggie, this is Ty."

Ty stuck out his hand. "Nice to meet you, Maggie."

Maggie looked slightly shell-shocked, but she recovered and reached out to shake his hand. "You too."

Ty gave her his signature smile and then turned toward the history hall. "See you guys later." I waved and watched him go.

Maggie waited till he was out of earshot and elbowed me hard in the ribs. "Damn, Styles." She grinned wickedly. "No wonder you skipped class."

"God, Mags, can you just not? It's not what you think."

"Oh, yeah? Then what was it?"

I stopped, the moment in the courtyard so perfectly undefined in my mind—I didn't want to ruin it by slapping a label on it.

"It was a just a sandwich, Mags. That's it."

Maggie scoffed and put her hands on her hips. "A sandwich?"

"Yup."

With a heavy sigh, Maggie rolled her eyes and started

walking in the direction of her next class, one we shared. "Fine, keep all the juicy details to yourself. Just remember, Styles. Friends before food . . . *and* hot boys."

I rolled my eyes and followed her, but when I turned the corner, I jolted to a stop.

There she was, staring at me again, the same mournful expression in her eyes.

"Josephine," I whispered.

I took a step toward her, but inky black spots appeared before my eyes, and the world slipped away.

CHAPTER TEN

JOSEPHINE

The wind outside was deafening as it ripped through the trees, but even louder than the howling gale was the uncontrollable chattering of Josephine's teeth.

Her skin was layered in gooseflesh, and her icy fingers fumbled with the knot of her shawl, untying it and pulling it even tighter around her shoulders. The threadbare fabric offered little in the way of warmth. She longed to light a fire—to be warm and dry for the first time in days—but the orange glow would be too easily seen. It had been pure luck that she had found shelter at all; to tempt fate further would be unwise.

The single-room shack must have been a logging cabin at one point in time, but it was clear from its state of disrepair that it hadn't been used in a while. The walls were bare, and the only pieces of furniture, a rickety wooden table and a single chair, were covered an inch deep in dust and cobwebs. Piled in the corner was a small heap of old burlap potato sacks. It was here that Josephine sank to her knees and tried as best she could to settle in for the night. She was weary and desperate for rest, but the hard floor was agony to her aching body, and the cold seemed to seep straight through her skin and resonate deep in her bones. The worst pain, however, was the deep hollow feeling of her stomach. How long had it been since she'd had anything to eat? She couldn't remember.

The days of running were taking their toll on her.

Tears pooled in her eyes, but she blinked them away. No matter what, she couldn't let herself fall apart. She had to keep going, had to keep running until she was safe.

Until *it* was safe.

Wiping her nose with the back of her hand, she unclasped the amulet from around her neck. She held it in her hand, a few whispered words on her lips. The crackle of energy and a warm green glow filled the small space. In the place of the amulet, Josephine held a large leather-bound book. It looked ordinary enough, with its worn cover and frayed edges, but it hummed with power. Magic tingled in her fingertips as she flipped carefully through the pages.

She knew she was being foolish; opening the book in its raw form would create an energy pulse. She might as well be sending a flare into the sky, signaling her location. Her resolve, however, had weakened, and a terrible grief, like an iron fist clenched around her heart, was threatening to crush her.

She'd lost her entire family. Everyone she loved was gone.

The book in her hands was the only connection to them that she had left, and she needed to feel it—even if only for a few precious moments.

You have to protect it, keep it safe, her father had urged her. *It must be protected at all costs.* Josephine's fingers dug into the worn binding as she clutched the book. "At all costs, indeed," she thought bitterly to herself, holding her family's heritage—their history, their lineage, their *magic*—in her lap. The fist around her heart clenched even tighter.

She had never felt more alone in her life.

A sob threatened to erupt from her throat, so she bit down hard on her lip to keep from crying out; she tasted copper on her tongue. The unbearable weight of the book grew heavier with every passing minute.

Choking back the tears, she held her palm down over the book and began to speak again. Her voice, although no more than a whisper, was confident and strong.

The air in the room shifted as the magic once again took hold. The book vibrated, and a pale green light draped around its edges. Soon, it began to shrink, and its form grew distorted. It twisted in on itself and formed new edges. The transfiguration was almost complete.

Josephine's cheeks flushed as the magic coursed through her, warming her chilled skin. It took only seconds, and when the green light faded, the book in her lap had been replaced once more with the small but ornate emerald amulet. Its oval face glowed slightly as the magic settled, before finally growing dark.

Her fingers trembling, she refastened the amulet around her neck. It was risky to use magic—stupid, even—but as the amulet came to rest at the base of her throat, right above her heart, the weight of her burden lessened. It was humming and pulsating as if it were alive, as if it had a heartbeat, and in that moment, the loneliness eased.

Yet there was one pain the amulet couldn't ameliorate.

Henry. Josephine's heart cracked open at the thought of him, and her mind recalled his face—an image that already seemed to be fading. She closed her eyes, savoring every detail: his unruly blond hair that was too short to be tied back in a tail; his calloused but gentle hands against her skin; the way he always smelled of pine and leather.

Outside, the wind had picked up. Its shrill whistle through the trees sent chills down Josephine's back. Wrapping her hands around her ears, she curled up in a tight ball and began to hum a soft lullaby, letting the image of Henry's face soothe her aching heart.

A bright flash of lightning illuminated the room, accompanied by a loud bang as the cabin door swung suddenly open. Josephine leapt to her feet, her heart pounding. A figure moved across the length of the floor. Her stomach pitched violently as she realized her worst fear.

They had found her.

Inching her way along the wall, she used the darkness as a cover, praying the old creaky floorboards wouldn't give her away. She'd have to make a run for it.

Mustering all her courage, Josephine threw herself at the

open door. Rain pelted her skin as she darted into the night and bolted for the tree line.

She had made it only a few feet when a pair of strong arms wrapped around her like a steel cage, lifting her off her feet. Josephine screeched and kicked her legs with all her might. A deep voice yelled against her scream, but the heartbeat pounding in her ears made it difficult to focus on the words. She thrashed about trying to break free, but the hands wrapped around her arms only tightened as her attacker moved back toward the cabin. No matter how hard she tried, she couldn't break free.

At the door of the cabin, her attacker lowered her to the ground and whirled her around.

"Josephine! It's me! Jo!"

The voice that broke through her screaming was familiar. In fact, she would know that voice anywhere.

Josephine opened her eyes and blinked away the tears and raindrops. When her eyes focused, the first thing she noticed was a pair of pale eyes the color of spun straw. She sucked in a breath.

"Henry?" she choked out. "You're alive?"

"Of course I am," Henry replied, helping her to an upright sitting position.

For a few seconds, all Josephine could do was stare. Was this a dream? Was the man who had captured her heart so long ago really standing in front of her?

She carefully reached out with trembling fingers and brushed his cheek. A layer of stubble covered his strong jaw.

As her fingers moved across the planes of his face, she began to tremble even harder. It was when he finally covered her hand with his own that she realized the man in front of her was no apparition or figment of her imagination.

He was real.

A hysterical cry erupted from her throat as she threw herself into his arms. She didn't care that she was covered in mud or that they were likely to be struck by lightning if they didn't take shelter soon. All that mattered was that Henry was *alive*.

Josephine sobbed against his chest, listening to the rhythm of his heartbeat for reassurance, as Henry wrapped his arms around her and murmured soothing words in her ears. She couldn't make out his words, but the deep tenor of his voice made her ache with relief.

"Shhh, Jo. It's all right. I'm here." Henry pried her away from his chest and pulled her face up to his. He pushed the matted strands of wet hair out of her eyes and gave her a gentle kiss. Despite the chill in the air, his lips were warm.

"Come on," he whispered, when they broke apart. "Let's get inside. This storm is likely to kill us both."

Still reeling from shock, Josephine was shaky on her feet, but Henry's strong arm wrapped around her waist and supported her as they made their way back to the cabin.

"I don't understand," she said, pulling Henry down beside her on the pile of potato sacks. "I thought you were dead."

"I probably should be. I was in the barn when those men attacked. One minute I was fighting with one of them, and the next minute I woke up on the ground with the barn going up in flames around me. I barely got out in time.

"It wasn't until I overheard the men talking that I realized I wasn't the only one who got away," Henry continued, squeezing her hand tight. "I knew it had to be you, Jo. As soon as it was safe, I headed south. I had a hunch you'd stick close to the river. It wasn't until a few days ago that I found your tracks. I was beginning to think I was wrong, that I'd never be able to find you."

"Well, you are the best tracker in the area." Josephine snuggled a little closer. "And you did find me."

"I wasn't going to give up until I did just that. I won't let anyone hurt you, Jo."

After days of running, terrified for her life, Henry's words were like a lifeline. A tear rolled down Josephine's cheek, followed by another. She clung tighter to Henry, and an almost peaceful silence settled over them as they held each other.

But Josephine knew it was a stolen moment.

"We can't stay here," she finally whispered into the darkness. "We should keep moving. He won't stop until he's hunted me down."

Her words had a sobering effect on Henry. He peeled himself away from her and looked into her eyes, his face solemn. "He? Jo, who are those men? I've never seen them before. Why would someone want to harm you and your family?"

Josephine bit her lip. Should she tell him the truth? And if she did, would he accept it? Her father had always warned her of this, of revealing their secret. But this was Henry. He had risked his own life to come after her. He loved her. He deserved to know.

She took a deep breath. "Henry, there's something you have to know about my family. I . . ." The words caught in her throat.

Henry's eyes narrowed in confusion, but he gave her hand a reassuring squeeze.

"My father," she managed to continue, "comes from a line of very powerful . . ." Her throat tightened, making it difficult to speak, and her mind was working overtime trying to come up with the proper words to say. "You see, my father's family . . . those men . . ."

A sob of frustration broke through her lips, and Josephine buried her face in her hands. The fear and anxiety crashed down upon her as heavy as her grief. She tried to swallow it down, to push it deep into the back of her mind, but after days of forcing herself to be numb, her resolve was disintegrating.

"Oh, Henry," she sobbed from behind her hands. "I'm so afraid. I don't know what to do."

With gentle fingers, Henry pried her hands away from her face. "I won't let anything happen to you, Jo. I swear it." He pushed her long hair away from her face, his hand tracing the contours of her neck before kissing the curve of her shoulder.

For a few precious seconds, the only thing Josephine could think about was the feel of Henry's lips, the heat that flushed her skin at his touch, but no sooner had he broken away than did her body begin to ache from the unbearable weight of her emotions.

She buried her face in the crook of his neck as hot tears pricked her eyes. "They're dead, you know," she finally whispered. "My father. Mother and Mercy. Everyone." She continued to weep.

As she clung to him, Henry rocked her back and forth. "I know, my love. I know."

The emotions tormenting her were excruciating, and with Henry's strong arms wrapped around her, Josephine finally gave in and let herself feel the full extent of her grief.

Her body shook violently, and sobs tore from her throat as she cried for the family she had lost. Henry held her against his chest, and Josephine was sure that his arms were the only things keeping her from breaking into a thousand pieces.

Henry kept his hold on her long after her tears subsided.

"I'm sorry," Josephine said, sitting up. "I shouldn't fall apart like this. I'm just so thankful you're here. I thought I was all alone."

"Listen to me." Henry leaned forward, his expression fierce. "You will never be alone, Jo. I will always look after you."

"Always?"

"Always." And as if to seal his declaration with a kiss, Henry pulled her toward him, capturing her lips with his own. It wasn't until she tasted salt that Josephine realized that the tears were not entirely her own.

Goose bumps rose on her skin and she shivered, but this

time, it had nothing to do with the cold. Henry's fingers traced down her arms, his lips like a gentle caress at the base of her throat. Warmth pooled in the pit of her stomach, and it wasn't long until her entire body burned. She wrapped her arms around his broad shoulders, pulling him tight against her body. Henry's lips moved from her skin, and Josephine barely had time to take a breath before his lips came crashing back down on hers.

Their kiss deepened, and Josephine gave herself over to it, letting her pain wash away like rainwater. The only thing she could think about was Henry. Of his strong hands moving across her back. Of the hot kisses he trailed up and down her slender neck. Everywhere he touched felt on fire, his fingers leaving a trail of what felt like tangible flames on her skin.

Her hands gripped his shoulders as she tried to pull him even tighter around her slender frame. Her arms were aching, but the burning inside her dictated her every move, and she couldn't let go.

She didn't want to.

So when he laid her against the worn wooden floor, she closed her eyes and gripped him tighter.

CHAPTER ELEVEN

"Hello?" A pair of fingers snapped in front of my face. "Earth to Styles. Come in, Styles."

I blinked several times before Maggie's face came into view. I recognized the row of lockers behind her head, and the chatter from people moving past us confirmed that we were still in the hallway, in the exact same spot we'd been standing when I saw Josephine.

"Um . . . are you okay?" Maggie was staring at me, one eyebrow raised.

I nodded my head. "Yeah . . . sorry." I glanced around for Josephine, but she was gone. "I just saw Josephine again. She showed me another . . . vision or whatever."

"Just now?" Maggie's face brightened. "What did she say? What did you see?"

"She was hiding, on the run from the people that attacked her family. But then someone found her."

Maggie gripped my arm, already deeply engrossed in the telling.

"It was her lover or husband, I think," I continued. "Josephine thought he'd been murdered like the others, but he'd managed to escape."

"And?" Maggie demanded. "What happened next?"

"They . . ."

I won't let anyone hurt you, Jo. The words echoed in my ears, and a hot flush crept up my neck as the corresponding images rippled through my thoughts. It was uncomfortable being so present in someone else's tender moment—especially considering my own experience in the love department was limited at best. I shrugged. "Nothing, they just . . . reconnected. That's all."

"Reconn—oh!" Maggie's knowing grin made the fire under my skin burn even hotter. Thankfully, she didn't press me further. "She's obviously showing you these things on purpose. Why, though?"

"I feel like she's trying to tell me something," I said. "But I have no idea what."

"Well, all the more reason for us to check out that supermoon, right?"

I nodded. "Right. I was doing some research earlier and—"

The shrill clang of the bell cut me off. I groaned. That red glaring "C" from earlier flashed in my mind. "I guess it's chemistry first. Paranormal investigation later."

Maggie looped her arm through mine as we headed toward the science lab. "I'll hold you to that, Styles."

I laughed. "I'm counting on it."

❧ • ❧

On Friday night when we pulled into the parking lot at the cemetery, the sky was dotted with stars. The moon was a big, shining orb in the sky, despite the thick layer of fog that had settled over the grounds. Drooping magnolia trees loomed eerily over the pathways and headstones, and Spanish moss hung from the low branches. Tendrils of ivy wound around the wrought iron gate that surrounded the premises, and everything looked gothic and full of mystery. The graveyard was spectacularly spooky—the perfect location for contacting a ghost.

"It looks like something right out of Edgar Allan Poe's *Tales of Mystery and Imagination*," I said, scrunching my nose.

"Doesn't it, though?" Maggie beamed, peering eagerly out the window.

"It's certainly creepy enough."

"This is one of the oldest cemeteries in the state," Maggie said. "I looked it up, and there are stones here that date back to the 1700s. My guess is if there's anywhere we'll find Josephine, it's here. Now, come on. It's time to track down a ghost!"

"It does look promising," I said, trying to ignore the way my stomach was churning.

Maggie stopped right outside the main gate and slung off her backpack. She began pulling things from inside— flashlights, a mirror, several pieces of chalk, matches, salt, candles, a thick white crystal on a string—and arranging them neatly on the pavement.

"Whoa, Mary Poppins," I said, staring at the supplies. "What's all this?"

I'd done a lot of reading on supermoons, but nothing I read mentioned the arsenal Maggie was assembling.

She rolled her eyes. "Contacting the spirit world is complicated, Styles. I wasn't sure what we'd need. I had to come prepared."

"Right. I guess I didn't know that," I deadpanned. "*Séances for Dummies* wasn't exactly high on my reading list."

Maggie glared at me for a minute before turning her attention back to her supplies. She pulled a composition book from her bag and flipped to a page covered in her messy scrawl. "Just give me a few minutes to make sure I've got it all in order."

Kicking loose pieces of gravel with my shoes, I walked toward a dilapidated picnic table off to the side of the main gate. The magnolia trees were blowing in the wind, casting strange shadows on the slabs of wood. I sat with my hand in a sliver of moonlight, watching the shadows dance across my skin. My stomach was in knots, and my hands and feet tingled with nervous energy. I began to run the facts through my mind—everything I'd gleaned about supermoons and then every little detail I recalled from the visions of Josephine.

"You're doing this to find the answers," I reminded myself. "Don't be a chicken shit, Lainey." I shook my shoulders out and took a deep breath. Whatever Josephine had to tell me, I needed to be ready.

I jumped off the table and turned to head back toward Maggie when I noticed that a figure was making its way toward me. My heart reacted before my brain did, jolting in my chest. The cemetery didn't get a whole lot of foot traffic during the day, and I doubted the evening hours were any different.

Panic lanced through me, and my mind immediately began imagining a scene from *Law and Order*. I almost yelled for Maggie, but the words caught in my throat.

There was something familiar about the strong set of his shoulders—I was sure it was a guy—and the way he shifted his weight from one foot to the other. Tension stretched across his back, and I watched as he reached up and entwined both his hands behind his neck—a gesture I'd seen Gareth make on several occasions when he was thinking hard about something.

As he came closer, I got a better look at his face.

"Ty?"

He stopped and trained his eyes on me. He was wearing a plain white t-shirt over a pair of worn jeans and looking more like James Dean than anyone had a right to. My heart began to race. I gulped. "Hey," I managed to squeak out.

Ty took a few steps closer to the table and nodded. "Hey," he replied, his expression changing into a smile. He sat down on the picnic table. "What are you doing here?"

I raised an eyebrow. "I could ask you the same question."

Ty shrugged. "I like to go for walks in the evening. Helps me clear my mind."

"And a cemetery is your idea of a good place for a leisurely stroll?"

A strange expression crossed Ty's face. I couldn't place it, and it was quickly replaced by his usual half smile. "Why not?"

A beam of light cut through the darkness, landing on Ty's face. He squinted and raised a hand.

"Oh, it's you," Maggie said, walking over, her flashlight still aimed at his face. "What are you doing here, Pretty Face?"

My cheeks flamed. "Maggie!"

"What?" Maggie looked at me for a second, then trained her eyes back on Ty. "Seriously, what are you doing here?"

"Just walking. It's a beautiful night." Ty gestured to the sky. The full moon was a silver orb shining brightly against the velvet backdrop of the night sky.

"Uh-huh," Maggie said. "Well, if you're here, you might as well help." She tossed him one of the flashlights and gave me an obvious wink. "Come on."

Ty grabbed the flashlight out of the air. "And what exactly are we doing?"

"We're—"

"We're doing research," I blurted out. "For a history project." There was no way I was about to admit the real reason behind our visit to the graveyard.

Maggie snorted but didn't contradict me. She just rolled her eyes and gave me a look that said, "Really, Styles?"

I pushed past her and walked through the front gate. I wasn't sure how I was going to explain Maggie's bag of supplies or keep Ty from thinking we were both complete nut jobs, but I was determined to try.

I moved through the headstones, reading off the names in my head as I passed.

Lainey.

I jumped, a cool shiver cascading down my spine.

The voice whispered again in my ear. *Lainey.*

I twisted my head back and forth a few times before I saw her. Josephine was standing under a tall tree, waving her arms. Her eyes were wide and her lips were moving, but no sound came out. The look on her face set an alarm bell off in my head.

"You okay?" Ty was at my shoulder, silhouetted by the moonlight.

"Yeah, sorry," I said, as Josephine blinked back into the shadows. "I . . . thought I saw something." I wasn't sure what else to say.

"Well, we *are* in a graveyard," Ty said with a smile, though it didn't reach his eyes. "Maybe it was a ghost."

I swallowed. "Yeah, maybe." *You have no idea how right you are.* I waited for a few seconds, but Josephine didn't reappear. I headed toward Maggie, a feeling gnawing at my mind: something was wrong.

Lainey!

This time, her voice was as light as the wind, barely above

a whisper, but with a resonating undercurrent that made my entire body tense.

"Josephine?" I whispered into the darkness. I was trying not to panic, but the look I'd seen on her face was disconcerting. A layer of goose bumps popped up, coating my skin. The air itself seemed suspended . . . as if it was waiting for something.

"Mags—" I broke off. A strange pressure wrapped around me and I couldn't breathe. My heart thumped in my chest, and every nerve cell in my body prickled.

"What's wrong?" Maggie appeared at my side.

It took all my effort to respond; the pressure squeezed me like a vice. "I don't know," I managed to whisper. "But I saw her."

"Josephine's here?" Maggie's eyebrows shot up. "That's great!"

The pressure lessened, but uneasiness still coursed through me. "No, something's wrong. It was like she was trying to talk to me but couldn't. I don't know, Mags . . . the look on her face was . . . something's not right."

"You guys okay?" Ty appeared beside us, and we both jumped.

"Holy crapkittens," Maggie squealed, smacking Ty with her hand. "Don't you know not to creep up on someone in the middle of a cemetery?"

"Sorry. Wasn't trying to scare you."

I tried to laugh, but it came out breathy and high-pitched. Cringing, I gave a little shrug and started walking toward another section of the cemetery. *Maybe if I'm alone, she'll come back.* Glancing behind me to make sure I was out of earshot, I whispered, "Josephine? Are you there?"

Though the moon was high in the sky, the trees in this part of the cemetery were dense and looming, not letting in much light. Another shiver darted down my back, and with shaky hands I reached in my back pocket for the flashlight I'd shoved there.

I clicked on the power. The beam of light was solid for a few seconds before flickering and going out.

"What the hell?" I tapped the flashlight against the palm of my hand and clicked the button a few more times. Nothing. It was completely dead.

I turned around, but it had become so dark I could hardly see two feet in front of me. The hair on the back of my neck stood up, and my breathing seemed to echo back at me across the eerily quiet grove of trees. Though I could hear their voices, farther away than I thought, I couldn't see Maggie or Ty from where I was standing.

Too far, Styles. A little too far. I shook my head and turned back the way I'd come. *I'm going to get back to Maggie and we're going to get the hell out of here. We're going to—*

The breath caught in my throat, and I stared at the ground—my eyes refusing to accept the sight: a long, thick vine was creeping toward me, slithering like a snake across the grass.

You're seeing things, the ever-faithful voice of reason whispered, but I shook my head. No, this was real.

The realization barely registered when the vine jerked toward me, snapping and twisting as it wrapped around my ankle and yanked me forward. I landed hard on my backside, all the wind knocked out of me. Another thick vine wrapped around my arm and encircled my hand and wrist. I shrieked and kicked at the vine, but it was too fast and too strong.

Using the flashlight in my free hand as a weapon, I tried to bludgeon the vine holding my wrist. The tree above me swayed, its limbs moving like a puppet master working his marionette. I screamed as one of the branches dipped down and wrapped around my waist, yanking me to my feet. It pulled me toward the thick trunk of the tree, the vines tightening around my arms and legs.

"Lainey!" a voice called, but it sounded a million miles away.

"Help!" I wailed, struggling against the tree. Hot tears burned my eyes, and I blinked rapidly, trying to clear them. The trunk of the tree was vibrating, and the rough bark against my back was hot, like the surface of an oven. Wind whipped through my hair, and I swore I heard laughter in the leaves as they enveloped me.

"Please," I choked out. "Please let me go."

The tree responded by squeezing me tighter. I cried out, and the movement created a painful pressure in my chest.

I'm going to die.

I tried to move, to scream, but every cell in my body was

wailing in pain. The tree held me so tightly I couldn't have moved if I wanted to. The branches continued to loop over my body, the leaves coarse against my skin. It was getting harder to breathe.

The vines rippled across me. My brain hurled the image of a boa constrictor in front of my eyes, and it was then that I knew: *I'm already dying.*

Uncontrollable tears gushed down my cheeks as I waited for the inevitable. The branches got tighter.

The tree isn't going to suffocate you. Like a boa, it's going to kill you from lack of blood circulation to your vital organs. The voice in my head spoke like a teacher giving a lecture. No emotion. Just the cold, hard facts.

Your circulatory system is malfunctioning. Your arterial pressure is dropping, and your venous pressure is skyrocketing. Your blood cells are beginning to close.

"Lainey!" The voice was closer this time, but I knew by the time they reached me it would be too late.

Your heart is going to give out. It won't be long now.

"No!" My voice was strained, and the cry was barely audible. *No! I don't want to die tonight!* I fought against the calm, scientific voice, *NO!*

Warmth bloomed in the pit of my stomach and began to spread throughout my body.

I will not die tonight!

Every part of me screamed in agony as both pain and heat surged through my veins. *I. Will. Not. Die. Tonight.*

I opened my mouth and with the last breath in my lungs, screamed into the darkness. "NO!"

A brilliant flash of green light exploded in front of my eyes, responding to my call. It lit up the dark space like a firework, and with a blast of cold air I slammed into the grass. The tree had released me.

My chest was on fire, and I gasped, nearly crying out as blood returned to my deadened limbs. A wave of nausea rolled in my stomach, and I turned my head, vomiting in the grass. I wanted to lie there until the pounding in my head eased, but I forced myself to move, crawling as best I could. My arms and legs were tingling, the same feeling as when you knock your funny bone or you sleep on your arm the wrong way. Every inch sent a spasm of pain through me. I clenched my teeth and kept crawling.

A shadow crossed over me, and something strong reached down and gripped my wrists, pulling me to my feet. I thrashed wildly and tried to pull away, but the hold was firm and unyielding. *Warm hands,* my brain quietly supplied. *Not vines.* But my mind was a separate entity from the rest of me; all I could focus on was the panic coursing through me.

"Lainey, it's just me! Open your eyes!"

The voice screaming at me was gruff, and my heart fluttered as if it recognized the sound. But it wasn't enough.

"Please, not again," I whimpered, waiting for the tree to claim me once more.

The hands around my arms tightened. "Dammit, Lainey! Open your eyes!"

My body obeyed, and my eyes shot open. A pair of wide, concerned eyes were peering back at me. My heart thumped, but the tremors that shook my body were more powerful, and the panic that held me captive was only gaining strength. Tears burned my eyes as I stared uncomprehending into those blue eyes.

"Don't worry, I've got you. You're safe."

You're safe.

The tiny voice in my head whispered those words in my ear, but before I had time to process them, the hands that held me pulled me forward and wrapped around me.

I resisted, pushing and twisting against my captor, my fingernails raking against the solid wall of flesh.

Ty tightened his grip. "It's okay, Lainey. I've got you."

"*Ty?*" The echo in my ears made my heart begin to pound. I smelled spearmint.

Ty! my mind whispered, louder this time; it was starting to reconnect with the rest of my body. I stopped struggling.

My senses were returning to me, and when I realized I was cocooned in the safety of Ty's arms instead of waiting for imminent death, I nearly collapsed, my hands twisted in the front of his shirt.

Lainey.

The sound of my name echoed in the breeze that blew through my hair.

Lainey.

"Please," I whispered against the fabric of Ty's shirt, my eyes squeezed shut. "I just want to understand."

I could tell from the vibrations in his chest that Ty was speaking, but I couldn't make out the words.

"Please," I whispered again.

Icy, but hesitant fingers gripped my shoulders, the hold unsure. I wasn't afraid. "I just want to understand," I whispered again. The acquiescence and permission in my voice was clear.

The fingers tightened, and I was yanked out of Ty's arms and into oblivion.

CHAPTER TWELVE

JOSEPHINE

The rain had slowed. Lines of pale moonlight streamed through the clouds, bathing the room in pools of silver light. Dawn was not far away.

They needed to move.

With the storm dissipating, Josephine knew time was running out. But as she traced delicate patterns on Henry's bare chest with her fingertips, all she could concentrate on was the rhythmic rise and fall of his breathing. Having him beside her was more than she ever thought possible, and the last few hours had been a welcome reprieve from the grief and fear that now crept back to claim her again.

Henry swore to protect her, to keep her safe from all harm, and as she lay wrapped in the warmth of his arms, she wanted to believe he would do just that. But the amulet that pulsed at her throat was reminder enough that there were forces at work much bigger than even the best of intentions.

She had to tell him. He had to know what he was getting involved with, that he was risking his own life every second he stayed with her. Her previous attempt had been a disastrous failure, but there was still time.

If she was being honest with herself, the thought of telling him the truth, telling him the one secret she had sworn she would never tell was terrifying. But after the days of running and the hours spent wrapped in his arms, she was more afraid of not having him by her side.

"Henry," she whispered, gathering her courage. "Henry?" She shook his shoulder.

He opened his eyes and gave her a sleepy smile. "I thought it was a dream."

Before she had time to respond, Henry grabbed her and pulled her back down on his chest, kissing her passionately.

"Henry!" Josephine gasped in between kisses, trying hard to balance her giggling and the need for oxygen. When he released her, he was grinning like a madman and Josephine couldn't help but laugh harder.

He tried to reach for her again, but she swatted his hands away.

"Wait," she tried again. "We have to talk. I need to tell—" The words died in her throat as the sound of horses broke through the stillness of the night.

Josephine leapt to her feet. Henry was at her side, pulling his tunic back over his head with one hand and throwing their small store of supplies in one of the burlap potato sacks with the other.

"Oh God," Josephine whispered, the blood draining from her face. "Oh God, Henry. He found us."

She yanked her clothes into place and pulled Henry from the cabin into the trees.

She stumbled over the uneven ground and the large roots from the trees. If it weren't for Henry gripping her elbow, she would have surely fallen.

Everything around her was fuzzy.

He found us.

The words, like a mantra, played over and over in her head.

Henry screamed at her, but the sound was distorted and she couldn't make out his words. The only thing that made sense was the circle of black horsemen moving toward them.

It was too late. They were surrounded.

Josephine stood rooted to the ground, every fiber of her being screaming for her to run. But there was nowhere to go. There was a sharp grappling as Henry was yanked from her side.

"Jo!" Henry screamed, thrashing around in the arms of the men who held him captive. "Jo!"

His frantic cries snapped her out of her daze. "Stop! Stop!" she cried, throwing herself into the center of the circle. "Please don't hurt him."

A man wearing a long, dark overcoat moved toward her. His tan face was twisted into a menacing sneer, and his eyes, almost the same color as his jet-black hair, were trained upon her face. Dark shadows clung to him as he walked, and the very forest itself seemed to bend beneath his darkness.

The fingers of his magic clawed toward her, cleaving through the night, and Josephine's heart nearly stopped, as the weight of his darkness settled around her. Her body recoiled as the shadows danced around her, sending shivers creeping along her spine and extremities.

Death incarnate had found her.

The Master.

The amulet around her neck began to vibrate, its gentle hum a reminder to stand strong.

Don't be afraid, Jo. Don't be afraid.

"Give it to me," he sneered, holding out his hand. His cold, slate-colored eyes were narrowed in disgust.

Somehow, she found her voice. "I don't know what you're talking about."

Faster than lightning, the man struck her across the face, knocking her to the ground. "Don't lie to me, you foolish girl. I know you have it . . . and I *want* it."

For a moment, she couldn't move. Her head throbbed, and her cheek was on fire. Henry was still yelling, but the men who held his arms managed to keep him secure between them.

"My lord." One of the other men came forward. A black tattoo—the same one she'd seen on the men who'd burned her house to the ground—covered his forearm. "It's not here. We searched the cabin but didn't find it."

The Master nodded his head before turning back to glare

at Josephine. Grabbing her by the hair, he yanked her to her knees. The pain was so intense that black spots dotted her vision, and she cried out in pain. "Tell us, girl! Where is the book?" he roared, his voice echoing across the trees.

As Josephine looked up into his angry face, all she could think about was the fact that this was the one responsible for murdering her entire family. *The Master.* Those two words burned her to the core, and anger coursed like venom through her veins. "You'll have to kill me first," she spat through clenched teeth.

The Master laughed, the same cruel laughter that had taunted her the night of the fire. "Oh, that can be arranged, little witch. But first . . ." He glanced over at Henry and grinned. "Bring him here."

Josephine's heart nearly stopped as the two men holding Henry moved toward her, yanking him between them. They forced him to his knees in front of the Master, who pulled a long dagger from the folds of his coat. With a sinister grin, he placed the blade across Henry's throat.

The sight of the blade at his throat made Josephine's knees wobble, but she forced her face to remain neutral, allowing only the anger to show. *Stay calm. You can save him. Just stay calm.*

"What about now, little witch? Care to change your mind?"

"Witch?" Henry's eyes were wide. "Josephine, what's going on? Who are these men?"

His words pierced her heart. "I'm sorry," she whispered,

meeting his gaze. The panic and confusion she saw there made her ache. "I was going to tell you. I . . ."

"Jo?" For the first time since she'd know him, Henry was staring at her as if she were a stranger.

She winced at that look on his face, so full of pain and doubt. *I have to fix this.*

She had only one option. She'd have to use magic.

Staggering to her feet, Josephine pushed her shoulders back and glared at the man in the overcoat. "You're a fool if you think there's anything in the world that would convince me to give it to you." The amulet at her neck pulsated in anticipation.

The Master laughed. "Just hand it over, girl. You have no leverage here." For emphasis, he dug the point of the knife into Henry's flesh. It was a shallow wound, but Henry's grunt of discomfort and the beads of blood that stained his shirt were almost enough to make Josephine lose her nerve. *Steady, Jo. Stay steady.*

"No amount of running and hiding will save you." The Master's wicked grin was back, his eyes fixed on Josephine. "I will hunt you to the ends of the earth, just like I hunted your father. Until there is nothing left but pain and death." He spit on the ground. "Be a good girl and give me what I want."

Mustering all of her courage, Josephine held up her hand, palm out. Magic sparked between her fingertips. "Let him go. *Now.*"

For the tiniest of seconds, Josephine swore she saw a flicker of panic flash in the Master's eyes, but then it was gone.

He sneered at her and yanked Henry to his feet. "Don't be stupid, girl. Give me the book."

"No!" Josephine screamed, a hysterical cry rising in her throat. The magic between her fingertips crackled like lightning. "Let him go. Now."

The Master's responding peal of laughter, cold and cruel, boomed across the trees, hitting Josephine like a slap in the face. Then, without pause, he took the dagger and sliced it across Henry's throat.

"No!"

It was as if time itself had stopped. Every part of her, body and soul, wailed as the light in Henry's eyes faded, as he sank to his knees, blood gushing from his wound. *No, no, no!* Her cruel mind began hurling images at her: her first glimpse at Henry's face, a stolen kiss among the trees, a dance underneath the moonlight, the feel of his fingertips tracing down her spine. *I can't survive this.* What was left of her heart splintered into a thousand pieces—a thousand wounds that would never heal.

"Take care of this." The Master flicked his hand toward Henry's body, addressing the man who has spoken earlier. "Then bring her to me."

"My lord?" The man with the tattoo cocked his head at Josephine, who stood unmoving. He had a peculiar look on his face, a vile hunger in his eyes that made the Master grin gleefully.

"You men have served me faithfully today," the Master replied. "Take your pleasure; then bring her to me. Maybe then she'll be willing to talk." He stalked back to his horse, mounted, and urged his steed forward.

Josephine's shattered spirit flickered a little as she caught sight of his long overcoat whipping in the wind as he rode away and disappeared into the shadows, the echo of his laughter on the breeze.

Everything inside her was broken beyond repair. It was as if she had lost all her ability to move or speak. There was nothing but silence and emptiness. She swayed and almost fell, but a rough hand gripped her by the wrist and yanked her forward.

The face in front of her was plain and covered with grime. The calculating, hungry eyes first roamed over her body, and then the hands followed.

Fight back! the tiny voice inside her head screamed at her, but it was her heart that was in control, or rather the aching hole where it had once been—nothing but silence and emptiness. *Please, Jo, fight back!* The man's foul breath was hot on her skin, but she couldn't move. The tiniest of sparks ignited between her fingertips, but quickly fizzled. Only silence and emptiness.

Over the man's shoulders, she saw two others walk over to Henry's body. One of them kicked at Henry's leg. The other chuckled. As they bent down to pick him up, something inside her snapped. A roar tore from her throat as fiery rage consumed her. She threw out her hands. The magic surged from her fingertips like bolts of lightning, ripping and shredding through the man holding her and the two next to Henry.

The screams of the men mixed with the harsh wails of the horses. The ground rumbled from the stamping hooves as the panicked animals broke the formation and fled. The sky filled with crackling green light and a tangible energy as she screamed, blasting man after man, until not a single person was left standing. It was only then that the scream died on her lips. She lowered her hands.

With tears pouring down her cheeks, Josephine crawled over to Henry's body. She called his name over and over as her fingers searched in vain for the rhythmic pulse in his neck. Desperate, she laid her head on his chest, praying the familiar beating would echo in her ears.

There was nothing but silence.

Crying bitterly, Josephine wept until her eyes began to ache, but that was nothing compared with the agony of her heart. *I can't survive this. . . . I can't survive this. . . . I won't survive this.*

She stayed there, the dead all around her, until the warmth had faded from Henry's skin.

The overwhelming sorrow had knocked the very breath right out of her, but she managed to pull herself to her feet. She placed a shaky hand over her heart, trying to stop the hammering pain from crushing her.

"Good-bye, Henry," she whispered through her tears. "Good-bye, my love."

With tears pouring down her cheeks and the orange glow of the morning sun streaming through the trees, she began to run.

Her emerald amulet hummed at her throat.

CHAPTER THIRTEEN

When I opened my eyes, a familiar face was staring worriedly back at me. It took several seconds for me to realize I was back in the graveyard with Ty's arms wrapped protectively around me.

"Lainey?" Ty whispered, his eyebrows furrowed.

"Ty," I whispered back. Then I burst into tears.

Ty's arms tightened around me, and I laid my head against his chest. Beneath my cheek, his heartbeat was fast, but sure. I closed my eyes and let the stable rhythm soothe me. When my tears had dried up, I pulled back, suddenly very aware of the way our bodies were pressed together. My ears burned. "I . . . uh . . ." I took a quick step back, looking down at my feet as I maneuvered out of his arms. My entire face felt like it was on fire. "I'm sorry, I—"

"Lainey?" another voice called from over Ty's shoulder. Maggie's pale face popped into view, and I launched myself at her.

"Oh my God, Styles. You scared the crap out of me. Are you okay?"

I pulled away and wiped my face with the back of my hand. "No, not really."

Maggie's arms tightened around me, and I snuck a quick glance at Ty. He had one hand resting on the back of his neck, and he looked confused.

"One minute we're standing there talking, and the next, you disappeared." Maggie's eyes were wide and she was shaking. "We heard you screaming, but we couldn't get to you. The trees . . ." She shook her head as if the words were too shocking to say.

"It's okay, you can say it. The tree attacked me," I said, as a hysterical giggle bubbled up in my throat. *I think I'm going into shock.*

"We need to get you out of here," Ty said, reading my mind. "Think you can walk?"

I nodded and allowed Ty and Maggie to guide me back toward the parking lot.

"Why don't you let me drive," Ty suggested. Neither Maggie nor I argued.

Maggie's car was parked near the street underneath the soft glow of a streetlight. When we were safely inside—I in the passenger seat and Maggie in the back—Ty turned the car on and cranked the heat on high. I didn't even realize how cold I was until the warm air came blasting through the vents.

"Here," Ty said softly, retrieving the leather jacket I still hadn't returned from the backseat.

I took it, looping my arms through the sleeves and pulling it around myself.

"Nice jacket," Ty murmured, the crooked smile on his lips.

Despite my frame of mind, I cracked a smile at the joke. But then my face crumpled, and I clamped my hand over my mouth to stop the cry that was building in my throat. I squeezed my eyes shut and let the panic pulsate through me. I waited for my heartbeat to slow before I opened my eyes again.

"Did you see her?" I managed to whisper.

"Who? Josephine?" Maggie leaned forward. "Was it her? I mean, the tree—"

"No," I shook my head. "She was trying to warn me, and I think she saved me. The green light. It was her, wasn't it?"

Maggie shook her head. "I don't know."

I looked over at Ty. "I guess I owe you an explanation."

"You don't owe me anything. I just want to make sure you're okay."

I sighed. "I wish I were." I took a deep breath and glanced back at Maggie, who was uncharacteristically quiet. "Mags?"

"It's up to you, Styles." She took a deep breath and gave me a small smile. "But the dude just saw a tree come to life and attack you. He might as well have the whole story."

I nodded, and before I had the chance to talk myself out of it, I blurted out the whole damn story: the attacks, the visions, the necklace. Everything.

Ty watched me as I spoke, his face unreadable. "And

you don't have any idea who Josephine is or why she keeps appearing?" he asked when I'd finished.

"I have no idea. I thought she was trying to hurt me, but after tonight . . ."

"We've been doing research," Maggie piped up from the back. "But there's nothing to find. We don't have a whole lot to go on." Her voice sounded as deflated as I felt. "And now, there's this thing with the tree." She bit down on her bottom lip. "Can we all agree that *that* did in fact happen? Because I'm starting to question my own sanity here."

"It happened, all right," I said, chewing on my bottom lip. The pain in my body was proof. "I have no idea what to do." I looked over at Ty. "You think we're crazy, don't you?"

"Not at all." His voice was soft but certain.

"So you're telling me that some girl you barely know just told you she's seeing ghosts and getting attacked by evil trees, and you're not even the slightest bit skeptical?"

Ty shrugged. "Not everything in the world makes sense."

That certainly wasn't the answer I'd expected. I stared at him for a moment, not sure what to think. "Well . . . thanks for what you did—helping me back there."

"You saved my life, remember?" He gave me a half smile. "I figured I owed you one. Besides, it's not every day I get to hold a pretty girl in my arms—even if she is screaming in my face."

A flush warmed my cheeks. "Sorry about that."

Ty waved his hand. "No apologizing. Aside from a few claw marks, I came out relatively unscathed.

"Claw marks?"

Ty smiled sheepishly and pulled up the hem of his shirt. His lower abdomen was covered in angry, red lines.

"Holy crapkittens, Styles." Maggie's head bobbed between the seats. "You put my cat to shame, and that's saying something. Frodo Fluffkins is as ornery as they come."

"Oh my God." I covered my face with my hands. "I'm so sorry."

"No apologies, remember?" Ty pulled his t-shirt back down in place. "It's nothing. I've had worse. And trust me, some of the guys at the gym have way longer nails than you."

He's trying to make me laugh. I cracked a tiny smile.

"So, what do we do now?" Maggie asked. "I mean, that was some freaky shit back there."

"We need to come up with some kind of plan," I said, even though every inch of my body was throbbing and achy. I wanted to go home and go to bed more than anything, but now more than ever we needed answers.

Plucking a leaf out of my hair, I pulled down the visor to open the compact mirror. I probably looked as awful as I felt. I was right. My eye makeup was running down my face in black streaks. Smudges of dirt mixed with the ruined makeup, and my skin was pale and splotchy. "Yikes," I muttered, leaning forward to wipe away some of the grime.

Then I gasped.

It's just your imagination, Lainey. Just your mind playing tricks on you. My mind began rationalizing away my fear, but as I stared at my reflection, I knew something was wrong.

"Ty?" I said, trying to stay as calm as possible. "Can you turn the light on, please?"

As soft yellow light filled the car, I sucked in a ragged breath. My fears were confirmed.

I turned slowly to Ty, my whole body trembling again.

"Lainey, what is it?" Ty asked, his face a stone mask.

"Styles?" Maggie was leaning forward, her hand on my shoulder. "What's wrong?"

"My eyes," I answered, my voice no stronger than a whisper. "It's my eyes," I tried again, my voice a little stronger this time.

Ty was clearly confused. "I don't . . ."

"What color are they?" I interrupted, shouting this time.

I looked in the mirror again, refusing to believe it, but the proof was right in front of me. "Ty, what color are they?" I snapped my head back to face him again.

He stared at me, his hands held up in front of him. But slowly, he leaned forward, his own eyes narrowing in the dim car light.

He exhaled slowly. "They're green."

Green.

I dropped my head to my chest and tried to keep from hyperventilating. Behind me, Maggie was making little noises of shock as though she were trying to speak but couldn't.

"Lainey?" Ty gripped my arm in concern. He didn't understand.

I raised my head. "Are you sure?" I whispered, staring at

the foreign irises in the mirror. I turned back to Ty. "What color are they?"

But the look on Ty's face was clear. There was no mistake.

My once golden-hazel eyes were now a vibrant shade of green.

CHAPTER FOURTEEN

"More coffee?" The waitress's tired voice broke the silence.

Ty shook his head, but Maggie and I both wordlessly handed her our mugs.

"I can't go home," I'd said when we left the cemetery. "Not like this. Gareth will freak, and I just can't deal with anything else right now."

After sending Gareth a text to let him know I was crashing at Maggie's, we'd ended up at the Waffle House—one of the only places in Lothbrook that stayed open twenty-four hours. Two rounds of coffee later, we still had no plan.

I tasted blood as I chewed on my bottom lip. My fingers, anxious for something to do, were busy playing with a piece of string I'd pulled off the fabric of my shirt. Over and over, I wound it tightly around one finger before unraveling it again.

I could have died tonight. That single thought kept running through my brain, along with images of snakelike vines.

I shivered and tried—unsuccessfully—to think of something else.

I sat back in the hard plastic booth and leaned my head against the windowpane. Outside, cars flew down the road. I couldn't stop the fleeting wish that I was inside one of them, heading somewhere my troubles couldn't find me. My reflection stared back at me, but the lighting of the restaurant made it impossible to see any distinguishing colors. I wasn't fooled, though. It was strange how alien my own face had already become.

Beside me, Ty shifted in his seat. His features were tight, his eyes cloudy as they darted back and forth between me and Maggie, who was furiously scribbling notes on a napkin.

I counted cars as they passed, trying to distract myself. My fingers were still busy with the string. I wound it tightly around one finger, cutting off the circulation. The tip of my pinkie turned dark red, then purple. I released the tension in the thread, sighing as blood pumped back into my finger—that tiny sense of control filling the aching parts of me.

"Lainey?"

I tore my eyes from the window. Ty was staring at me. "Yes?"

"When my dad was . . ." He broke off for a moment and exhaled. "The night I lost my dad was the worst night of my life. Aside from the grief, the one thing I remember most clearly is how alone I felt." As he spoke, his hands tightened against the empty coffee mug he held.

"What happened to him?" I didn't have any right to ask, nor was it polite, but I was too frazzled to consider decorum.

"He was killed," Ty answered, staring at his hands as he spoke. "Because he refused to bend to someone else's will."

The tangible sadness of his words made my chest ache. I wanted to ask more questions, but the pained look on his face kept my mouth shut.

"After it happened," he continued, "I didn't know what to do or where to go. I couldn't understand why. I had so many questions, but no one seemed to know the answers. I just felt so . . . so lost. I *was* lost—sometimes it still feels that way." He glanced over at me, his eyes blazing. "I know it's not the same thing. I can't possibly understand what's going through your head right now, but I just want you to know that . . . that you're not alone, okay?"

I bit down on my lip again. *I was lost.* The words played over and over in my head, until Ty's voice faded away and my own voice whispered back at me. *I am lost.* The words settled on my shoulders like a ton of bricks, as if at any moment, they would crush me.

Ty gave me a small smile, and as he turned his attention back to Maggie, he reached over and entwined my fingers with his, giving my hand a gentle, reassuring squeeze.

My mind was overwhelmed with fear and confusion, but as I held his hand, a small part of my brain made a mental note to later marvel at the strange boy sitting next to me—the mysterious one who was fierce and aloof one second, and incredibly kind and gentle the next.

"Okay!" Maggie said triumphantly, looking up. "I think I might be on to something." She indicated the scribbled napkins. "I wrote down everything that's happened so far. I thought there might be a pattern or something that could give us some clue about what we're dealing with."

A flicker of hope danced through me. "Is there? A pattern?"

"Not at all," Maggie said, with a sigh.

My stomach turned, and I gulped down a mouthful of coffee to keep from gagging.

"Everything just seems kind of random, to be honest," she continued. "But I do think I know what we should do next."

"What?"

Maggie bit her lip. "Just go with me on this one, okay? I really think we should go see Serena."

"No." I shook my head. "Maggie, I already told you. I don't think she can help us."

"How do you know? She's the closest thing we're gonna get to an expert on this sort of thing. She's reads tarot cards and performs cleansing rituals on your house—which makes a whole lot more sense now, come to think of it." Maggie waved her hands to punctuate her words. "She gave you a tiger's eye for protection on your twelfth birthday."

"Exactly. She's a complete nut job."

Maggie leaned forward. "But what if she's not? What if she's just the one other person in this town who sees what others don't?" She shoved the napkins toward me. "It's the only lead we have, Styles. There's nothing else to go on. Besides, after tonight . . . I think it's obvious we're in over our heads. We need help."

I stared at the messy scrawl on the napkins in front of me. "She *is* good with weird."

I let out a deep breath. Maggie was smirking, knowing she'd already won. I looked at Ty, who said nothing but gave my hand another reassuring squeeze.

"Fine. But I'm gonna need more coffee."

ও • ৩

The sidewalk was full of antique buyers and the usual Saturday morning brunch crowd. The crisp air was blowing through the golden amber leaves of the trees, and the street had recently been decorated for the upcoming Harvest Festival. Lampposts were festooned with orange twinkle lights, and the shop windows were full of hay bales and pumpkins.

Next to me, a smiling scarecrow waved jauntily from his perch atop a parking meter. I adored this time of year, but right now the only thing I could focus on was moving my feet down the sidewalk.

This is ridiculous. Such a stupid idea! one side of my mind yelled, while the other fired back, *It's not! After everything you've seen, can you really say that?*

I maneuvered through the crowd, Ty and Maggie in step beside me, and tried to ignore the bickering in my mind.

The storefronts in this area of Main Street were all much the same: large windows and brightly colored doors. I kept an eye on the numbers as we passed, but more to keep my mind busy than for direction. I could find Serena's shop blindfolded.

The small storefront looked like a rainbow had thrown up on it, especially compared with the sensible, clean look of the dry cleaner's and dental office that neighbored it.

Several clay gnomes and garden fairies lined the windows, and a large mask of unknown provenance hung from the ceiling like a piñata. There were also hundreds of crystal stars and moons that had been suspended from various strands of patterned ribbon. Stacks of books were arranged in an ornate pattern, and old posters heralding the benefits of reading plastered the windows. Above the bright blue door was a sign that read, *"Too Good to Be Threw: Secondhand Books."* Underneath that, a small hand-painted sign read, *"Madam Serena: Spiritual Advisor."*

I stopped walking. Maggie bumped into me from behind.

"Walk much, Styles?" Maggie said, then she noticed the look on my face. "What? What's wrong?"

"My uncle's here." I pointed to the rusty red Ford parked in front of the store.

"Maybe you should—" Maggie started.

"No. I'm not ready to talk to him about what's going on. He can't know why we're here. Not yet." Ducking low, I crept toward the window and peeked into the shop. The front of the store looked empty. There weren't any customers milling about, and there was no sign of either Serena or Gareth. "We'll just sneak in and wait until he's gone."

Maggie shook her head at me but didn't argue.

"I think they're in the back or something," I said, motioning for Ty and Maggie to join me in my crouch. I put my finger to my lips and eased the door of the shop open, careful not to jingle the bells attached to the door. I poked my head inside and, still seeing the coast was clear, waved Ty and Maggie inside. We dashed behind a tall row of bookcases.

"Does anyone else hear the *Mission Impossible* theme song right now? Or is it just me?" Maggie whispered, a grin spreading across her face.

"Shhh," I said. "I don't want them to hear us."

We moved around the bookcases slowly, inching toward the back of the store. The muffled undertones of a heated conversation drifted toward us.

"They're in the office," I said, leaning around the bookshelf to listen more closely. The words floated clearly through the air, chilling the blood in my veins. "Oh my God."

"What is it?" Maggie hissed.

"My name. I heard my name. They're arguing about *me.*"

Inching farther around the bookcase, I could just make out Gareth and Serena through the open door of a small office. Serena had her hands on her hips, her face flushed, and Gareth had his arms crossed, his posture rigid.

"You don't understand, Gareth. You *have* to tell her.

Events are in motion, things are already happening. I've *seen* it. Haven't you felt the pulses? She's getting stronger."

"Of course I have. That's why I'm here," Gareth said, rubbing his forehead with his fingers. "But your sight is subjective, Serena. You know that. You told me when she was twelve that she'd be killed by a bounty hunter, and that never happened. There's no reason to think that she's in immediate danger now. If someone were coming for her, we'd know it." He began pacing. "We stick to the plan. Keep cloaking her as long as possible."

"But she *is* in danger. I can sense it. Even with all the wards we've placed around her, we can't hide her forever. You need to bring her to me. If I could just do a proper reading, I might be able—"

"*No,*" Gareth argued. "There's still time. I *know* I need to tell her, but . . . we still have time."

"Gareth," Serena pleaded, "if he finds out about Lainey, who she is, *what* she is, he will hunt her down just like he did her mother. You know it's true. You always said you were going to tell her, that you were going to protect her. Why can't you see that time is now?"

"Don't talk to me like every single thing I've ever done hasn't been to protect her," Gareth practically growled. "I swore to her mother that I would take care of her, and I've kept my oath. I won't let anything happen to her now."

Serena exhaled slowly. "I know that, Gareth. But you cannot protect her from her destiny. She deserves to know the truth—and to hear it from you."

"She's still so young. How can I possibly burden her with that?" Gareth's forehead creased and the lines made him look a hundred years old.

"You tell me all the time that she's strong. That she's got her mother's spirit. She can handle it."

"She's not ready."

"She's not ready? Or *you're* not ready?"

"Serena, how can I look her in the face and tell her that everything she knows is . . . is a lie?" Gareth's voice cracked.

"It will break her heart," Serena whispered, her eyes sparkling with unshed tears. "But you must help her understand. We're running out of time."

"Her seventeenth birthday is still a few weeks away."

Serena clasped her hands together in frustration. "Gareth, please. I know it's hard, but you have to do right by her. The pulses I've felt? They're unlike anything I've felt in a long time. She's her mother's daughter, and she is capable of far more than we can possibly imagine. If I've sensed the power, and you have sensed it, then it won't be long before others come searching for the source."

"You're right," Gareth said. "I'll tell her." He let out a long sigh. "When I find the right moment, I'll tell her."

I couldn't move. The wheels in my head were whirling, trying to process the information I'd overheard, but it was like trying to punch through a brick wall—nothing was getting through. My stomach pitched and rolled, and I wanted to throw up. I would've put my head between my knees if not for Maggie yanking on my arm.

Serena and Gareth were now talking in more hushed tones, her arm looped through his as they slowly made their way toward the front of the shop. We needed to move or we'd be seen.

Following Maggie's lead, I crawled toward another row of bookcases.

"Over there?" Ty was gesturing toward a door off a small alcove.

Maggie nodded, and it was all I could do to follow them. We crawled inside the tiny space and Ty shut the door behind us, careful not to let it slam. The smell of old books, incense, and cleaning supplies burned my nose. It must have been the supply closet.

"Lainey? Are you okay?" Maggie was whispering to me, but I'd lost all ability to speak. My brain was spinning out of control, and my heart thumped against the walls of my chest. *If he finds out who she is, what she is, he will hunt her down just like they did her mother.* Serena's words reverberated in my ears. Every inch of my skin was covered in goose bumps, and a cool shiver danced up and down my spine.

"I don't understand," I managed to whisper. "I don't understand."

My entire body was shaking. Maggie wrapped her arms around me and held me tightly. Ty watched from his post at the door, his fists clenched at his sides.

"I don't understand," I kept whispering.

Who am I?

What am I?

CHAPTER FIFTEEN

Maggie held me long enough for the shaking to subside. "Are you okay?" she asked me when I pulled away.

"I don't know," I whispered. The weight of that horrible conversation between Gareth and Serena weighed down on me, but I sucked down a large gulp of air and exhaled slowly. I would not let it crush me. "But I'm going to find out."

Neither Maggie nor Ty said anything as I pushed past them and out the door.

Who am I? What am I? Like a cadence, the words bolstered and guided my steps as I marched past the rows of bookshelves.

The wooden planks of the floor creaked as I walked into the main room of the shop. Maggie and Ty walked wordlessly behind me.

"Serena?"

Serena's head popped out of the office. She was holding a ledger and small stack of papers. She looked at me first with confusion; then her eyes widened. "Lainey, what are you doing here?"

I ignored her question. "I heard what you said to Gareth. I heard everything."

The color drained from Serena's face.

"You need to tell me what's going on." My voice wavered but grew louder as a rush of adrenaline coursed through me. "You said I deserved to know the truth. What truth?"

Serena squared her shoulders. "You need to talk to Gareth. He—"

"*No,* Serena," I said, the volume of my voice causing us both to jump. "I want the truth *now.*"

We stood staring at each other, locked in a silent show-down, but then Serena lurched forward, closing the distance between us, and yanked me forward. Her other hand reached up to grip my chin, angling it to see better.

"Your eyes," she whispered. "They're green." She let go of my chin. "It's happening." The words were barely more than a whisper. The hand that held my arm tightened.

I squealed as Serena jerked my arm closer and forced my clenched fist to open. Behind me, Maggie muttered a curse word under her breath and Ty moved closer, his eyes darting between the two of us as if he were trying to decide whether or not to intervene.

"What are you doing?" I squirmed, trying to pull my hand from Serena's surprisingly firm grip. "Stop!" I tried to push her away, but Serena was unhearing as she pored over my hand, her fingers tracing over the lines in my palm.

Abruptly, Serena gasped and dropped my hand as though it were on fire. She muttered something incomprehensible under her breath, swept past Ty and Maggie—whom she seemed not to even notice—and rushed back into her office.

"Where are you going?" I cried out, my hands clenching into fists. "Serena!" I bellowed. "What the hell is going on?"

She didn't answer me, but when she came flying back out of the office, she had two lit candles in her hands. She was still murmuring under her breath.

"Serena!" I tried again, louder this time.

If Serena heard me, she didn't acknowledge me in any way. She walked over to the large table between the two blue reading couches and pulled a stack of thick, colorful cards from the front pocket of her long skirt. She cut the deck, shuffled the cards with nimble fingers, and placed the cards on the table.

I marched over and yanked the remaining cards from Serena's hands. "Talk to me! What is going on?"

At my touch, Serena seemed to snap to her senses. "Oh, Lainey," she whispered. "I'm so sorry." Her large brown eyes were full of sympathy and regret. "We should've told you. It's not supposed to happen like this."

"Told me what?" I cried out. Hot tears burned my eyes as emotion after emotion slapped me in the face. *Anger. Frustration. Confusion, Fear.* "Please . . ."

Serena's shoulders slumped in resignation. With a sigh, she pointed to the cards in my hands. "Choose one."

I was about to protest, but Serena eyed me fiercely. *"Choose one,"* she repeated, her voice firm.

I wanted to scream, but instead I clenched my teeth together and pulled a card facedown from the stack.

"Place it on the table," Serena instructed.

Rolling my eyes, I slammed the card down on the table. A pair of pillar candles sitting nearby rattled from the vibration. Serena swooped in and carefully flipped the card over so its image was facing up. Her eyes grew wide, and as I peered down at the image, I didn't need Serena to tell me that it wasn't a good sign.

The tower itself looked innocent enough, sitting atop a mountain, but the bolts of lightning and flames that rose from the windows made my stomach turn. On both sides of the tower, a body was pitched forward, falling to the craggy depths below.

"The Tower," Serena whispered, her tone eerily reverent. She turned to me, her eyes brimming with tears. "It's worse than I thought." She leaned forward, as though to embrace me, but stopped suddenly when she saw the look on my face. "Please," she said, indicating the sofas. "Sit down. There is much to say."

It was then that Serena seemed to notice Ty and Maggie standing stiffly near the wall, their faces narrowed in seriousness. She looked at me with raised eyebrows. "Perhaps we should speak privately."

"No," I said, surprised by the strong tone of my voice. "They stay with me."

Serena nodded, though her eyes were still narrowed in suspicion. After a moment, she turned back to me, her face grave. She took a deep breath before she spoke again, her expression both serious and concerned. "What do you know about your mother?"

"I know there's some connection," I said. "Am I right? Did my mother have something to do with whatever secret you and Gareth are keeping from me?"

"She has everything to do with it, I'm afraid." Serena began to wring her hands. "Lainey, your mother didn't die in a car accident like you were told. She was murdered."

"What?" I stared at Serena. Her words made no sense to me. "That's impossible. My mom was a schoolteacher. Why would anyone—"

"She wasn't just a teacher, Lainey," she interrupted. "She was a witch."

"A witch?" The word tasted bitter on my tongue. "My mother was . . . a witch?"

"Yes. A very powerful one." The look on Serena's face was absolute.

This can't be real. I'd always know Serena was a little . . . well, kooky, but she didn't actually believe all that hocus-pocus mumbo jumbo, did she? "This has to be some kind of a joke, right?"

"I wish it were, dear, but the truth is even far more complicated than the mere fact that your mother was a Supernatural." Serena leaned forward, grabbing my hands. "Lainey, your mother was killed by someone very dangerous—someone who, if they knew of your existence, would come after you also."

She paused for a moment and looked at our clasped hands. "I knew your mother. We were all friends, Gareth, your mother, and I." She broke off and sniffed. "When she realized she'd have to go, she came to me for help, and I've done what I can for you all these years. I've done my best to watch out for you like she asked." A single tear rolled down her cheek.

"Please understand that Gareth and I swore to keep you safe, and so far we have . . ." She trailed off.

All the moves, never staying in one place for too long. It was all starting to make sense.

"Events are in motion," Serena continued. "Things that are beyond our control. It's only a matter of time until they discover the secret that we've kept hidden these sixteen years." She heaved a sigh and placed a palm on my cheek. "*You*, Lainey."

"But why . . ." I trailed off.

She's her mother's daughter and she is capable of far more than we can possibly imagine. The words poured over me like a bucket of ice-cold water.

"I'm a witch, too." My voice was barely stronger than a whisper as the realization came spilling out. "Like my mother."

"Yes." Serena pulled her hands away and stared down at them, picking at the dark blue polish. Her voice was soft as she spoke, indicating that the next part was both important and painful for her to say. "And if anyone finds out about you," she pointed to the card lying ominously on the table, "you're likely to share her fate."

CHAPTER SIXTEEN

My brain was working overtime to make sense of Serena's words, but it all seemed so nonsensical. I half expected someone to jump out from behind the sofa and announce I was on one of those hidden camera shows. *Please let this be some sick joke.*

Beside me, Serena was pacing back and forth. She had her tarot deck clutched in her hands, and her eyes kept darting between me and the tower card still lying faceup on the table.

"Why my mom?" It was the easiest of the questions to ask. "There have to be hundreds of . . . *witches* in the world, right?" I nearly choked on the word. "Why would someone target my mother?"

Serena took a deep breath as if to steel herself. "Your mother was the last living descendant of one of the most powerful lines of witches our kind has ever seen. Your mother was targeted because of the blood that flows through her veins—and yours—because she was a DuCarmont witch."

"DuCarmont?" My tongue was like sandpaper. "But my

mother's maiden name was . . ." The lump had formed in my throat again. "Is it all a lie, then? Everything I've ever known about my family?"

Serena's eyes brimmed with tears as she leaned over to grip my hand. "No, not everything. Your mother and father loved you very much."

"What about my dad? Was he some kind of witch too?"

"No," Serena answered, a slight smile at the corner of her lips. "He was entirely human and a wonderful man. Your mother never told him about who she was. The DuCarmonts had been all but eradicated, and as the last remaining DuCarmont still alive, she was forced into hiding. She thought it was best to keep your father in the dark—better to protect him that way."

I felt a strong kinship with the father I barely remembered. "At least I'm not the only one that was lied to." Serena winced at the rancor in my voice.

If it wasn't bad enough that Gareth has been lying to me my entire life, now it seemed that everything I knew about my own mother was also a lie. I had only a few memories of my mom, but now even those I did have felt tainted, as if the warm smile and the melodious sound of a lullaby I remembered weren't even real.

An unfamiliar emotion surged through me, threatening to break me in half: betrayal. The ache of it resonated in my bones, and it was only the notion that my father had also been left in the dark that kept me from completely erupting in the middle of Serena's store.

"Was my father murdered, too?"

"He *was* killed in a car accident. Although your mother had suspicions that the crash that killed your father was somehow meant for her—orchestrated by those who wanted to kill her, of course. She could never prove it, though."

A different kind of ache rippled through my chest as I thought of my dad. My brain offered up a fuzzy mental picture of his face, full of kindness with warm brown eyes and a thick beard. Another tear rolled down my cheek. "So, who *are* these people?"

"I'm not sure the 'who' is important just now." Serena's voice was flat. "It's the 'why' that matters."

"Okay, then. Tell me about the DuCarmonts," I said, swaying a little as the vertigo threatened to reappear. "Tell me about my family."

Serena stood up and crossed to the bookshelf on the far wall. She pulled a large, old-looking book from the shelf and began to flip carefully through the pages. When she found the appropriate page, she handed the book over to me. The page was open to a spread of antique photographs.

I eyed the photographs, not understanding, but then I gasped, my hand flying to my mouth.

There was a picture of a grand plantation with wide columns and a wraparound porch staring back at me. A family stood in front of the house. I recognized the house—I'd watched it burn. I leaned closer, taking in the images of the family. Two women, one older and one younger, with light-colored hair, stood side by side, wearing long dresses with wide hoopskirts. Their likeness was uncanny—clearly mother and daughter. But it was the other people in the picture who nearly stopped my heart.

There was a man with his arm wrapped around another young woman at his side. The man was wearing a long overcoat, and though the photograph was black-and-white, I knew the coat was green. The woman next to him had long dark hair that tumbled across her shoulders in waves. I'd know that face anywhere.

"Josephine," I whispered.

"You know her?" Serena was confused. "You know the woman in the picture?"

As if I needed confirmation, there was a tiny caption underneath the photograph penciled carefully by a steady hand. *The DuCarmont Family, 1860.*

I nodded. "Josephine . . . DuCarmont." I turned to Serena with wide eyes. "That means . . ."

"Yes," Serena finished. "Josephine DuCarmont is your ancestor."

It was as if someone had punched me in the stomach, knocking all the air out of my lungs. Several seconds passed before I was able to suck down a mouthful of air.

Serena looked perplexed. "Lainey, how do you know her?"

In answer, I pushed up the sleeve of my shirt. The handprint was almost gone, but the faint outline of her fingertips was still visible. "The first time I saw her, she left me this."

Serena's face was already pale, but the last bit of color drained away. "Of course. I should have known." She reached out and touched the lines on my skin, then jerked her hand back like it was on fire. "Magic always leaves a mark," she intoned, her voice eerily quiet.

"What?"

"It's like a fingerprint. The more powerful the magic, the more potent the mark." Serena's eyes were wide, almost reverent. "Josephine DuCarmont was one of the most powerful witches of all time." She stared at me.

"But what does it mean?" I pulled my sleeve back down.

Serena pursed her lips. I could see an internal debate going on in her head. Finally, she let out the breath she had been holding. "I believe she . . . established a Continuance."

"A Continuance?"

"It's like a bond, or a link, between the two of you. She's trying to communicate."

"Josephine just wants to talk to me?" I recalled the pain that had lanced through my body at her touch. "She could've just sent a text."

"Lainey, you don't understand. It is exceedingly rare for a witch to perform a Continuance from the other side. A link forged through the veil can only be created by channeling enormous amounts of energy, and sustaining it requires tremendous power from both parties."

"But why create a link in the first place?"

"There's only one reason I can think of." Serena swallowed. "You're in danger."

Those three little words echoed in my ears. I shivered,

feeling the branches of the tree slithering across my skin. I nodded slowly. "I almost died tonight."

Serena gasped, but before she could ask questions, I told her of how the tree in the graveyard had attacked me.

"I know it sounds crazy," I said, "but it happened. I don't know how or why, but—"

"It was a dryad." Serena's face was still pallid, but she spoke with certainty. "A tree spirit."

"A tree . . . spirit." I swallowed. All I knew about dryads was what I remembered from a Greek mythology book I'd read a few years ago. "Aren't they supposed to be . . . nice?" I swallowed again, feeling both confused and ridiculous for asking.

Serena shook her head. "Not all of them—that's like asking if humans are nice. It depends on where their loyalties lie."

"Oh," I said, though the answer made little sense to me. "Well, I think Josephine saved me. There was a flash of green light right before the tree dropped me. Afterward, my eyes looked like this.

"Yes . . . green eyes," Serena said, her knowing eyes staring into my mine. "Oh Lainey, do you know what this means?"

"Oh yeah, of course." I rolled my eyes.

Serena's eyes were closed, and she looked as if she were going to cry. "The cloaking spells aren't working anymore." She looked at me, tears brimming in her eyes. "Oh God, I told Gareth!"

The hysteria on her face made my heart race. "I don't understand."

"It's called the Awakening," Serena began, her tone resembling that of a teacher giving an important lecture. "Although witches are born with their powers, they don't manifest until the witch is grown—usually around one's seventeenth birthday. There are rare cases, though, of premature witches being able to perform small feats of magic. We call them pulses."

"And these pulses?" I said, trying to grasp the situation. "They're bad?"

Serena's lower lip was trembling when she spoke, her voice barely louder than a whisper. "Powerful magic attracts attention."

"And these pulses are coming from me?"

Serena nodded gravely. "You are your mother's daughter."

I swallowed. "So the tree was feeding off my . . . my magic?"

"I believe so, yes."

My chest was starting to tighten. I sat down on the edge of the couch and tried to take a few deep breaths.

"And it wasn't Josephine who saved you." Serena knelt down in front of me. "It would be almost impossible for her to perform that kind of magic from the other side. No, I think it was *you*, Lainey." She pointed to my eyes. "Magic always leaves a mark."

I tried to speak, but the words were stuck in my throat.

"Gareth and I have been cloaking you your entire life, using magic to hide the pull of your power. But you're getting stronger, Lainey. The spells . . . they're failing. If Josephine has linked the two of you, it must mean she's trying to warn you." Her eyes flitted once again to the tarot card lying faceup on the table. "You're in terrible danger."

The words made me shiver. "You're psychic, right? Can't you look into your crystal ball or something? Give me something more concrete than that?"

"I'm a Seer, but my Sight doesn't work that way," Serena argued. "I'm afraid modern entertainment has painted a rather unrealistic portrait of my abilities. I can't just tap into people's lives and see what I want to see. I see flashes, things that will come to pass or might merely be a glimpse of what could be. And magic also distorts my Sight—it's very susceptible to spells and charms. Even protection wards." She indicated me. "It's all very subjective."

"Then what good is a Seer?" I seethed. Anger boiled under my skin until it exploded through me. "You say you knew my mother, that she was your friend. Did it ever occur to you that maybe her daughter deserved better than a life full of lies?"

Serena winced as though she'd been struck.

I wanted to keep yelling. I wanted to throw things and scream at the top of my lungs, but as quickly as it'd come, the fire leaked out of me. My entire face crumpled as the anger gave way to something much deeper. "You're the closest thing I have to a mother anymore. Didn't you think I deserved to know the truth?"

Serena didn't bother wiping the tears that streaked down her cheeks. She stared at me with eyes that were full of guilt as she struggled to respond. "Lainey, I wanted to, but Gareth . . ." She trailed off and looked miserably down at her lap. Tears fell from her cheeks and made tiny wet spots on the fabric of her skirt. After a few moments, she looked back at me, the remorse in her eyes clear. "You're right. We should've told you. But you have to understand, we've only ever tried to protect you."

I nodded and tried to take the words to heart, but when Serena tried to wrap a comforting arm around my shoulders, I couldn't help but pull away. I knew Serena's words were genuine, but the betrayal I felt still burned around the edges. "No more lies, okay?"

Serena nodded her head gravely. "I promise."

I turned my attention back to the book in my lap, focusing once more on Josephine's smiling face. "So what happens now?"

Serena stood up from the couch and ran her fingers anxiously through her hair. "That part, I don't know. This is practically unprecedented, and I'm no expert on witches."

"Well, Gareth will know what to do, right? I mean, he's my uncle, so that makes him a witch, too—or rather a warlock."

Serena's eyes darted around the room, her shoulders tense. But almost immediately, she relaxed her posture and looked at me with a knowing smile. "Yes, you're right. Gareth will know what to do."

I closed the book and stood up, wiping my hands on the fabric of my jeans. "Guess I'm just gonna have to talk to him, then." A feeling of dread washed over me at the thought of confronting him.

"In the meantime," Serena interrupted my thoughts, "please be careful. Don't attempt anything foolish."

"Oh, right, my powers." I looked down at my hands and laughed—the alternative was to succumb to the panic that gnawed at the back of my mind and burst into tears. "Don't worry. If I have the sudden urge to yell 'Expelliarmus!' at passersby, I'll try to refrain."

It was a terrible attempt at a joke, and Serena didn't laugh. "I'm serious, Lainey. Don't do anything stupid. There are eyes everywhere."

Serena's words knocked the smile right off my face. *If anyone finds out about you, you're likely to share her fate.*

I gulped. "What do I do?" I held out my hands away from my body, afraid magic might start shooting from my fingertips.

"First of all, don't panic," Serena answered. "That will only make things worse."

My head was beginning to throb, and I wasn't sure if it was the massive brain overload or my body going into shock. I pinched the bridge of my nose and squeezed my eyes shut.

"I'm going to keep consulting the cards," Serena continued. "See if there's anything I missed and reach out to some fellow Seers. Something is going on, I can feel it. Go home, now. You need to talk to Gareth."

I nodded. I was suddenly exhausted in every possible way. All I wanted was to sleep until the world made sense again.

Practically in a daze, I shuffled over to where Ty and Maggie were standing stiffly by the bookcases. Maggie looked as overwhelmed as I felt; Ty's face was unreadable. His shoulders were tense. He had his hands intertwined behind his neck, and his eyes were trained on the ground.

"You guys ready?"

Maggie nodded and Ty looked up, his strained eyes softening. "Yeah, let's go."

"Just a second, young man," Serena called as they headed for the door. "A word, please."

Ty muttered something under his breath and then jogged back to where Serena was standing.

"What do you think that's all about?" Maggie asked, watching as Serena and Ty spoke in hushed tones.

"I'm too overwhelmed to even guess," I said. I swayed a little, leaning on Maggie for support.

"Well, whatever it is, he doesn't look happy," Maggie observed.

Ty said good-bye to Serena and made his way back toward us. "It was nothing," he said in answer to our expectant faces. "Something she saw in my aura or whatever." He waved his hand in dismissal and pushed open the door to the shop.

I took one last look at Serena, who was already hunched over her tarot cards, and followed Ty out into the bright sunlight.

The car ride to my house was quiet, but I was grateful for the silence. Now that the adrenaline from everything that had happened had drained away, I was physically and emotionally spent. I doubted that I could've carried on much of a conversation even if I'd wanted to.

Maggie was passed out in the backseat, and I was having a hard time keeping my own eyelids from drooping. The radio was playing softly in the background, and as I stared out the window, I tried to not to think about anything other than the reassuring pressure of Ty's hand holding mine.

It wasn't long before he pulled the car into my driveway.

I glanced at the clock on the dash. It was a little after eleven in the morning. Gareth's truck was missing from its spot in the driveway, and I was relieved. I wasn't ready to face that conversation just yet.

"Thank you for the ride home." I turned to Ty. "And . . . for everything else, too."

Ty inclined his head. "Anytime."

I gently shook Maggie' shoulder, waking her. "I'm leaving, Mags."

She sat up, looking bedraggled. "I'll call you soon."

I opened the car door and managed to keep myself upright long enough to unlock the front door and stumble inside. I gave a small wave to Maggie and Ty as he backed his car out of the driveway, and then I turned and fumbled up the stairs toward my room.

Sinking down onto my bed, I shrugged off my clothes and pulled my favorite worn sleep shirt over my head. The picture of my parents, of my mother wearing Josephine's necklace, stared at me from the bedside table. I'd forgotten to ask Serena about the necklace.

There's still so much I don't understand.

An invisible hand wrapped around my heart and squeezed until I was sure it would break, the smiling faces of my parents as the only witnesses.

With one hand clutching at my chest, I pulled the comforter over my head, blocking out the world.

CHAPTER SEVENTEEN

"There you are."

I turned to see Maggie walking toward me, her hands plunged into the pockets of her jeans. Her face was pale, and there were purple circles underneath her eyes, similar to my own.

"How'd you find me?"

"It wasn't hard to guess." Maggie shrugged. "Besides, it's a really small town."

I nodded as she settled beside me on the picnic table.

"Why *are* you here, Lainey?"

"I really don't know," I replied after a minute or two. I'd woken up restless from my nap and grabbed my car keys. After driving around aimlessly for a while, I'd ended up back at the cemetery. "I guess I just didn't know where else to go. I thought maybe if I came back here, where I saw her last, that Josephine might show up. Explain a few things."

"Has she? Shown up, I mean?"

"No. It's been frustratingly quiet."

"And the trees?"

"I haven't gotten close enough to find out."

Maggie reached over, took my hand, and gave it a gentle squeeze. "I know all of this . . . isn't what you expected. But it's better to know, right? The truth will set you free and all that?"

"I *did* want answers," I said. "But I don't know what to make of the ones I got. Two weeks ago, I was plain ol' Lainey Styles, and now I'm apparently some all-powerful . . ." I couldn't say the word out loud. "The truth about my mom and Josephine. All the lies. How am I even supposed to process it all?"

"Well, step one is to *not* freak out." Maggie gave my hand another squeeze.

"Yeah, but how can I not freak out? It seems easier to completely fall apart than to accept any of this as true."

"But it *is* true. What else could explain all the weird stuff that's been happening to you?"

"I know." I pulled away from Maggie and dropped my head in my hands. "But it shouldn't be. I had my life all planned out, ya know? Since middle school, I've been killing myself to be the best at everything, to be number one. All I ever wanted to do was to get into a good school with a great science program and be on my own, have the opportunity to see and discover the world. I wanted the chance to figure out who I really am. But this?" My voice cracked. "It's not exactly what I had in mind. . . . It's not fair."

"No, it's not," Maggie agreed. "But this *is* your life now. *This* is who you are, and you can't run away from it. You have to face it."

My shoulders sagged. The whole story sounded too ridiculous to be real, but there was a ring of absolute truth to Serena's words. And even stranger than that was the feeling of acquiescence that was gnawing away at me deep down—it was like being reunited with a long-lost friend or finding something valuable you didn't even realize you had lost. It felt as though a part of me had already accepted the news of my newfound "witch" status without so much as a blink of an eye, while another part of me was convinced I had lost my mind.

It made me uncomfortable to feel so at war with myself, but I was trying not to let it show. "How are you so calm right now?" I asked Maggie. "You're handling the news way better than I am."

Maggie shrugged. "I think you're forgetting who you're talking to, Styles. I'm the girl who spends more time with fictional superheroes than I do with actual people, the girl who spent an entire summer learning Elvish, the girl who already believed in magic. It's not that far-fetched for me, if you think about it. Besides, you're my best friend and I believe in *you*."

"But what if I really am a . . . *witch*." The last word came out in a whisper, and I grimaced.

"Then you'll learn to deal with it," Maggie said. "I think you're looking at this all wrong. You know, before he was part of the Super-Soldier Project, Steve Rogers was this puny, unimpressive guy who was more likely to break his arm playing checkers than to accomplish anything noteworthy. But then he became freaking Captain America! You get what I'm saying?"

"Um, yes?"

Maggie laughed. "God, Styles, you have got to read more comic books." She leaned forward. "Do you have any idea how many times I've dreamt of being bitten by a radioactive spider or finding a magical thunder hammer? I've spent my whole life wishing to be more than just *ordinary*. But I'm just me, just Maggie, and that's probably all I'm ever going to be." Maggie grabbed my hand again. "But *you,* Lainey, you get to be anything but ordinary, and maybe that's not such a bad thing."

The words settled over me, wrapping around me and covering me with calm reassurance. I smiled. "You know, Mags, even if things go to hell, I'm glad to have you by my side."

"Oh, don't get all emotional on me now," Maggie chided, but she was smiling too. "I've got your back, you know that."

"I know. Thank you. I really don't know what I'd do without you."

"Well, for starters, you'd be stuck hanging out in a graveyard all by yourself."

"It's not so bad in the daylight."

"I don't know about that," Maggie said, glancing around. "But you are a witch now, so I can understand if this place speaks to you."

I sucked down a gulp of air. Maggie was just teasing me, but it was the first time anyone had actually called me a witch. It was jarring.

Well, Lainey, you're gonna have to get used to it sooner or later. I took another deep breath. *I'm a witch.* I tested the phrase in my mind. It was strange, but not completely wrong.

It reminded me of the time I bought my first pair of cowboy boots. I remembered pulling the soft-soled boots out of the box and marveling at how the rustic leather looked vintage and worn in all the right places. I'd bought them immediately and worn them out of the store, but that night my feet were sore and blistered. It wasn't until I'd properly broken in the boots that they fit without pain. Maybe, like the boots, I just needed to give myself some time to get used to the idea—to break it in, so to speak.

I'm a witch, I tried again. This time, the words didn't completely jar me. *I'm a witch.* Better still. *I'm a witch.* It was getting better every time.

"I'm a witch," I whispered under my breath, testing the words on my tongue. I closed my eyes and allowed myself to completely surrender, to try and reconcile the two warring sides of myself. Warm energy crackled underneath my skin. "I'm a witch," I said again, a little louder this time. "I am—"

"Um, Lainey?" Maggie suddenly interrupted.

My eyes flew open. "Sorry. I was just trying to—"

"No," Maggie interrupted again. "Look." She pointed over my shoulder.

Unsure of what to expect, I turned around slowly. At first I didn't realize what I was supposed to be looking at, but then I gasped.

The tombstone behind me was a small worn piece of polished stone. It was so old, the inscription of the name was barely visible, and weathering the elements for so many years had coated it in a dark layer of grime. But it wasn't the stone that stole my breath; it was the rosebush behind it.

Most of the plants in the cemetery had grown wild, covering the tombstones around them like ivy, while others had simply succumbed to the Georgia heat. This was one of the latter, its withered, brown leaves brittle and lifeless.

But as I watched, slack-jawed, the rosebush had begun to change. The base of the bush turned green again, and tiny pink buds sprouted from its branches.

Maggie's eyes were as wide as saucers, and it took several gulps of air before I could speak.

"Did I . . ." I trailed off. "Did I do that?" I finally squeaked out.

Maggie looked back and forth between the rosebush and me. "There's only one way to find out." She stood up, pulling me with her, and pushed my hand toward the bush. "Say it again."

I nodded, swallowing hard. I leaned forward and touched one of the tiny buds. "I'm a witch," I whispered.

Immediately, the bud responded, blossoming into a large pink rose with wavy petals and a darker center. I'd never seen a rose look so *alive* before. A tiny squeal of both laughter and amazement escaped my lips. Behind me, Maggie had her hand clamped over her mouth.

"I'm a witch," I said again, louder and with both hands stretched out over the rosebush. I was still overwhelmed and absolutely terrified by the prospect of the future, but watching as the entire bush began to bloom and teem with life just felt *right*.

I turned back to Maggie, whose face mirrored my own amazement. "I probably shouldn't have done that. I'm guessing that was a pulse?"

"Looks that way," Maggie replied, and she started laughing. "God, Styles, if you get your Hogwarts letter before me, I'm gonna be so pissed!"

The look on Maggie's face was so comical I couldn't help but laugh.

It was surprising how easily the sound spilled out, how easy it was to laugh off the anxiety that was gnawing at me from the inside out. Was I really accepting that this was my fate?

I glanced over at the rosebush that was continuing to bloom and flourish, and then back at Maggie, who was still giggling. "I'm a witch," I said, and for the first time since I'd discovered the truth, the word didn't seem so foreign. It would still take some getting used to, but it was a start.

"So," Maggie asked a little while later, "what's the next step in all of this?"

I sighed. "I have to talk to Gareth." It was the logical thing to do, but I was dreading it. I was so angry with him for lying to me, I wasn't sure I'd be able to calmly and rationally discuss the issues at hand. What I really wanted to do was punch him in the face.

"Does he know you know?"

"I assume Serena has told him by now. I had a few missed calls from him."

Maggie scrunched her nose in thought. "What do you think he'll say?"

"I don't know." I shrugged. "But he's got some serious explaining to do."

A short tritone chime chirped from inside my bag. Sighing, I dug around until my fingers wrapped around my phone. "Maybe that's him now." I slid my finger across the screen to read the text.

The number was unfamiliar, but as I read the message, a smile crept across my face. "It's from Ty." A rush of adrenaline shot through me, and my heart fluttered. "I didn't even know he had my number."

"Oh, I gave it to him."

I rolled my eyes. "Gee, thanks, Maggie."

"You're welcome," Maggie replied, her cheeks pulled up into a devilish grin.

I snorted and turned my attention back to the text. "He wanted to make sure I was okay."

"How sweet!"

"I guess so." I tossed Maggie the phone so she could read the message. "But all things considered, why in the world is he still talking to me? Last night was like a freaking episode of the *Twilight Zone*. What normal guy would be into that?"

"Eh, normal is overrated," Maggie replied matter-of-factly.

I thought of the sympathetic look in his eyes as I'd spilled my guts about all the freaky stuff that had been happening, of the reassuring pressure of his hand in mine. Most of the guys I knew would've run for the hills by now. But Ty hadn't.

I took my phone back from Maggie and stared at the screen, contemplating a reply.

"Hey, Styles?"

"Yeah?"

"You're blushing." Maggie giggled and then winked at me.

"Oh, shut up!" I reached over to smack her, but she darted out of the way with a laugh. "I am not. I'm just trying to figure out a response that doesn't make me sound like a complete psycho."

"Say what you want, Styles. But I can read you like a book." Maggie smirked again and started making kissing noises.

"God, Maggie! What are you, five years old?" I pulled a comic book from the messenger bag around her shoulders and tossed it at her. "Here, read about that green lamp guy and quit distracting me."

"*Lantern,*" Maggie corrected. "It's the Green Lantern!"

"Whatever. Same thing!"

Maggie mockingly gripped her chest as though she were in pain. "You wound me, Styles. You wound me."

"Maggie!"

"Okay, okay." Maggie threw her hands up in surrender. "Be sure to tell Pretty Face I said hello." And with one final kissy noise, she turned her attention to her comic book.

With Maggie's teasing voice echoing in my ear, I recalled the moment Ty had brought me back from the brink with Josephine. The whole evening was starting to blur together, and the moments after Josephine's appearance were the fuzziest of all.

Yet, I could distinctly remember the feel of Ty's hands, the way his fingers had pressed into my back as he held me. I could still see the worry burning in his eyes as he tried to calm me, and the very thought of how his strong arms had wrapped around me, forceful yet gentle at the same time, was enough to get my heart pounding again. I remembered the undeniable feeling of security I'd felt wrapped in his arms, the sound of his husky voice murmuring words of comfort in my ear. I shivered just thinking about it all.

Beside me, Maggie giggled. "I saw that, Styles." She eyed me suggestively, and this time my whole face ignited, betraying me. "I knew you were thinking about it."

I rolled my eyes and quickly tapped out a short reply on my phone. I hit send and tossed the phone back into my bag. "You're something else, Mags."

"I know. That's why you love me," Maggie replied sweetly, flipping her comic book shut with an audible snap.

"Oh, yeah? Well, that's debatable." I laughed. "Now, come on. I should get going."

"Heading home, then?"

"Yeah." I sighed. "Gareth will be home soon. It's time he and I had a talk."

လ•ಲ

Gareth's truck was parked in its usual spot in front of the house. I parked next to it and opened my car door, wincing as the creaky hinges grated against my frazzled nerves.

I walked slowly up the walkway. I hated how nervous I felt; I'd wanted to confront Gareth with strength and confidence, but now that the conversation was moments away, I was the exact opposite of brave. I was a lamb being led to the slaughter.

Stop it, Lainey. He's your uncle, not an executioner. I straightened my shoulders and walked toward Gareth's office. It was where he spent most of his time when he was home.

Pushing the door open, I stuck my head inside.

Two of the four walls of the room were lined with floor-to-ceiling bookcases, and a large antique desk sat near a large window with a wide bench seat. The other wall was decorated in large maps that were covered in Post-it notes, Gareth's neat handwriting scrawled across them.

I'd always loved the way the room smelled of old, well-loved books. Some of my favorite childhood memories were of Gareth and me sprawled out together on the large rug, flipping through antique encyclopedias and atlases, of reading *The Lion, the Witch, and the Wardrobe* and *The Hobbit*.

I scanned the room and frowned. It was empty. *That's strange.*

The rest of the house was quiet, and I'd been certain I'd find Gareth behind his desk, poring over papers. I shrugged, turned toward the door, and stopped.

One of the bookshelves on the far wall was leaning precariously forward, and there was a dim, hazy glowing coming from the right side of the shelf.

I blinked. Maybe it was the sunlight that poured in through the window creating some kind of optical illusion. Or maybe it was the lack of sleep that was making me loopy, but it almost seemed as if the bookshelf had come unattached from the wall and was floating in midair.

I moved closer to get a better look.

I stopped again, my breath hitching in my throat.

It had been an optical illusion after all. The bookshelf wasn't floating or about to fall over.

It was a door.

CHAPTER EIGHTEEN

I stood there staring, utterly gobsmacked at the door that shouldn't exist.

What the hell? I reached out my hand.

The hinges creaked when I pushed the large, book-covered panel even farther away from the wall to reveal a narrow passageway. I couldn't see much—the only source of light was a small yellow lantern that hung from the ceiling—except for the fact that the walls were made of large gray stones. I stepped inside.

The narrow passageway was long and winding, with lanterns placed sporadically to light the way. The floor was nothing but dirt.

Where am I? The passageway looked like it belonged in an ancient castle in medieval England, not a conservative, two-story house in the middle of Nowhere, Georgia. Was it possible that I'd stepped through some magical portal, transporting me to another time and place entirely? I shook my head but kept inching along.

The passage began to widen, and after rounding the last curve, I found myself standing in a large, dome-shaped room with walls that were a strange mixture of polished metal and compacted dirt. A web of ropes hung from the ceiling, and there were wide hooks attached to the metal paneling of the walls that held a large collection of weaponry. My mouth dropped open as I took in the assortment of long and short swords, sabers, scimitars, rapiers, daggers, spiked maces, longbows with matching quivers of arrows, and other strange, yet dangerous-looking objects I couldn't identify.

I turned and nearly jumped out of my skin. Gareth was standing a few feet away, holding a long, heavy-looking sword in his hand. His back was to me, and he was wearing a plain white t-shirt and some loose sweatpants. The sword in his hands was long and curved, the blade a deep copper color.

I stared as Gareth began to move, flinging the blade around his head as though it weighed nothing. He lunged forward, striking the air, and the sword moved so gracefully it might have been a natural extension of his arm.

I think my eyes may have bugged out of my head as I watched Gareth attack his invisible opponent with a skill and ease that bespoke long years of practice. I gasped in sheer admiration and astonishment as he executed a maneuver I'd only ever seen in movies.

At the sound, Gareth whirled around and darted forward, the sword aimed at my chest.

I screeched and threw myself backward, landing hard on

my ass. I was more shocked than hurt, but my entire body was shaking as I stared up at my uncle.

"Dammit, Lainey, I could've killed you!" Gareth roared, moving the blade away from my chest. He wiped the sweat from his brow and reached down to help me to my feet. "What are you *doing* down here?"

"What am I doing down here?" I dusted the dirt from the back of my pants. "What am *I* doing down here?" I threw my arms out. "I don't even know where the hell I am!"

Gareth let out a long sigh and shifted from one foot to the other as if he wasn't sure what to say next. "Serena told me—" he started, then shook his head. "No, let's start with the easy stuff first. You're in the training room." His casual use of the term—as if he'd said 'grocery story' or 'library'— sent a surge of anger through me.

"Oh, the training room?" I glared at him. "Well, that explains everything."

"Look, I know you're upset—"

"Upset?" My voice was rising, shrill and punctuated. "Now, why would I be upset? Oh, I know! Maybe it's because I just found out that I'm a witch—a fact that you conveniently forgot to tell me *for almost seventeen years!* Or it could be that I just got attacked by a freaking tree. And let's not forget the fact that my house has a hidden dungeon in it where my uncle likes to show off his secret ninja skills and throw around a sword!" I tilted my head in mock thought. "Nope, can't see any reason at all why I should be upset."

"A ninja?" Gareth scoffed.

"Fine. Warlock." I threw my hands in the air. "Whatever."

The smile faded from Gareth's face, and he blinked a few times before he spoke again. "Come on. I'll explain everything." He walked over to a pair of chairs near one of the weapon racks. I huffed and followed him, plunking myself down in one of the seats.

After he had wiped down his sword with a soft cloth, Gareth hung the weapon in its rightful place on the wall and sat opposite me. "Okay," he said, his face serious. "Where do you want me to start?"

"How come you never told me the truth about Mom?"

Gareth sighed. "I *was* planning to tell you. I had it all thought out in my head, what I was going to say and do, but I could never seem to find the right time."

"The right time?" I clenched my hands into fists. "You should've told me when I was old enough to understand. I deserved to know the truth about my mother, about what happened to her and my dad." My voice cracked, but the words kept coming. "I trusted you."

Gareth cleared his throat, visibly trying to keep his emotions at bay. "I'm sorry, Lainey. I was just trying to do what I felt was right."

His face was pained, and his eyes sparkled with unshed tears. "Children don't come with an instruction manual, and in your case I didn't know what to do because I had to keep you safe. That was everyone's priority. I let that stand in the way of my judgment. Telling you would have been the best thing, I know that now." He wiped a hand across his face. "But I never meant to hurt you or break your trust. I'm so sorry."

The remorse in Gareth's eyes hit me harder than I thought it would. My throat constricted, making it hard to swallow. "What about telling me I was a witch? Were you just gonna wait until I woke up levitating or turned my English teacher into a lawn gnome?"

"No, of course not."

I fidgeted in my seat, fighting the urge to scream. "You can't say 'of course not.' Serena told me about the pulses, how your cloaking spells are failing. Were you planning to wait until something bad happened to finally clue me in?"

Gareth sighed and put his head in his hands. "I was wrong not to tell you, to keep you in the dark about who you are, but this life isn't easy. There is danger everywhere—people who would stop at nothing to harm you just for who you are, what you can do. I guess I just wanted you to have as normal a life as possible for as long as possible." He sat up straight in his chair. "Does that make sense?"

"It does," I replied. "But you should've told me."

"You're right. I should have."

A few minutes passed, and then Gareth leaned forward. "It's true, then. The Continuance?"

I nodded. "Apparently. Although Serena doesn't really know why Josephine established the bond. She said it's extremely rare."

"It is," Gareth confirmed. "And I think I might know the answer to that." He took a deep breath and exhaled sharply.

"What did Serena tell you about her—about Josephine DuCarmont?"

I shrugged. "Nothing, really. Only that we're related, and that the DuCarmonts were a very powerful family of witches. That's why Mom was . . . murdered." I swallowed. It was still hard to wrap my head around. "Because she was a DuCarmont."

Gareth's face was as serious as I'd ever seen it. "Yes, but that's not the only reason." He glanced around the room, almost as if he were afraid of someone listening. His next words were hardly louder than a whisper. "Lainey, she was killed because she was the Keeper."

"The Keeper?"

Gareth nodded. "Yes, the Keeper of the Grimoire."

"The what? Gareth, I don't—"

"A grimoire is basically a textbook of magic. It's specific by coven and contains all of the spells, charms, and rituals performed by those witches. Each coven has one, and the books themselves are very powerful talismans of magic. To keep them from falling into the wrong hands, a Keeper is destined to protect it, to keep it safe. The more powerful the coven, the more valuable the grimoire would be."

Gareth took a deep breath and continued. "Josephine DuCarmont was the Keeper of the Grimoire. And like her, your mother was as well."

I didn't know what to say. I stared at Gareth, trying to wrap my head around the new information. "So Mom was killed because of a book?"

"Yes," Gareth breathed out. "But Lainey, you have to understand, the Grimoire isn't just any old book. The DuCarmonts were the most powerful witches of our realm, and their grimoire contained magic more potent than any other in existence. Power like that—well, let's just say the DuCarmonts had their fair share of enemies, people who would stop at nothing to get their hands on the book."

In my mind, remnants of my visions flashed before my eyes: the worn book in Josephine's hands, the man in black demanding to know where it was hidden, the emerald amulet, the picture of my mother.

"The necklace," I whispered. "It's the Grimoire." I wiped my face with my hand. "Did they take it?"

Gareth looked confused.

"When they killed my mom," I supplied. "Did they take the Grimoire?"

"Yes." He frowned. "They did."

The knot in my stomach grew. I nodded, not sure what to say next.

"The Continuance," Gareth continued. "I think it's a warning of some kind." He began to pace. "You see, Keepers don't just protect the book. They are the only ones who can truly wield its power. It's as if the book is the lock, and the Keeper—"

"Is the key," I finished for him. "But they killed her. My mother. If she was the Keeper, why would they kill her?"

"It's a well-protected coven secret." Gareth stopped pacing and faced me. "Your mom told me the night she left. It's likely that they killed her before realizing she was the only one who could harness the book's power. Lainey, you have to understand that you are the only living person with DuCarmont blood running through your veins. Which means—"

"By default, I'm the new Keeper." I sucked in a breath of air. "Aren't I?"

"Yes," Gareth said. "Serena thinks you are in some kind of danger, but I've kept you hidden from the Supernatural world for years. No one knows you exist." Gareth's face was grim. "But you're strong, like your mother, and the cloaking spells aren't working anymore. The dryad was proof of that. Lainey, if more people find out about you—"

"I know," I said. "The big, bad wolf will come after me. But who—" A knot formed in the pit of my stomach. "Wait. You just said I'm the only one left with DuCarmont blood. Serena said the same thing. But that's impossible. What about you?"

All the blood drained from Gareth's face.

"Gareth," I tried again, louder this time. "You're my uncle. You were her brother. You're a DuCarmont, too . . . aren't you?" I searched his face, anxious to see recognition of his mistake, but there was nothing but guilt. That look said everything.

"I'm gonna throw up." I pushed out of the chair and crossed the room. A worn bucket sat in the corner, and I snatched it up, gripping its sides while my stomach pitched and rolled.

Gareth walked up behind me but didn't say a word. I

waited until I was certain I wasn't going to hurl before I turned to face him. "You're not my real uncle." It wasn't a question.

"No," he confirmed, "I'm not."

I took a deep breath and turned back toward the trash can just in case. I squeezed my eyes shut, refusing to spill the tears of frustration that were forming.

I gripped the can for a moment before finally shoving it away. It fell to its side with a loud clatter, and I whirled around to face Gareth, my chest heaving. "Was *anything* real?" I spat. "God, how many more secrets are you keeping from me?"

"None," Gareth replied. "I swear."

"How can I even trust you anymore?" I demanded, trying not to let the hurt show on my face. "I don't even know who you are."

Gareth grimaced. "Lainey, I will explain everything if you'll give me the chance." He took a hesitant step forward. "Please, you have to understand, everything I did, all the secrets, it was to protect you."

I stepped backward, away from him. I wasn't going to forgive as easily this time. "Start talking."

With a heavy sigh, Gareth began to speak. "Your mom, Serena, and I were friends; more than that, really. We were family. We grew up together, did everything together." He swallowed. "So when things got bad and your mom had to go into hiding, Serena and I went with her. We thought it would be safer, that the three of us would be strong enough to protect each other."

Gareth broke off, his voice choked. He took a few deep breaths and kept going. "Everything was fine for a few years. Your mom met your dad, and they had you. It was the happiest I'd ever seen her."

Gareth walked back over to the table and sank down into one of the chairs, as if the burden of his story weighed heavily upon him. "After your dad was killed, she knew it was only a matter of time. She knew she had to leave, to run, so that you would be safe. She made me promise to take you away, to hide you from everyone." He looked up at me, his eyes full of grief. "You were calling me Uncle Gareth from the time you learned to talk. It was just easier."

He sniffed. "I loved her, Lainey, and I swore to look after you, to keep you safe. And that's what I've tried to do these last sixteen years."

My head was swimming. It made sense, and I even understood *why* he'd kept so many secrets from me, but it still didn't diminish the betrayal and anger boiling underneath my skin.

"I was planning to show you this place," Gareth said, his voice breaking through my thoughts. "I can't help you with your magic, but I can show you how to protect yourself." He stood up and walked over to the weapons wall. He retrieved the bronze sword he'd been using earlier, as well as a sheathed dagger the size of my forearm.

He walked back to me, the smaller sword in his outstretched hand. "I'm good with most weapons, but long swords are my specialty." He had a sheepish grin on his face; this was a side of Gareth I'd never seen before.

"I don't understand," I said, staring at the sword in Gareth's hand but refusing to touch it. "Why can't you train me to use my magic? If the pulses are the problem, I have to learn to control them, to keep my magic in check."

Gareth's face flushed, and he smiled sheepishly again. "Witches are incredibly secretive about their magic." He motioned for me to take the sword. "My expertise is elsewhere, I'm afraid."

I stared at him. Even though I knew the truth, it was still hard to fathom that the man in front of me, the man who had taken care of me my whole life, wasn't who I thought he was. The ache in my chest nearly crippled me.

"And I'm guessing the reason you don't know much about magic is because you don't have any, right?" It seemed a logical enough question.

"Oh, I have magic," Gareth replied. "Just not your kind of magic." He pointed to the ceiling. "I created this room, for example." He chuckled at little at the confusion on my face. "I'm one of the Fey. Warping dimensions is a specialty of ours."

"The Fey?"

Gareth nodded. "Lainey . . ." He leaned in closer, resting his hand on my shoulder and looking me in the eye. "I'm a Faerie."

I blinked. "A Faerie?

"A Faerie."

"What the hell?" The words tumbled out before I could stop them. Everything I knew about Faeries involved clapping, pixie dust, and tiny shimmering wings. As I stared at Gareth, tall and broad with muscular shoulders and a menacing sword in his hand, I was having a hard time reconciling the two images in my brain.

"Like with wings and stuff?" I finally asked, unable to get the image of Tinkerbell out of my head.

Gareth laughed loudly. "In a manner of speaking, but with less glitter," he replied, almost as if he could read my mind. "I'm a bladesmith by trade." He took a step forward, urging me to take the dagger he was offering.

Not knowing what else to do, I gripped the thick handle of the dagger. It was heavy in my hand and incredibly foreign.

"Move around a little," Gareth encouraged. "Get a feel for the blade. You might like a short sword better, but I thought we should start small."

I took a step forward, holding the dagger awkwardly away from my body. My brain was muddled, and the longer I stood with the blade in my hand, the more overwhelmed I felt. With my pulse echoing in my ears, I dropped it onto the ground.

Gareth started to rush over, but I held out a hand to stop him.

"I can't do this." My voice was shaky, but strong. "I'm trying really hard to process all of this, but every time I think I have a handle on things, something even crazier happens."

I clenched my hands into fists. "One minute I find out

that everything I know about my family is a lie, then it's 'oh, hey, guess what? You're a witch!' And now, I find out that my mother was some kind of guardian for a book that got her killed, and my uncle is actually not my uncle at all. He's friggin' Tinkerbell!" My voice was high and shrill by the end of my tirade, and Gareth was staring at me, pain and guilt etched across his face.

"Lainey," he began.

"No!" I shouted at him. "Just leave me alone."

I turned on my heel and ran across the room to the pathway that led back to the house. Gareth called my name, but I kept running. It felt like the walls were closing in on me; I needed to get out of there, and fast.

I plowed into Gareth's office. It was disorienting to return to the modern world, and I shook my head to clear it, slamming the door behind me.

I grabbed my purse and keys from the table in the hall and walked outside. There was no way I was spending one more minute in that house.

I threw myself into the car. I didn't pay attention to where I was going, and I didn't have a destination in mind. All I knew was that I needed to get away from my life for a while. I needed some kind of distraction.

So, I kept driving, determined to find one.

CHAPTER NINETEEN

My phone continued to ring.

I rolled my eyes, not even bothering to glance at the screen. Gareth had been calling nonstop ever since I'd fled from the house, but I had nothing to say to him.

It was getting late. The sun had set hours ago, and I'd already driven to the state line and back. I knew I should probably just go back home or at least stop wasting a perfectly good tank of gas, but the anger coursing through my veins only made my foot press down harder on the accelerator. I didn't have a specific destination in mind; I was driving on autopilot.

When I pulled into the familiar gravel parking lot of the cemetery, I wasn't completely surprised. I didn't know what had drawn me back, but then I saw her, standing beside the wrought iron entrance gates. Josephine. Unlike earlier when I had hoped to see her, the very sight of her made my blood boil.

I slammed the car into park. "Seriously?" I glared at the

apparition across the blacktop. I shoved the door open and stalked toward her.

"Now you're here?" I threw my arms out. "What do you want from me?"

She just stared at me, her face sad.

"Oh that's right, you're here to warn me. Well, message received," I yelled across the parking lot. "You can go now!"

Lainey. The whispered word came from behind me. I whirled around, but there was nothing but my car. I looked back toward the gate. Josephine was gone.

"What game are you playing?" I yelled into the wind. I wanted to punch something, just beat the crap out of it until the ache in my chest stopped hurting, until all the anger and frustration flowing through me evaporated.

I sagged against my car. *This isn't my life.* The truth about my parents, my own supernatural lineage, the sightings of Josephine, Gareth—it was all hitting me like a slap in the face. "This isn't me," I whispered, but the words tasted like ash on my tongue. *Don't lie to yourself, Lainey. This is you. Who you are, and who you've always been.* The voice in my head was my own. I thought how good it had felt in the graveyard with Maggie, how those three little words had felt: *I'm a witch.* But now everything was muddled, and I wasn't sure how to wrap my head around it all.

I got back in my car and kept driving. Still reeling from the emotional cyclone swirling inside me, I drove slowly down the darkened streets, not really paying much attention to where I was going.

Before long, I ended up near the railroad tracks on the outskirts of town. It wasn't the nicest or safest area, but it was fairly secluded, and a lot of the local teenagers used it as a place to hang out away from the watchful eye of adult supervision. From the looks of things—a slew of parked cars, loud music, and a large bonfire—there was some sort of party going on.

It wasn't a smart idea to stop—the tracks were known as a place where bad decisions were made—but I couldn't go home. Not yet.

Besides, this looks exactly like the type of distraction I need. I pulled off the main road and parked next to an old, rust-colored Bronco.

My phone started ringing again. This time it was Maggie. I almost didn't answer it, but on the very last ring, I slid my finger quickly over the screen. "Hey, Mags."

"Where the hell are you?" she breathed into the phone. "Your uncle just called me. He's freaking out. He said ya'll had some kind of fight and you ran out, said you'd been gone for hours."

I snorted. "A fight? Yeah, I guess you could count me calling him out for lying to me my entire life as a fight. Oh, and by the way, he's not really my uncle."

Maggie sucked in a quick breath of air. "Wait, what?"

Sighing, I quickly recapped the afternoon, from finding the hidden passageway and room to Gareth being a Faerie.

"Holy cra—holy shitkittens, Styles!" Maggie said, when I was finished. "I don't even know what to say."

"Tell me about it," I said. "I just feel kind of blindsided. I don't know really how to process all of this. I'm a facts girl. And these are the facts, but I cannot seem to reconcile them in my mind. I'm trying, but . . ." I trailed off.

"God, Styles, I'm so sorry. I can't imagine how you must be feeling right now."

I could only respond with a choked sigh.

"Oh, Lainey." Maggie's voice was soft and full of sympathy. "Where are you? Why don't you come over? We'll stuff ourselves with mint chocolate chip ice cream and watch movies until you feel less crappy, okay?"

I sighed again. Maggie's offer was incredibly tempting, but what I needed was a distraction, a way to completely shut off my brain. As much as I loved her, spending hours talking and analyzing the situation wasn't exactly what I had in mind.

"Thanks, Mags. But I just need to clear my head for a little bit. I'll come over tomorrow, okay? I gotta go for now." I opened the car door. The loud music from the party echoed across the trees that surrounded the clearing.

"Okay," Maggie replied hesitantly. "Wait, what's that noise? Lainey, where are you?"

"I'm . . ." I figured I might as well tell someone just in case. "I'm at the tracks."

"What!" Maggie demanded. "What are you doing there?"

"I drove by and saw a party, so I stopped."

"And you're just gonna go? All kinds of crazy stuff happen at those parties."

"I'll be fine, Maggie."

"I'm serious, Styles. This is not a good idea!"

"I'll be fine," I repeated, already stepping out of the car. "Don't worry about me."

Maggie continued to yell, but I'd already made up my mind. "I'll call you later!" I yelled over her tirade and ended the call. I knew I'd have to deal with her wrath later, but I figured I'd cross that bridge when I came to it.

Shoving my phone in my back pocket, I shut and locked the car door and headed toward the party.

There were about twenty or so people sitting near the bonfire, drinking beer and laughing loudly. There was another group a few feet away dancing next to an iPhone that had been rigged to play through a large set of speakers.

I recognized some of the people from school, but the rest were strangers. A few gave me curious looks as I walked by, but didn't bother to stop and make conversation.

Plopping myself down next to the bonfire, I stared into the flames and tried to think about nothing except the way the colors moved and danced together. Beside me, a boy with stringy blond hair and pasty skin popped the top of a beer can and alternated between swigs of beer and taking drags from the lit cigarette in his hand. I shook my head when he offered me the can. He shrugged and turned his attention back to his cigarette.

A few minutes later, an excited squeal rose over the music playing from the iPhone. "It's almost time!" a voice called out.

All at once, the partygoers around the fire and those dancing began to move toward the tracks.

I looked around. "What's going on?" I asked the blond boy. He took a quick drag of his cigarette before responding.

"It's almost eleven," he said, blowing smoke in my face.

Wrinkling my nose, I fanned the smoke from my eyes. "Yeah, so?"

The boy shakily got to his feet, squeezing the beer can tightly in his hand. "The freighters," he said, stumbling toward the tracks. "They're always right on time."

I watched him walk away, feeling more than a little confused. In the distance, a shrill whistle cut through the darkness, eliciting cheers from the group by the tracks. *What's the big deal? It's just a couple of trains.*

I was trying to decide whether to go down to the tracks and see what all the fuss was about or just go home when a familiar voice whispered in my ear.

Lainey.

Josephine was standing a few feet away, underneath the canopy of the tree line, the orange glow from the bonfire lighting her face.

I leapt to my feet. "Go away," I said, glaring at Josephine. I clenched my fists at my sides as hot anger ignited inside me.

Huffing, I stalked toward the group gathered by the tracks. A small orb of light was bouncing along the darkness—the headlight of the freight train coming closer.

"So what's the big deal with the train?" I asked a girl with long braids and a nose ring.

The girl rolled her eyes as if I'd just asked her to analyze *War and Peace.* "It's the eleven o'clock freighter," she answered matter-of-factly.

"Yeah, I got *that.*" I narrowed my eyes. "But who cares?"

"You're new here," the girl spat out, glaring at me like I was an interloper in some secret society. She rolled her eyes again. "It starts at eleven, and then they run every eight minutes. Last man standing wins."

"Wins what? What are you—" I stopped as two boys stepped over the metal railing and stood side by side in the middle of the track facing the train. Almost in response, the train gave a loud whistle. It was still several hundred feet away, but it was moving fast.

The boys were laughing as they stared down the train, daring each other to move while the rest of the group cheered and placed bets on who would wuss out first. I wasn't sure whether to laugh or be appalled, but I stayed where I was, watching the boys with wide eyes.

Lainey.

The voice came from behind me. I didn't have to look to know who it was. "I told you to go away," I grumbled beneath my breath, refusing to turn around. The train was getting closer, and there was a tangible energy churning through the air. The boys on the tracks were no longer laughing, but focused on the train itself, both posed in a stance that would allow them to jump from either side at the last second.

I stood half horrified, half amazed as the boys played chicken with the train. One of them was swearing loudly and his whole body was shaking from exertion. The train was getting closer, its harsh whistle echoing across the trees. The boy who had been swearing turned and jumped off the tracks shaking his head. The other boy, the one still on the tracks, raised a fist triumphantly in the air but continued to stare at the train—now dangerously close. At the very last second, he threw himself from the tracks and landed on his stomach in the grass while the train roared over the very spot on which he'd been standing. The crowd cheered as he got to his feet and dusted himself off, grinning like a madman.

I was surprised to find myself clapping. The whole thing was incredibly stupid, not to mention dangerous, but there was something about the look in the boy's eyes, how his whole face glowed. He looked entirely *free*. I was envious of him for that.

In the distance, another whistle began to sound and the crowd began crowing once more. Two more boys hopped up onto the tracks. I watched as they stood there looking confident and brave, the train barreling down the tracks.

Lainey.

I jumped as the voice called again. This time it was right next to me. I turned my head; Josephine, her mournful eyes trained on my face, was standing on the other side of the girl with the braids. She was close enough that I could swear she was a solid, living person instead of an apparition. Her long, dark tresses were blowing in a breeze I couldn't feel, and the flames from the bonfire danced in her eyes.

I stared back, but when Josephine took a step toward me, something inside me snapped. "Enough!" I growled. "Leave me alone!"

The girl with braids whipped her head in my direction. "What the hell is your problem?"

I didn't answer. I was already pushing my way through the crowd. No one tried to stop me, and I wasn't fully aware of exactly what I was doing until I stepped over the metal rails and felt the wooden slates and the gravel crunch underneath my feet.

Behind me, a murmur of confusion was circulating through the crowd as I walked toward the boys and shoved myself between them.

"What the—?" one of the boys shouted, while the other jumped in surprise. I ignored them. As the light of the next freighter appeared, a rush of adrenaline kicked in, and I took a breath to steady myself.

What are you doing? Get off the tracks! the tiny voice of reason screamed inside my head, but the sense of absolute control swirling around inside me kept my feet grounded.

The train's harsh whistle sounded again, and my hands began to shake. My breath was hitching in my lungs, but I forced myself to plant my feet. Small bits of gravel dug into the worn soles of my sneakers, but I didn't move. The two boys were still staring at me as the train continued to wail.

The ball of light from the train's headlight grew bigger.

The sounds of laughter and catcalling drifted toward me as the crowd yelled taunts and encouragements at the three of us on the tracks. A single voice seemed to echo in my ears, louder than the rest—though it couldn't have been more than a whisper.

Lainey.

Grinding my teeth, I took a step forward. I forced my shoulders back and stood a little straighter.

The train was still several hundred yards away, but I rose up on the balls of my feet, throwing my arms out wide. The beam of light from the train was warm on my face, the scream of the whistle deafening in my ears.

A bit of air whooshed past me as one of the boys behind me jumped off the tracks with a yell. The other swore loudly. The voice in my head screamed at me to move, but the heady euphoria coursing through me held me in place.

Just when the tang of metal hit my nose, I threw myself sideways and off the tracks, only a second or two before the train roared over the very spot on which I'd been standing.

I landed in a soft patch of grass, rolling until I came to a stop on my back. My chest was heaving, but the weight I'd felt from the conversation with Gareth was lighter somehow. I let out a laugh.

That is, until a large hand clamped down on my wrist, yanking me to my feet.

I yelped and tried to pull my hand free when I came face-to-face with a familiar pair of blue eyes.

"Ty?" I stared at him as he dropped my arm. His mouth

was set in an angry line, and his shoulders were tense. "What the hell are you doing?"

He cocked one eyebrow and glared at me. "What are *you* doing, Lainey? Standing in front of a train? How could you do something so stupid?" he spat, his eyes flashing.

The adrenaline pumping through my system kicked up a notch as I processed his words. "It wasn't stupid." My cheeks flared, and heat seared through me.

Ty threw his arm out, gesturing to the freighter that was still making its way across the crossroads. "Right, because standing in front of a moving train isn't some sort of death wish."

"It's not!"

"Yeah, okay."

I rolled my eyes. "I don't need you or anyone else telling me what I can and can't do."

"I wasn't trying to—"

"You just don't understand, okay?" I ran a hand through my tangled hair, trying to find the right words. But with the adrenaline rush slowly ebbing, I wasn't exactly feeling confident about the motive behind my little daredevil stunt.

I looked around; Josephine was nowhere to be seen. The rational part of my brain was resetting itself, and I stared at the train, only now understanding the danger I'd put myself in. *What was I thinking?*

"Just tell me," Ty said, with a sigh. "What were you thinking?" It was as if he had plucked the words right out of my head. I stared at him blankly for a moment. I tried to come up with an explanation.

"I don't know," I finally answered, my voice soft. "I don't know."

Ty's face softened. He sighed heavily and took a step toward me. "It's okay."

"No, it's not."

As the train continued to roar down the tracks and the shouts of strangers from the other side mixed together in a strange cacophony of sound around me, all I could think about was just how close I'd come to death. Bile began to rise in my throat, and my chest began to tighten.

"It's not okay. I could've died tonight." My voice cracked on the last word. Ty took another step closer.

"No, don't," I warned him, holding up my hand. My emotions were spiraling to the point of physical pain, but I forced myself to feel them.

"I just wanted to feel the control," I pleaded with him, needing him to understand. "I watched the others, and they seemed so confident, so in control. I wanted to feel that. I wanted to remember what it felt like to have my life in my own hands again, without all the lies and the secrets." I thought of Josephine. "Without all the ghosts."

"Is that what you think is happening?" Ty asked gently. "You're losing control?"

"Well, aren't I? The variables keep changing. Every time I come close to a conclusion, an answer, I have to adjust to a whole new set of parameters." The words were pouring out of me. "How can I analyze the data and figure this out when there's no constant?" My shoulders sagged. "I've always seen my life one way, and now it feels like a lie."

"That doesn't mean your life isn't your own."

"How can you possibly know that?" I whispered. "We've known each other for, what? Like, two minutes? And every time you're around me, I'm falling apart because something crazy happened." I snorted. "I just stood in front of a moving train. Sounds like a lost girl to me."

Ty hesitated, thinking. "I don't know if I'd call it 'lost.'"

"Oh, yeah? What would you call it, then? Stupid? Reckless?"

"Oh, it was definitely stupid." Ty gave a crooked smile and crossed the distance between us, taking hold of one of my hands. "And reckless. But I also think it was kinda human."

"What do you mean?"

Ty shrugged. "You've had a lot thrown at you. Anyone in your shoes would be freaking out."

I gave a tiny smile. It wasn't at all the answer I'd been expecting from him. I cleared my throat. "You really think so?"

"Yeah, I do." He chuckled softly. "Did you know I think you're the only girl I've met that talks in scientific metaphors when she's upset?"

I laughed. "Well, I guess I'm not like most girls."

"No," Ty said, "you're definitely not."

The smell of his cologne—warm with a hint of spice— hit my nostrils. We were standing closer than I thought. My heart began to beat faster.

"So . . . um . . ." I said, shifting from one foot to the other. "How did you even know I was here?"

"Maggie texted," Ty replied. "She's worried about you."

My eyebrows shot up. "Maggie texted you and told you where I was?"

"Yeah, she told me what happened with your unc—er, with Gareth, and she said something about the Punisher, but I didn't follow."

I raked my brain trying to remember all the useless facts Maggie was always pouring into my brain. "Oh, that's the marine guy who became a vigilante in hopes of seeking revenge for his family's death!"

Ty looked confused. "Uh . . . not following you."

I burst into laughter. "She's pissed I came here, and probably even more pissed that I hung up on her."

"Still not following you."

"I guess this is her revenge, calling you instead of coming to get me herself."

Ty let go of my hand; he looked unsure. "And me coming here, that's a bad thing for you?"

My cheeks warmed. Up close, I could see his eyes had flecks of gold in them. Ty was watching me carefully, but his eyes sparkled in the moonlight. My heart beat wildly.

"No," I whispered, taking a step closer. I stared up into his face. "No, not at all."

He lowered his head, our noses brushing. "Lainey . . . I . . ." The husky tenor of his voice sent a rush of adrenaline through me.

With a boldness that was surprising even to me, I stepped up on my tiptoes and pressed my lips to his.

CHAPTER TWENTY

Ty stiffened at first, but a moment later, his hands found the curve of my hips and pulled me closer.

His lips were warm. I shivered as Ty reached up to cup one of my cheeks, his thumb tracing lines across my cheekbone. I tasted the spearmint gum on his breath, and I gripped the front of his shirt, pulling myself closer.

It wasn't a hurried kiss, but as Ty's soft lips moved against mine, a fresh rush of adrenaline surged through me just the same. Like fire, it burned through my veins, warming my skin and speeding my heart. I was so acutely aware of the loud hammering of my own heartbeat that I barely registered the rumbling sound in my ears. It was only when the rain began to pelt us that the noise made sense.

Ty pulled away first, looking around in surprise. Thick raindrops poured from the sky, but all I could focus on was the feel of Ty's warm hand trailing what felt like fire down my arm. He smiled at me and leaned in once more, pressing his lips gently against mine. Standing on my tiptoes, I reached up and wrapped my arms around his neck, running my fingers into his hair as the rain fell around us.

The kiss deepened. A strange sensation began to hum inside my chest. Warm wisps of energy danced across my skin, and a sense of magnetism enveloped me. The impression was so intense, I broke away from Ty with a gasp.

"I'm sorry, I—" I began, but stopped. Ty was staring down at me, his blue irises tinged with a ring of golden light.

"I knew it was you," he said. His voice was low, almost a whisper.

"Ty?" I took a step back. A gust of wind whipped my hair across my face, and a low peal of thunder rumbled across the sky. "What's going on?"

He stared at me for a moment. The golden light had faded from his eyes, returning them to their normal color. "Lainey, there's something I need to tell you."

I'd seen that look before. On Serena's face. And on Gareth's.

"Stop." I held up my hand. My stomach rolled with nausea. "I know that look, and what you're about to tell me is going to change everything again, isn't it?"

He didn't have to reply. His face said it all.

"God!" I cried. "I'm so sick of this. Every time I turn around, someone is lying to me or keeping some massive secret from me. I can't trust anyone!" I rubbed my forehead where a pounding headache was building in my temple. "What is it this time, Ty? What's your big secret? Tell me!" I spat out the words. A loud clap of thunder seemed to echo my anger.

A thought struck me, and I glared at him. "You walked by Auntie Marmalade like you were invisible." I swore under my breath. "When Serena said I was a witch, you didn't even blink an eye. What happened in the graveyard—you weren't surprised at all, were you?"

I sucked down a quick breath, squeezing my hands into fists. "Of course you weren't. Because you must have seen it all before." Another loud clap of thunder responded to my words.

Ty looked up at the sky and then back at me, a peculiar expression on his face. I'd seen that look cross his face before but could never identify it. Now it made sense. My heart sank.

"You're a part of this somehow. Aren't you?" I took a step backward.

Ty hesitated, but reached for me, his eyes full of guilt. "Lainey, I—"

"Just answer the question."

"Yes."

That single word was a slap in my face. I recoiled, wrapping my arms around myself.

Ty started to move toward me again, but stopped when he saw the look on my face. He plunged his hands into the pockets of his jeans instead. "You're right. I wasn't surprised. I know about Supernaturals . . . because I am one." He shrugged, his face one of resignation. "I'm a Praetorian."

I stared at him.

"It means guardian," he continued. "It's what we do, what *I* do—protect other Supernaturals."

"Like a bodyguard or something?" I asked through clenched teeth.

"Yes." Ty moved closer to me. "We're like . . . marines, or the army, or something, but we're faster and stronger. We train our whole lives to be the best at what we do. Weaponry, hand-to-hand combat, tracking." He ticked the items off on his fingers. "We do it all."

"Right . . . and what? You just go around protecting and saving random people?"

"Well, no. It's a little more complicated than that. We're drawn to the people we're meant to safeguard, and they to us—like magnets. It's . . . the Calling. I wish I could explain it more than that, but it's just a feeling we get. The instinct to travel in a particular direction, to be in a certain place at a certain time, to speak to someone we've never met."

"And the whole glowing eyes thing?"

Ty's flush deepened, and the look in his eyes intensified. "I knew it was you from the moment I saw you. And in the gym, when I touched you . . . I've never felt so drawn to anyone in my life."

I swallowed, remembering the spark of electricity. "So, I'm your . . . your Calling, then?"

"Yes."

I didn't know what to say. The rain began to pick up, coming down in solid sheets.

"The street fights?" I asked, eyeing the almost faded bruise on his cheek. "They're not just for fun, are they?"

"I have to stay sharp, strong." Ty shrugged. "It's easier to practice with an opponent."

"Serena knew, didn't she? When she spoke to you at the shop?"

"She could See what I was," Ty confirmed. "Apparently Praetorians have a different color aura then everyone else." He cracked a smile. "She threatened to flay me alive if I hurt you."

I didn't laugh. "What am I supposed to do with all of this?" I asked. "I barely know you, but you're supposed to be some kind of protector magically assigned to me? Sorry, but I'm not a 'knight on a white horse' kind of girl."

"I never thought you were," Ty said, his brow furrowed. "And it's not like that. Being my Calling doesn't mean I fight your battles for you. It means I stand beside you."

"I don't even know who you are," I whispered. "And yet, when I'm with you, things seem clearer . . . Is that really how I feel, or just some magic trick?" My lower jaw started to tremble, and I bit down hard on my lip. I would *not* cry.

"Lainey, I—"

"No, don't say anything else. Pretty sure I'm at my limit of magical confessions for the day." Brilliant streaks of lightning flashed across the sky. *Breathe. Just Breathe.*

Kissing Ty had been an impulse, a rash action with very little thought behind it, much like standing in front of the train. Remembering his guarded expression from the boxing studio, I'd half expected him to push me away, but instead he had wrapped me securely in his arms and kissed me back.

I flushed at the thought of his fingertips pressing into the small of my back, his warm breath on my skin. In spite of the fact that my life was a hot mess and I knew nearly nothing about him, kissing Ty had felt so incredibly *right*.

Now with the declaration of who he truly was hanging in the air, the kiss itself felt like a lie.

Everything is so screwed up right now.

The small semblance of acceptance I'd gained in the graveyard earlier that morning had evaporated after the conversation with Gareth; the pangs of hurt, anger, and betrayal stirred up by the whole situation refused to be ignored. I already felt like I was at my emotional capacity—but then I'd kissed Ty, and I'd been woefully unprepared for it.

It wasn't just the physicality of the kiss; it was the warmth that radiated from Ty himself, a sense of certainty and purpose. The notion that even if everything in the world was wrong, *this* was right. *He* was right. But now, everything felt even more jumbled and confused.

"What do I do?" I whispered.

Another loud crack of thunder jolted me back to reality. This time it was so loud, the ground rumbled beneath my feet.

The wind picked up, and the rain fell even harder. Nearly everyone from the party had already made a mad dash for the row of parked cars, and the only remnant of the gathering was the smoke from the dying bonfire.

I tried to look at Ty, but the wind was howling around us, whipping my hair into my face. I tried in vain to wrangle my hair into place, but the wind was impossible and the rain was starting to come down so hard that it was like tiny nails pricking my skin. It was dark, but overhead angry clouds swirled together. Panicked, I scanned the surroundings for some kind of shelter from the storm.

Ty shouted, but I couldn't make out the words over the wind. A flash of lightning split the sky about us, and I shrieked. Ty grabbed my arm and pulled me close, his lips at my ear. "Lainey!" he shouted over the storm. "I think you're doing this."

"What?" I cried. Had I heard him correctly? I wiped the rain off my face and leaned forward. "What did you say?"

"The storm! It's you, Lainey!"

I shook my head. He wasn't making any sense. Ty grabbed me by the wrists, pulling my hands up in front of my eyes. A startled cry erupted from my lips.

Tiny sparks of green light flashed like lightning between my fingertips.

"No!" I wrenched myself away from Ty. "No!" I stared at my hands, then looked up at the clouds rotating dangerously above my head. "What do I do?" I cried as a loud crack of thunder echoed across the trees. "Ty, what do I do?"

As if in response, a streak of lightning struck a tree several feet away from where we were standing. Wood splintered everywhere as a large branch crashed to the ground. I shrieked and nearly tumbled to the ground. Ty shouted again, and gestured with his hands, but all I could focus on was the fear shooting through my entire body. "I don't know how to stop it! I don't know what to do!"

The physical storm and the torrent of emotion raging

inside me were too much. I turned away from Ty, covering my face with my hands. *I just want it to stop. Please let it stop.*

A loud peal of booming thunder shook the ground. Accompanying bolts of wild lightning streaked across the sky.

I would've collapsed, but then there were hands gripping my shoulders. Ty pulled me closer, trying to shield me from the violent wind. I could tell from the vibrations in his chest that he was talking, but his words were lost to the storm. Despite the fact that the earth whirled around him, he radiated steadiness.

Taking deep breaths, I closed my eyes and leaned into Ty, trying to block out the storm. I refused to allow myself a peek at my hands to see if the light was still dancing between my fingertips. Instead, I forced myself to take deep breaths, keeping my eyes squeezed shut. *Just breathe, Lainey. Just breathe.*

"That's it," Ty's voice murmured in my ear a few moments later. "It's almost over. Just relax."

Opening my eyes, the first thing I noticed was the sky. The rotating clouds were scattering. The wind, though still blowing, was no longer a howling gale, and the rain had dissipated to a light sprinkle. I turned to face Ty. His blue eyes were wide and fixed on my face. "Are you hurt?"

I shook my head. "I don't think so." I disentangled myself and took a few steps away. I looked around; the sky was clearing, and the stars were peeking out brilliantly overhead. The only evidence of the storm that remained was a few mud puddles, the damp smell of the trees, and a palpable humidity.

"But how?" I looked back at Ty. "I wasn't trying to—" Realization smacked into me. "This isn't the first time it's happened, either." I remembered the warmth that had spread across my skin as the rosebud had started to bloom, the feeling of strange acceptance as the plant came to life before my eyes.

Ty's eyebrows rose. "You mean the dryad?"

"Well, that, but earlier today in the graveyard. I made a dead rosebush bloom. I wasn't trying; it just kind of happened." My mind flipped backward through my memories, and I gasped. "The red lights . . . and the clock. The morning of the SATs. That was . . . *me*." I stared at Ty, my mouth hanging open. "Is it possible that every weird, unexplainable thing that's happened to me the last few years . . . was *my fault?*"

I staggered backward. "But those were small things. I just nearly unleashed a freaking tornado on top of us." My voice was getting higher and shriller the more I talked. In the distance, there was a low rumble of thunder.

"I could've killed someone, and I don't even know how I did it!" I bent over, clutching my knees for balance as a rush of vertigo had me swaying on my feet.

A streak of lightning flashed across the sky, and there was another low rumble of thunder. Ty looked up at the sky and then back at me. "You have to calm down. I think it's reacting to your emotions."

"Calm down? I don't think I can." Raindrops pelted my shoulders.

Ty quickly walked over and grabbed me by the shoulders. "Lainey, look at me." With one hand, he pulled my chin up so that he was staring into my eyes. "It's going to be okay. Just breathe."

I mentally urged my lungs to function, and using Ty's eyes as an anchor, I took a few deep breaths, forcing my mind to go blank.

After several long minutes, Ty broke his gaze and glanced around. When he looked back at me, he was smiling. "See? You just can't freak out."

I looked around. Ty was right. The rain had disappeared and the sky was clearing once again. I exhaled sharply. "My powers are linked to my emotions," I stated, not really needing the confirmation.

"Yes, it would appear that way."

"Well, that's just great," I groaned. "Not only do I have power that I can't control, but it's influenced by my emotions."

I began pacing, throwing my arms around as I ranted. "What kind of sick joke is that? Is the universe trying to make me go completely insane? I'm a teenage girl! It's in my genetic code to be a big ball of mess! How do I know the next time I get stressed out, I'm not going to accidentally blow up a building or turn the entire swim team into goldfish?"

"I doubt you'll blow up any buildings, Lainey," Ty replied, his face kind. "But turning the swim team into goldfish? *That* I might like to see."

I rolled my eyes.

"You just have to learn how to control it," Ty continued.

"But how?" I twisted some of the water out of my pony-tail, eager for even the smallest sense of normalcy.

He shook his head. "I'm not sure. But you'll figure it out. You have to . . . I'll help you."

I groaned. "There's just so much about all of this that I don't understand. I'm trying to make sense of things that shouldn't make sense." I looked over at Ty, almost pleading. "I'm a witch. My uncle is a Faerie. You're some kind of magical bodyguard. I have lightning that apparently shoots through my fingers when I'm overwhelmed. It's absolutely crazy! This kind of stuff just doesn't happen in real life, and it certainly doesn't happen to me."

"You make it sound like a death sentence."

"Well, isn't it? There are people out there who would *literally* kill me for my powers. Powers that I didn't know I had and certainly don't want! Am I just supposed to accept all of this with a grain of salt? Don't I get a say at all?"

"I won't try to tell you what to feel," Ty said. "But have you stopped to think that maybe all of this is what was *meant* to happen? I mean, what if your destiny is something bigger than even *you* imagined?"

I was at a loss for words. Ty's sapphire eyes stared deep into mine, and for a moment, he looked much older and wiser than his eighteen years.

"But I'm nobody," I whispered. "There's nothing special about me at all. I'm just . . . *Lainey*."

"Well, Lainey Styles, I haven't known you for very long,"

Ty said, "but from what I can tell, you're far from being a nobody. Besides, no one can tell you who or what you're going to be. Destiny or not, you get to choose."

Ty was silent for a moment. Then he reached out and took my hand. "The point is, you can do this, Lainey. I know it. I mean, come on," he continued, the half smile curling on his lips. "How many girls do you know who can create thunder like that? Maybe I should start calling you Thor."

"You sound exactly like Maggie." I tucked a loose strand of hair behind my ear. "Thank you . . . for helping with the storm."

"You don't have to thank me for anything. You were the one who stopped it. It was all you."

"I'm also the one who started it." I sighed. "But you know what? I don't want to be the kind of girl who finds out her life is about to change and just freaks out about it. I'm angry, don't get me wrong, but the sooner I stop yelling and start accepting that this is what my life is going to look like from now on, the better. Like you said, the universe has a bigger plan for me than I have for myself, right?"

Ty nodded. "Just remember, it is your choice."

Gareth's words echoed in my thoughts: *A person's destiny is not a concrete certainty. There are people who live their entire lives and never fulfill their true purpose. Free will and choice, you see, are powerful tools of alteration. A simple choice can change everything.*

"It's my choice," I whispered. "I have a choice."

"Yes, you do."

I took a deep breath and nodded, squeezing Ty's hand.

He reached out with his other hand to cup my cheek, running a thumb across my cheekbone. "Come on, let's get out of here."

We crossed the tracks and started walking to where I'd parked my car.

A familiar sensation filled me, tugging at me as we walked. I stopped, my wet shoes sinking into the mud.

Josephine stood a few feet away.

Her eyes, both lovely and sad, were trained on me. She didn't speak this time, but we stared at each other—a thousand words between us.

I don't want to be afraid anymore.

The words echoed all around me, mimicking the fire that burned in her eyes. When it ignited inside me, I knew I'd never be the same again. I took comfort in that tiny spark; it was small, but steadily growing warmer.

I have a choice.

Too many decisions had been made for me, but no longer.

It's up to me. It's my choice.

Like molten steel in cold water, my resolve was forged.

I gave Josephine a tiny smile, finally understanding. *It's my choice, and I choose my destiny. I won't walk away.*

I didn't need confirmation, but as I turned away, I heard a soft word in my ear.

One last time, my name whispered in the wind.

CHAPTER
TWENTY-ONE

I pulled the car into its usual spot in the driveway. With the exception of the porch light, the rest of the house was dark. *Gareth must have gone to bed.*

Feeling more than a little relieved, I got out of the car and made my way inside. I couldn't avoid him forever, but I just wasn't ready to face him again. Gareth's deception had cut me deeply, and while the events at the train tracks had afforded me a small sense of clarity and acceptance, the truth was still just as painful as it had been when I'd fled the house hours before.

My wet shoes squished around my toes as I tiptoed upstairs trying to make as little sound as possible. Crossing the hall to my room, I walked inside and shut the door silently behind me.

"Hello, Lainey."

I whirled around. A figure sat in the darkness, silhouetted

by moonlight. Swearing, I fumbled for the light switch on the wall and grabbed the baseball bat I kept beside the bed. Gripping the wooden handle, I flipped the switch, bathing the room in bright light.

Gareth sat in the armchair by the window staring at me. The dagger I'd seen earlier was resting across his knees.

"Oh my God, Gareth! You scared the crap out of me!" I said, loosening my grip on the Louisville slugger.

"I scared *you?*" Gareth's eyebrows shot up. "You've been gone for hours. You wouldn't answer my calls, and I had no idea where you were. I was about to have Serena perform a tracking spell when Maggie finally called back and said she spoke to you. Do you have any idea how worried I was?"

"Well, no need to worry anymore," I spat. "I'm home now. You can go." I hadn't meant to sound so cold, but the sight of him had refueled my anger.

"Lainey . . ." Gareth trailed off and hunched over, pinching the bridge of his nose.

When he sat back up and looked at me, pain and concern were etched all over his face. "Lainey, I—" He broke off as a rough sound choked him.

I swallowed the lump that had formed in my throat. I was absolutely furious at Gareth for keeping the truth from me, but as I watched him wrestle with his emotions, it was obvious that, real uncle or not, he cared about me. I suddenly felt very small.

Sighing, I propped the baseball bat back against the wall and plopped down on the edge of the bed. "I'm sorry I ran out like that," I said. "I didn't mean to worry you. I just needed time to process everything."

With a sigh of his own, Gareth nodded. "I get it, I do, but you can't go running off like that. It's dangerous. Now more than ever." He ran his fingers through his hair and leaned forward, his eyes pleading. "I know you hate me right now, but I swore to protect you, and you have to promise *never* to do that again."

"I won't."

Gareth, relieved at my words, sank back into his chair. "Thank you."

I watched him for a few moments. "I don't hate you," I whispered, struggling to keep my own emotions in check.

He looked surprised. "You don't?"

"No, I don't," I replied. "I'm angry at you for lying to me and keeping all those secrets from me—*really* angry—but I know you care about me, and I know you'd never intentionally try to hurt me." I offered a small smile. "It's been just you and me my whole life. You're my *family,* Gareth. No matter how mad I am at you, I could never hate you."

Gareth's shoulders sagged, his eyes swimming with tears. "I didn't think you'd still feel that way when you found out the truth." He nervously tapped the sword in his lap. "In fact, after you left, I thought you'd never want to speak to me again."

"I didn't at first," I admitted, "but now I think I understand why you lied to me. Finding out who I really am, what happened to Mom—it's a lot to take in. I'm not sure I was ready before now. I'm not sure I could've handled it."

Gareth nodded. "I never meant to keep this from you for so long. I just wanted you to be happy . . . and safe." He picked up the blade in his hands. It was the smaller version of the sword I'd seen him practicing with, the dagger he had offered me down in the training room. "I made this for you, you know. I was planning to give it to you when I told you. It's probably stupid, but I thought it might help you feel less afraid . . ." He blushed crimson. "I really *am* sorry, Lainey."

"I know." I leaned forward. "I'm fine. But no more secrets, okay? From this moment on, I need to know what I'm up against. There's still so much I don't understand." I exhaled. "It scares me, but I have to know everything."

Gareth nodded and placed a hand over his heart. "I promise. No more lying and no more secrets," he vowed. "I'll tell you everything I know."

"Good." I gave a tiny smile. "So, can I have it?" I indicated the dagger.

"Oh!" Gareth jumped up and placed the weapon in my hands. "Yes, of course."

The dagger still felt foreign in my hands, but up close, I saw that the blade was engraved with an intricate design of greenery and daisies, my favorite flower. The meticulous design was not only beautiful but clearly one of a kind.

"They were her favorite too," Gareth said. "Your mother loved daisies."

I ran my finger across the smooth metal. "It's beautiful."

"If you let me, I'd like to teach you how to use it properly. You need to know how to protect yourself."

I gripped the hilt tightly. It was more than a little strange to be sitting in my bedroom, holding a Faerie-made weapon—and even more so to imagine myself using it—but I nodded my head anyway.

"Great!" Gareth jumped up from his seat, his eyes wide and bright. "We can start right now."

I stifled a laugh at his excitement. This was a side of Gareth I'd never seen before. "How about tomorrow? It's late, and I need a shower." I pointed to my clothes, which were still damp from the rain.

"Right, of course," Gareth smiled and kissed me on the top of my head. "Get some sleep. We'll talk more about training tomorrow." He smiled again as he moved toward the door.

"Uncle Gareth?" I called out. "Before you go, can I ask you a question?"

"Sure."

I took a deep breath. "You want to teach me how to use a weapon to protect myself, right? Well, what exactly am I supposed to be protecting myself from?"

Gareth's face paled, and his smile disappeared.

"Serena mentioned that the same person who killed my mother might come after me," I continued. "I need to know what I'm up against."

Gareth swallowed and sat back down in the armchair facing me. The light in his eyes had faded, and his face was as somber as I'd ever seen it.

With a sharp exhale, he nodded and began to speak. "Centuries ago, there was a war between the various factions of the Supernatural realms. Witches, Lycans, Elementals, the Fey—everyone was involved. Even the Seers, who don't normally get involved in such things."

My eyes widened at Gareth's words. I shouldn't have been surprised by anything at this point, but Lycans? Elementals? Was *everything* real? Shaking my head, I forced myself to focus on the story.

"It was a bloody war, and thousands of lives were lost. It was as if the very fabric of our world was ripped apart, never to be whole again." Gareth took another breath, as though to steady himself.

"You see, our world is meant to be balanced, each faction equal with every other. This balance is the only thing that protects us—our anonymity—from humanity. This civil war between the factions was threatening the system. If the humans were ever to discover our existence, an even greater war would be inevitable."

"What were they fighting about?" I asked, leaning forward.

"Power. *All* great wars are fought over power," Gareth said. "When the bloodshed became too great to continue, the leaders of each faction agreed to meet to discuss a peace treaty. The result of that meeting was the formation of a fellowship of sorts, a group of Supernatural representatives—one from each faction—chosen for the task of keeping the balance. They called it the Hetaeria."

Gareth held up a finger and quickly darted down the hall to his room. When he returned, he had a large antique book in his hand. Sitting next to me, he flipped the pages until he reached an old painted portrait of ten or so men and women dressed in long black capes. Behind them, several rows of severe-looking men all in black stood at attention.

"The Hetaeria created a new set of laws to ensure that no one faction had more power or more control than any other. They also enlisted other Supernaturals to serve as militia. The Guard, as it was called, was tasked with enforcing the new laws and working as protectors for Supernaturals in peril." Gareth indicated the photo and sighed heavily. "They're the ones who hunted down your mother, Lainey."

I leaned over and studied the faces of the men in the photographs. They didn't look like killers to me.

"But I don't understand. If the Hetaeria was created to keep the balance, to be peacekeepers, then what happened to my mom? Why would they or the Guard want to hurt her?" I trailed off, feeling overwhelmed by the complexity of Gareth's story. "Why would they want to hurt *me?*"

Gareth closed his eyes for a moment, as if in pain, and then continued. "The Hetaeria *was* successful in keeping the peace for quite some time, until a young man by the name of Emmett Masterson infiltrated it and began to pervert its mission."

The ominous tone in Gareth's voice made me shiver.

"He was power hungry, even from the time he was a

young man. He had a cruel nature and saw himself as king of the Supernatural realm."

"There's a king?"

Gareth shook his head. "No. That was the purpose of the Hetaeria: to balance the power among the factions. But Masterson sought control of the factions—to hold dominion over them all. He ended up selling his soul to a Sorcerer of Darkness and began using black magic to amplify his abilities. He became incredibly powerful. Then he began to strike down those weaker than himself."

Gareth took a deep breath, clearly affected by his own story, but steeled himself. "First, he manipulated the Guard. He is incredibly charismatic, you see. He began to poison their minds with talk of a new order, of overthrowing the Hetaeria, of a world united under a single rule: *his* rule. He quickly gained a following among them, and any who opposed him either fled or were murdered. It wasn't long until Masterson had overthrown the faction leaders and eradicated the Hetaeria altogether. He dropped the last part of his surname and began calling himself 'The Master.'"

The Master. My heart skipped a beat. I thought back to my visions of Josephine, of the man cloaked in shadows. *Don't lie to me, you foolish girl. I know you have it . . . and I want it.* I shuddered at the memory. It was all starting to make sense now.

Gareth and I were both silent for a moment, lost in our

own memories. Then Gareth began to speak again, his voice even once more.

"The Master began using the Guard to hunt down Supernaturals. Witch, Warlock, Shape-Shifter, Nixie—faction didn't matter. Any who opposed the Master's reign was disposed of."

"But they fought back, right?" I interjected. "The other Supernaturals?"

"I'm afraid it wasn't that simple." Gareth smiled sadly. "Fear and greed are powerful motivators, Lainey. Without the Hetaeria allying them, the factions drew into themselves, untrusting of each other. There were also a number of Supernaturals who disagreed with the initial creation of the Hetaeria—people who would rather die than see the factions at peace. They didn't like the fact that the Hetaeria was imposing what they saw as unnecessary laws upon them. The Master allied himself with those people—with those *traitors*."

Gareth looked disgusted. "He imbued the members of the Guard with black magic, turning them into assassins. Not only are they deadly, but they're also damn near indestructible, even for the strongest of our kind. The Master's greed sparked another bloody civil war—one we've been fighting ever since."

"How is he even still alive?"

"Supernaturals tend to have longer life spans, particularly if they're powerful. In the Master's case, his use of dark magic has given him unnatural longevity, even by our standards."

A sudden dread settled in my stomach. "It was the Master who killed my mom, wasn't it?

Gareth leaned forward, his piercing brown eyes never straying from my face. "Yes."

His words from earlier floated back to me. *Lainey, she was killed because she was the Keeper, the Keeper of the Grimoire.*

I shook my head. "Wait, you told me that my mom was killed because she was the Keeper, right? If the Master is so powerful, why would he need the Grimoire?"

"Magic always leaves a mark," Gareth said. "And the Master never anticipated the price the black magic he used would exact from him. Over time, his powers began to weaken, only allowing him to sustain small bits of power at a time."

He flipped back to the page of the original faction representatives and pointed out one of the members—a strapping young man with dark hair that was pulled back in a low ponytail. He looked familiar, but I wasn't sure I'd ever seen him before.

"That," Gareth said, "is Lane DuCarmont. He was the representative for the witch and warlock faction. He was also Josephine DuCarmont's father and the man you were named after."

I remembered the picture Serena had shown me of the DuCarmont family. In that picture, a much older Lane was calm and relaxed, his arm wrapped around Josephine's shoulders. In this picture, there was no kindness on his face.

"It's said that Lane DuCarmont killed a dark sorcerer

who was carrying a spell that would allow the Master to bleed magic from other Supernaturals. If he collected magic from every faction, he could use the spell to fuse it all together and be all-powerful—immortal even. No one would be able to stop him."

"But Lane stole the spell."

"Yes," Gareth said, "and contained it in the one place where he knew it would be safe."

"The DuCarmont Grimoire," I finished for him.

I thought back to my visions of Josephine. "But Lane knew the Master would kill him for what he'd done, so he made someone else the Keeper, didn't he? Someone he trusted above all others."

My mind was busy replaying the scenes of my visions over and over in my mind as the pieces of the puzzle were starting to come together.

Lainey.

The whisper in my ear was hardly a surprise, and I looked over at Josephine's face for confirmation. "He made Josephine the Keeper, and when the Guard came for Lane and his family, Josephine escaped with the Grimoire." I looked back over at Gareth and smiled. "She kept it safe."

"Yes," Gareth confirmed. "But she sacrificed her own life to do so."

"What?" I tore my eyes away from Gareth. In the last vision I'd had, Josephine was alive. I looked over at Josephine, whose sad eyes confirmed the truth.

"What happened to you?" I said, standing up and moving

toward Josephine. I balled my hands into fists, stirred by conviction. "You have to tell me the rest. I have to see it."

Josephine nodded and held out her hand.

I was vaguely aware of Gareth's voice calling my name, but as I reached out to take Josephine's hand, everything else faded away.

CHAPTER
TWENTY-TWO

At first, there was nothing but darkness. But then my insides began to twist, and it was as if I was being pulled in two. I yelped, but then the sensation suddenly gave way, and a bright light sliced through the darkness, nearly blinding me. Instinctively, I squeezed my eyes shut and raised a hand in front of my face. When I opened my eyes again, the light was gone and I was no longer standing in my bedroom.

A dense thicket of pine trees loomed over my head, and a symphony of crickets chirped around me.

"Whoa," I muttered under my breath. "We're definitely not in Kansas anymore, Toto."

Rubbing my abdomen with the palm of my hand, I glanced around to get my bearings. I was in an unfamiliar wooded area with the sun dipping slowly toward the horizon.

I turned to find Josephine standing a few feet away. Her lovely face was cloaked in sadness, and her eyes were full of tears.

My stomach did a somersault. "What is it?" I asked. "Show me."

Josephine said nothing, but slowly reached out her hand and pointed away from us, to where the sound of laughter wafted through the air.

With dread settling in the pit of my stomach like a heavy stone, I nodded and made my way through the trees toward the noise. Josephine followed beside me, silent tears dripping down her cheeks.

I picked my way carefully over the uneven ground until I stepped through a break in the trees and out into a wide meadow that appeared to be a campsite of sorts. There were forty or so large canvas tents arranged in rows with several campfires blazing between them.

People were milling about, moving between the tents, and two young girls nearby hung wet linens on a thick piece of rope that had been strung between two trees, their soft chatter muffled by the sound of the sheets whipping in the breeze. Both of the girls wore long skirts that were patched in several places, the fabric thin and faded. Their shirts looked homemade and were equally worn.

"Hello?" I called out, but there was no response. Neither of the girls acknowledged me. They kept casually chatting, hanging more of the bedclothes on the line.

They can't see me.

I looked over at Josephine, who pointed again, this time toward the first row of tents. We kept walking.

At first glance, the camp had seemed unimpressive, but as I moved among the tents, two boys ran past me with a third trailing behind. The two boys in front were taunting the straggler and calling him slow.

"Come back here, you toadlickers!" the little boy shrieked at them. "I'll show you slow!"

Then the little boy exploded out of his skin, leaving a large gazelle in its place. I gasped as the gazelle darted into the woods after the other boys.

I glanced around to see if anyone else had noticed the boy, but the people in the tent village continued on with business as usual, as if a little boy morphing into a large antelope was hardly out of the norm.

Several feet away, a group of women sat huddled together, knitting blankets. They looked quite normal except for the fact that, aside from holding balls of yarn, they weren't actually doing anything. Their knitting needles hovered near their heads, carefully creating tiny loops, as though held by invisible hands.

If that wasn't proof enough that this village wasn't an ordinary one, there was a girl—she looked about twelve—sitting under the shade of a large oak tree. Her skin had a greenish tint to it. As I watched her, the young girl held out a long piece of dried-out ivy. Brown and brittle, it had clearly been dead a long time. Cradling the plant in her hand, the girl smiled and gently began to blow on the stalk. My mouth dropped open as the plant began to turn green and sprout tiny purple flowers.

Supernaturals, I realized. *All different kinds. But what are they all doing here?*

We came to a tent in the back, set apart from the others. Josephine was standing in front, tending to the fire. She was wearing a long blue dress, and the emerald amulet hung around her neck. Her long brown hair fell loose around her shoulders. Her cheeks were flushed, and her eyes sparkled in the firelight. *This* Josephine radiated life.

The dread in my stomach grew heavier.

The living Josephine added several sticks of kindling to the fire and wiped her hands on the thick folds of her skirt. Turning back toward the tent, she walked through the opening flap without saying a word.

When she emerged again, she carried a cast-iron pot. Singing softly, she knelt down next to the fire and began slicing various vegetables from a basket sitting near the kindling. The amulet at her throat sparkled in the light from the flames.

I took a step closer to the young woman by the fire just as a shrill cry sounded in the back of her tent. It startled me, but Josephine just smiled, wiped her hands once more on her skirt, and walked through the flaps of the tent. When she returned, she was holding a tiny bundle wrapped in blankets. The bundle was wriggling and squirming in her arms.

"Oh my God," I said. "It's a baby." I looked back at the

other Josephine, whose solemn face was streaked with tears. "Yours and Henry's." She nodded.

Josephine was staring down at the tiny face completely enraptured and overjoyed, the way new mothers always look at their children. As she began to coo softly to the baby, a tiny hand reached for her face.

It was in that moment that the ground began to tremble. A pulse of energy shot through the camp and slammed against the walls of the invisible shield surrounding it—some kind of protection ward, I realized.

"No!" Josephine cried, staring at the magical shield disintegrating before her eyes. The air all at once filled with piercing cries. The baby began to wail, and Josephine clutched the amulet at her throat.

People ran in all directions—some toward the conflict and others away from it. Magical energy permeated the air until it was as thick as fog. A large plume of black smoke rose into the distance, and the ground rumbled again as another electrical pulse assaulted the remnants of the protection wards.

Josephine clutched the baby tighter to her chest with one arm, while the other she held in front of her, green lightning dancing around her fingertips.

A young woman with long blonde hair ran toward her, tears streaming down her face. "Jo!"

Josephine reached for her, wrapping an arm around the girl's trembling shoulders. "Eliza!" she cried, struggling to juggle the infant in one arm and her hysterical friend in the other. "What has happened? Is it them? Have they found us?"

The younger woman nodded before slumping against Josephine's shoulder, her entire body shaking from fear. She mumbled something under her breath. I couldn't understand much of what she said, but the two words I did pick up stole my breath: "The Guard."

Josephine instantly paled. "No," she whispered against the young woman's hair. "No!"

She stood still for a moment, as if in disbelief, but then a look of fierce resolve crossed her face and prompted her into action.

Grabbing the woman's arm, Josephine yanked her upright and stared into her face. "Eliza, listen to me!" she barked, her eyes blazing. "It's time. You have to take her and run."

The young woman's eyes grew wide. "You're not coming?"

"I'll hold them off as long as I can." Josephine looked down at the child in her arms. "You have to get her to safety."

"But you're her mother," the girl argued. "You can't just . . . I don't know—"

The rest of her sentence was cut off as Josephine placed the screaming infant in her arms.

"Please," Josephine urged, staring at Eliza with wild eyes. "Please. I'm begging you."

She hesitated for a moment, but as the terrible cacophony of sound rose around them, Eliza squared her shoulders, took a deep breath, and nodded. "I'll keep her safe. I promise."

Josephine exhaled sharply in relief. "Thank you." She

squeezed Eliza's shoulder in gratitude. Tears poured down her cheeks as she hastily bent over to kiss the child's brow. Pulling the shawl from around her shoulders, she tucked it tightly around the child and nodded at Eliza. "Run east along the river," she instructed the girl. "Find the others. I'll try to hold them off as long as I can. And please, remember what I've told you. You have to tell her one day. Promise me?"

Eliza nodded, tears dripping down her cheeks. "I promise." She turned to run.

"Wait!" Josephine reached out and caught her by the arm. "One more thing." With trembling fingers, she reached up and unclasped the emerald amulet from around her neck and quickly fastened it around the baby's tiny throat.

"Good-bye, my sweet daughter," she choked out, as Eliza turned and ran toward the woods, the tiny bundle held tightly against her chest.

Tears poured from my own eyes as Josephine clutched her chest with one hand and let out a wail that ripped through my heart.

Another boom of energy ricocheted through the small village. Josephine sucked down a breath of air, her features twisting from anguish to determination. Yanking up her shirtsleeves, she planted her feet and flexed her fingers. The green lightning crackled between her fingertips like live wires.

Up ahead, a swarm of men dressed in black with dark linen masks covering their faces were wreaking havoc on the tent village. A few feet away, two of them terrorized an old man with a walking stick. The old man hobbled along, desperately shooting balls of fire at the men, but the guards merely laughed. One of the Guard waved his hand, and the old man sprawled to the dirt, his eyes frozen open forever.

I tasted bile.

The soldiers moved quickly through the village. A few Supernaturals attempted to fight them off, but were quickly subdued. Desperate to help, I raised my hands. Magic sparked between my fingers, but the other Josephine placed an icy hand on my shoulder.

"I have to help them!" I cried, but the look in her eyes was clear. There was nothing I could do. My heart sank to my feet.

Beside me, the living Josephine tensed. A tall figure in black strode toward her. A thin piece of black fabric covered the lower half of his face, but his eyes—full of hatred and disgust—were fixed upon Josephine.

"My lady," the man boomed, "the Master thanks you kindly for your hospitality." He bowed low at the waist, sweeping his free hand out in mockery. "But he's done playing your little game. Give me the book, and we will show mercy. Refuse, and my men and I will slaughter every last man, woman, and child in this village."

Josephine narrowed her eyes and took a calculated breath. "You're a fool if you think I'll believe such a lie." Her voice was strong and clear. "The Master's thirst for blood will never end, not until every last Supernatural who defies him is dead. He knows nothing of mercy."

The guard laughed coldly. "How right you are." He leaned forward, his murderous eyes blazing. "And what he has planned for you, little witch . . . well, *that* definitely isn't mercy."

Josephine snarled and threw her right hand out toward the soldier. A brilliant beam of emerald light shot from her palm and knocked the soldier to his knees.

The guardsman emitted a grunt, but leapt quickly back to his feet. "My, my, my, aren't you the feisty one." He sneered. "You don't know a trap when you see one, do you?"

Six men suddenly appeared out of nowhere, encircling Josephine. Each bore the mark of the Master—the two interlocking triangles, made to form an M. They were chanting softly.

With a wail of pain, she clamped her hands on the sides of her head and fell to the ground, the lightning in her hands extinguished.

"No!" I yelled, rushing toward Josephine. "Stop it!" I cried, feeling utterly helpless as Josephine writhed in pain. The guardsman's laughter echoed across the trees and mixed with Josephine's anguished cries.

"Enough," the man said. The effect of his quiet command was immediate. The other men stopped chanting and Josephine lay unmoving on the ground.

"Now," the leader said, "tell me where the book is."

Josephine did not move or speak.

"Come now," the man said more loudly. "We mustn't waste any more time." Crossing the space between them, he grabbed Josephine by the arm and yanked her to her feet. "Where's the book?" he roared.

With a visible effort, Josephine raised her head and met the man's glare with a steady gaze. "Go to hell," she hissed and spat into the man's face.

He staggered backward, releasing her. She leapt away and pulled a small knife from the inner pocket of her long skirt.

Josephine lunged at the man, but another soldier grabbed her arm, yanking it behind her while the leader ripped the knife from her hand. She screamed, struggling against the man's firm grip. They grappled back and forth until finally the man threw Josephine to the ground.

"Enough!" the man shouted, reaching up to yank the strip of cloth away from his face.

An identical cry of shock erupted from both my and Josephine's lips.

Standing in front of us, his face twisted in unadulterated hatred, was Henry.

"Henry?" Josephine whispered, her eyes wide with tears, her face deathly pale. "I saw it with my own eyes. I held you in my arms. You were *dead*." Her voice broke on the last syllable, and the mask of strength she had painted across her features crumbled in an instant.

Henry smiled cruelly and bowed in jest once more. "Compliments of the Master, my lady."

Josephine cried out again, but managed to stagger back to her feet. "Oh, Henry," she sobbed. "I'm so sorry. This is all my fault. It's all my fault."

"Oh, yes, dear one," Henry jeered, "it is."

But then he took a step closer, his face suddenly softening.

He looked once more like the man he had once been. "But, Josephine, my love, I'm still here. You just have to give him the book. He promised to restore me to you." He placed a tender hand against Josephine's cheek. "Please, Jo. We've been apart for more than a year, and my heart cannot bear our separation any longer. Do this for us, Jo. Do it for *me*."

He was gazing upon Josephine with such tenderness and love that my own heart felt it would break. Josephine carefully reached up and touched the hand against her cheek. "I'm so sorry," she whispered. "I'm so sorry . . ."

Then, acting so quickly her movements were blurred, she spun around out of Henry's grasp, her own knife back in the palm of her hand and against Henry's throat.

She was nearly choking on her own tears, but she held the knife steady.

"Jo!" Henry cried out in surprise. "What are you doing?"

"Don't call me that!" Josephine cried, hysterical. "You're not my Henry. The Master killed him! I saw it! You're some creature of black magic created to torment me! But it won't work! I'll kill you, I swear it, I will."

The features of Henry's face suddenly relaxed—any traces of the old Henry disappearing—and he laughed. There was nothing left but cold, calculating hatred. He gripped Josephine's wrist and pushed the knife harder against his throat. Droplets of blood rolled down his neck. "Do it, then," he growled.

Josephine's hands were shaking. She was losing the fight.

"Hang on, Josephine!" I cried out, wishing there was more I could do to help. "Don't let him win!"

"Give me the book," Henry spat, gripping Josephine's hand so hard she whimpered. "Give me the book or kill me for good. Those are your options."

Josephine sagged as though her own body weight was pulling her down. "I can't," she whispered over and over. "I can't."

I wasn't sure if she meant the book or Henry.

"I can't . . . Oh, God, Henry, I can't."

For one brief moment, I saw again the familiar face of Henry fight its way to the surface before the mask of malice slammed back into place. Prying the knife from Josephine's hand, he sneered down at her, his cold eyes unforgiving and expressionless. "Pity," he whispered against her hair. "Such a pity." And with that, he drove the knife into Josephine's gut.

I screamed as Josephine crumpled to the ground, a blossom of crimson blood staining the fabric of her dress.

The air around me rippled, and the images in front of me grew distorted. The scene before me was fading away, and as the familiar twisting sensations claimed me, wrapping me in darkness, the last thing I heard was a cold, calculated laugh.

Then there was nothing but silence.

CHAPTER TWENTY-THREE

This time when the darkness lifted, I was standing in an unfamiliar, empty room. Shadows danced around me, and the energy of the room pulsed like a heartbeat.

"Hello," I called out. "Josephine?" I was shaking from what I'd just witnessed, and my face was wet with tears. *Where am I?* I stepped forward, but there was only emptiness in every direction

"Hello?" I tried again. Still no response. A jolt of panic shot through me.

I was seconds away from completely freaking out when a burst of light erupted in front of me. The light twisted and spun, evolving into a swirl of vivid colors that morphed into the picturesque scene of a garden. A young girl with long dark hair and wide green eyes was playing with a doll and singing to herself.

It was like I was standing in the middle of an IMAX

theater, except the picture was vivid, so real I could smell the scent of lavender and honeysuckle in the air, could feel the breeze that blew the child's long locks.

She looked familiar, but I was sure I'd never seen the little girl before. She continued to sing, her sweet little voice soft and breathy. I smiled, but when she twisted toward me, I got a glimpse of the necklace that hung around her slender neck. It was Josephine's amulet. I sucked in a breath, the ache of Josephine's death still resonating within me.

"It's her," I said, leaning forward. "Josephine's daughter."

Now I recognized the high cheekbones, the slightly up-turned nose, the black hair, the green eyes that could've only come from her mother. I put a hand on my heart to stop it from beating out of my chest.

The scene abruptly shifted; the garden was the same, but the child had grown. She was a young woman now, lovely as the rosebush she stood beside and looking just like Josephine. She stood tall, gripping the front of her full skirt. Her face was pale, and in her hand was the emerald amulet. "What do you mean, Eliza?" she said, her voice quivering. "You told me my mother died in childbirth."

Another woman stepped into view. I recognized her as the young girl who'd taken the baby at Josephine's urgent request. "I know, but it's time you learned the truth about who you are, Lily, about your destiny."

As I watched, Eliza put a comforting arm around the young woman and told her about her mother, about what had really happened to Josephine. The pain etched across Lily's face was so familiar I felt a pang in my chest.

After Eliza left, Lily took a deep breath and squeezed the amulet in her hand. "I won't let you down, Mother," she whispered, her face set with resolve. She whispered something, and the amulet began to glow and change. Pale pink strands of light wrapped around the necklace, covering it in a rosy glow. It was so bright I had to look away, but Lily stood strong, her head held high as the magic flowed through her.

When the light faded away, the amulet was no longer an emerald stone but a small pendent in the shape of tiny pink rose. Lily smiled and pinned the pendent across her heart.

The colors began to swirl again, and the image that appeared caused my throat to tighten. Lily was locked in a battle with three guardsmen. Electric pink lightning flew from her fingertips, but she was outnumbered. Her neck was bare. The amulet was gone. Her scream as they moved to overcome her was a knife in my chest.

The scene changed again. A new face this time: a young woman with a warm smile and long blonde hair piled on top of her head. Though there were less similar features, her wide green eyes were unmistakably DuCarmont. In her hands was a thick, leather-bound book: the Grimoire. The woman ran her hands across the book, whispering words under her breath. The book began to glow, streams of crystal blue light enveloping it. When the spell was complete, a blue-jeweled bracelet rested in place of the book. The woman secured the bracelet to her wrist and moved from the room.

I sank to my knees as the colors transformed again. The blonde woman was lying in a pool of crimson blood, her eyes open and unblinking. A young girl with fiery red hair knelt beside her, tears streaming down her face. "Good-bye, Mama," she whispered, ripping away the bracelet.

Another scene materialized. A woman with chestnut brown hair moved into view and transfigured the Grimoire into a ruby brooch. Her eyes—the same unmistakable pair of green eyes—were the confirmation of what I'd begun to suspect.

This is my family. All the Keepers who came before me.

In between scenes of the Keepers were horrific flashes of the Master and the Guard—of their hunt for the Keepers. Every single pair of green eyes—the green eyes *I* now possessed—closed in death at the Master's hand.

The tragedy of my heritage rolled before me like a filmstrip, and my entire body shook from the kaleidoscope of emotions swirling inside me.

Then, at last, came an image that nearly stopped my heart.

It was my mother.

She was holding the Grimoire in her hand, her forehead scrunched as if she were thinking hard about something. Then with a little shrug and a half smile, she muttered an incantation and the book began to glow. When the light faded, the emerald amulet sat in her palm, pulsing as if it were happy to be in its original form again. A fresh batch of tears rolled down my cheeks.

The final face I saw was gaunt and severe. A tall member

of the Guard with blood staining his uniform walked toward the Master, his face triumphant. In his hands was the amulet. "It is done, my lord," he said. "The witch is dead."

I crumpled in on myself, losing the tiny scrap of control I still clung to. Everything faded away as my sobs grew louder. My heart was utterly broken for the family who had tried so hard, yet ultimately failed to keep the Master from getting the book. They sacrificed so much, only to fail in the end. It shattered me.

I cried even harder as I thought of my mother. The mother I'd never gotten a chance to know. I didn't fight it when the colors began to swirl away and the darkness enveloped me again.

❧ • ❧

"Lainey? Can you hear me?"

I flinched away from the sound—the image of Henry stabbing Josephine was burned into my eyelids. The faces of the other Keepers. My mother. I clenched my fists together and fought the urge to scream.

I became aware of a warm pressure on my arm, the voice from before murmuring in my ear. As my eyes fluttered open and adjusted to the sights around me, it took several minutes for my brain to register where I was.

The tall pine trees were gone, replaced by pale yellow walls and white linen curtains. The smell of gunpowder and smoke had vanished, leaving in its place the delicate scent of clean laundry. Josephine, Henry, and the Guard were nowhere to be seen, but a single face hovered over mine with wide eyes. Gareth. I was back at home in my bedroom.

"Gareth?" I whispered, relief flooding over me. Sitting up so fast it made me dizzy, I launched myself into Gareth's arms.

"Lainey, are you okay?" he asked, holding me against his chest. The anxiety in his voice was clear. "What happened?"

I shook my head, not yet ready to relive the horrible moments in the tent village, nor the flashes in the dark room.

"I was so worried," Gareth whispered against my hair. "One minute you're talking to the wall, and the next minute you're unresponsive on the floor."

Taking a deep breath, I pulled myself out of Gareth's embrace and brushed the hair out of my face. "I wasn't talking to the wall. I was talking to *her*. To Josephine."

Gareth's eyebrows rose.

"She showed me the rest of the story, what happened to her," I continued. "You were right. The Master hunted her down; he wanted the Grimoire." I took a deep breath. "He . . . he killed her." I felt a lump rising in my throat, and I gulped.

Gareth nodded solemnly. "Yes. But she protected it."

My brain supplied me with the image of a tiny baby girl with rosy cheeks, clear eyes, and a large emerald amulet fastened around her neck. "Yes," I agreed. "She kept it safe."

Now that the shock of the whole ordeal was over, my body sagged with exhaustion. I wanted to curl up in my bed and lose myself in the oblivion of sleep, but seeing the Guard in action had ignited a spark of fury deep inside me, and

Josephine's words echoed in my ear: *The Master's thirst for blood will never end, not until every last Supernatural who defies him is dead. He knows nothing of mercy.*

I thought of Lane and Josephine, of my mother, and finally of the card that meant death held gingerly between Serena's shaking fingertips. I couldn't go to sleep now if I tried. I had to do something.

Pushing myself off the bed, I walked over to where the bronze dagger lay on the carpet. Kneeling down, I reached out and grasped the hilt. Its weight in my hand was terrible, but also reassuring. It promised dreadful things to come, but that I might now have a chance to survive them. I turned back to Gareth. "Ready for that training session?"

"Now?" he questioned. "I thought you said—"

"Let's go." Without waiting to see if he was following me or not, I turned on my heels and headed downstairs toward Gareth's study.

It's my choice. A flame blazed within me, the warmth spreading throughout my entire body. *I'm choosing my destiny.*

Gripping the hilt of the dagger even tighter, I straightened my shoulders and kept walking. I wasn't going to sit around and let my mother's sacrifice be in vain.

I was choosing to fight.

§•§

When I drove to school the next morning, the sun was

obnoxiously bright. It was entirely too cheerful, given my mood. Gareth had coached me well into the morning hours, and everything hurt.

First, he taught me the basics of self-defense and hand-to-hand combat. Then we'd moved to weaponry. The dagger wasn't heavy, but after hours of holding it out and slashing it through the air, the muscles in my arm were cooked spaghetti. Not to mention that every other inch of my body felt like it had been beaten black and blue. Between the train tracks, the magical leap through time, and the combat training, I felt like I'd been mauled by a bear.

I arrived at school just as the first bell rang. I parked my car and attempted a mad dash across the parking lot, my muscles screaming in protest.

As I limped toward the door, though, laughter bubbled in my throat. In the last twenty-four hours, I'd come to terms with the fact that I was a witch, created a massive thunderstorm, and watched the Master's Guard slaughter innocent people—yet here I was running like a normal teenager across campus just to avoid being tardy to English class.

I skidded down the hall and then stumbled to a stop. Ty was waiting at my locker, leaning against the wall with a steaming cup of coffee in his hand. My heart started beating a little faster.

"Good morning. Nice of you to join us."

I rolled my eyes. "I overslept."

"I see," he said, smirking. "Well, perhaps this will help?" He offered me the cup of coffee.

"Oh my God, thank you!" I took a large swig. "What are you doing, anyway? Aren't you going to be late for class?"

"Late? Nah, it's making an entrance." Ty winked at me. "Besides, I wanted to check on you."

"Check on me?"

"Well, yeah. After last night . . . I just wanted to make sure you were okay."

My heart skipped a beat. My mind flashed to last night's kiss—the way Ty had held me in his arms, the feel of his lips against mine. *Get it together, Styles!* I took another sip of coffee to clear my head. "Oh, right. The Calling and all that."

"Well, yes, but . . ." Ty shifted from one foot to the other. "That's not the only reason." A slight flush colored his cheeks.

The tips of my ears grew hot, and I didn't know what to say. We stared at each other until the final bell rang shrilly, making us both jump.

"Well, I guess there's no point in rushing now," I said. "Might as well take my time." I started walking down the hall.

"Are you sure you're okay, though?" Ty asked, falling into step beside me. "You look—"

"Like crap?"

"I wasn't going to say that."

"It's okay." I grinned. "I know I look pretty rough. I only got two or three hours of sleep last night."

"Just couldn't sleep?"

"No, Gareth was teaching me the proper way to stab someone. Did you know that if you stab someone here," I indicated the soft spot underneath the corner of his jaw, "it will kill them almost instantly?"

Ty's eyebrows shot up.

I laughed. "Let's just say there's a lot to fill you in on."

"Well, you know, Ms. Runyan probably already marked us absent." Ty pointed down the opposite hallway. "We could always take the long way to class."

The voice in my head, the one that was still desperately clinging to the old order of things, protested weakly at the notion. Old Lainey would've been more concerned with getting to class than anything else. *But I'm not that girl anymore,* I thought to myself, and for the first time in my life, I didn't feel a flood of anxiety when I thought about my future. *I'm not that girl.*

I smiled. "You walk and I'll talk."

જે • ર્

"So let me get this straight," Maggie said, brandishing her celery stick like a wand. "In the mere twelve hours since I last saw you, you played chicken with a train, made out with Pretty Face, and became Storm from X-men?"

"Yep."

"And," Maggie continued, gesticulating wildly, "you also pulled a Time Lord and somehow traveled back in time to see your long-lost grandmother get murdered by her resurrected lover?"

"It's true," I confirmed. "Don't forget about the part where I found out my uncle was a Faerie."

Maggie was silent for a moment, celery stick paused mid-air. "Holy crapkittens, Styles!" she finally squealed, sending the stalk flying behind her.

"Yeah, that was pretty much my reaction too." I chuckled, then winced. The headache I'd woken up with had become a massive migraine, and every time I moved or turned my head, the dull ache behind my eye sockets throbbed.

Resting my head on my arms for a second, I tried to block out the noisy cafeteria. I'd already taken some ibuprofen, but it had had little to no effect, and the noisy commotion of lunch wasn't helping either.

"Um, excuse me, ladies?"

I lifted my head to see Ty standing beside me, Maggie's celery stick in his hand. "I believe this belongs to you." He smirked.

I smiled up at him, warmth spreading through my body. Maggie leaned over, grabbed the celery stick from his hand, and pointed it at him. "You. Sit," she commanded.

Ty chuckled. "Yes, ma'am." He sat beside me, his shoulder brushing mine. A warm shiver skipped down my back.

"Just so we're clear," Maggie said, leaning across the table. "You're Wolverine. Got that?"

Ty looked at me, his brows scrunched. I was equally puzzled. "Uh, Mags?"

"Oh, good gravy," Maggie said. "Don't you people read?" She pointed at me. "You're Jean Grey, and I'm Scott Summers.

He," she indicated Ty, "is Wolverine." She looked expectantly at me and Ty, as though things were suddenly crystal clear. When neither of us showed any sign of comprehension, Maggie groaned and shook her head. "Look, most people assume that Jean Grey and Wolverine were the 'it' couple when it comes to X-men, but in reality, *Scott Summers* was the true love of her life. Do you get what I'm saying?"

I was still confused, but Ty leaned forward and nodded his head. "Absolutely." He smiled. "You're the best friend and I'm . . . just Ty."

Maggie raised her arms above her head in the touchdown sign. "Yes! Well done, Pretty Face!" She winked at me. "He's quick too! You picked a good one, Styles!"

"Maggie!" I hissed. Beside me, Ty chuckled and nudged my shoulder.

Maggie and Ty continued to chat, but I couldn't concentrate on their conversation. My headache was getting worse, and all I really wanted to do was find a nice quiet spot where I didn't have to think.

I glanced around the cafeteria, watching my classmates interact with one another. A bunch of football players were throwing balls of wadded-up paper at one another, and a few kids from the drum line were tapping out beats on their lunch trays with pencils. There was a group of mathletes working on what appeared to be advanced calculus, and several cheerleaders were hanging neon posters advertising the upcoming Halloween carnival. It was exactly the type of scene you would expect to see in a normal high school cafeteria.

It was strange to think that, only days ago, I'd been just like them—completely oblivious to the fact that the world was home to an entire realm of people only believed to exist in fairy tales and bedtime stories. A realm *I* belonged to.

The cheerleaders moved closer, hanging a large banner on the wall near my table. Their cheerful chatter seemed to amplify the pounding in my head. The other sounds—the rhythmic tapping, the thwack of the paper balls, the rustling of pages turning—all seemed to be getting louder. Every single decibel grated against my nerves. Groaning, I put my head down on the table.

I just need it to be quiet. I flipped the hood of my sweatshirt up over my head, and immediately I noticed a difference. The sounds were slowly fading away. "Just a little peace and quiet," I murmured.

"Uh . . . Lainey?"

"Yeah?" I replied, not moving from the sanctuary of my hoodie.

"I think you need to see this." There was something in Maggie's voice that made me sit up. Ty and Maggie were both staring at me.

"What?" I demanded. "What is it?"

That was when I noticed that the entire cafeteria had gone silent. The students were still moving around, laughing and talking, but it was as if someone had pressed a gigantic mute button.

"What the . . ." I looked around, watching as a tall, lanky boy tripped on his own shoelaces and dropped his tray to the floor. Where the loud clatter should have been, there was nothing but silence. I turned back to Ty and Maggie, my mouth hanging open. "What happened?"

Maggie shrugged. "We were hoping you'd tell us."

"I didn't—" I sucked in a breath. "Oh . . . it's because of my head. I just wanted some quiet."

"Well, I'd say you got your wish. Nice job, Styles."

"Nice job?" I jerked my head around to look back at my classmates. "Maggie, this is not okay. I don't know how to fix it!"

"I think it's an improvement, personally."

I groaned and threw my hands up in the air. I glanced around again trying to figure out a way to undo . . . whatever it was I had inadvertently done, but I wasn't sure what to do and I was beginning to panic.

"Just take a deep breath and relax, Lainey," Ty's calm voice whispered in my ear. "Your magic reacts to your emotions, remember? Just take a deep breath and focus on the sounds you heard before the silence."

I nodded, grateful for a game plan. I closed my eyes and took several deep breaths. After a few minutes, my heart rate slowed. Relief rushed through me when the silence suddenly broke and the loud sounds of the cafeteria flooded in on me again. Pain shot through my temple, but I was so thankful that the spell was lifted, I hardly noticed.

"Thank you," I said to Ty. "I don't know why this keeps happening. I'm definitely not doing it on purpose."

"Maybe you should talk to Serena," Maggie suggested.

"Maybe she knows why your powers are going all haywire on you."

"That's not a bad idea, actually." I reached into my bag for my cell phone. As soon as I pulled it from the zipper pocket, it began to vibrate and chirp in my hand. Serena's name appeared on the caller ID. "That's a weird coincidence." Swiping my finger across the screen, I answered the call.

"Hello?"

"Lainey!" Serena's exasperated voice came through the speaker. "Where are you?"

"I'm at school. I was just getting ready to call you, actually. I—"

"Lainey!" Serena shouted into the receiver. "You have to get out of there now!"

"What?" I gripped the phone tightly as a cold shiver ran down my spine. "Why?"

"You're in danger, Lainey! You have to leave right now!"

"What are you talking about?" I stood up, throwing my backpack over one shoulder, and headed toward the double doors of the cafeteria, beckoning Ty and Maggie to follow me. "Serena, what's going on?"

There was a long pause. Finally, Serena exhaled sharply and started talking. As she spoke, all the blood drained from my face.

"We'll be right there," I managed to whisper, hanging up the phone.

"Lainey, what is it? What's going on?" Maggie yanked on my arm, trying to get my attention.

"It's the Guard. They're coming."

Ty and Maggie began talking over one another, asking me questions, but the only thing I could focus on was the rapid pounding of my own heartbeat.

"They're coming . . . for *me*."

CHAPTER
TWENTY-FOUR

S erena paced back and forth, muttering to herself.
I sat with Ty and Maggie on one of the blue couches in
Serena's shop and drummed my fingers against my knees.
With so much adrenaline pumping through my system and
the frustrating lack of information, I was like a caged animal
waiting to pounce.

"Hey," Ty leaned over and whispered in my ear. "Breathe.
It's okay." He nodded at my hands. Tiny green sparks were
shooting from my fingertips.

"This whole mood ring power situation is getting old,"
I said, forcing my hands to lie flat.

"Just take a few deep breaths now and then," Ty said,
grabbing one of them in his own. He smiled at me—the
crooked smile I'd grown to adore—and despite my mood, I
managed a small smile back.

The front door flew open with a bang, and Gareth rushed

in, his face red and eyes wide. "What is it?" he demanded. "What's happened?"

Serena dashed over and gripped Gareth's arm. "Nothing yet." She looked over at me, her face pale. "But I had a vision about the Master. He knew about Lainey, knew who she was. He wants to use her to unlock the Grimoire. He sent the Guard after her."

"Wait, let me get this straight." I held up a hand. "The Master knows I'm alive, knows that I'm the last remaining Keeper, and is coming after me."

"If my vision is correct," Serena swallowed, "then yes."

"That's impossible," Gareth said. "Everyone who knows Lainey exists is either in this room or dead." He scanned the room, landing on Ty. He coughed and straightened his shoulders. "That is—"

"This is Ty," I said, trying not to roll my eyes at the overprotective uncle routine. "The guy I told you about last night."

Gareth narrowed his eyes. "Praetorian, right?"

Ty nodded, standing up to shake Gareth's hand. "Pleasure to meet you, sir."

Gareth shook hands, but still looked wary.

"I'm afraid there's more," Serena said, pulling Gareth's attention back to her. "I also saw Scavengers."

The word didn't mean anything to me, but Gareth swore under his breath and Ty stiffened in his seat.

Maggie leaned forward on the couch. "What's a Scavenger?"

"A traitor," Gareth spat. "Supernaturals from all different factions who earn money by rounding up Supernaturals who either oppose the Master or who they think might be of interest. He gives them a reward for every one they capture."

"Like some kind of supernatural bounty hunter?" Maggie asked.

"Exactly. They can sense magic," Gareth said. "They track it like a bloodhound on the hunt."

"And they're coming here?" I asked.

"Yes." Serena nodded. "In my vision, I saw you through their eyes. I could *smell* the magic emanating off of you, could feel how it fueled their urge to hunt—"

"But it makes no sense," Gareth said, waving his hand to cut her off. "They can't be sensing her, so what trail are they following?" He raked a hand through his hair and started to pace.

Oh. My stomach did a somersault. *Of course.* I cleared my throat. "You're wrong."

"The storm," Ty said, reading my thoughts. "And today in the cafeteria."

Maggie was just as quick. She leaned forward and snapped her fingers. "The rosebush! And the dryad! At the cemetery."

"The clock," I said, nodding my head. "And the streetlights—that was all me."

Gareth and Serena were quiet, staring at us like we'd failed to deliver the punch line of a joke.

"It *is* me. The trail they're following is mine," I explained, quickly pouring out the details of all the strange occurrences . . . what I now knew were pulses.

Serena sank down on the edge of the couch. "We knew our cloaking spells were failing, but—"

"But we underestimated one very important thing," Gareth finished. He looked at me. "You're a DuCarmont. And more powerful than even we realized." Emotion flashed in his eyes, but he blinked it away. "Power like that . . . of course they'd be drawn to it." He sank down next to Serena. "How long?" He looked at her with a face that had seemed to age at least ten years.

She jumped up, unsteady on her feet, and darted over to the table where her stack of cards lay. She waved her hands over the deck, her whispered words unintelligible, and then expertly cut the deck in half.

She placed the first card faceup on the table. The tower card. The terrifying, yet familiar sight of the burning structure stared at me from across the room. A wave of nausea rolled in my stomach. Then Serena placed another card on the table.

It depicted a young woman kneeling at the edge of a small stream with two containers of water. She was pouring one of the containers back into the stream and the other she was pouring onto dry land. Behind her, there were several stars shining brightly. It was a sharp contrast to the bleak tower card lying next to it.

Serena looked up at me, relief etched on her face. "The star card," she said, pointing.

"Please tell me that one doesn't also predict my impending doom."

"Oh, no." Serena held up the star card and smiled. "*This* means there's hope."

"So what do we do now?" Gareth asked, moving toward the table. "Do we run? Go into hiding?"

Serena shook her head. "Well, now that we know what's drawing them in, it's possible that the vision will change. The future is subjective, after all, much like my visions. Nothing is set in stone until it happens."

"Okay," I said. "So, just so we're clear—the Scavengers are tracking my magic. If I stop using magic, then they won't be able to track me, right?"

Gareth nodded, his eyes lighting up. "Yes, that's it. We just have to change the vision."

"There's only one small problem," I said. "Changing the vision is contingent on me not using my magic. So far I haven't consciously attempted to use it—it just happened. How am I supposed to stop doing something I apparently have no control over?"

Gareth and Serena shared a look.

"You'll need training for your magic," Serena said. "But there's no time . . ."

I rolled my eyes again. "Okay, so we need something to draw the Scavengers' attention away. Something to distract them."

Gareth looked to Serena. "Would that work? If the Scavengers began to sense magic somewhere else, somewhere close enough to be connected, but far enough away that they wouldn't be able to track it back to Lainey?"

"A diversion?" Serena's eyes were wide, but she nodded. "Yes, I think it's possible."

"A diversion?" Maggie echoed. "How will that help?"

"We need to get the Scavengers off my trail," I answered. "If my magic is drawing them into Lothbrook, then we need someone to draw them back out. Someone whose magic is more noticeable than mine."

"But you're a DuCarmont." Maggie turned to Gareth and Serena. "Didn't you just say that she was really powerful? Will you even be able to find someone with more power?"

"Probably not," Gareth admitted. "But we won't necessarily need to find someone with more power. We just need to find someone with more frequency. Someone who is using large quantities of magic on a daily basis. Any small spell that Lainey might accidentally cast would barely be a blip on their radar by comparison."

"But it's a crazy idea," I argued. "How in the world can I ask a perfect stranger to go out there, perform magic, and potentially be captured by Scavengers?"

"Well, it's obvious, isn't it? It wouldn't be a perfect stranger. It has to be me."

I stared at Gareth, his words and the horrible realization of their meaning slamming me in the face. "No," I said firmly when I found my voice again. *"No."*

"There isn't another option."

"But you could be hurt . . . or worse. There has to be another way."

Gareth crossed over to me and placed his hands on my shoulders. "I'm not afraid for myself. My only fear is what might happen if the Scavengers get their hands on you." He gripped my shoulders even tighter. "They would deliver you directly to the Master, and *that* fate is not one I'd wish on my greatest enemy."

I felt the tug of old Lainey on my psyche, the girl who would have accepted Gareth's words as law without another thought—but I had made my choice and that wasn't who I wanted to be anymore.

I stepped out of his hold and looked him square in the face. "I know you're trying to protect me, but I won't let you risk your life for me."

"It's not up for discussion."

"Like hell it isn't!" I hadn't meant to raise my voice, but the words were fuel for my flames. "My mother died sacrificing herself for me. I won't let you do the same."

"This is the only way. We have to act now before it's too late."

"I refuse to believe that. I'm saying no, and I—"

"ENOUGH!" Gareth roared, his eyes flashing. "That's *enough*, Lainey."

I stared at him, my chest heaving.

"You think you understand what's at stake here, but you don't know the Master like we do. You don't know what he's capable of." Gareth began to pace again, raking his fingers through his hair. "For years, the black magic in his veins has kept him alive, fueling his malevolence. He kills for sport and tortures his own kind for entertainment. If he gets his hands on you . . ." He whirled to face me. "I *need* to do this. Please, let me do this for you . . . and for your mother."

Tell him no, the voice in my head whispered. *There has to be another way.* I opened my mouth, my lips already forming the words, but the look in Gareth's eyes stopped me.

"Okay," I finally whispered.

He didn't wait for me to change my mind. Instead he moved back over to Serena and they began to discuss the logistics of the plan.

My entire body was shaking, a physical protest to the whole thing. Tiny arcs of green lightning were sparking from my fingertips again.

But my mind was made up.

"Don't tell me to breathe," I warned, when I saw Ty looking at my hands.

"Wasn't going to," he responded. Instead, he leaned over and pressed his shoulder against mine in a silent show of support. I bit my lip as an ache bloomed in my chest. It was a nice reminder of something good, even if it lasted only a second—even if my entire world was consumed with chaos.

"I'm gonna head home and pack a few bags," Gareth was saying to Serena. "If the Scavengers are as close as you say, I'll need to leave tonight for our plan to work."

"What will you do?" Maggie asked, ever curious. "Where will you go?"

Gareth shrugged, a half smile on his face, though you could still see the worry painted across his features. "I'll head toward the neighboring towns and search for my own kind. And I'll do what I've always done—make swords. I'm a blade-smith, after all," he explained. "And Faerie blades are infused with quite a bit of magic—it's what makes them so powerful. It should be enough to draw the Scavengers away from here."

Maggie's face must have conveyed some hint of doubt, because Gareth winked at her. "Don't worry, we Fae are tougher than we look." He kissed Serena on the cheek and headed for the door without a single glance in my direction. Serena followed him, the murmur of their voices carrying down the hallway.

Maggie walked over to the couch and sat on my other side. "Hanging in there, Styles?"

I dropped my head in my hands. "This is never going to work. He's going to get hurt. How can I let him do this?"

"How can you *not?*"

I sat up, looking at Maggie. "What? You agree with him?" My heart started racing again, and heat flooded through me.

"Hold on, now, Styles." Maggie held up her hand. "No need to go all Dark Phoenix on me. All I'm saying is that Gareth has spent his entire life keeping you safe. Don't you think you owe him a little bit of faith?"

The words were like a punch to the gut. "I guess I *do* owe him that."

Maggie wrapped an arm around me and pulled me close. "It's gonna be okay."

I sighed. "I hope so . . . but a big part of this plan is contingent on me not drawing attention with my magic. How can I avoid something I have no control over?"

Maggie didn't have an answer this time. We sat in uncomfortable silence for several minutes before Ty offered to take us home.

We walked down the hall and, after saying good-bye to Serena, headed toward Ty's car. Maggie quickly crawled into the backseat, leaving me alone with Ty outside the car.

"Can I ask you if you're okay now?" He grinned.

I laughed. "Yeah, I guess so, but I honestly don't know how to answer." I leaned against the car and looked up at the sky. It was dotted with hundreds of stars, twinkling against the velvet backdrop next to the half-moon shining brightly. It looked so calm and peaceful—the exact opposite of how I felt.

"You can do it, you know." Ty's words were soft but clear.

"Do what?"

"Control it." He seemed to be reading my mind again.

"Can I, though?"

"Yes, you can. You just have to believe it."

I took a deep breath. "I just . . . I mean . . . they should've told me years ago. My powers are the reason we're in this mess, and if I'd known, I could've trained or at least learned how it all works. I wouldn't be sending my uncle on a death mission just to buy me some time."

I frowned. "Now that I know the truth, I can't just sit here and do nothing."

"So don't."

"What do you mean?"

"Ride out this plan, but start preparing yourself. Serena said you need training. So, find someone who can train you in magic. Learn not only how to control it, but how to *use* it."

Ty stepped closer and gripped my hand. "You'll need it if you ever come face-to-face with the Master."

The words sent a chill down my spine. I tried to laugh it off. "Isn't that what Praetorians are for?"

Ty's eyes flashed. "Don't do that. Don't diminish who and what you are. You're stronger than you think. You're a DuCarmont witch. Don't forget that."

The strength of those words filled me, the truth in them ringing true in my heart.

I nodded. "I won't."

Ty took a step back, breathing deeply. "Good." Then he stood up straight and crossed his right arm across his chest. "The protection of my hands, my blade, and my life . . . is yours, Lainey Styles. You're my Calling, and whatever you may face, I will be at your side."

The words, so formal and irrevocable, struck a chord within me. My whole soul vibrated as an image of Lancelot taking the oath at King Arthur's table flashed in my mind.

Ty's eyes burned with intensity, and there wasn't any doubt that he meant every word of his pledge. Any notions of protesting quickly dissipated. I stayed silent, choosing my words. "Thank you," I said, finally. "Truly."

There was a moment when something passed between us, something ancient and binding, and I accepted it, the knowledge that our fates were now entwined. The Praetorian and his Calling.

"Come on, you guys. I'm aging here!" Maggie called from the backseat, breaking the mood. I rolled my eyes.

"I guess we better go," I said. "I need to talk to Gareth before he leaves and somehow figure out how to keep from completely losing my mind while he's gone."

Ty thought for a moment. "A distraction, perhaps? You could go with me to that Halloween thing that I keep seeing signs about at school."

"Oh, the carnival." The tips of my ears blazed. "You mean like a date?"

Ty chuckled. "Well, we don't have to call it that if you don't want to, but yeah."

"No," I said, a little too quickly. "No, a date sounds great. I'd really like that." I smiled, hoping the blush burning my skin wasn't visible in the darkness.

Ty opened the passenger side door for me, and I slid into the seat. Maggie was sitting in the backseat grinning from ear to ear, clearly having overheard the exchange outside.

"Just remember," she said with a laugh after Ty had climbed into the driver's seat and turned the ignition, "you're Wolverine."

CHAPTER
TWENTY-FIVE

"Do you really have to go?" It wasn't the first time I'd asked, and I was sure it wouldn't be the last either.

Gareth looked up from the pile of clothing and supplies he was arranging. "I thought we covered this already."

"We did," I said. "But I'm hoping if I keep asking you, the answer might change."

Gareth sighed, came over, and sat next to me on the bed. "Look, I know you think this is a bad idea, but everything's going to be fine. The plan will work."

I rolled my eyes. "You have no way of knowing that." I balled my hands into fists. "This whole thing could end badly."

He offered a small smile, but his eyes narrowed in what looked like sadness. "No," he said. "You're just new to this, that's all. Lainey, Serena and I have been hiding from the

Master our whole lives. Every day that we wake up breathing, our death is a possibility."

His words were like ice water, dousing the anger and frustration burning inside me. I swallowed. "You must think I'm pretty selfish," I said. "All I can see is how this affects me, when in reality there's a much bigger picture here." I looked down and unclenched my hands. "This is what it's like for all Supernaturals, isn't it?"

Gareth nodded. "I'm afraid so. The Master has Scavengers all over the country watching us. Small uses of magic are typically allowed—Serena's visions, for example. That type of power rarely entices a Scavenger, but if a Supernatural is doing something that could be seen as a threat to the Master's power, the Scavengers report it to the Master, and the Guard moves in."

"Just like that? Don't the Supernaturals try to fight back?"

"Some do," Gareth replied, "but it's rare. The Scavengers have one motivation: money. They care about nothing except the cash they make when they deliver someone of value to the Master. If a Supernatural tries to fight back, the Scavengers just call the Guard and wash their hands of the whole thing. Plus, as long as they're valuable to the Master, they're safe from his wrath."

He took a deep breath and exhaled slowly. "I can understand why the Guard hunt us. They're corrupted with dark magic. But I've never been able to understand the Scavengers.

To turn on your own kind like that . . . for nothing but money." He shook his head in disgust. "It makes me sick."

I nodded, not really sure what to say, so I squeezed Gareth's hand in lieu of words.

"So," he continued, "you're not the only one who understands the severity of the situation. We've just gotten used to it, I suppose."

"It makes me angry," I said. "It just doesn't seem fair. One dude has control issues, and a whole lot of people have to suffer for it."

Gareth shrugged. "History is full of people like the Master, people determined to destroy and dominate for no real reason."

"Yes, but it isn't fair. And it isn't right."

"No, it isn't. But unfortunately, that's the way the world works."

My stomach rolled with nausea. Was that really how the world worked? One man decided that another group of people didn't deserve to live free, and that was it? There was nothing to be done?

"Why don't we fight back? Why don't the Supernaturals combine their powers or something?"

"You don't think we've tried?" Gareth shook his head sadly. "Those with enough power to stand against him were exterminated long ago. Now our kind stays hidden, never grouping together to avoid unwanted attention. What can one or two Supernaturals do against soldiers like the Guard? Against the Master himself?"

"So everyone just stays hidden and hopes the Master doesn't find them?" I asked. It seemed like no way to live. "That seems so . . . so . . ." I trailed off, not wanting to speak the word out loud.

"Cowardly?" he finished for me. I nodded.

"Well," Gareth sighed again, "perhaps it is, but fear can be a powerful motivator—or a de-motivator in this case. At the end of the day, I think most of us just want to make it through to the next day." He squeezed my hand. "Most of us have families that we want to keep safe. It just isn't worth it to declare war on an adversary we have no hope of defeating."

"So we just tuck our tails between our legs and run?"

"We do what we must to survive," Gareth replied with a shrug of his shoulders, standing and moving back over to his pile of clothes. "Can we ask any more than that?"

I didn't reply. I didn't want to fight with him again right before he left, though I was tempted to grab him by the shoulders and shake him. He might be okay with the status quo, but now that this was my fight too, I certainly wasn't. Was this how all Supernaturals felt? Just sit back and wait for the Guard to come after them? I shook my head. There had to be another way.

Gareth finished packing the small stack of clothing and toiletries into the duffel bag at the foot of the bed. "Well, I think I have everything I need. I should probably get going."

He walked over and wrapped his arms around me. I clung to him, and he to me. Finality seemed to wrap around us in the moment, but I shoved it away with all my might.

"You have to promise me you'll be careful," Gareth said, squeezing me tighter.

"Don't worry about me. I'll be fine. Just, please . . . whatever you do, come back home."

"I promise, Lainey Bug," he whispered against my hair. "I promise."

When we broke apart, Gareth walked over to his closet and pulled a small leather sheath from the shelf. I recognized my dagger.

"I cleaned it for you," Gareth said as he handed it to me. "And I sharpened the blade, so be very careful. I know we didn't get to train with it for very long, but it would make me feel better to know that you have it."

I took the small scabbard in my hand, running my fingers over the smooth leather. "Thank you. I'll keep it with me."

"Good," Gareth said, grabbing his duffel from the bed. "Walk me to the door?"

We walked down the steps in silence, both of us at a loss for words.

I hugged him one more time and watched as he walked to his truck.

"You'll be at Maggie's till this all blows over, right?" he called out over the open door. I nodded. "Okay, good. I'll call you when I can. Oh, and Lainey? One more thing." Gareth smiled. "I love you. You know that, right?"

I flew down the stairs and into his open arms one last time. "Love you too, Uncle Gareth. . . . Thank you." There was so much I wanted to say, but I hoped those two little words were enough.

When Gareth pulled back, his eyes were swimming with tears. "No," he said. "Thank *you.*"

We embraced a moment longer, and then with one more smile, he was in the truck and driving down the dark street.

I watched until the red taillights of the truck disappeared from view. Trudging back into the house, I headed toward my bedroom to pack my own bag, trying to ignore the terrible feeling gnawing at the back of my mind.

Everything's going to be fine. The plan will work. Gareth's words swam in my head.

I sure hoped he was right.

❧ • ❧

"What about this one?" I held up the sweater for Maggie's approval.

"It's fine, but I think my grandmother has the same one in green."

I groaned and threw the sweater over my head where it landed on the pile of already discarded clothes. "That's it! I'm not going!" I flopped down on Maggie's bed and covered my face with my arms.

"Don't be so dramatic, Styles," Maggie calmly called from the bathroom. "And could you cut that out? I'm trying to put mascara on, and you're gonna make me poke my eyeball out."

I uncovered my face to see the lights in Maggie's bedroom and bathroom were flickering on and off. Yelping, I jumped to my feet. "Argh, not again!"

Maggie walked from the bathroom and put her hands on my shoulders. "Relax, Lainey. You have to relax."

"I'm trying," I said through clenched teeth. "But the more I try not to use my magic, the more it keeps happening! The freaking Scavengers could be right outside for all we know!"

"You're just nervous. You need to calm down."

I sighed. It'd been four days since Gareth left town. I'd spent hours poring over books about magic in Serena's shop, but the distraction did little to quell my worry. Gareth had called once to let me know he was safe, but that was two days ago. Every time the phone rang and it wasn't him, my nerves grew more frazzled.

It didn't help that Ty was due to pick us up for the carnival in half an hour.

Date. The very word made me want to crawl under the covers and never come out. I'd been on a few dates before, and I'd had the sporadic boyfriend or two. But this felt . . . different, and it made me ridiculously nervous.

I groaned and covered my face with one of Maggie's pillows.

"It's just a date, Styles," Maggie said. "Not an act of congress. It will be fine." She hopped up and pranced back to the bathroom, fluffing her voluminous curls. "Besides, I'll be there to back you up. You got this."

I let out a breath. "Thank goodness for that." I'd insisted

Maggie come along—using my unstable magic as a feeble excuse for not being alone with Ty—but even her usual perkiness couldn't alleviate the churning in my stomach.

"Here," Maggie said, coming out of the bathroom to pull an off-the-shoulder, midnight-blue sweater from her closet. "Wear this."

I took the sweater and threw it on. It hit just below the waistline and sat perfectly across my collarbones. It was exactly the look I'd been hoping for. "How is it that you can dress me better than I can dress myself?"

Maggie laughed. "'Cause I know you better than you know yourself."

I grinned and sat down to put my boots on. Then I pulled the dagger Gareth had given me from my bag and carefully tucked it in the waistband of my jeans. I pulled the sweater over it and checked in Maggie's full-length mirror to make sure it was covered.

A few minutes later, I was putting on a thin layer of lip gloss when headlights flashed across the wall. "He's here," I said, peering out Maggie's bedroom window. Ty's familiar black car was parked in the driveway. "I think I'm gonna throw up," I continued as Ty walked toward the door.

"It's not like you've never hung out before, Styles."

"I know, but this is . . . different." I tugged on my hair, trying to smooth it into place.

Maggie walked over and pulled my hands away from my scalp. "Stop that. You look beautiful, and he's gonna think so too."

"You really think so?"

Maggie put her hand on her hip. "Please, when have I ever been wrong?"

"Never." I grinned. Downstairs, the doorbell rang. I jumped, and the light overhead gave a tiny flicker.

"Come on," Maggie said with a laugh. "Let's go save him before my dad starts doing his 'famous' impressions." She cocked her head at me and, with a voice that perfectly mirrored her father's phony Humphrey Boggart accent, said, "Here's looking at you, kid."

Giggling, we linked arms and walked down the stairs to where Ty was talking casually with Maggie's dad. He was wearing his leather jacket—which I'd finally returned—and a long-sleeved gray thermal with a pair of dark jeans and boots. He looked incredible.

Swallowing, I forced myself to focus on the stairs so I wouldn't trip and fall on my face.

After listening to Donald Duck and Bill Clinton remind us several times to stay safe and wear our seatbelts, we managed to say good-bye to Mr. Dawson and head outside. Maggie dutifully crawled into the backseat with a wink as Ty walked me to the passenger side of the car and held the door open.

"Thank you," I squeaked as I sat down. *Oh my God.* I cringed at the shrill sound of my voice. Behind me, Maggie snickered. I turned around and gave her a quick glare. She responded by kicking the back of my seat, as if to say, "Chill out! Take a deep breath!"

I rolled my eyes but sucked down a mouthful of air anyway.

Ty walked around the car and got inside. He cranked the car and backed down the driveway in one fluid motion. "I didn't want to say this in front of Maggie's dad," he began, his cheeks turning slightly pink, "but . . . uh . . . you look gorgeous tonight."

My cheeks burned, but I smiled. "Thank you," I said, grateful that my voice seemed to have returned to its normal state.

"And we all know, *I*, of course, look fabulous!" Maggie chirped.

My laugh had always been a little too breathy for my liking, but it blended with the deeper tones in Ty's laughter as we chuckled at Maggie's comment. I liked the way it sounded—our two voices together in harmony. A flash of warmth rushed through me.

"How've you been?" Ty asked. "I haven't really had a chance to talk to you much since Serena's house."

"I'm okay. Worried about Gareth. I can't reach him on his phone. He called a few days ago, but since then nothing. Everything else's been quiet."

"He's probably just being extra cautious," Ty suggested.

"Yeah . . . maybe."

"No sign of the Scavengers?"

"No, not that I know of anyway. I haven't seen anything strange, and Serena hasn't had any more visions about them, so I'm guessing whatever Gareth is doing must be working."

"Are they still in the area?"

I nodded. "She thinks so, but she's too afraid to do any real spell that would tell her for certain. She doesn't want to attract any more attention."

"Well, no news is good news, right?"

"Right," I agreed. "Although I really wish Gareth would call. I'll feel a whole lot better once I hear from him."

"I'm sure he'll call soon," Ty said.

"I hope so."

"And how about you, Maggie?" Ty turned his attention to her, and Maggie immediately launched into an animated narrative of her week. I watched Ty's face as he listened, my heart fluttering as I studied the planes of his cheekbones, the strong set of his jaw, his lips that were quirked up into his crooked grin. I resisted the urge to fan my warm cheeks.

After parking the car and paying for out tickets, we walked into the carnival grounds. The cheerleaders had really outdone themselves this year. The fairgrounds were brightly lit with colorful lights, and speakers hanging from the light posts blasted popular country music. There was a large selection of rides, including a Ferris wheel and a Tilt-A-Whirl, and there were tons of booths that had games where you could win prizes. The smell of popcorn and funnel cakes wafted through the air, and my mouth began to water. In the back corner of the fair there was a haunted house, and there was also a haunted corn maze as part of the festivities.

"Wow," I said, taking it all in.

"What you said," Ty replied, his face in equal awe. Maggie, who was grinning like a five-year-old, nodded.

I bounced up and down on the balls of my feet. "What do you want to do first?"

"Oh, look," Maggie said, pointing toward one of the booths. "There's Lily Owens!" She waved, and a girl I recognized from school with strawberry-blonde hair waved back. "I think I'll go hang with her for a while."

I opened my mouth to protest, but snapped my lips back together when Maggie glared at me.

"You guys have fun. I'll meet up with you later, okay?"

I let out a huff. I'd been counting on Maggie as a wingman, but as she wiggled her fingers at Ty and grinned at me with a smile that would've made the devil cringe, I knew that wasn't going to happen.

I mumbled under my breath as she winked at me and then skipped over to where Lily Owens was waiting. "Why, that little—"

"So," Ty said, "are you hungry, or do you want to hit up the rides first?" He was beaming a smile that made me feel all gushy inside.

"I could definitely eat." I tried to say it casually, but in truth I was starving. I'd been too nervous to eat earlier.

"I was hoping you'd say that," Ty said with a grin, "because there is a booth over there that claims they have corndogs so good they'll make you want to slap your mama!" he finished the last part with an over-exaggerated Southern accent that made me laugh.

"That sounds great! Although I must warn you, I can pretty much eat my weight in corndogs. They're my favorite."

Ty grinned and put one of his hands over his heart in mock surprise. "Beautiful *and* loves corndogs? Be still my beating heart!"

Laughing, we headed toward the food vendors.

The crowd was thick and difficult to maneuver through. As Ty was getting the food, I jumped to the side as a mother wrangling three young boys almost trampled me on the way to the ice cream stand, and I stumbled into somebody on my other side.

"Excuse me, sir!" I said to the tall gentlemen I'd accidently bumped into. The man grunted in response, pulling his black baseball cap lower over his eyes. He stalked off without a word.

"Geez, rude much?" I muttered.

Before I could think on it further, Ty walked over triumphantly with a tray full of corndogs in his hands.

"You ready for this, Styles?" he crowed. "'Cause I'm about to kick your butt in a corndog-eating contest." He did a little box step with his feet.

"Already practicing your victory dance?" I laughed.

"Yep, just want you to have a little taste of what's to come." Ty's smile lit up his entire face.

"Ha!" I chortled. "Dream on, pal! I never met a corndog I didn't like!"

Laughing, we made our way toward the picnic tables.

"You ready for this, Styles?" Ty asked, handing me a corndog.

"Let's do it."

CHAPTER
TWENTY-SIX

"There's still time to back out, you know," I yelled over the din of laughter and childish shrieks.

Ty leaned forward and gripped the wheel of his electric-blue bumper car. "I never back down from a fight." I got a brief flash of smirk before a loud bell jangled and the cars went live.

I yanked my wheel and sped down the shiny linoleum track, trailing Ty's car by a few feet. Just when I was close enough to ram the bumper, a yellow car driven by a kid in a Minions shirt t-boned me and sent me spinning into the middle of the track. The kid's gleeful giggle echoed in my ear as I maneuvered my car back into the flow of traffic, scanning the sea of color for electric blue.

I heard his shout before I felt the impact that sent my car spinning. Squealing, I tried my best to control my car, but I was laughing too hard to make a real go of it. Ty rammed me again, knocked my car off the main course and into a small corner. I was trapped. I held my hands up, feigning defeat.

"Do you yield?" Ty joked, as if we were in the middle of a duel. He held out his arm like a sword and pointed at me. I tried to maneuver around him, but he had me pinned. He grinned smugly at me.

"Never!" I yelled, abandoning all attempts of going around him and stepping on the gas pedal instead, ramming my car into his. The impact knocked his car to the side just enough for me to squeeze through. The expression on his face made me burst out in another fit of giggles. The wind whipped my hair around my face as I raced toward the opposite side of the track, his laughter booming behind me.

By the time the bell jangled again, I was doubled over in my seat, laughing so hard my stomach ached. Ty's car was parallel to mine, his own shoulders shaking nearly as much.

It took several minutes, but he finally stood up and managed to pull me to my feet. I was out of breath and the muscles in my face hurt from smiling so much, but I couldn't stop the stupid grin I knew was plastered on my face.

"How about now?" he said, trailing a hand down my arm. "You yield?" His eyes were bright and sparkling.

The touch of his skin on mine sent a wave of heat through me.

"Never," I whispered. Every fiber of my being began to sing as he reached out and ran his fingers lightly over my cheek. My breath hitched in my throat as he leaned forward to kiss me.

"Um . . . excuse me."

We both jumped. Ty took a step backward, and we both looked down at a kid wearing a baseball hat staring at us with crossed arms. "Blue's my favorite color," he said, looking pointedly at the car Ty had exited, the one our bodies were currently blocking.

"Oh," I said, moving out of the way. "Sorry about that." I tried to smile at the kid, but disappointment was coursing through me. I think I grimaced instead. The little kid gave me a weird look before hopping into the car.

Ty chuckled and reached for my hand. "Come on, Road Slayer. Let's go get some lemonade."

I let him lead me back outside where the night air was cool against my flushed skin. I'd expected him to drop my hand once we were outside, but he didn't. His warm hand was still wrapped firmly around mine. I gave his fingers a gentle squeeze, and when he looked down at me, I swear my heart dropped right out of my chest.

I was so busy enjoying the gushiness of my emotions that when Ty stopped abruptly, I didn't notice. I tripped as the tether of his arm yanked me backward. It was then that I saw the tight set of his shoulders, his rigid posture.

"Ty?"

When he looked at me, golden light ringed his irises.

"What's wrong?"

He scanned the area, ignoring my question. Whipping his head back and forth, he pulled me toward the food vendors, tension pulsating down his arm.

"Ty, what is it?" He was walking briskly, and I did my best to keep up. I looked around but saw nothing out of the ordinary. "Ty!" I yanked on his arm and pulled him to a stop. "What's going on?"

He was breathing easier now, and the golden light had faded slightly from his eyes. "I don't know," he said, focusing on my face. "Something's not right."

"Praetorian senses?" I asked, pointing to his eyes.

He nodded. "I think maybe we should get out of here."

The look on his face made me swallow hard. "Is it the Scavengers?"

"I'm not sure, but whatever it is, it's not friendly."

That was good enough for me. "Okay, we have to find Maggie first. I don't want to leave without her."

Ty nodded, and we moved through the crowd, both of us alert. We were near the back corner of the grounds, the one adjacent to the corn maze, when I heard someone call my name.

"Styles! Styles, up here!"

I looked up, and Maggie was waving from one of the passenger pods on top of the Ferris wheel. Next to her, Lily Owens also gave a cheerful wave.

"Shit," I muttered. Maggie's pod was at the very top of the wheel.

She waved again, but her smile faded when she saw the serious look Ty and I were sharing. She disappeared from over the side of the pod, and a few seconds later, my phone buzzed in my pocket.

What's wrong? Scavengers?

Maggie was lightning-fast when it came to texting.

We're not sure, but Ty has a bad feeling. We need to go.

Roger that. As soon as I get down.

I sighed and shoved the phone back into my pocket.

Ty was standing stiffly at my side, his eyes scanning the crowd, looking for any signs of trouble.

I had no idea what to look for, but I scanned the crowd too. Adrenaline was pumping through me to the rhythm of my pounding heart. Every sound made me jump, and the bright lights of the carnival suddenly felt too warm. Shivers were racing up and down my back, and there was something hanging in the air that made my stomach churn with nausea.

"Ty," I said, my voice strained, "you're right. Something's wrong." I sucked in a shallow breath. "I can feel it."

The golden rings around his eyes were growing brighter. He pulled me closer to his side, his arm a welcome and protective weight around me. "We really need to get out of here."

"I know," I whispered, watching as Maggie's pod moved inch by inch toward the ground. The operator seemed to be giving each individual pod a turn to stop at the very top. I chewed on my bottom lip, my fingers tapping an impatient rhythm at my side.

There were only three pods left in front of Maggie's when the screaming started.

The air erupted with horrified wails and shrieks of terror. I twisted my head back and forth but couldn't locate the source of the cries. The people around me had grown eerily quiet as the screams floated through the air. Then I saw it.

I stood frozen, trying to make sense of what I was seeing. There was a strange orange glow illuminating the sky. The amber hue seemed to glow against the contrast of the dark night, but the feeling in my gut told me this was no carnival trick. This was deadly.

Ty stood beside me, his eyes too fixated on the sky.

"Ty, what is—" I broke off. The realization came crashing down. "Oh my God. It's fire. The corn maze is on fire!"

As if my words had broken some kind of spell, the crowd around us erupted in panic and began running toward the exits. Carnival workers and volunteers were yelling at the crowd to remain calm, that everything was under control, but the air was already thick with smoke, and a wave of heat seemed to blanket the grounds. The corn maze bordered the fairgrounds on two sides, and with each passing minute, the screams grew louder, the thick orange haze growing brighter.

I wasn't sure what compelled me, but I pushed through the crowd and ran toward the main entrance of the corn maze. As the blazing field came into view, I skidded to a stop and assessed the scene. About five feet away from the entrance to the corn maze, three carnival workers with fire extinguishers were trying to put out a large blaze that appeared to be one of the kettle corn vendor carts. Though the cart fire looked frightening, it was nothing compared with the flames that rose up behind it in the midst of the dry cornfield.

Ty stood wordlessly at my side, the bright flames dancing in the reflection of his eyes.

"The wind must have carried the embers!" I shouted over the noise, indicating the cart. "The cornstalks are so dry they burn like paper."

A small contingent of policemen were trying to organize a rescue plan for those trapped inside the maze, and a tall carnival official barked into a walkie-talkie. People were running in all directions as the tall orange flames flickered and danced along the edge of the field, engulfing everything in their path. Black smoke billowed out behind the flames, and the air was filled with the roar of flames and burning cornstalks.

With the cart fire finally out, the carnival workers ran over and tried to extinguish the blaze with the fire extinguishers, but their efforts, however admirable, were no match for the appetite of the all-consuming fire.

Sirens sounded in the distance, but as the flames continued to spread, it became clear that in a matter of minutes there would be nothing left of the maze but ash and smoke.

"Lainey." Ty's gruff voice was low in my ear. "I don't think it was the kettle corn cart." He nodded at the burning stalks. "Look at the flames. Even with the dry conditions, it's moving too fast."

I stared at the fire. Nearly the entire corn maze had been consumed by the flames in a matter of seconds. Ty was right; even with the dried-out stalks, there was no way it could've burned that fast. It wasn't possible . . . No, it had to be magical.

"Oh my God," I said, feeling my knees start to weaken. Ty gripped me under the elbow. "Someone's using magic, aren't they?"

The hard look on his face said it all. My knees weakened again. "But why?"

"It must be the Scavengers. Only they would resort to something like this. They must be trying to draw out magic-wielders—only someone with a lot of power could stop the fire."

"Well, then, we have to do something," I shouted over the noise. "There are people trapped in there!" I held up my hands, the green lightning already crackling between my fingertips.

"You can't!" Ty shoved my hands back down at my sides. "It's too dangerous. We need to get you out of here, *now!*"

"We can't just let them die!" I screamed at him.

He stared at me, his face a mixture of emotions. "We don't have a choice. If the Scavengers find you—"

"There's always a choice." I gripped his arm, my fingers digging into his skin. "*You* taught me that."

We stared at each other, a silent showdown of wills, until a new wave of screams—this one from a different direction—filled the air.

The vendor and game booths nearest to the maze were starting to catch fire. The flames licked through the cheap fabrics covering the wooden structures and ignited them like kindling. The fire was spreading through the fairgrounds, and in minutes the entire place would be a maelstrom of flames.

Including . . .

"Oh my God! Maggie!"

I was running again, willing my feet to fly as I shoved back through the crowd of people trying to exit the grounds. The Ferris wheel operator was doing his best to move and unload the pods as quickly as possible, but the other attendants had abandoned their posts, and the flames danced along the metal piping, scorching the polished metal black. Maggie's pod was still high in the air.

"Maggie!" I screamed her name and ran faster.

"Lainey!" Her face appeared over the side of her pod, her eyes wide. "We're not moving fast enough."

"Don't worry!" I shouted over the noise. "We're gonna get you down."

Ty had already run over to the Ferris wheel operator. They were arguing, and Ty's hands were clenched into fists.

"It's too hot," the man was saying, his face dripping with sweat. "The controls are overheated. We'll never get them down before the flames spread." He wiped a hand over his ash-streaked face.

Ty looked like he wanted to punch the man. "In minutes, this whole place is going to be nothing but ashes. You need to get them down *now*. The wheel could tip."

As if in response to his words, the Ferris wheel began to groan and creak, the metal protesting the heat of the flames.

"Ty!" I shouted. "We're running out of time!"

Embers were falling from the sky like snow. I hissed as one landed on the back of my neck. The Ferris wheel operator took advantage of the distraction and shoved past Ty, running toward the exit like a dog with its tail tucked between its legs. Ty swore and started to run after the man, but then dashed over to the operating box and stared at the controls.

"I'm not sure how to work it," he said, when I ran over, coughing on the smoke.

"We don't have any more time!" I shouted. The sound of sirens was louder now, but as I stared at the empty corner of the fairgrounds where we were, I knew they'd never get to us in time. The remaining people on the Ferris wheel were wailing for help, but it wouldn't come.

"Lainey! Help us!" The sound of Maggie screaming my name tore at my heart.

Sweat dripped down my neck as I moved to where I could see her leaning over the side of the pod, panic written all over her face. "We're coming, Mags. We're gonna get you down, I promise."

The Ferris wheel groaned louder this time, the creaks and pops making me jump.

I looked at Maggie's face for a second longer before making up my mind. I held out my hands in front of me, the green lighting already growing. "Ty!" He turned to look at me. "I have to! We don't have any other options. I have to save Maggie!"

Ty's face was conflicted, but he nodded to me and pulled me over behind the tall metal operator's booth. "No one can see you," he said, peering around the small building. "Okay, if you're gonna do this, now's the time."

I nodded and pushed up my sleeves. I had no idea what to do; I hoped some sort of instinct would kick in.

The nerves must have been showing on my face because Ty grabbed me by the shoulders, looking deep into my eyes. "You can do this, Lainey."

"I know."

Stepping around Ty, I faced the blazing cornfield and closed my eyes, holding my hands out in front of me. I had no real idea how to go about summoning my powers, but this seemed right, so I went with it.

I have to do something. I have to help those people. I have to save Maggie.

A deep warmth was beginning to spread throughout my body, and a strange tingling sensation—like a thousand tiny pinpricks—licked across my skin. An electric flow of energy began to course through my veins, enveloping my senses and taking over my self-control.

The heat from the fire burned my face and skin, and glowing embers fell from the sky, singeing tiny holes into my sweater. Sweat poured down my back, and glistening beads of perspiration fell down the sides of my cheeks.

I have to do this. I have to help them.

Over and over, I said the words carefully and with purpose in my mind. My hands ached as the lightning between my fingers grew brighter.

I'm going to do something. I will help those people. I will save Maggie.

Overhead, the sky erupted with an explosion of light. Lightning streaked across the darkness, its silver fingers reaching and stretching to every corner of the night sky. Deafening peals of thunder boomed across the valley, accompanying the streaks of light, and a strange wind began to blow.

I raised my shaking hands in the air. A force unlike anything I'd ever known took hold of my conscience and dominated my every thought and action.

My hands began to glow, the light as bright as the flames themselves. My whole body convulsed, and I heard Ty yelling my name, but I couldn't stop.

I cried out in a mix of exhilaration, terror, pain, and pure adrenaline as a huge pulse of energy shot through my entire body and out through the palms of my hands.

My cry seemed to echo across the valley, and suddenly the heavens opened up and torrents of rain began to fall.

CHAPTER
TWENTY-SEVEN

As the wave of energy left my body, I sagged and struggled to stay upright. I barely felt the raindrops on my skin. All at once, the overwhelming energy had completely evaporated, leaving me drained and depleted.

"Easy now," Ty said, helping me to the ground.

"Ty," I croaked, my throat both raw and dry, "where's Maggie?"

"I'll get her. Wait here."

I leaned against the wall of the tiny building, breathing deeply. *Had I done it?*

Several minutes passed. I was too exhausted to move, but the sounds of bustling activity filled the air. Footsteps approached the building, and then Maggie's face appeared.

"Styles?" she asked, her voice quavering.

"Maggie!" I winced a little as the movement caused a stabbing pain in my temple. "Are you okay?"

"I'm fine." She knelt down and squeezed my hand. "All thanks to you. Ty was able to get everyone down. You saved us, Lainey."

My brain was fuzzy on the details. I looked at Ty. "It worked?"

"It worked," Ty said, his voice strained. His face was a hard mask, though he offered me a tiny smile. "How are you feeling?"

"I'm okay . . . I think." I was exhausted, and every inch of me ached, but I was otherwise unscathed. I whipped my head toward the corn maze. A gentle rain was still falling, and the air was thick with smoke, but the orange haze was gone. "The fire?"

"Extinguished. Every last bit of it," Maggie exhaled, breaking into a smile. "You really did it, Lainey."

I looked to Ty for additional confirmation, and he nodded, though his face was still grim. A wave of relief rushed over me. "Are they okay? The people that were in the maze? Everyone else on the Ferris wheel?"

Maggie nodded. "I think so. I heard someone say there were injuries, but everyone was lucky." She leaned over and squeezed my hand. "You saved them, Styles. It was *so* amazing. You conjured this huge storm, and in minutes, the flames were all out. They're calling it a miracle."

I sucked in a deep breath; the relief I felt was so tangible it was almost as if I could wrap my arms around it. I'd *saved* them, saved *Maggie*. Warmth spread through my body, and I smiled. "Well, it wasn't just a miracle. It was magic."

"Do you think you can stand?" Ty held out his hand. His eyes darted back and forth, and his shoulders were tense and rigid.

"The Scavengers. Are they still here?" I asked, allowing him to pull me to my feet. The movement unsettled my equilibrium and I swayed, but Maggie moved quickly to my side. "I got you, Styles."

"Yes, I think so. We need to get out of here." Ty peered around the building shielding us from view.

"Did they see me?"

Ty shook his head. "No, I made sure of that. But . . ." He stopped, listening to something too low for my ears to hear.

"The Scavengers are here?" Maggie squeaked, struggling to support my sagging weight.

Ty moved to my other side and wrapped a strong arm around me. I leaned against him, trying to relieve Maggie. "Yes. The fire was magical," I explained.

"I can't be sure," Ty continued. "But there are three men that keep looking in our direction. One of them is wearing a black hat. I think the smoke is confusing them, but they keep sniffing the air."

My heart nearly stopped. "They're tracking me."

Ty nodded. "I think so."

"What are we gonna do?" Maggie squealed. "If we try to run they'll see us."

Lainey.

I jumped at the sound of my name, but I wasn't afraid— I'd know that voice anywhere. Josephine. I turned, and there she was, standing a few feet away, her fierce gazed locked on my face.

"Is it them?" I whispered. "Did they find me?"

Josephine nodded gravely.

Lainey. Her voice inside my head was growing louder. *Lainey!* My name whispered over and over until it was as if Josephine was shouting in my mind.

I sucked in a breath and gripped the front of Ty's shirt. "Ty, we have to go now!" I grabbed Maggie's hand, yanking her close. "Josephine's here to warn me. It's definitely Scavengers."

Ty's face was serious, his features hard and focused. "Right." He turned to Maggie. "We'll have to try to outrun them." He tightened his grip around my waist. "You ready?"

Maggie nodded, wrapping her own arm around me, my weight supported between them.

"Okay then . . . now!"

We began to run.

The gravel parking lot was fairly empty. I glanced around, desperate for a cop or anyone who might be able to help us, but now that the fire was out, the authorities were herding people back toward the main entrance, taking down statements and checking for injuries. Most people were moving back toward the carnival grounds, while we were moving away.

Flashing red and blue lights illuminated the sky. Ty stuck close to the tree line, trying to stay hidden in the shadows of the parked cars. My head was throbbing, and though he and

Maggie were trying to be gentle with me, the jostling from the running wasn't helping.

We stopped behind a large pickup truck, all of us out of breath. "It no use. I can hear them behind us. They're too fast," Ty said. He peered out from behind the truck and swore. "We're out of time." He grasped Maggie by the shoulder. "Think you can get Lainey to the car?"

I could see from the hard lines on his face what he was planning. *The protection of my hands, my blade, and my life . . . is yours.*

"No," I said, gripping his shoulder. "No knights on a white horse, remember? We do this together."

"It will give you a better chance of getting away."

"Yeah, and it will give *you* a better chance of getting hurt . . . or worse."

"Well, we have to do something," Maggie said. "No offense, Styles, but you're kinda heavy."

"I can help you." I ignored her and turned to Ty. "I'm not gonna let you face them alone."

"Um . . . Styles?" Maggie piped up. "I'm not saying to send Pretty Face to his doom or anything, but, um . . . you can barely stand up."

I opened my mouth to protest, to declare that I was okay, but the argument died in my throat. "I'm fine, really," I tried, but I was fooling no one.

"Remember, being my Calling means I stand beside you," Ty said, his eyes shining with gold. "But in cases where you can barely stand—"

"I'm fine," I broke in, stronger this time.

"But in this case," Ty continued, unconvinced, "it means I give you a head start."

He stared at me with such intensity I knew there was no other choice. "Okay."

Ty looked to Maggie. "You got her?"

Maggie nodded and readjusted her arm, supporting my full weight now.

"You'll only get one shot," Ty said. "Get ready."

My erratic pulse was booming in my ears, but the vertigo was dissipating. I tried to steady myself as much as possible. Beside me, Maggie tightened her grip.

We waited, pressed against the cool metal of the pickup. Peering over Ty's shoulder, I nearly choked when I saw the man in the black hat from earlier. Two other men I didn't recognize, one with long, stringy hair and the other with short, cropped hair, flanked him on either side. They were trying to act casual, but the leader was muttering under his breath, pointing directly at the truck we were crouched behind. They were getting closer.

Lainey! Josephine's warning was louder than ever. *Lainey!*

With a mighty roar that mirrored Josephine's cry, Ty launched into action. Darting around the shed, he flung himself at the closest Scavenger, slamming into him and knocking him to the ground. The man grunted, but Ty jammed his fist into the man's throat, breaking off the sound. He slammed his other fist into the man's jaw. A spray of blood splintered the air.

I bit back a scream as one of the other men dove forward, grabbing Ty by the arm and wrenching him free of his fallen comrade. They fell to ground, rolling together. The man was growling and snapping at Ty like a feral dog, his hand tearing at Ty with what looked like long, sharp claws. I lunged forward, but Maggie's arm pulled me back.

"Lainey, we have to go!"

"No, we have to help him!"

"You're not strong enough! You need to—"

Maggie's voice cut off. Her eyes were wide, her skin ashen. I tore my eyes away from Ty and saw what Maggie was seeing: the Scavenger that hadn't yet joined the fight—the one in the black hat—was slinking toward us, his face twisted in a savage grin.

I lifted my hands, but the effort left me panting. "Run!" I shouted, willing my legs to move. My body was still weak, though, and we fled through the rows of parked cars, tripping and stumbling the whole way.

Behind us, someone laughed, and I said, "He's toying with us, Maggie. We're not going to make it."

Maggie didn't answer, but she yanked on my wrist, trying to pull me along even faster. We didn't even have time to scream when a solid mass came out of nowhere, colliding with us in a tangle of limbs and snarls.

I was wrenched from Maggie's hold and slammed into the ground face-first. I sputtered and coughed as the heavy weight on top of me forced the air out of my lungs.

Maggie screamed my name, but I couldn't move or speak.

My right arm was pinned underneath my chest, but my left arm was down at my side.

The dagger! The dagger Gareth had given me was tucked into the waistband of my jeans; the hilt was stabbing me in the hip. *If I can just reach the dagger!* I squirmed and twisted, reaching for the metal that was just out of reach.

My fingers were inches from the hilt when the Scavenger yanked me to the side and onto my back, what felt like claws digging into my shoulders. I screamed as the man's face came forward revealing a pair of round yellow eyes. He laughed, his breath hot on my cheek.

"Now, now, love. Don't be like that," he sneered, tracing the lines of my jaw with a grimy finger. "My God, you smell delicious." Inhaling deeply, he shoved his nose into my hair. I squealed and tried to pull away, my fingers still clawing for the weapon at my waist.

Over the man's shoulder, Maggie's face popped into view. Before I could scream at her to stop, Maggie let out a yell and launched herself on top of the man's back, pulling hair and kicking anything in reach.

I gasped under the weight of them both, and black spots appeared before my eyes.

The Scavenger was roaring as he swatted at Maggie while trying to keep me pinned beneath him. With an angry growl, he threw himself backward, sending Maggie flying through the air at an unnatural speed. She slammed into a car with a sickening thunk and collapsed on the ground. She did not get up. She didn't even move.

"Maggie!" I screamed, but the Scavenger slapped me hard across the face.

"Quiet! I've had enough of these games."

My cheek immediately began to burn and puff, and my eyes watered. There was a putrid smell of rotten meat stinging my nostrils, and as I tried to move, a snarl ripped through the air. Teeth grazed my skin, and I screamed.

When my eyes cleared, I found myself staring into the face of the largest wolf I'd ever seen. I screamed again.

Then the weight that was pressing me to the ground lifted, and large hands pulled me roughly to my feet. The man in the black hat gripped my arm so tightly I was sure it was going to break. His yellow eyes were glowing now, and his lips were curled up into a snarl revealing a row of sharp canines. *Lycan!* My mind supplied the word.

I tried to pull my arm out of his grasp, but the man growled, tightening his grip. With my other hand free, I yanked the dagger from my waistband and, with the last bit of strength I had, rammed it into his gut.

Blood sprayed from the wound, and the Scavenger screamed, releasing me.

Circulation returned to my arm, and I cried out from the pain of it. I staggered backward, clutching the bloody dagger in my hand. The Scavenger was doubled over, his hand clenching at the wound as blood ran down his fingers.

The dagger was shaking in my hand, but I gripped it tighter and lunged at the Scavenger, angling it upward toward his throat.

The tip was inches from driving home when the Scavenger twisted at the last second, the dagger slicing his cheek and jawline instead.

With a roar, he leapt at me. One hand clamped around my throat while the other pried the dagger from my fingertips. He tossed it on the ground and roared again, rivulets of blood dripping down his face. The gash, from hairline to jaw, was deep, but looked like it was already beginning to heal.

"Stupid bitch!" he spat, both hands now at my throat. He growled and pressed his fingers deeper into my skin. I clawed at his hands, desperate for air. My chest was on fire, and I couldn't see anything but a swirl of black and red.

Just as I was about to lose consciousness, I heard a warlike cry, and Ty was there, his face contorted with rage. He slammed into my captor, driving his fist into the man's face. There was a loud crunch, followed by another spray of blood that spattered over my face. The Scavenger screeched in pain and released me. I dropped to the ground like deadweight, choking and coughing.

Ty leapt on the man's back and wrapped his arms around the Scavenger's head, entrapping him in a tight headlock. The man was transforming again, his features snarling and snapping. But then it was over—the muscles in Ty's arms tensing as he jerked the Scavenger's head to the side with a sickening snap.

The body hit the ground. The body of another Scavenger, the one with short hair, lay a few feet away. The third was nowhere to be seen. Ty was panting, and blood poured from the split knuckles on one of his hands. Another trail of blood dripped down his face from a cut above his eyes, but that appeared to be his most serious injury.

I was frozen on the ground, numb and unable to move.

"Lainey?" Ty knelt down, inching toward me the way one would approach a wounded animal. He reached out a hand. "It's over now."

His fingertips grazed my cheek, and I launched myself at him, nearly knocking him over.

He groaned, but wrapped his arms around me, holding me tightly. "I've got you."

The warmth of his skin and the beating of his heart beneath my cheek brought tears to my eyes. I blinked them away, but gripped him tighter.

I closed my eyes, only to jerk them open a second later. "Maggie!" I wrenched myself away from Ty and stumbled to where Maggie lay unmoving in the grass.

"Maggie, can you hear me?" I tried to shake her awake.

"Looks like she hit her head," Ty said, examining her.

"Will she be okay?"

"I think so, but we should get her somewhere she can rest." He gingerly scooped Maggie into his arms. "Come on, before anyone notices us."

I picked up my dagger, wiping it on the grass, and followed Ty.

People were starting to flood the parking lot. Given the general scene of mayhem that surrounded the corn maze, no one had seemed to witness the fight in the parking lot. My head was pounding and my limbs were like lead, but I forced myself to focus on Ty's back, to keep moving.

By the time we made it to the car, my last ounce of energy had evaporated, and I slumped against the cool metal of the door, gripping the handle to keep from toppling over. After laying Maggie in the backseat, Ty helped me inside and ran around to throw himself into the driver's seat, slamming the keys into the ignition. The back tires squealed on the gravel road as he tore out of the parking lot and onto the dark road.

My eyelids drooped despite my best efforts, and the gentle hum of the engine and the movement of the car as it sped down the road were making it difficult to stay awake. Every cell in my body was depleted, and even though I knew we weren't out of the woods yet, the only thing I could focus on was how much I wanted to close my eyes. Instead I forced my mind to go through the ordeal again, frame by frame. Now that the shock was wearing off, the details were crystal clear.

"He got away, didn't he?" I finally asked. "The third Scavenger."

"Yes," Ty answered, his voice strained. "He was a Shifter, and he kept changing form. I thought I had him, but then that one in the hat had his hands on you and I . . ." His cheeks turned pink. I wasn't sure if it was from embarrassment or guilt.

"We're alive," I said, reaching over to squeeze his shoulder. "*That's* what matters here, okay?"

Ty nodded, but the muscles in his back were still tight under my hand.

"We should probably get off the main road," he said, his eyes flitting to the surrounding area. "He may still be tracking us."

"What about Maggie? Should we take her to the hospital?"

"Serena's place is probably safer." Ty leaned over and trailed a gentle finger down my sore neck. "Too many questions at a hospital."

I nodded, but a thought struck me and I gasped. "Serena!"

"What?"

I didn't answer. I pulled my purse into my lap and starting digging around for my cell phone. "Why didn't Serena warn us that the Scavengers were so close? Her vision would've changed, right?" I glanced over at Ty, whose face had paled.

"Yes," he answered. "She would've seen it. So why didn't she call?"

I stared at the phone in my hand. "She did."

I flipped the phone over so he could see the screen. Twenty-five missed calls. "I must have accidentally put it on silent," I whispered as a feeling of dread washed over me, but then an icon in the top left-hand corner of the phone caught my attention. "She left voice mails."

With a shaky hand, I pressed the voice mail button and placed the phone against my ear. The first few voice mails were what I expected, Serena urging me to call her back. But as the voice mails progressed, Serena's tone grew more and more frantic. By the time I got to the last one—left only a few moments ago—I felt like I was going to throw up.

I listened carefully and hung up the phone.

"What did she say? Lainey, what is it?"

I gripped my cell phone tightly as though it were the only thing keeping me anchored to earth. "The vision changed," I whispered, my voice eerily calm. "Serena saw me die."

❧ ✦ ☙

"I still think we should take you to the hospital."

Maggie plucked a fresh ice pack from the table and applied it gingerly to the knot on the back of her head. "No way. I'm fine. Just a bad headache. I promise, I'm okay."

"You really scared me back there," I said, trying not to yell. "What were you thinking? Jumping on that guy's back like that, huh? He could've killed you!"

"He could've killed *you*. I wasn't going to let that happen." Maggie reached over and squeezed my hand. "We're in this together, remember?"

"Like Batman and Robin?"

Maggie grinned. "See? Now you're catching on, Styles."

I reached over and hugged Maggie's shoulders. "Seriously, though, if you do that again, you might just find a few of your precious comic books with pages missing."

"You wouldn't!"

"Wanna bet?" I smiled but fixed my eyes on Maggie's face. "Maggie, you have to promise me that you won't take unnecessary risks me for me, okay? Things are going to get dangerous—more than they already have been. I don't want you getting hurt."

"You're not getting rid of me that easily."

I started to protest, but Maggie clamped a hand over my mouth. "Like I said, you're my best friend, Lainey, and we do this together. I'll be more careful, I promise."

"I know you will, but it's not a good idea. If something happens to—"

"*Together,* Styles. Batman and Robin. You and me." Maggie's face was set in a determined line, and I'd seen that look before—I was more likely to convince a mule to take a bubble bath than talk Maggie into leaving.

"Fine. Batman and Robin." I sighed. "Now, will you please lie back and try to rest?"

Maggie snorted. "We both know there's no time for that." She peered around my shoulder where the sound of heated discussion was coming from the office in Serena's shop. "What have I missed?"

"A whole lot of nothing. If you're feeling all right, you should join us."

"I'm guessing we still don't have a plan."

"No. All we've really managed to do is argue back and forth about what we should do next." I wiped my face with my hand, kneading at the tension in my temple. "Despite the visions, Serena thinks the Master still doesn't know I exist, but she said the power I used at the carnival is enough to raise suspicion. The third Scavenger got away; he will have reported back to the Master by now. We need to act now."

"But it's not like the Scavenger knows who or what you are."

"No, but he has my scent. The Master is cunning. It won't take long for him to figure out that there's another DuCarmont witch to contend with. He *will* come for me. I think it's just a matter of when at this point." I sighed. "Serena is spooked enough. She thinks we should go into hiding." The words settled in the pit of my stomach like rocks, and I frowned. "We can't get in touch with Gareth. I keep calling, but his phone goes straight to voice mail. It's freaking Serena out—that and her vision."

"Well, what do you want, Lainey?"

I stopped chewing on my bottom lip and stared at Maggie. "I . . . I don't know."

"I think you do," Maggie said. "You're just afraid to say it out loud."

I shrugged. "I'm absolutely terrified of what the future might hold for me . . . But I keep thinking about Josephine, and my mother, and all of the other Keepers who came before me. They didn't run." I looked down at my hands and took a deep breath. "I don't want to run either. I'm through with being afraid and refusing to accept that this is my destiny. When I saw what the Master did to Josephine . . . it sparked something inside of me. I'm afraid . . . but I'm more afraid of failing myself."

I reached for Maggie's hands, needing her to believe it too. "And I know this is right. I can't walk away from this."

"That's my girl, Styles." Maggie grinned at me. "So what now?"

I bit down on my lip again. "I think I have a plan. But it's absolutely crazy and it probably won't work."

Maggie scoffed. "You know, I think *all* great ideas are a little crazy."

I cracked a smile and helped Maggie up from the couch. "Come on."

We walked arm in arm to the office where Serena and Ty were still arguing.

"I have a plan," I said, interrupting the conversation. Ty and Serena turned to face me. "I know what we need to do."

"What we need is to get you someplace safe," Serena said. "Something's wrong. The vision I had . . ." She shook her head as if to shake the image from her thoughts. "I promised Gareth I'd look after you while he's gone. We need to get you far away from here."

"No."

"What?" Serena stared at me.

"I said no. I'm not going to hide, Serena. It doesn't matter where we go, or how long we run. Eventually the Master will find me."

Ty reached over and grabbed my hand. "You know we'll protect you, Lainey. *I* will protect you. No one will hurt you."

"I know," I said softly, "but I'm not gonna run from this. I know who . . . *what* you are, Ty, but you can't protect me from my destiny. I'm not going to let you or Serena or *anyone* hide me away from the world again." I took a breath, my voice stronger now. "I've always wanted to find out who I really am, to go out and see the world, to make my own discoveries—sure, it's not how I always pictured things to be, but this is it. This is *my* time."

I smiled at him, my own version of the half smirk he was always flashing me. "Besides, once the Master figures out who I am, he'll never stop hunting me. I refuse to spend my life hiding." I took a deep breath, bolstering my courage. "Therefore . . . I propose an alternative."

Serena looked uncertain. "But Gareth said—"

"Let her talk," Maggie said, moving to stand beside me. "It should be Lainey's call."

I squeezed Maggie's hand. "It's simple, really. If the Master gets ahold of me, he'll force me to unlock the Grimoire, right? For the spell Lane DuCarmont stole from him?"

Serena nodded. "Yes. The dark magic has made him incredibly vulnerable. He needs that spell."

"Well, isn't it obvious, then?" I couldn't stop the grin from forming on my face. "We have to steal back the book."

Serena's laugh made me jump. "You're joking, right?" When I didn't respond, her smile faded. "Lainey, you can't be serious. Stealing the Grimoire from the Master? It's suicide. He'd kill us all."

"The way I see it, if the Master unlocks that spell, we're dead anyway. We can't just sit back and hope he never finds me. He may have already figured out some other way to unlock the Grimoire. Some other form of black magic, for all we know." I moved to Serena and grabbed her by the shoulders.

"If that spell is the one thing that's keeping the Master from completely conquering the Supernatural realm, then we can't let him have it. We'll steal the book and destroy it. He'd never get the power he needs."

Serena shook her head. "It's not that simple. You can't just destroy the Grimoire. It's infused with generations of DuCarmont magic. The effort alone would kill you."

"Well, we'll hide it, then," I said. "Put it someplace that he can never find it. As long as the Master possesses the Grimoire, I'll never be free to live my life, and there's a good chance he'll figure out some other way to open it. If the Master gets ahold of that spell . . ."

"He'd be unstoppable," Serena whispered. "More powerful than anything our world has ever known."

"So don't you see? Stealing the book is the only way."

"But Lainey, you'd be putting a target on your back. Gareth would never agree to this."

"Gareth's not here. I'm deciding this. Besides, I already have a target on my back. I'm the last DuCarmont Keeper, and it's my job to guard that book. My mother died protecting it, and now the job belongs to me. I have to get it back. My death is . . ."—I let out a breath—"inevitable."

Serena flinched away at my words, but I gripped her tighter. "You've *seen* it. If I do die, I want to know I died fulfilling my destiny. Or at least giving it my best shot."

"We're not sentencing you to death just yet, Lainey," Ty said, his voice low and serious. "The vision can change."

"I hope you're right, but if it doesn't, I need to know

I've done everything in my power to keep the Master from getting his hands on that spell. Or else Josephine, the others, my mother—everything they have done has been in vain." I stood a little taller. "I'm the Keeper, and I'm going to get that book back."

Ty's eyes were pulsing with gold—his Praetorian senses on high alert. "Lainey," he said, "we can find another way."

I reached for his hand. "You told me that I have a choice in all of this. That I'm the one who chooses my own path, my own destiny." I gave him a small smile. "Ty, this is what I choose. Are you with me or not?"

He stared at me for several long moments. Then, with a deep breath, he nodded, leaning forward to whisper in my ear. "My hands, my blade, and my life. Yours."

I squeezed his hand. "Thank you."

"We're really going to do this?" Serena asked, sinking down onto the couch. "I don't know. I don't think this is a good idea. Gareth—"

She looked at me, her eyes wide as she choked on the words.

Then all sound cut off from her throat, and her entire body went rigid.

"What's happening?" Maggie asked, her voice shaky.

"I think she's having a vision," I said, my own heart pounding in my chest. I reached for her, but Ty held me back.

"Don't touch her," he said. "It can be dangerous to interrupt a Seer's Sight. All we can do is wait for it to pass."

I nodded, and we all stood frozen, waiting for Serena to come back to us.

CHAPTER TWENTY-EIGHT

S erena shot up from the couch.

It startled Maggie and me so much we both jumped, butting heads. "Ow," she mumbled, as I moved over to Serena. I rubbed the throbbing pain in my temple but didn't comment.

"Serena! Are you okay? What did you see?"

Her face was pale, but life danced in her eyes. "I didn't think it was possible," she said, propping herself up on the pillow. "We heard whisperings and rumors, but we never thought—" She laughed then, covering her mouth as tears sprang up in her eyes.

I stared at her, wondering what in the world she was talking about. Ty and Maggie looked equally puzzled.

"Um . . . Serena?"

"Sorry," she said, wiping the tears from her eyes. "Let me

explain. You see, no one's been able to confirm it, but I Saw it myself. Just now. The Hetaeria has gathered."

The painting Gareth had shown me what felt like years ago popped up in my mind. The faction leaders, the balance keepers, *the Hetaeria*.

"But . . ." I was confused. "But I thought the Master destroyed the Hetaeria."

Serena nodded. "He did, and for thousands of years the factions have lived in fear of what another alliance might cost us, but I *saw* them, Lainey. Supernaturals who are no longer afraid, who are willing to fight. Don't you see? This is the answer."

I shook my head, but before I could speak, she leaned forward and gripped my hands. "We need some sort of plan to steal the Grimoire, right? In my vision, I heard the leaders of the Hetaeria talking about a Gathering."

"A Gathering?" The word in this context was unfamiliar to me.

"The Master likes to throw extravagant parties as a way to reward his followers and flaunt his power to anyone who would dare oppose him," Ty answered. "He throws one every few months."

"The Hetaeria must be planning some kind of coup or takedown. We can ally with them. They'll help us, I know they will." Serena ran a hand over her excited face. "If we can rendezvous with them at the Gathering, they can help us find the Grimoire. They have far more resources at their disposal, and we wouldn't be going in blind." She was smiling now, her eyes bright.

"Can't we just call them?" Maggie asked. "It seems to me that the best plan is to avoid showing up at the Gathering at all if it's possible. The Master wants Lainey. If we can get to the Grimoire without putting Lainey at risk, then—"

"No," Serena said. "It's too dangerous to try to reach out to them, through human channels or otherwise. If the Master gets wind of this . . ." The little color that had returned to her cheeks drained away. "No, our best plan is to go to the Gathering and try to find the Hetaeria before the Master finds us first."

I swallowed, trying to wrap my head around the plan. "But how?"

"I don't know," Serena said, wringing her hands. "But if we're to have any shot at finding the Grimoire, stealing it, and getting out alive, we'll need the Hetaeria's help."

"The Scavenger will have reported to the Master by now," Ty argued. "If he attends the Gathering and catches Lainey's scent—"

"We won't need long. I saw their faces," Serena said. "If we can just get into that room, I can find them. I know I can." She looked at me, her expression fierce. "It's what Gareth would say if he were here. He wouldn't want us to do this alone."

I sighed. It was exactly the type of thing Gareth would insist on. I pulled out my phone and stared at the screen. Still no calls or messages. *Where are you, Gareth?*

"You're right," I said, ignoring the voice inside my head

that was screaming how absurd the whole thing was. "Finding the Hetaeria is our best chance of getting out alive. So now we just need a plan. We'll have to sneak into the Gathering and figure out some why to buy us time in case the Scavenger is hanging around. Any ideas?"

Silence fell over the room. It was almost comical how quiet the room became—I could practically hear crickets chirping.

I was trying to decide whether to laugh or burst into hysterics when Maggie stood up suddenly, a wide grin on her face.

"I've got it!" She laughed and did a little dance. "Mystique!" She held out her arms and waited as if she had just told us some gigantic secret of the universe.

When we all stared at her blankly, she rolled her eyes and placed her hands on her hips.

"Seriously? You guys have *got* to read more comic books."

CHAPTER
TWENTY-NINE

My hands were shaking. I swore under my breath and considered throwing the necklace—and its pesky clasp—against the wall.

"Here, let me." Serena came up behind me and nimbly fastened the necklace around my neck. The jeweled pendant came to rest at the base of my throat, right above the sweetheart neckline, and helped hide the ugly, yellow-purple bruises coloring my skin—my parting gift from the Scavenger.

She smiled at me, an approving glint in her eye. "You look lovely. Gareth . . ." Her voice wavered. "Gareth would be so proud." She smiled again, but I could see the worry she was trying to hide.

"Hey," I said, squeezing her hand, "I'm sure he's fine. He's probably just not somewhere he can call." It was the same thing I'd been telling myself for days. I hoped it sounded more reassuring to Serena than it did to me.

"I know." Serena sniffled. "I just wish I could See him." She was quiet for a moment, her forehead scrunched. "It never occurred to me to be annoyed with my Sight until now—how little control I have." She huffed, her fists clenching. "Just one glimpse, that's all I want."

"I know, but we have to stay focused." I gave her what I hoped was a calm, reassuring smile. "After this is all over, we'll find him, okay?" I had no idea where my motivation was coming from, but I wasn't going to question it. I had a feeling I'd need it. An undercurrent of nerves vibrated beneath my skin, but I forced the feeling away.

Serena sighed then, but offered me a small smile. "Right." She waved her hand. "Well, you do look lovely, you know."

I understood her need to change the subject, so I didn't press the issue. "Thank you," I said, tugging at the neckline of the dress, "but I'd feel a whole lot more comfortable in jeans."

The dress itself was stunning: the deep emerald color of the gown brought out the hue in my eyes, and the beaded waistline that sat below the fitted lace bodice gave me more of a shape than my usual t-shirts and hoodies. The full skirt, layered with tulle, swished around my ankles. It was the most beautiful garment I'd ever put on, but I was showing way more skin that I was used to, and it made me feel too exposed, too vulnerable.

"That makes two of us," Serena said, looking ill at ease in her elegant white gown compared with the eccentric pat-terned skirts she usually wore. She clutched absently at her chest, her fingers searching for the blue lace agate medallion that usually hung from her throat.

"How'd we let her talk us into those again," I grumbled, pointing to the heels Maggie had insisted complemented our dresses, though I thought they looked more like strappy torture devices.

Serena eyed the shoes and grimaced. "It's Maggie. We didn't really have a choice in the matter."

"Right," I said with a laugh. "What was I thinking?"

We smiled at each other, and for a moment it felt good, normal even to be joking around with Serena. It was almost too easy to pretend that we weren't standing on a precipice— hell, hanging off it, really—with more than just one life at stake. My smile faded.

We'd arrived in Savannah that morning. The fact that the Gathering was taking place only a few hours from home wasn't lost on me—the Scavenger had no doubt reported my power to the Master.

I'd always imagined myself leaving Lothbrook and moving somewhere where adventures would find me. Savannah, with its beautiful architecture, tall, billowing live oaks, and rich history, was exactly the type of place I could see myself. With the Gathering only an hour away, however, all I could think about was how much I wished we were all safe and heading back home to simple little Lothbrook, where nothing ever happens.

I sighed. *Things are never going to be the same again.*

I looked at Serena, who was adjusting her hair in the

mirror. "So, tell me about the Gatherings." I'd already grilled her multiple times over that very topic, but I needed to distract myself. "Why so formal? Are they always like this?"

"Usually. The Master likes luxury, and he chooses to lavishly reward those who have remained loyal to him."

"But not every guest is loyal. The majority of the guests are forced to attend, right?"

"Yes. It's a show of power," Serena said. "I guess you could say the Master has a flair for the dramatic. If you're going to terrorize people, you might as well do it in top hat and tails, or in our case, at a masquerade ball."

The whole thing sounded grotesque and utterly terrifying. I thought of our plan, and my nerves responded by clenching into a ball that sank like a rock in the pit of my stomach. I shivered, her words like ice down my back.

"It's okay to be afraid, you know," she said, reading the expression on my face. "I'd be worried if you weren't."

I sighed. "I know, but . . . if we fail . . . if something happens to you or Maggie or—"

"We've gone into this of our own volition, Lainey. You can't shoulder the responsibility if something goes wrong."

"How could I not? We're in this mess because of me."

Serena gave me a hug, squeezing me tightly. "You're so much like your mother. She was always worried about everyone but herself." She gave me a warm smile. "You have her spirit."

I swallowed, the lump in my throat growing bigger. I couldn't think about my mother right now; I had to focus. I cleared my throat and gently pulled away from Serena. "Let's just hope I don't get anyone killed tonight."

"Lainey—"

"You ready?" I plastered a smile on my face and checked my hair one last time. "I think it's time."

Serena's expression was guarded. I could tell there was more that she wanted to say, but she nodded, linking her arm through mine. Arm in arm, we walked into the adjoining room.

Ty was standing next to the window in a black suit, but instead of a white shirt, he had opted for a black one, with a black silk tie to match. There was the tiniest bit of gel taming his hair, and he was smiling at me.

I blinked several times, all words having escaped me.

He smiled as he moved beside me. "You look beautiful," he said. His husky voice in my ear made me shiver.

"And what about me?" Maggie called from the open bathroom door. She waltzed toward us and did a little spin. Her dress was identical to the one I wore.

"You look so pretty, Maggie." I was being sincere, but the sight of Maggie in the same dress brought the logistics of our plan back to the forefront of my mind. We knew what we needed to do—find the Hetaeria and steal the Grimoire— but the Scavenger had my scent, and if he caught wind of it, our whole mission might be over even before it had a chance to begin. So we'd come up with a plan. Maggie called it "Operation Mystique"—fitting since the inspiration came from the blue-skinned shape-shifter from the X-men comics—and it involved confusing my scent with someone else's. A decoy. A fake Lainey.

Maggie had been more than eager to volunteer for the job, despite my objections. Options were limited, and I knew that. But knowingly putting my best friend in danger while I searched for the Hetaeria made my stomach pitch and roll.

"Stop it, Styles," Maggie said, noticing my frown. "I volunteered, remember."

"I know, but I don't like it." I looked to Serena. "Are we sure there's not another option?"

"Unfortunately not," Serena said, her face mirroring the worry I knew was written across mine. "The Scavenger will be present tonight. If we're to stay hidden as long as possible, we need to confuse his sense of smell. It will be harder to track two of you."

"I just can't stomach the idea of using my best friend as a decoy." I turned to Maggie. "You could get hurt."

Maggie rolled her eyes and placed her hands on her hips. "Batman and Robin, remember?"

"It only has to work long enough for us to find the Hetaeria," Ty said, reaching over to still my trembling hands.

With his reminder and Maggie's determined face, I knew there was no way I would win that argument. "Fine," I grumbled. "Let's just get this over with."

Serena nodded. "Join hands, please."

Maggie grinned excitedly and grabbed my hands.

"Gareth would've been better at this," Serena said, pulling a small vial from her purse, "but the Sage I bought this from promised me it was genuine, and Sages are usually trustworthy."

"Usually?"

She grimaced at me. "Usually."

Sprinkling the contents into her hands, she walked around us murmuring under her breath. I did not understand what she was saying but recognized that she must be speaking in some sort of Fae tongue. As she walked faster, she raised her hands, and Maggie's countenance began to shimmer. Her features began to distort and change: her thick curls began to grow and straighten, and her lovely, rich brown skin lightened, turning fair beige. Her tall frame shrank a few inches. It was really strange to watch, so eventually I closed my eyes, still feeling uneasy about the whole thing.

I felt the hum of magic around us, felt it vibrate within me. When it faded, I heard a murmur of approval from Ty. "It's done," Serena said.

When I opened my eyes, my own face was staring back at me.

"Well?" The face might have been my own, but the voice still belonged to Maggie.

"The glamour worked." Serena passed her a handheld mirror. "It won't last for more than a few hours, but it should buy us the time we need."

"This is so cool." Maggie was gingerly prodding her new face with her fingertips.

Ty checked the clock on the wall. "We should go."

I sucked in a deep breath. There was no turning back now.

"Okay. Let's do it."

ᪿ • ᪿ

There was a slight breeze coming off the Savannah River, and the low-hanging Spanish moss swayed back and forth like a flag. It wasn't cold, but I was shivering just the same. The planation home in the distance looked like something out of *Gone with the Wind,* with its wraparound porch and tall, wide columns. The place was illuminated with the golden hue of candlelight, and the air around the house seemed to twinkle like fireflies. It was chilling how something so picturesque could cloak such evil. It reminded me of Lily of the Valley—lovely, yet deadly to all who came near.

I clutched Ty's arm and tried to focus on keeping myself upright in my heels, the brick walkway an adequate distraction from the dread that threatened to choke me.

The sidewalks leading up to the main entrance and the lush front lawn were cluttered with people in formal wear. Laughter filled the air, and I reached up to make sure my mask was still in place.

There was every variety of dress and fabric, all in varying colors with matching masks. Small pockets of guests were laughing and mingling among themselves, but the majority of the line waiting to enter was eerily somber. It reminded me of a viewing at a funeral.

At the door, several men in tuxedos stood guarding the

entrance. They were checking each guest's name against the master list of guests.

"Warlocks," Ty whispered in my ear. "Training with the Master."

Our first obstacle.

I ground my teeth, feeling my nerves crackle under my skin.

When it was our turn at the door, Serena and Maggie sidled up to the two men not holding the list and began inquiring about the plantation house, the Gathering, anything to keep them occupied. I pushed my shoulders back and bolstered my courage. "The Lady Seraphine, her brother, Maxwell, and their guests," I said grandly, with a lilting accentuation on my words. I hoped the fake names sounded less false to the doorkeeper than they did to me. *Please let this work.*

The warlock stared at me with narrowed eyes for a few seconds but then bent to check his list. "You're not on the list," he said curtly, turning his head to the other men.

"Could you please check again?" I asked quickly. I needed to keep his attention on me. I batted my eyelashes and placed a hand on the warlock's forearm. "I would be so grateful." I smiled warmly.

The man huffed and bent to check again. Ty took a slight step forward, angling his back, shielding the man from the view of the other warlocks and the other guests awaiting entrance. He spoke softly, reading off a piece of paper Serena had written out for him, and when the man looked up from the list, I blew a bit of shimmering dust into his face.

"Your name's not—" The man's face grew comically blank before returning to his normal scowl. "Your name's here. Go on in."

I wanted to whoop in excitement, but I smiled demurely and thanked him. He moved to let us pass through.

I noticed Ty looking at me. "What?" I asked him as we stepped through the doors.

He was grinning at me, his smile sitting crookedly on his lips. "I would be so grateful," he intoned, doing a perfect imitation of my horrible accent. Then he batted his eyelashes, almost making me snort.

I smacked him in the chest. "I never claimed to be any good at flirting."

"You did quite well, I think." He winked at me, and the tips of my ears grew hot.

We followed the crowd down a long hall until we hit a wide foyer with a large winding staircase at one side and pair of double doors open to the ballroom on the other.

When I stepped through the doors, I sucked in a breath. I'd never seen a more beautiful room. The walls were covered with a lush, pale-golden tapestry, the swirling lines of the fabric mirroring the design of the building. The ceiling wasn't vaulted, but it made up for the lack in black tiles dotted with tiny white lights, giving the illusion of a star-filled sky. Candles and crystal vases adorned the tables that were set up sporadically throughout the room, and the air smelled sweet, fragrant from the white roses that decorated the space.

There was a small orchestra playing softly in the corner, and the wide dance floor was already spotted with a handful of couples spinning across the floor.

When the room was nearly full, the conductor silenced the orchestra. Almost at once, the room grew silent in anticipation. The whole atmosphere of the room had shifted, like a drop in temperature. I blew out a breath, half expecting to see it as a puff of frozen air.

There was a slight commotion as one pair of double doors opened grandly. Standing on my tiptoes, I craned my neck to see what was happening, but my view was blocked by a group of men in tuxedos.

Then I saw him.

"The Master."

CHAPTER THIRTY

My heightened nerves prickled in the base of my spine, and my heartbeat pounded in my ears.

He doesn't look a day older than I am, I thought to myself with a mixture of awe and confusion. He looked exactly the way he had in Josephine's visions. I knew Supernaturals had a longer life span, yet I still half expected to see a stooped old man, not the strong, youthful man in front of me.

His slick-back hair was black, and his tawny face was sharp with angles. His gray eyes were cold and unfeeling. It was a cruel face—though an admittedly handsome one—and though he was the host, the Master seemed to have no notion of warmly greeting his guests. He made his way from the far end of the ballroom, wearing a crisp black suit. His shirt, however, was blood red.

Uncertainty, fear, and nervous anticipation seemed to hang in the air, and it was as if the whole room held in a collective breath as he made his way to a plush, high-backed chair placed in the front of the room. When he was seated, he waved a hand and sneered at the crowd. "Dance."

That single word seemed to reverberate throughout the room, and the crowd shifted so fast it was as if the word he'd uttered was "stampede."

Before I had time to get out of the way, I was engulfed by a crowd of couples, practically running to take their place on the polished floor.

Behind me, Maggie hissed my name. I reached for her, but my fingertips met nothing but air as I was shoved into an open spot on the dance floor.

The strain of music floated through the air, and I glanced around trying to find a way off the floor that wouldn't draw much attention. There didn't seem to be an easy escape route. The Master's face was trained on the sea of couples, his roving eyes scrutinizing each one.

I couldn't move. My heart was hammering in my chest; I was certain those around me could hear it over the music.

As the couples began to move, a tall figure glided in front of me, his hand extended. The familiar blue eyes immediately slowed my heart.

"Ty," I breathed, placing my hand in his.

His face was serious as he draped the other arm around my waist, pulling me close.

"I can't dance," I whispered, as panic of a different kind washed over me.

"I've got you," Ty whispered back, his voice husky in my ear. "Just look at me."

His words wrapped around me, his fingertips gentle against my skin. "I've got you," he whispered again, his words as soft and as warm as a caress. He led me backward, one slow step at a time, and we began to glide across the floor in the gentle rhythm of the music.

We didn't speak, didn't smile, but as he pulled me closer, his deep voice humming along to the melody, I was floating.

The music swelled, and we moved together, two leaves twirling in an autumn wind, while the rest of the world melted away. There was nothing but the beating of both our hearts.

"Lainey," Ty whispered, as the music began to slow. His breathing was uneven, and his eyes were blazing. He pressed his forehead against mine and pulled me closer. I couldn't speak; I was lost in the sea blue of his eyes, so full of emotion I couldn't name it.

Then he pressed his lips against mine, and something within me ignited, burning through me—something new, forever forged in the flames.

When the sound of applause shattered the stillness around us, we broke apart, both of us breathless.

We stared at each other, frozen in place, as new couples were moving onto the dance floor to replace those returning to their seats.

"We should probably head back," I whispered.

Ty nodded and tore his eyes away from my face. He reached for my hand, and I saw his shoulders rise with an inaudible sigh.

I led him off the dance floor to where Serena and Maggie were waiting, seated inside a small, dark alcove.

My face was hot as I sat down beside Maggie. It was strange seeing my own face, but the smirk it wore was entirely Maggie.

"What?" I asked.

"*That* wasn't part of the plan," she said, grinning.

My cheeks burned, and I swatted at her, not knowing what to say. I leaned back against the cushioned seat and hoped the shadows hid the flush I felt covering every inch of my exposed skin. Ty glanced over at me, his eyes locking on mine in the darkness. There was so much to say, but neither of us said a word. My cheeks blazed even hotter.

"I think it's time," Serena said, standing up. "We should split up now."

The music was building, and dancers were swirling across the floor. Waiters were busy bringing hor d'oeuvres and trays of sparkling drinks to the various tables, and more and more people seemed to be milling about. Despite the tension that still lingered in the air, the room had relaxed into a milder atmosphere. If there was any hope of finding the Hetaeria, now was the time to start looking.

I leaned forward, sneaking a peek at the Master. A line of servers in white uniforms promenaded toward him, presenting trays of delicacies. He sneered at each of them before selecting a tall glass of red wine and waving the others away. A trio of Guards wearing masks stood behind him at attention, ready and waiting.

I stared at the Master, trying to read his face, but there was nothing but a pair of cold, calculating eyes. My hands shook as I reached up to make sure my mask was still firmly in place.

I nodded. "Okay, let's do this." I stood up and adjusted my dress, trying to ignore the waves of nausea rolling around in my stomach. If something were to go wrong . . .

"None of that, Styles," Maggie said, reaching for my hands. "I know what you're thinking. Everything is going to work out exactly we planned."

I sighed. "You don't know that."

Maggie nodded. "You're right, I don't know, but I'm choosing to believe that it will. You should do the same." She squeezed my hands. "Besides, it's simple really. Ty and I will walk around and try to get some clue as to the Grimoire's whereabouts, while you and Serena find the Hetaeria. Easy peasy."

I rolled my eyes. "Yeah, but only a hundred things could go wrong. Like the Scavenger, for example."

Maggie waved her hand. "That's what I'm here for, re-member? If he does catch your scent, it will be much harder to sniff out two of us." She beamed at me, confidence shining in her eyes.

I wrapped my arms around her with a laugh. "Please, just promise me you'll be careful."

"Don't worry about me, Styles. I'll make like Barry Allen and be back in flash—you can count on it." Maggie hugged me tightly and pulled back with a smile. "You be careful too. Find the Hetaeria."

"I will, I promise."

Maggie moved over to Serena, and Ty stepped in front of me. His face was serious, but there was a storm swirling in his eyes. "I'll keep her safe," he said.

"I know, just keep yourself safe too, okay?"

With a nod, he turned toward Maggie as if to go, but then turned back to me, closing the gap between us. "Lainey, I . . ." He trailed off, running a hand up to squeeze the back of his neck. He let out a deep breath, and instead of speaking, he reached for one of my hands and then gently placed it across my chest. My own heart pulsed against my fingertips.

"You feel that?" Ty asked. His eyes were flashing, and there was a desperation in his face that I didn't understand. I managed to nod.

"It's the one thing he can't take away from you." Ty leaned forward, his forehead touching mine. "Do you understand?"

I squeezed my eyes shut, knowing it wasn't my mortality he was speaking of. I was consumed with fear and doubt, but every beat of my heart was a reminder of something so much stronger. Goodness. Courage. Strength. Determination. *Heart.*

We were dangling from the edge of a cliff, and in the moment before we hurled ourselves completely into the void, Ty had given me peace.

Tears sprang up in my eyes. I blinked them away as I lifted my head and met his gaze. "I understand."

He nodded, the tiniest trace of a crooked smile on his lips.

I watched as Ty and Maggie headed toward the orchestra, weaving in and out of the crowd until I could no longer see them.

Serena wrapped a hand around my arm. "You ready?"

"Ready as I'll ever be." I smoothed the front of my dress and stood a little taller. "Let's find the Hetaeria."

We moved through the room, sticking to the shadows. We linked elbows and giggled playfully to each other to give the appearance of two silly partygoers; all the while we were busily scanning the faces around us.

Serena had given me a vague description of the people we were looking for, but no one seemed to fit the description. Pockets of people dotted the room, but the masks and elaborate costumes made it difficult to see features clearly. There was a feeling of unease that permeated the room, and despite the facade of merriment many wore, the crowd seemed to be waiting for something to happen.

Shivers waltzed up and down my spine. *Don't think about that now. Focus on finding the Hetaeria.*

We'd stopped to accept a glass of sparkling cider from a waiter when Serena's hand flew to her temple. She let out a gasp and squeezed her eyes shut.

The waiter seemed startled, but I let out what I hoped was a realistic laugh and waved my hand. "Parties! Aren't they just exhilarating?" I didn't wait for a response before grasping Serena by the elbow and ushering her away from his wide eyes.

"What is it?" I hissed when we were out of earshot.

"A vision," she wheezed, surprise coloring her cheeks. "It's the Scavenger. He's here."

I whipped my head back and forth, but there were no familiar faces that I could see. "How much time do we have?"

"I don't know. But we need to move fast."

We continued canvasing the room. My heart was pounding, and worry pulsed through me in time with the music. Serena kept whispering words of encouragement in my ear, but I could tell from her faltering smile that she was every bit as worried as I was.

What if we can't find them? What if the vision about the Hetaeria was wrong? What if the Scavenger catches up to us first? The voice inside my head was screaming. It took every ounce of strength I had to keep my face neutral.

"Breathe, Lainey," Serena whispered, feeling the tension in my limbs. "We'll find them."

But the more we searched, the more panicked I became. I felt like Cinderella, racing against the clock—except I doubted my story would end with a happily ever after. I walked with my hand pressed against my hammering heart, desperate to keep it from clawing its way out of my chest. *Deep breaths, Lainey. Just breathe,* I coached myself, ignoring the ranting inside my brain.

"Lainey," Serena said, pulling me to the side. "Over there." There was a large round table tucked behind a pillar. In the dim light of the room, it was difficult to see the faces of those sitting around the table, but there was one distinguishing feature that made my heart stop.

A woman with fiery red hair was facing us, her face hidden behind a large lace mask. The flame color of her hair was like a beacon in the darkness. It also matched the description that Serena had given me.

"Is that them?" I asked, watching as the red-haired woman caught my gaze and leaned over to whisper something to the gentleman next to her.

Serena's face was pale, and indecision seemed to be written all over it. She turned to me, her eyes blazing. "I can't be sure, but there's only one way to find out."

It was a risky move. If we exposed ourselves and our purpose to the wrong people, it wouldn't end well for us. Our whole plan would go up in smoke.

I squeezed Serena's hand. "Let's go." The clock was ticking; it was a risk we had no choice but to take.

We walked slowly toward the table. The red-haired woman nudged her counterpart, and they watched us from their seats, scrutinizing our movement the way a cat stalks its prey.

We were only a few feet away when a loud commotion broke through the peaceful melody of the orchestra. There was the sound of scuffling, a loud smack of skin against skin, and someone crying out. The crowd began to murmur, and the din of the ballroom rose as people craned their necks to see what was happening.

That cry sent a chill so deathly cold down my back that

my knees nearly gave way. Before my brain even had time to catch up, I was moving, pushing through the crowd. The crowd was beginning to clump, everyone trying to see what the fuss was about. I elbowed and shoved, trying to force my way through, but there were too many people in the way. I got stuck in a mass of people but could see the Master clear enough.

He looked irritated and waved his hand, the way one would swat at a fly. "Come forward," he said. The words were quiet, but they reverberated through the room as if he had shouted them.

Several guests near him flinched visibly. The crowd quieted and there was a mass shuffling from the people trying to get out of the way as a tall figure pushed toward the Master, dragging someone behind him.

My heart plummeted to the floor.

It was the Scavenger.

Though dressed in dark slacks and a white shirt, his clothing couldn't hide the layer of grime that covered his skin or detract from the greasy stringiness of his hair. His face was twisted in a triumphant grin. He yanked his arm forward, plucking his captive from the crowd and into the open space before the Master.

It was Maggie.

CHAPTER
THIRTY-ONE

I staggered backward, bumping into Serena. A scream rose in my throat, but her urgent voice hissed in my ear: "Don't. You'll only make it worse." Her fingertips wrapped around my arm, steadying me, but it was as if the room was spinning on its axis and I couldn't tell which way was up. I swallowed hard, forcing air into my lungs.

"Serena, we have to do something. We—"

Another cry from Maggie stopped me short.

The Scavenger had yanked Maggie by the wrist until she was standing in front of the Master. Rivulets of blood dripped from a wound on her left forearm, spotting the emerald dress she wore with crimson. The fear was plain on her face.

A pulse of electricity lanced through me. I didn't have to look down to know green lightning danced between my fingertips. The current pulsing through me was alive and ready. *I have to help her.* I stepped forward, welcoming the energy igniting inside me. *I have to save her.*

A strong yank on my arm made me stumble. Serena's mouth was set in a hard line, her eyes locked on mine.

"Serena?" I asked.

"I'm sorry, Lainey," she said, her grip firm. "I can't let you do that. I promised Gareth I'd keep you safe."

I shoved her hand away. "It's not your call to make." I glared at her, the anger fueling the fire that burned inside me. "I won't just stand here and do nothing. She's my best friend."

Serena opened her mouth to refuse me again, her hand already reaching up to latch onto me. I shoved her hard, and she stumbled backward, tottering on her tall heels. I pushed my way forward, as much as the crowd would allow. I reached for the energy inside me, but before I could act, a roar filled the ballroom.

"Let her go!" Ty pushed through the crowd. He wasn't wearing his suit jacket anymore, and there was a shoulder holster of long knives across his back. He rushed toward the Scavenger, his face twisted in fury. Then he turned slightly and bowed deeply to the Master. "My apologies, my Lord, but that woman belongs to me." He pulled one of the blades from the holster and pointed it at the Scavenger. "I do not mean to interrupt, but I intend to get back what is mine."

I let out a strangled cry, but the sound of it was lost in the cacophony of surprised gasps, squeals of alarm, and even laughter from the other guests.

The Scavenger looked surprised at first, but narrowed his

eyes and tightened his grip on Maggie's wrist. She winced. "What claim do you have on her?" He took a step forward, sniffing the air. "Oh, I see. You were there that night in the woods. You're the one who killed my brothers." The Scavenger opened his mouth and snarled, the feral sound echoing across the walls. The murmur of the crowd grew louder.

"You will return what is mine," Ty said coolly, slashing his blade through the air. The Scavenger jumped back.

There was surprised gasp from the crowd as Ty swung the knife again. The Scavenger shoved Maggie farther from reach and pulled a long dagger of his own from the inner folds of his shirt. He laughed, his features rippling between man and wolf.

They skirted around each other. The din of the crowd grew louder, an excited murmur pulsing though the observers. The sound of steel striking steel filled the ballroom. Ty moved like the wind, twisting and rolling, always out of the Scavenger's grasp. When he thrust an elbow into the Scavenger's face, there was a loud crunching sound and a spray of blood. The Scavenger stepped back holding his nose and howling. The crowd clapped in appreciation, but Ty stood stone-still, gripping his blade.

The Scavenger spit a mouthful of blood on the floor and then made a move to lunge at Ty.

"Enough." The command wasn't loud, but it cut through the room silencing the crowd and stopping the Scavenger. The Master rose from his chair, his eyes flicking back and forth between the two men. He beckoned the Scavenger forward.

"Explain yourself." His voice was cool, but there was steel in the undertone.

"My lord." The Scavenger dropped to a bow in front of his feet. "This is the witch I told you about, the one with more magic than I've tracked in years. I've brought her to you." He beckoned to the Guards, who brought Maggie toward them. Her face—*my* face—was streaked with tears, but she stood with her head held high, her back straight.

There wasn't the slightest bit of emotion in the Master's face as he walked around Maggie surveying her. "You are a fool and not worth the coin you think you deserve."

The Scavenger looked confused. "My lord?"

The Master sighed and then turned smiling to address the crowd. "Someone had been sampling too much wine, I think." There was a murmur of polite laughter from the crowd. He looked back at the Scavenger, but there was no amusement in his features. "Do you not know your own kind?" His voice wasn't loud, but it was full of venom and the Scavenger winced. "This girl isn't one of us. She is *human*."

"Human?" The Scavenger looked taken aback. "I swear it's her, my lord. Her scent. I . . . There must be some mistake."

"I do not make mistakes." The Master waved his hand across Maggie's face. Her features began to shimmer and distort as the glamour faded away. "Sage magic," he said simply, eyeing Maggie curiously.

The Scavenger dropped to his knees and began murmuring words of apology. His features blurred and his form flickered in and out—clearly a nervous habit.

The Master looked almost bored. "And now, you've interrupted a perfectly good party." He sighed and turned to the Guard nearest him. "Take this underling outside—I'll deal with him later."

The Guard bowed and dragged the Scavenger to the nearest exit. The double doors slammed shut behind them.

The Master swiveled on his heel and looked to Ty. "Your turn." He held out a hand, waiting for Ty's explanation.

"Thank you, my lord," Ty said. He nodded toward the door where the Scavenger had been taken. "That vagrant is nothing but a money-grubbing liar who would seek any opportunity to earn a coin or two. I know nothing of the witch he speaks of, but I do know that he planned to use her for his own purposes—to fool you and get revenge upon me."

The Master had settled back in his chair, but at the word "revenge," he leaned forward, interested.

"As he said," Ty continued, "I killed his comrades. They were trying to harm my . . . my . . . I have a thing for humans, my lord." He indicated Maggie. "That vile creature kidnapped her the minute my back was turned and planned to turn her over to you, disguising her with magic as a witch." Ty paused to bow graciously. "I do apologize for the interruption; however, I am glad to have been able to foil his subterfuge."

I'd managed to shove my way through the crowd far enough that I was only a few feet away from where Ty was standing. I stared at him standing there with a posture and formal manner of speaking that were entirely foreign to me. It was as if he had stepped into another time and place entirely.

I barely recognized him. Where was the boy with the half smile?

Fear and suspicions rolled around in my stomach, but I forced the feelings aside. *Everything will be fine. Ty will save Maggie, and we'll all make it out alive.* I had to believe it.

"I heard him boasting of the reward he anticipated for his treachery," Ty went on. "Everyone here knows that the clink of coin is the only language those dogs understand."

There was a murmur of agreement from the crowd, and even the Master nodded his head in accord. Pulses of fear and anxiety coursed through me with every rapid beat of my heart, and a thin sheen was forming on my skin. I forced myself to take a few deep breaths. I glanced at Maggie. She was on the floor near the Master's chair, her eyes narrowed on Ty. I could tell from the look on her face that she was as confused as I. *She doesn't know either.* Whatever Ty's plan was, he was the only one in on it. I turned my attention back to Ty.

The Master was regarding him. He wiped a hand across his brow. "I know you." He leaned forward. "What's your name, boy?"

"Tyler Marek, my Lord."

"Marek." The Master clapped his hands together. "Of course, now I remember. What was it? A year ago? Such a brooding, angry young man. Why, I hardly recognize you now. I see your training was effective."

Ty swallowed. "Most effective, my lord."

The words didn't make sense. My head was screaming at me, but my heart refused to acknowledge, to even consider the thoughts roaring inside my mind. Still hidden in the shadows of the crowd, I took a deep breath. *I have to trust him. I have to trust Ty.*

The crowd was growing restless. The murmur of voices grew louder.

"Peace, friends." The Master stood from his chair and held out his hand. "There's no need for discord." He turned to Ty. "Show them who you are."

With a slight inclination of his head, Ty yanked off his tie and unbuttoned the top few buttons of his shirt, which he pulled down to reveal a dark tattoo across his chest.

I knew that mark, had seen it before in my visions of Josephine.

"No," I whispered, shaking my head. *No.*

Two interlocking triangles that formed a capital M. It was the mark that denoted the Master's most loyal followers. The mark of the Guard.

"My name is Tyler Marek." He bowed his head in reverence. "I am one of yours, my lord."

CHAPTER
THIRTY-TWO

I cried out, a strangling sort of sound, and stared at the tattoo on Ty's chest. "No," I breathed. *Ty? Part of the Guard?* I didn't want to believe it, but the proof was there, inked across his skin. Flashes of heat flushed my skin, and I tore my gaze away as hot tears burned my eyes. *He's been working for the Master all this time.*

Pain ripped through the walls of my chest and ricocheted throughout my entire body. *Ty betrayed me.* Those three little words sliced right through me, and I glanced down expecting to see blood—the physical evidence of my internal agony. I choked down a sob.

"My apologies again, my lord, for the interruption to your party," Ty said with another bow. He moved toward Maggie. "Allow me to take the human to a more secure location until you are ready to deal with her." He took a step forward, straightening his shoulders. "I will personally see to it that she is . . . *looked* after." He grinned, a wild look in his eye. My stomach rolled, and I was sure I was going to vomit.

The Master seemed to consider this for a moment before rising to his feet. "There's something about you," he said to Ty. "You're far more civilized than most of the men in my Guard. I like that. Civility is all but lost these days."

A strange look flashed across Ty's face, but then it was gone behind his congenial smile once more. "My father was a gentleman, my lord. He taught me well."

The Master nodded, impressed. "I see."

Ty bowed his head again. "Thank you, my lord." He bent down and yanked Maggie to her feet. *My hands, my blade, and my life.* His words echoed in my thoughts, twisting my heart. Every word a lie.

"Where might I secure her, my lord?"

"Oh, that won't be necessary," the Master said, settling back into his seat. "After all, what's a party without a little . . . *entertainment?*"

"My lord?" Ty stared at him, not understanding.

The Master held up a hand, waving him off, and fixed his stare on Maggie. He cocked his head a little, amusement dancing in his eyes. "Come here, girl."

Maggie jerked her arm out of Ty's grasp and walked toward the Master, trying to keep her shoulders back and head held high. She was shaking all over, but it was obvious she was trying not to let her fear show.

"Such a pretty face," the Master mused, running a finger

across her cheek. "Yet the face you wore as a disguise . . . *that* is the face that interests me the most." He turned to the crowd, scanning the faces of the guests. "For you see, it belongs to someone I'm dying to know better."

Oh my God. My stomach turned inside out. *He knows who I am. He knows I'm here.* All of the planning, the details, everything we'd prepared for tonight was all for naught. Our plan was always going to fail.

I glared at Ty through angry tears. His face was void of all emotion, and he was standing at attention next to the Master. I directed all the malice and hatred I felt burning through me toward him. *I hate you. I hate you, Tyler Marek. I will never forgive you for this.*

It might have been wishful thinking, but I swore I saw him wince.

"You can come out now, love," the Master projected, his voice filling every inch of the ballroom. "There's no point in hiding from me."

What do I do? My feet were frozen to the floor and my head was spinning. *What do I do?*

"Oh, come now, there's no need to be shy." The Master took a step forward, his arms open. "No? Well, perhaps then you need a little motivation." He walked back to where Maggie was standing and reached for her hand. "I have no use for the human girl," he said, his features twisting into a vile grin. "But it *is* a party. Perhaps some of my men would appreciate a little company."

Several in the crowd murmured appreciatively as the Master flicked his wrist. One of the Guards moved to Maggie, pushing her toward the crowd.

"Stop!" I yelled, pushing my way through the crowd. "Leave her alone!"

The Master's face was positively gleeful. "Ah, yes. Come, my dear. I've been expecting you."

The Guard was still towing Maggie toward a group of men who were waiting, their expressions hungry.

Overhead, the lights flickered as a surge of magic rushed through me. "I said, leave her alone." I was surprised how strong my voice sounded as it carried through the room.

The Master grinned. "See? Was that so hard? I knew you wouldn't be able to resist. You witches and your code of goodness. A pity, really. You miss out on *so* much fun." He leaned in and smelled Maggie's hair. "Lovely. Yes, I can think of quite a few of my guests who would love a little . . . taste of this delectable flower, hmmm?"

My heart was pounding, and every nerve cell in my body was crackling with energy. "Leave her alone." The lights flickered again with another wave of power.

The Master leaned forward, his grin so wicked that my heart plummeted to my feet. "But what would the fun be in that?"

He motioned to the Guard who had seized Maggie by the shoulder, and he pushed her forward, the hands of the eager men waiting.

They pulled at her, an audible snap of jaws and competing

snarls filling the air. As the men's faces began changing into something more feral, Maggie's cry erupted in my ears, catapulting me into action.

"Stop it!" I screamed, throwing my hands out in front of me. A pulse of energy shot through my fingertips. It expanded, the hazy wave rippling forward and engulfing the men who held Maggie. With a whoosh of air and the crack of lightning, the men flew backward, landing unconscious on the ground. Maggie was left standing, and though her dress was torn and she was visibly trembling, she was otherwise unharmed—save for the wound on her arm that still dripped blood.

I sagged, exhausted from the magic still effervescing underneath my skin.

The sound of laughter and applause brought my attention back to the Master. His face was full of joy, and he was applauding me along with the stunned crowd. "Yes, that's more like it. But now, I'm being awfully rude. Come here, love, and tell my guests here who you are." He held an arm open as if to embrace me warmly.

When I hesitated, the Master snapped his fingers. "Marek. If you will, please."

Strong hands gripped my shoulders. I tore my gaze away from the Master and focused on the cold blue eyes staring into mine. Gone was the boy I had kissed in the rain, the one who had challenged me to a corndog-eating contest, who had danced with me like we were the only ones in the room. I didn't recognize this person at all.

I yanked myself out of his grip. "*Don't* touch me!" I sneered.

"Just do what he says, Lainey," Ty replied, his voice cold, void of any emotion. For a brief second, something flashed in his eyes, but as quickly as it had come, it was gone, replaced with nothing by empty promises and lies.

I hate you, Tyler Marek.

He reached for me again, his hand on my arm. I yanked it away, reared back, and spat in his face. "You can burn in hell," I said. My voice was strong, but my heart throbbed as I watched him merely reach up and wipe the spittle from his cheek.

The Master laughed. "My, aren't you a spirited one?" He leaned forward. "Come now, love. I haven't got all night."

Seeing as I had no choice in the matter, I walked toward him and allowed him to wrap his arm around me and pull me close. I swallowed the bile that rose in my throat.

"Lainey Sty—" I said, staring out into the crowd. "Lainey DuCarmont." Warmth bloomed inside me. It was the first time I'd claimed the name as my own. I smiled a little. *That one's for you, Jo.*

The crowd began to murmur, their whispers rising to an audible murmur of concern and confusion. The word "DuCarmont" began to spread; like the call of a minor bird, its echo floated through the air.

"That's right, darling." The Master kissed the top of my head. "Lainey DuCarmont," he said with a flourish, his voice loud and carrying. "The last remaining DuCarmont witch." He motioned to one of the Guards, who nodded his head and left the room. Then he turned back to me. "I've been expecting you."

I swallowed. "But how?" My heart ached with the answer I already knew, but I wanted to hear the Master say it out loud.

"Ah, ah, ah," The master waved a finger at me. "Let us not get ahead of ourselves. You'll spoil the surprise." He winked at me then, tapping playfully at my nose. I fought the urge to bite his hand.

"My friends." The Master's voice boomed across the room. "Welcome. Tonight, as promised, will be truly magical, as you're here to witness history in the making." He laughed again, the maniacal sound loud in my ear.

The double doors to the ballroom opened, and the Guard had returned, carrying an ornate black wooden box in his hand, which he handed to the Master.

"My lord," he said with a bow.

The Master released me and took the box from the Guard's hand. He laughed again and opened the box before flipping it around for all to see.

My knees buckled, and I nearly collapsed.

Sitting inside the box on a cushion of blood-red crushed velvet was a sparkling emerald amulet. *The Grimoire.* I felt myself sinking to the floor, but the Guard grabbed me and held me upright, before yanking me over to the Master and whirling me around to face the crowd.

The Master's face had lost some of its glee. He was staring

at me with such intensity that I felt shards of ice slice through my veins.

His gaze never leaving mine, he removed the necklace from its place and, tossing the box behind him, walked behind me to fasten the amulet around my neck.

It was heavier than I had expected, and the energy emanating from it set my heart racing. At the same time, the magic was strange. It was like putting on someone else's shoes. It made me slightly uncomfortable. The metal was hot against my skin, almost too hot, but I welcomed the pain. I needed to keep my mind clear.

The Master was facing me now, his features solemn again and harsh. "A long time ago," he began, his voice eerily calm as though he were speaking to children, "a foolish warlock took something from me, and now I want it back."

His words were laced with venom, and I flinched.

"You, Lainey DuCarmont, will undo what your family has done. Do so, and you walk away with your life. Deny me, and the consequences will be beyond your reckoning."

I shook my head, fighting back tears. "I can't."

Behind me, Maggie whimpered.

"I'm sorry," I whispered. The amulet felt like a fifty-pound weight around my neck. "I can't do that."

The Master sneered at me, his eyes flashing.

"My lord," a voice called out. "Perhaps I may be of some service."

The Guard who had retrieved the Grimoire stepped forward.

"Yes." The Master's face relaxed back into a grin. "Oh, yes," he crooned, "I think you shall." He waved his arm forward. "Proceed, sir."

The Guard walked forward and bowed mockingly at the waist to me. "My lady," he said, something oddly familiar in his tone. "The Master is a benevolent man, and you try his patience."

"Benevolent, my ass." The words were out of my mouth before I could stop them. A tiny spark of amusement bubbled under my skin as the crowd gasped and murmured.

The Guard laughed out loud, but it was a cold laugh. "Give the Master what he seeks and no harm will come to you." He stepped closer and said so only I could hear, "Unlock the Grimoire, you stupid girl."

Everything within me was screaming in warning, but I stood my ground, refusing to say a word.

The Guard chuckled again and then looked to the Master, who nodded. His eyes were full of light, and he looked very much like a child who has received a present. I tasted bile again.

"Very well." The Guard moved closer to me and slowly removed the mask he wore from his face.

Gareth.

I cried out, clamping a hand over my mouth to stop the sound.

The look in his eyes told me the answer, confirmed what I already knew in my heart to be true. My Gareth, the man who had raised me, the man who had always made me feel safe and loved, was not the same man that stood in front of me. This man's face was severe, his features hard, his eyes dead and unfeeling.

"Gareth?" I finally whispered, not wanting to believe what was in front of me. "What happened to you?"

Gareth smiled, a cruel smile, and bowed again. "Compliments of the Master, my lady." The words were a knife to my heart.

Lainey.

Josephine appeared, standing a few feet away, tears streaming down her face. As our eyes met, it hit me: those exact words, the look in Gareth's eyes. I'd seen it all before.

Henry.

I bit down hard on my lip to keep from screaming.

"Are you . . ." Every ounce of courage left in me evaporated, and I began to shake, a torrent of emotions rushing over me. "Are you dead?" My voice cracked on the last word and swallowed hard, nearly choking on the panic and tears that were forming.

"It appears we Fae aren't as strong as we seem," Gareth replied coolly. "We break fairly easily given the right amount of . . . encouragement." He grinned.

"Oh, allow me," the Master said. He snapped his fingers, and then, with a blinding flash of light, the world split open.

At first there was nothing but darkness and haze, but when the perspective shifted, images and figures shot before my eyes, moving so quickly they seemed to blur.

I could still feel the Master's eyes trained on me, could

tell I was still standing in the ballroom, but I was lost in a sea of swirling color—blind except for the flashes he was sending through me.

A swirl took shape, and Gareth stood before me with his back pressed against a brick wall, three of the Master's men surrounding him. Blood poured down the side of his face, and he was weaponless, but his face twisted in rage and determination as he launched himself at the Guards. He fought like a man with nothing to lose, though I could see his strength was failing. "Lainey," he said, seconds before they overcame him.

I opened my mouth to scream his name, but before I could even squeak out a syllable, the flash was gone, replaced by a new frame: Gareth, bent and broken, lying on the floor of what looked like some kind of holding cell.

"You will tell me what you know." A voice, strong and melodious, ripped through the air. My body jerked, reacting to the voice: the Master.

Gareth winced as he tried to move, to sit up. His movements were jerky as though he were fighting against invisible restraints. His face was a swollen mask of blue and black, and blood poured from a wound in his shoulder, but I could tell that it was neither of these that was paining him enough to move like that. He smiled, his teeth coated crimson. "Go to hell," he spat, and blood splattered the floor.

"Bravery only gets you so far," the Master fired back, laced with fury. "I guess we'll have to see how brave you really are."

Gareth's body began to twitch and arch violently. His

limbs contorted and twisted while his face was a picture of pure agony. As he began to scream, I felt my knees give way and I cried out for him through the haze of colors. "Gareth! Gareth!" It was no use, though. He couldn't hear me. Instead I watched the man who raised me endure more suffering than I could possibly imagine for one reason only: *me*.

The terrible wail of his screams punched a hole in my chest, and tears rolled down my cheeks as the scene faded away.

The Master released me, and I doubled over, covering my ears with my hands, desperate for the echo of the screams to end. I was trembling violently, and every cell in my body seemed at war with the images that flashed through my mind like a movie on repeat.

I couldn't speak, my heart trapped in my throat. I knew I'd never forget that sound; it was tattooed upon my soul.

I waited until I could breathe again, choking down my tears, and looked back up at the stranger in front of me.

"He tortured you to death."

Gareth nodded, and the Master gave a delighted giggle. The sound was a slap in the face. I couldn't hold it in any longer. I cried out, unable to stop the tears. "Gareth," I sobbed.

I put my face in my hands and let the tears take over. It was all over now. "I'm so sorry. . . . This happened because of me. . . . I'm so, so sorry." Each word punched a hole in the fragments of my heart.

"Lainey?" The voice that called to me was soft, familiar.

I looked up from my hands. Gareth was staring at me. *My* Gareth.

"I'm still here, Lainey," he whispered. "Underneath the darkness and beyond death, he has me bound. He promised to bring me back to you if you just do what he says." A tear rolled down his cheek. "We can be a family again." He took a step toward me, his hand outstretched. "Please, Lainey, I don't want to die. Do this for us, Lainey. Do it for *me.*"

The tortured expression on his face broke me in two. My hand started to lift to meet his.

But another voice, from another time, echoed those same words in my head. I clenched my hand into a fist and forced it down to my side. I looked over at Josephine. Her hand was pressed against her heart, and she was staring at me with such understanding eyes that I nearly lost it completely. "I don't know what to do," I whispered.

"Just unlock it, Lainey. Give him what he wants," Gareth pleaded with me, thinking my words were meant for him.

Josephine's face was smattered with tears, but she nodded resolutely at me. *What you must,* her face seemed to say. *What I could not do.*

A fresh wave of tears poured down my face. It was all I could do to keep my face from showing the anguish that was ripping me to shreds on the inside.

I stepped forward, closing the distance between Gareth and me.

I stared into his face, looked at the man who'd been my

only family for my entire life. I could hear his voice in my head, hear his laugh. What I would've given to have him wrap his arms around me one last time, to go back to the way things used to be.

As I looked into his eyes, what was left of my heart shattered into a thousand tiny pieces.

"Gareth." My voice was low, but he could hear me. "I love you so much."

His eyes softened and he reached for me, pressing his palm against my cheek. "I love you, Lainey Bug."

"I'm so sorry," I whispered, pulling back just far enough to reach the dagger I'd hidden in the bodice of my dress.

When he reached for me again, to pull me close, I yanked the blade from its hiding spot and pointed it at the soft skin of his neck.

The kind face went flat, and my Gareth was gone. The face that looked at me now was one of pure evil, the eyes full of hatred and cruelty.

He grabbed my wrist and pushed the blade in just enough to send several rivulets of blood coursing down his skin, where a brand new triangle tattoo was branded into his skin.

"Do it," he sneered. "Go on."

My hand was shaking, and the tears made it hard to see. I gripped the handle of the dagger.

He laughed seeing my struggle and released my hand. "You're weak. You always have been."

The Master's face came into view over Gareth's shoulder, his eyes alive. He was positively gleeful.

"Poor little Lainey," Gareth continued to taunt me. "Such a scared, weak little girl."

Just as I was about to lose my nerve, my fingers already loosening on the hilt, a hand reached out and touched my back. *Lainey.*

I didn't hesitate.

With renewed strength flowing through me, I let out a wail and thrust the dagger up under the corner of Gareth's jaw.

You must strike hard and fast, he had once said in our training session. *Never lose the opportunity to take down your enemy. He won't hesitate and neither should you.*

The memory was sharp and clear as a spray of warm blood coated my hands and ran down my arms—the very maneuver he had taught me.

Gareth's eyes went wide as blood gushed from the wound, the color immediately leeched from his skin. His legs gave way, and he swayed forward.

He would've fallen face-first, but I caught him and wrapped my arms around him. I couldn't hold his weight, so we sank to the floor, blood pooling around us.

"I'm sorry," I whispered over and over again, rocking back and forth, choking on my own tears. "I'm so sorry."

"Lainey." His voice was faint, and there was a sickening gurgle as Gareth suffocated on his own blood. I stared into his eyes, and as the last bit of darkness faded away, he was my uncle again. *My Gareth.*

The room was silent. The crowd stared at me as I held my dead uncle.

Maggie had both hands clamped over her mouth, and tears streamed down her face. Serena was standing a few feet away, at the front of the crowd. Her head was down, but her shoulders were shaking with quiet sobs. Ty stood a few feet away, stoic and unfeeling. I hated him, hated everyone in the room.

I would've sat there forever, the whole world titled on its axis, if it hadn't been for the laughter, such delighted, overjoyed laughter.

I picked my head up.

The Master was clapping his hands, almost doubled over in merriment.

He stood up, whipping his arms out, and addressed the crowd. His smile was so feral the crowd shrank back from it.

"Now," he said, his voice loud and booming, "how's *that* for entertainment?"

CHAPTER THIRTY-THREE

The words hung in the air like smoke.

No one moved; no one breathed a word. The only sound that filled the room was the rise and fall of the Master's laughter.

Gareth's head lay cradled in my lap. His blood—still warm—stuck to my skin. Heat pulsated through me, enflaming the gaping hole where my heart had been.

Time itself seemed to stop. There was only this moment, every detail searing itself into my brain, etching into my bones. Only *this*.

The Master's laughter grew louder, echoing in my ears like a drum. I was moving, before my mind even registered the movement. I slipped out from underneath Gareth's body, laying him gently against the ground, and stood up.

His blood had soaked through my clothes, staining the fabric of my gown. I didn't care, though. The crimson banner was my war paint now. Inside me, something was taking hold. It was surging through me, eating away at my senses. Green lightning crackled between my fingertips, and I shivered from the flashes of energy and heat that swelled within me.

"You killed him." My voice didn't sound like my own. It was cold and flat. The crowd had grown restless, but quieted at my words. "You. Killed. Him." The heat underneath my skin was getting hotter, boiling me from the inside out.

The Master stopped his cackling long enough to plop down in his chair, throwing his legs over the armrest. "Oh, no, love." He smirked at me. *"You* did that."

I could hardly hear his voice over the sound of my own blood rushing in my ears. I was on fire, every cell within my body drunk on the flames that no one could see. Power. Pain. Heat. It wouldn't take much now. Lighting a match into my endless supply of gasoline. I could feel it rising, and I welcomed it.

"You *killed* him." My voice was louder this time, and energy surged through my body, taking hold. I stepped forward, a burning inferno, every part of me engulfed in flames and fury.

"You killed him!" I screamed, letting go of the last ounce of control I had left. I threw back my head and unleashed the magic within me. It shot outward, a massive shock wave of electricity that exploded from my fingertips.

The sconces on the wall reacted first, growing brighter and brighter until they shattered in a rain of sparks. The guests screamed as the lights overhead began to burst, one after another.

My screams grew louder, and I raised my hands over my head, consumed by my own power and magic. I wasn't in control anymore. There was no Lainey, nothing but the insatiable heat, the conflagration of flames that consumed me.

The crystal chandelier hanging in the center of the ballroom detonated like a bomb, showering the room in broken glass and tiny sparks that danced with a life of their own. They floated through the air like fireflies, setting fire to everything they touched. The tapestries on the walls went first. The flames spread like wildfire, devouring everything in their path. They moved unnaturally fast, and screams filled the room as it quickly turned into a firestorm.

I stared unseeing, as everything began to blur together into hazy patches of gold, crimson, and amber. I couldn't make sense of anything anymore. There was nothing but the flames. As the last ounce of my strength evaporated, I sank to my knees.

My hands were red and blistered. Black spots swam in front of my eyes, and when my vision finally failed, I welcomed the darkness.

I didn't fight the hands that caught me, yanking me to my feet. I didn't resist when I felt the swaying motion of someone carrying me.

Just let me go. I wanted to stay in the comforting darkness forever.

The last thing I heard before I sank into nothingness

was a terrible wail, a visceral scream of rage that resonated in my bones.

Then, at last, stillness.

৩•৶

It was the light tap of fingertips on my face that woke me. I opened my eyes to a glittering sky, the moon a shining silver orb nestled among a blanket of stars. Maggie's face appeared then, blocking out the moon.

"Lainey?" she said, her voice hoarse, as though she'd been screaming for hours. "Can you hear me?" She prodded at my face again, unsure if I was really conscious or not.

I nodded, though I didn't speak. Seeing the movement and realizing that I was at least somewhat coherent, Maggie's face crumbled and she began to sob. She launched herself at me, squeezing my shoulders and gripping me as though she'd never let go.

It was her tears that broke through the fog inside my head. I struggled to sit up, but Maggie's weight made it nearly impossible. "I'm okay, Mags," I said, wincing at the rawness of my throat.

I managed to push her off of me enough to pull us both upright. Her face was pale, and her nose was red from crying. "Are *you* okay?" I ran my eyes over her, landing on the wound on her arm. I yanked the arm closer for inspection. The wound had stopped bleeding but was puffy and red. Bluish-black lines ran in all directions like a spiderweb from the indentation that looked like . . . teeth. All of the blood rushed from my head. I looked up at her face.

"Maggie . . . is that . . ." I broke off, unable to say the words.

"Yeah." Maggie nodded, eerily calm about it. "The Scavenger bit me."

Somewhere nearby, I caught the sound of a whispered conversation, but for the moment all I could do was stare at my best friend's face. The best friend I had willingly thrown into the lion's den. Shame colored my face. I had no idea how dangerous a shifter bite could be, or what might happen as a result, but if the black lines running from the wound were any indication, it wasn't good.

"This is all my fault." My voice cracked as the weight of my guilt threatened to crush me. I felt a surge of energy but forced it back. I took a deep breath. "I'm so sorry, Maggie. I never should have let you come."

"We both know you couldn't have stopped me." Maggie took her own deep breath and wiped her cheeks clean of tears. "And look, we don't really have time for this right now. We'll deal with it later, okay?"

I nodded, finally looking around at my surroundings. "Where are we?" We appeared to be outside in a small wooded area. Everything was fuzzy, but my memory was clear enough to remember the fire. "How did we get away?"

Maggie smirked at me. "Well, after Gareth . . ." She faltered as a fresh wave of tears filled her eyes, but she swallowed and went on. "You incinerated the plantation, Lainey.

Everything went up so fast, I thought for sure we were all dead." Her eyes were wide. "They said you were powerful . . ." There was awe in her eyes, and it made me feel uncomfortable. I looked away.

"So how are we alive now?"

A voice rang out from behind me. "I believe we had a little something to do with that," it said. I turned around and four figures—three men and one woman—moved toward us. Serena was with them, her face covered in soot, her eyes sad.

The woman had thick red hair that hung down her back in tousled waves. Her eyes were ringed with black, and her thick, prominent eyebrows were knitted in disgust. She was glaring at me.

"The Hetaeria," I whispered, recognizing her face from the ballroom.

The woman nodded as if it were the most obvious thing in the world. "Of course, and you're lucky you didn't burn yourself out up there, little witch." The words were sharp and full of mirth. "Don't you know how foolish that was?"

"Don't you talk to me like that," I snapped, indignation welling up inside me. "You have no idea . . ." My voice cracked and I swallowed, unable to say anything else without bursting into tears.

The woman's face was still severe, but it softened slightly. She knelt down, her face level with mine. "Oh, I do know, little witch." There was understanding in her eyes. "I do know." She held out her hand. "My name is Zia."

I hesitated for a moment before shaking her hand. "And you work for the Hetaeria?"

"I do," she nodded. "And my orders are to get you somewhere safe."

There was something in her face that made me nervous. I looked at Maggie and Serena and then back at Zia.

"How do I know I can trust you?"

Zia leaned forward, her brows furrowed. "You don't. But consider your alternatives. If you'd rather, I'll have Julian here skip you right back to the ash heap you created. I'm sure the Master is dying to thank you for . . . redecorating." Her tone was cold, and she waved her hand in the direction behind me. I looked, and through the tree line I could just make out the dark pillar of smoke.

"Is that how we got away? We . . . skipped?"

Zia shrugged her shoulders. "Well, you pretty much brought down the house all on your own. We just provided the getaway car, so to speak." She motioned her comrades forward. "Julian, Blake, and Morgan are Skippers," she explained.

I eyed the men carefully. One was tall and stocky with broad shoulders and tan skin—he could have easily passed as a linebacker. The one in the middle was fair skinned and short, but what he lacked in height he made up for in girth. He looked like one of those bodybuilders from the supplement infomercials. The third man had dark onyx skin and short, cropped hair. His eyes were cautious, but friendly.

"Skippers?"

"Teleportation," the linebacker answered. "We can 'skip' from place to place." He smiled at me then, and I nearly cried at the kindness I saw in his face.

A chorus of deadly cries broke through the night air.

"We need to get out of here now," Zia said, grabbing my hands and yanking me to my feet. "He's sent the Guard after us, and we're not prepared for a battle."

Zia motioned the linebacker forward and turned to me. "Julian will get you and your friend here to safety."

I nodded and leaned over to squeeze Maggie's hand. She looked as nervous and unsure as I felt.

There was another chorus of howls, closer this time and more frenzied.

"We go now," Zia ordered.

Julian gave me a tentative smile. "Ma'am," he said, politely, "you're gonna want to hold on tight."

I shook my head and allowed him to pull me close. He did the same for Maggie, and we were both pressed against his chest as if he were giving us a giant bear hug. I reached around and locked my own arms around his waist as best I could, gripping her wrists. Maggie did the same. Beside us, Serena and Blake were wrapped in a similar embrace next to Zia and Morgan.

"I'll count to three," Julian said, his voice low. "It will be disorienting and scary for you, since it's your first time, but *I've got you.* Just don't let go. Are you ready?" He waited for the confirmation from Maggie and me. "Good. Here we go, then. One."

I've got you. The words sent of jolt of pain through me. Ty's face appeared in my thoughts, and pain lanced through me, but I blinked, forcing my mind to go blank.

"Two."

I took one last look at the pillar of smoke, sucked in a deep breath, and squeezed my eyes shut.

"Three."

There was a strange tingling sensation, and then it was as if we'd been thrown backward out into nothingness. The cool breeze whipped my hair in my face, and the sensation that we were free-falling made my stomach flip-flop. I bit back a cry, but Maggie was squealing loudly, the sound making my eardrums ring. Then there was a strong jerk, and I was wrapped in a swirling vortex of color and wind. I screamed then, unable to stop it this time, and buried my face in Julian's broad chest.

Moments later, I hit the ground hard, knocked from Julian's arms and onto the ground. I looked around but had no idea where we were. It looked like an abandoned patch of highway.

"Up you go," Julian said, pulling me to my feet. There was a van parked on the shoulder, hidden in the shadows of the trees. Zia motioned us forward.

Julian tugged at my hand, towing Maggie and me toward the vehicle.

More of the fog in my head was dissipating, and as more and more images became clear, the more pain I felt surging through me. By the time we made it to the car, I was barely hanging on.

"Here," Zia said, reaching into the back of the van. "You'll want to get out of those clothes." She pulled several pairs of dark clothing from a bag and handed them to us.

Then she whistled and the men quickly turned around, giving us some privacy. Maggie and Serena immediately began to change, eager to be free of the ball gowns.

I rubbed my hand over the fabric. The dark green pants and white cotton tank top were worn but clean. I knew I should put them on, but I couldn't bring myself to remove my dress. It was covered in Gareth's blood. As crazy as it sounded, I didn't want to take it off. It was the last piece of my uncle I had left. I wasn't ready to let go.

Maggie and Serena, seeing my distress, walked over and wrapped their arms around me.

The warmth of their skin made me realize just how cold I was, how hard I was shivering, and the hold I had on my emotions crumpled.

I began to sob uncontrollably.

They didn't say anything, but I could see understanding in their eyes. Together, they helped me out of the gown and into the fresh clothes.

I cried even harder as they pulled the wretched heels from my feet and replaced them with warm socks and a worn pair of boots.

I had been so certain that there wasn't anything left of my heart, but as they helped me into the back of the van, I thought of Gareth and Ty, and something inside me broke in two, obliterated by grief and guilt and sorrow.

It was *me*. I was broken. Broken beyond repair.

My stomach ached and my body convulsed as the sobs ripped through me, tearing me to pieces.

I heard Maggie's tearful voice. "Please," she whispered, though I didn't understand.

There was a slight shuffling sound, and then I felt a hand against my forehead. "Rest now, little witch."

Zia's cool voice filled my thoughts, and then I met the darkness of sleep.

CHAPTER THIRTY-FOUR

It was cool outside. The night air had a slight nip to it that made me shiver. The wool blanket I'd wrapped around my shoulders scratched against my skin, but I didn't care.

The cot underneath me was rigid and stiff. By proxy so were my limbs, but the discomfort of my body could hardly touch the deep ache from the gaping hole in my heart. I lay with my arms wrapped around myself, as if to keep the ragged edges from caving in. I squeezed, my fingers digging into my skin. Crescent-shaped indentions covered my arms, but I felt nothing. I was completely numb, encased in a fog that dulled my senses.

Zia and the Skippers were sitting around a small campfire a few feet away. The men were drinking coffee and laughing, while Zia pored over a map and offered a few small smiles in response to their goading. The warmth of the fire was enticing, but I couldn't bring myself to join them.

The golden-orange flames that flickered in the darkness reminded me too much of another fire—the one that had cost me everything.

We'd been on the road for days now, and every night it was the same. Despite my best efforts to stay awake, my body was drained, still exhausted and weak. Sleep came for me like an executioner, torturing me with sights, smells, and sounds that plagued me until I finally woke screaming in the darkness.

Serena and Maggie kept reassuring me that it would get better, but every night I woke with Gareth's blood on my hands, the Master's scream of rage in my ears, and Ty's blue eyes, cold and unfeeling, staring into mine.

I can never come away from this. That thought reverberated in my mind, a never-ending loop of unspoken truth. I'd read an article once about people who experience trauma. The study showed that while many are able to move past their experiences, a small number remain lost, living their lives within themselves. The article called them the "living dead," and while it had seemed so entirely strange and sad when I read it, I now understood what it meant to be alive but not living.

I stared at the flames of the campfire. They also perfectly mirrored the anger that flowed within me—the only thing that could reach me past the numbness. I was so angry I could hardly bear it—angry at Ty, at the Master, at Gareth, and worst of all, at *myself.*

There's nothing more you could have done, the voice of reason whispered in my ear. *You have to keep moving forward.*

"No. I can't . . . I *won't,*" I hissed back, raking my hands over my face. I deserved every ounce of pain and suffering I got. Tears sprang up in my eyes, but I blinked them away. I'd spent too many days lost in sobs and heartbreak. It made me sick. Being numb was better.

"It's not your fault." Maggie's voice broke through my thoughts. She was staring at me from her own cot a few feet away. Serena was on a similar cot, snoring peacefully. "I know what you're thinking right now, but it's not."

"Stop saying that." My voice was harsher than I meant it to be. "It *is* my fault. I never should have let him go."

Maggie sat up, wincing as she put weight on her injured arm. "You have to stop beating yourself up. Gareth wouldn't want you to blame yourself for what happened. You did everything you could've."

I balled my hands into fists. "No, I could've done more. I could've tried harder. I could've done *more.*"

"Styles." Maggie's voice was soft. "There was nothing else to do. The Master had already . . . Gareth was already gone, Lainey. You have to know that."

"And Ty? Is that not my fault either?" I clutched my chest as the hole spasmed painfully. Even his name on my lips was unbearable. I squeezed my eyes shut, fighting against the agony.

Maggie let out a soft sigh. "At least we have the Grimoire."

The emerald amulet had still been around my neck when we escaped from Savannah. Our plan to steal it back had worked after all . . . yet, considering the cost, it hardly felt like a victory.

"So easy for you to say," I growled, rolling on my side away from Maggie. I didn't want to talk anymore.

"We should get some sleep." Maggie sighed again and settled back down on her cot. I waited for the sound of her even breathing before I rolled back over.

She was asleep, but restless. She shivered, though there was a sweaty sheen to her skin. The bite on her arm had been cleaned and bandaged, but the black veins that spidered from the wound were spreading up her arm. They nearly reached her shoulder; the poison from the bite was working its way through her system.

"Will she be okay?" I had asked Zia when we had stopped to camp on the first night.

"Shifter bites aren't usually lethal." The other woman shrugged. "But the change won't be comfortable for her."

"The change? Does that mean she . . ."

"Yes," Zia said. "Your friend is transitioning. She's becoming a Shifter."

"Is there a way to stop it?"

"I'm afraid not." Zia thought for a minute, and then added, "But if it helps, Shifters have unique magical abilities—the kind that are not only useful but admired by many of our kind. If she can learn to control it, that is."

I'd broken the news to Maggie as gently as possible.

"So . . . what you're saying," Maggie had said after a long pause of silence, "is that once the transition or whatever is complete, then I'll have the power to change into any kind of animal that I want?"

I gulped and nodded. "That's the way I understand it." I had reached for Maggie's hand to comfort her, but she'd already jumped to her feet, her face bright with excitement. "This is amazing!"

I stared at her. Was it possible that shock was making her loopy? "It is?"

"Don't you get it, Lainey? This is my radioactive spider, my super-soldier serum! My chance to be something more than just ordinary!"

I'd tried to reason with her, to explain the challenges of what she might face, but Maggie smiled and waved her hand. "Semantics. Don't worry, Styles. They're gonna write a book about us one day. Just wait and see."

The pain from the transition had gotten worse with every passing hour, but Maggie had continued to bear it with a smile, her eternal optimism never faltering.

Guilt pulsed through me as I stared at her sleeping face. "I'm so sorry," I whispered. "I'm sorry for what happened to you, Mags. And I'm sorry that I'm not being a good friend right now." Hot tears brimmed in my eyes. "But most of all, I'm sorry for not being brave like you."

I rolled over again, the tears streaking noiselessly down my cheeks. I reached underneath my pillow and pulled out the Grimoire. It hummed in my hand, though the magic felt stale and disjointed in a way. I gripped the necklace, willing it to transform. Green lightning flashed between my fingertips, but the necklace remained a necklace.

I tried again, but it remained sealed shut. I had no idea how to transform the amulet into a book, much less how to use it or keep it safe.

With an angry curse, I shoved the necklace back underneath the pillow. My chest was throbbing, and my breath was coming in short bursts as my lungs fought back the hysterics that gripped me.

I wrapped my arms around myself again and squeezed my eyes shut. It didn't help. I opened them again and stared up at the star-filled sky. I began to count—distraction was the only thing I could tolerate.

Lainey.

The familiar voice was barely audible, and I wasn't sure if my subconscious had made it up or not. I looked around, looked at Maggie, but with the exception of Zia and the Skippers a few feet away, the campsite was still.

Lainey.

This time I sat straight up, my eyes searching. I saw someone waiting in the shadows of a small grove of trees. I didn't hesitate this time.

I grabbed the Grimoire and eased off my cot, careful not to wake Maggie and Serena or draw attention to myself from the Skippers. I hedged my way out of the light of the fire and then dashed as quietly and quickly as I could to the trees.

I nearly cried when I saw her standing there.

Josephine. Her long dark tresses danced in the breeze, her face so full of sorrow that I had to clutch my chest to keep from crying out.

"Where have you been?" I croaked, my throat full of emotions. I hadn't seen Josephine since the Gathering, and I'd feared I might never see her again.

She said nothing, but her own eyes began to fill with tears. She pointed to the Grimoire in my hand.

"Yes, I have it, but something's wrong with it," I said. "I can't open it, can't transform it. Shouldn't I be able to?"

Josephine took a deep breath and held out her hand. I paused for only the slightest second before I placed my hand in hers. I was ready for the vortex of color as it swirled around me. This time the pain was familiar, and gripping the Grimoire, I welcomed it.

When I felt solid ground underneath my feet, I opened my eyes. I was standing on the bank of a small river. Across the water, there was what looked like a thick wall of smoke or a gauzy curtain. People were moving behind it, but I couldn't make out faces or features. The place was peaceful, but there was something heavy hanging in the air that made me grip the necklace a little tighter.

"Lainey."

I whirled around. Josephine was standing behind me, though for the first time, her garments were clean of blood. Her hair was combed and pulled back in a loose braid, and she was more solid than ever before. For the first time, Josephine looked nothing like a ghost. She looked human.

"Josephine?" I reached out to touch her, but hesitated and pulled back.

She smiled at me and reached out, squeezing my hand affectionately. I stared in shock at the hand in mine, the feeling of warmth around my fingers. "How is this possible? Where are we?"

"I've brought you to the Veil," Josephine explained. "Some call it the In Between. It's the only place I could appear to you like this. There is much to be said, and my time with you grows short. I wanted you to see me like this, if only for the last time."

"I don't understand."

"Lainey, it's exceedingly difficult to communicate from the Other Side. It requires incredible power, and I'm afraid that I am growing weak. My magic is running out. I will only be able to speak with you this one last time." She smiled, though her eyes were sad. "Our parallel destinies made this connection possible, so that I might warn you of the dangers and be with you in that final moment when you needed strength the most—when you had to do what I could not do. But now, I must go."

Panic rocketed through me. "But you can't leave. I have so many questions. I don't know what to do." I sucked in a large breath, trying to keep it together. "The Master, he . . . he . . ." I broke off as a sob lodged in my throat.

Tears dripped down Josephine's cheeks, the pain in her eyes mirroring mine. "I know." She wrapped her arms around me, pulling me close. I clung to her as a torrent of emotions poured out of me. Josephine held me, rubbing my hair until my sobs had subsided. I knew I didn't have to say the words. Josephine had been through it all.

The crater in my chest felt ragged and raw, but for the first time in two days, I felt like I could breathe again. I pulled back and wiped my cheeks with my hand. "I'm sorry."

"Please don't apologize to me, Lainey. I know your pain well. Our paths are connected; your pain is my pain."

I nodded, remembering Henry and the loss of her child. I took a deep breath. "Why can't I open the Grimoire?"

Josephine gently took the necklace from my hand. "Because *this* is not the Grimoire." She waved her hand, and the necklace began to bubble and ripple. With an audible pop, the magic surrounding it evaporated, and it transformed into a thick, leather-bound book.

She handed the book back to me. Gripping the spine, I flipped through it. Every single page was blank.

"But . . ." I kept turning the pages, unwilling to believe it. My mind was whirling, trying to come up with some kind of explanation, but there wasn't one. "It's a fake," I finally whispered. My fingers dug into the covers of the book. "It's a fake."

Josephine nodded gravely. "Yes."

Pain shot through me, followed by hot flashes of anger and frustration. "Then it was all for nothing?" I cried. "Oh, God!" I clutched at my heart as I thought of Gareth. "Oh my God."

I whirled on Josephine. "Why didn't you tell me?" I was nearly hysterical.

"Please hear me," Josephine urged. "I swear to you, Lainey. There are secrets even in death."

"You didn't know?"

Josephine shook her head. "No, I did not. Things are not always as simple as they seem. Not even here." She gestured at her surroundings.

"So is that why you're here now? To tell me that I've failed? That everything I did was for nothing?"

"No, I've come to show you something."

Josephine waved her hand, and a small block of color swirled into view.

An image took shape. It was my mother.

I bit back a cry as I watched her kneel beside the bed of a sleeping child.

"That's me," I whispered, staring at the tiny version of myself curled up beneath a fuzzy pink blanket, my thick hair spread across the pillow like a fan. My mother reached for my hand, her eyes full of tears.

"My darling girl," she whispered, pressing my fingers against her cheek. "My sweet baby. I know you won't understand this and you'll probably hate me, but please believe I'm doing this for you. You have such a big heart, and you're so strong. You've always been so brave."

My lip began to quiver as I listened, and tears of my own began rolling down my cheeks.

She kissed my palm and then reached down and picked

up a book, the Grimoire. "Now you'll both be safe," she said, her voice clear and full of resolve.

She began to murmur words soft enough that I couldn't make them out. But the Grimoire responded. The book began to glow, and then it began to smoke as if it were on fire.

I cried out as I watched the book become consumed with glowing green flames. As the pages burned, their essences seemed to gather into a cloud of vapor that swirled like a tornado on the ceiling.

When the entire book had been consumed and eradicated, I watched my mother say one final word and wave her hand over my head. The swirling cloud of vapor plummeted downward and poured into the sleeping child's mind. I did not even stir.

When the room was dark again, my mother kissed me once more and then walked out of the room, shutting the door softly behind her.

"Are you sure you have to leave?" A younger Gareth rounded the corner, his face mournful.

"You know I have no other choice." Her voice was ragged. "I won't let anything happen to her, Gareth. I won't!" My mother's tears were flowing freely now. "You have to keep her safe. He can never find out about her."

Gareth nodded solemnly. "I promise." He reached out his hand and my mother shook it, a golden glow emanating from their touch.

The image faded away, leaving me alone again with Josephine.

"Promises forged through magic can only be broken by death. Your mother sealed the truth of what she'd done in the vow Gareth made to keep you safe," Josephine said. "He had no way of knowing the secret he was carrying, and neither did anyone else. Not until . . ."

"Not until I killed him," I finished. The words sliced through me, but I forced the pain away. "But I still don't understand," I said. "What did my mother do to me? What secret? She destroyed the Grimoire."

"No," Josephine said softly. "You mother did not destroy the Grimoire. She transfigured it. The book no longer exists in physical form. What your mother did has never been done before, but she thought it was the best way to keep you both from the clutches of the Master."

"If the book no longer exists in physical form, then where does it exist?"

Josephine gave a tiny, encouraging smile. "In you, Lainey."

"In me?" I swallowed hard, feeling my body sway as adrenaline and panic swam through my veins.

"Yes. Lainey, there is no Grimoire anymore. *You* are the Grimoire."

I blanched. For several moments I couldn't speak. "What does that mean?"

"It means that everything that was in the Grimoire—all of the information, the spells, the power—it's all a part of you now. You are the last remaining Keeper, and it is your job, your *destiny* to keep it all safe."

"But I don't even know how to use my powers." I felt very small, like a child who's just been given an impossible responsibility. "How can I be responsible for something of this magnitude when I have no idea how to use it?"

Josephine reached out and caressed my cheek. "You'll learn in time. Go with Zia to the Hetaeria base camp. There are people there who can help you, train you. The Master is coming for you, Lainey. You must be ready."

I swayed on my feet but managed to stay upright. I was shaking all over. "I don't know if I can do this." My words were barely louder than a whisper.

"You must."

I sucked in a breath as I remembered Gareth's words. *You can't control what happens to you, but you can control how you react to it. Those choices are what will determine your destiny.*

I realized then that, despite my pain, I wasn't one of the living dead, and in that moment, I knew I didn't want to be.

"I know," I finally said. "I know." The words filled me with renewed strength, and though I was still raw and aching, my fear and anger dissipated.

I thought of my mother, of Josephine, of all the Keepers that came before me—their strength, their courage was mine now, flowing through my veins. I was a DuCarmont witch, and I was choosing to be strong.

"I am the Keeper of the Grimoire," I said, my voice clear and strong. "Now and forever."

Josephine smiled proudly and nodded.

"Won't I see you again?" I asked hopefully.

Josephine's smile was a little sad. "One day, I hope." She looked over her shoulder, as if someone had called her name. "I'm afraid I must go now. My power isn't strong enough to sustain me much longer. But there's one last thing I must show you." She pointed to the gauzy barrier. "Look."

I followed her gaze and saw the outline of three figures standing beyond the shadows. One was tall with broad shoulders; the other two had their hands linked. One was small and petite, yet strong, and the other was solid and of a medium height. The tall one raised an arm in greeting, and I felt the tiniest beat of life in my chest.

And I knew.

"Mom and Dad . . . Gareth . . ." I smiled, though I tasted salt from my tears. "They're okay?" I asked Josephine. "They're happy?"

"Yes, dear one. They are together and happy. And *so* proud of you."

Her words jump-started my heart, and for the first time in days, I felt it beating with life. I was bruised and weary, but I was *whole* again.

I wrapped my arms around Josephine, squeezing her tightly. "Thank you," I said. "For everything." I pulled away. "Will you do something for me? Will you tell them I love them, that I won't let them down. Can you do that?"

Josephine's eyes were full of tears and she nodded. "Of course." She leaned over and kissed my forehead. "Be brave, Lainey," she whispered. "As you always are."

She gave my hand one last squeeze and then stepped

across the river and through the Veil. I watched her go, and when the swirling vortex of color came for me, I was ready.

With one last look at the shadows, I closed my eyes and waited for the darkness.

It was the sound of birds chirping in the trees that let me know I was back at the campsite. When I opened my eyes, Maggie was sitting up in her cot, yawning and stretching. "Morning," she chirped.

I sat up slowly. The sun was just beginning to peek through the trees. It was a new day. A fresh start. I smiled to myself.

"Hey, Styles? What's that on your arm?" Maggie was staring at me with wide eyes.

I looked down to see a small emerald tattoo on my wrist. It was green and the exact shape of Josephine's emerald amulet. *You are the Grimoire.*

I ran a finger over the tattoo and smiled. "Magic always leaves a mark," I said simply. *Thank you, Josephine.*

I stood up from my cot, ignoring the bewildered look on Maggie's face, and walked over to where Zia and the Skippers were packing up the camping gear.

"How long till we reach base camp?"

The Skippers looked up in surprise, but Zia didn't even glance away from the map she was folding. "Couple of days. We're going to take a few back roads just to make sure no one is following us." She tucked the map into her back pocket and gave me an indifferent glance. "We need to leave in ten minutes. Are you ready?"

I took a deep breath. My future was uncertain, and there was no telling what new trials and tribulations awaited me, but there was one thing I knew for certain.

I looked Zia in the eye and smiled.

"I'm ready."

ACKNOWLEDGMENTS

I used to think writing a book was the hardest thing I'd ever done. Yet, as I sit here trying to articulate just how thankful I am for all the people who have helped me and encouraged me on this journey, I realize I was very wrong. *This* is the hardest thing I've ever done. So please bear with me as I try to express my thanks—although, to be honest, there just aren't words adequate enough to express my gratitude.

First and foremost, thank you to my heavenly father from whom all blessings flow. It is by his grace and his grace alone that I am standing here today.

To my incredible beta readers: Megan Addison, Cheryl Baker, Marlena Bell, Francesca Bartolomey, Brayden Fraser, Bethany Gallahair, Jessica Henderson, Adrienne Johnson, Claerie Kavanaugh, Mindy Kloka, Shannon Lane, Stephanie Mitchell, Kate Pilarsh, Rebekah Rose, Bobbie Stanley, Haley Street, Jamie Young, and Killian Zimmerman. Thank you for taking time out of your busy lives to read my little book. Your enthusiasm meant so much to me, and I cannot tell you how grateful I am for your kind and constructive criticism. Thank you for treating Lainey, Maggie, and Ty with such care! You guys are the best!

To Summer Spence: Thank you for telling me that I was starting my book off in the wrong place! Your advice led to a complete rewrite and a new beginning that I love! I owe you a lifetime supply of *Grey's Anatomy* hot doctor gifs!

To Dea Poirier: Thank you so much for helping me polish this book until it shone! Your excitement, encouragement, and feedback truly meant the world to me, and I cannot thank you enough for choosing me! You deserve every single gel pen and piece of Godzilla memorabilia in the world!

To Stephanie Fowler: Thank you so much for my beautiful author photos! I absolutely adore them and working with you is always so easy and so much fun. Thank you for your art and your friendship! You're the best!

To Naomi Hughes: You were one of the first people to ever read *Keeper,* and bless your heart for that! Thank you for reading those early versions and seeing the potential buried underneath all the junk. Your encouragement and feedback not only helped mold *Keeper* into what it is today but gave me so much more confidence as a writer. Thank you so much, Naomi! I couldn't have done it without you!

To Kate Angelella: I will forever be grateful to you for pushing me outside of my comfort zone. Without your help and advice, *Keeper* would likely still be written in third person and still be a hot mess. Thank you for your guidance, overwhelming kindness, support, and encouragement. I think the world of you, Kate!

To my amazing critique partners, J. M. Miller and Christine Danek: You read the earliest and crappiest drafts of this story and still encouraged me to keep going. I can never thank you enough for that! You not only helped me shape this story but you also helped shape me as a writer. Thank you for believing in me and this book!

Megan LaCroix: Without you, Lainey wouldn't be who she is today. Thank you for helping make her as strong as I always envisioned her to be. I am so grateful to have connected with you, and aside from being an excellent critique partner, you're an amazing friend. Thank you for everything!

Ashley Zarzaur: I can honestly say that this book would not exist if not for you. You have always believed in me, even when I didn't believe in myself. You helped me through the rough patches, talked me down from the ledge, and saved me from "the creepy car scene." Thank you for your never-failing support, friendship, and encouragement.

To Mari Kesselring, Megan Naidl, and the team at Flux: Thank you so much for taking such wonderful care of me and my book! This experience has been a dream come true and I am SO grateful to all of you for taking a chance on me and *Keeper*. You helped make my dream come true!

To my editor, Reece Hanzon: Thank you for being an advocate and supporter of this book from the beginning. I cannot begin to tell you how truly grateful I am for your kindness and encouragement throughout this process. Working with you has been such a wonderful experience, and I am so thankful *Keeper* landed in your hands. Thank you for helping me turn my dream into a reality.

To my amazing agent, Caitlen Rubino-Bradway: You changed my life the day you offered me representation, and I will never stop being grateful to you for taking a chance on me. Thank you so much for being so encouraging and supportive and for working so hard to make sure *Keeper* found a home. I couldn't ask for a better agent, and I hope you know how wonderful I think you are! Also, thank you to Lauren Galit, whose behind-the-scenes efforts have not gone unnoticed. And I haven't forgotten that I owe you both pie!

To Mom, Dad, and Amiee: I couldn't ask for a better family! Thank you for always encouraging me to go for my dreams and for always believing in me. Your love and support are everything to me, and I hope I make you proud!

To my beautiful children, Shiloh, Harlee, and Rhys: Thank you so much for sharing mommy with the writing world. I love you more than life itself, and I want this book to always be a reminder that dreams can and do come true! Always reach for the stars, my darlings!

To Jim: My love, you are *everything*. I thank God every day that you chose me and continue to choose me every single day. You are my life's greatest blessing, and I will never be able to put into words how much I love you or how grateful I am to have you by my side. Thank you for never letting me quit and for always believing that I could do this. Thank you for taking on more than your fair share of kid duty so that I could write and for always being willing to talk through plot holes, writer's block, and self-doubt with me. Thank you for being you and for being absolutely everything to me. The Big C always! I love you!

ABOUT THE AUTHOR

Kim Chance is a high school English teacher and Alabama native who currently resides in Michigan with her husband and three children. Kim is also a YouTuber who has a passion for helping other writers. She posts weekly writing videos on her channel, www.youtube.com/kimchance1. When Kim is not writing, she enjoys spending time with her family and two crazy dogs, binge-watching shows on Netflix, fangirling over books, and making death-by-cheese casseroles.

For more information, please visit www.kimchance.com.